THE
DISCOVERY SAGA
COLLECTION

THE
DISCOVERY SAGA
COLLECTION

A 6-Part Series from
Lancaster County

WANDA E.
BRUNSTETTER

New York Times Bestselling Author

SHILOH RUN PRESS
An Imprint of Barbour Publishing, Inc.

Published by Shiloh Run Press, an imprint of Barbour Publishing, Inc.,
P.O. Box 719, Uhrichsville, Ohio 44683, www.shilohrunpress.com

*Our mission is to publish and distribute inspirational products offering
exceptional value and biblical encouragement to the masses.*

ecpa Member of the
Evangelical Christian
Publishers Association

Printed in the United States of America.

GOODBYE TO YESTERDAY

To all my Amish friends who live in Pennsylvania.
I appreciate your friendship and hospitality.

Thou wilt keep him in perfect peace,
whose mind is stayed on thee:
because he trusteth in thee.
ISAIAH 26:3

CHAPTER 1

Bird-in-Hand, Pennsylvania

"Would you like another piece of bacon?" Meredith Stoltzfus asked her husband, barely able to look at his grim expression as he sat across from her at the breakfast table.

"No thanks," Luke mumbled. The sparkle was gone from his beautiful turquoise eyes, and there was no joy on his bearded face. They'd only been married a little over a year, and already the thrill seemed to have worn off. At least for Luke it must have. Meredith had been so sure about his love for her during their courting days and throughout the first eight months of marriage. But now Luke's attentiveness had been replaced with worry and defeat. When Luke lost his job at the nearby furniture store, everything had changed. Oh, not at first. Luke had been optimistic, saying he was sure the economy would turn around and that he'd either get hired back or would find another job where he could use his woodworking skills. But that had been six months ago, and he was still out of work, as were some of the other Amish men the store had let go. Luke hardly talked about it anymore, but Meredith knew it was eating at him.

"Would you like some more juice?" Meredith asked, reaching for the pitcher of apple juice.

He shook his head. "I'm fine. Haven't finished what's in my glass."

"No, you're not fine, and I wish you would talk about it instead of sitting there, staring at your plate."

He shrugged. "There's nothin' to talk about."

Meredith sighed. Lately, all she had to do was look at her husband to

7

know he was depressed. Luke's stance was no longer confident. He walked slightly hunched over, with a look of uncertainty and doubt. Gone was his open-minded manner, replaced by edginess and impatience. Luke's folks had offered to help out financially, but Luke had turned them down. Since Luke's dad had sold his bulk food store and worked part-time for the man who'd bought it, Luke's folks were getting by okay, but they weren't well off. Meredith's parents wanted to help as well, but they had seven other children to raise—all still living at home. And Grandma Smucker had moved in with them two years ago, after Grandpa died of a heart attack, so she, too, needed their financial support. On more than one occasion, Meredith had suggested that she look for a job, but Luke wouldn't hear of that. He insisted that it was his job to provide for them.

Meredith, trying to be optimistic, was thankful that while Luke had been working at the furniture store, he'd put some money into a savings account he had started even before he'd met her. They'd been given some money from several people who'd attended their wedding, and that had gone into the bank as well. Since losing his job, Luke had sold some of his handcrafted projects at the local farmers' market, as well as at a few gift shops. That had helped some; but for the most part, they'd been living off their savings. That money wouldn't last forever, and Meredith feared they might be unable to meet all their financial obligations if Luke didn't find a job soon.

She sighed. Being forced to pinch pennies had put a strain on their marriage. When Meredith and Luke had first gotten married she'd been convinced that the love between them could withstand any hurdle. Now, she wasn't so sure. To make things more complicated, Meredith felt pretty sure she was pregnant. She'd sometimes been irregular but had never missed two consecutive months. After her appointment with a local midwife next week, she'd know for sure. She hadn't told Luke, though, and felt apprehensive about doing that before she was certain. He was already uptight about their finances, without worrying about the possibility of having another mouth to feed in about six months.

But if the midwife confirmed Meredith's suspicions, she'd have to tell Luke soon because it wouldn't be long before she'd start to show. If Luke could just find another job, all their worries would be put to rest.

She cleared her throat. "Uh, Luke, I need to do some shopping today, and

I was wondering—would it be okay if I buy some paint for the spare bedroom next to ours?"

Luke's eyebrows furrowed as he pulled his fingers through the ends of his thick blond hair—so blond it was nearly white. "Using our money for groceries is one thing, but paint will have to wait till I'm working full-time again."

Meredith clenched and unclenched her fingers. *What would he say if he knew that spare room I want to paint is for the baby I believe I'm carrying? Should I go ahead and tell him right now, or would it be better to wait?* "I know we have to be careful with our money," she said, "but paint shouldn't cost that much."

"It costs more than I want to spend right now." Luke drank the rest of his apple juice and pushed away from the table. "Now, if we're done with this discussion, I need to go out to the barn."

"But Luke, I really would like to paint that room because—"

"I said no, Meredith," Luke said firmly. "We can't afford to do any painting right now. The spare room can stay like it is for the time being. There's no need to paint anyways, since we're only using it for storage. Until we get on our feet again, we should leave well enough alone."

"But Luke, if you knew—"

"Mir sin immer am disch bediere iwwer eppes." He frowned. "And I'm gettin' tired of it."

"It does seem like we're always arguing about something," she agreed, "and I don't like it, either."

"Then let's stop arguing and talk about something else." Irritation edged Luke's voice.

"You can be so *eegesinnisch* sometimes," she muttered, looking away.

"I'm not being stubborn; I'm being practical. And as far as I'm concerned, this discussion is over!"

Luke grabbed a dog biscuit and went out the back door, letting it slam behind him. Meredith flinched. It wasn't right for them to be quarreling like this. It wasn't good for their marriage, and if she was pregnant, it certainly wasn't good for the baby. She would never have imagined that their lives could change so drastically in such a short time.

Meredith jumped up, moving quickly to the kitchen window, watching through a film of tears as Luke tromped through the snow to fuss with his dog, Fritz, before going into the barn.

She ran her fingers over the cold glass. *I wish Luke would communicate with me as easily as he does with his dog.*

Sometimes Meredith wondered if it would be better for her to not even talk to Luke unless it was absolutely necessary. It was ridiculous to be thinking this way, especially since up until recently they'd always discussed things and made important decisions together. But wouldn't it be less stressful to keep quiet than to quarrel with him all the time?

A year ago, those thoughts would have never entered her mind. How was it that they were either behaving like total strangers or snapping at each other these days? When they were newly married, with their future spread out before them, Meredith had been full of hopes and dreams, and every day had been blissful. Now the discouraging job outlook was swallowing Luke up and affecting every aspect of their marriage.

Despite it being a nice idea to spruce up the terribly drab spare bedroom, Luke was probably right about not spending the money on paint with their finances so tight. Paint wasn't that expensive, but in Luke's eyes, it may as well cost a million dollars. Even a few cans of paint were a luxury they really couldn't afford. If the midwife confirmed Meredith's suspicions, then maybe she could start moving some boxes up to the attic. That would need to be done anyway, before it became a baby's room.

She reached for the teapot simmering on the stove and poured some hot water over a tea bag in a cup. While it steeped, she cleared the breakfast dishes and ran water into the sink. Then, blowing on the tea, she took a cautious sip. The warm liquid felt good on her parched throat. For now, she would forget about painting the room and stop adding to the anxiety her husband already felt.

Lord, she silently prayed, *please help Luke find another job soon, and while we're waiting, help us learn how to cope.*

⁂

"Sure wish I could find another job," Luke mumbled as he crunched his way through the snow toward the barn. He and Meredith hadn't argued at all until he'd gotten laid off. Now it seemed like all they did was argue. *Guess it's mostly my fault, but I can't help being fearful that we'll lose everything if I don't find something soon. Maybe I should quit being so stubborn and let Meredith look for a job. Maybe she'd have better luck finding one than I have.*

Luke had made good money working at the furniture store, but he'd been one of the newest men hired, so when things got tight, he was the first to go. He guessed during these hard economic times that people were buying less furniture, even the finely crafted kind. Luke had applied for several other jobs in the area, but no one seemed to be hiring. Even though he'd sold a few of his handcrafted items, that income wasn't enough to fully support them. This whole situation sure was discouraging!

"How are you doin' there, Fritz, ole boy?" Luke asked, hearing his German shorthaired pointer bark out a greeting and feeling glad for the diversion. "Don't worry, I hear ya." Entering the pen, he petted the head of his beloved companion and bird dog. Good ole Fritz. Luke loved that faithful critter, and he was glad Meredith loved the dog as much as he did.

Last winter, Meredith had insisted on bringing Fritz into the house, where she felt he would be warmer. Luke would have preferred to keep the dog outside in the kennel like he had when he was still living at home. But after a while, Meredith convinced him to let Fritz become a part-time house pet. Those times that he was allowed to stay inside, Fritz would lie right by their feet while Luke and Meredith ate popcorn or played board games. At night while they slept, Fritz was like their guardian angel, lying on the floor by the foot of their bed, watching over them and keeping the house safe from intruders. So now only on rare occasions did Fritz stay outside in his kennel at night.

Luke squatted down and scratched the soft fur behind the dog's ears, while Fritz gazed back at him with trusting brown eyes. Fritz was beautifully marked. His head was a solid liver color, and his body was speckled with spots and patches of liver and white. Fritz was affectionate and gentle with everyone. He'd no doubt be good with their children when Luke and Meredith started a family. Luke didn't have that in mind when he'd first purchased Fritz, of course, but it just so happened that the breed produced not only excellent hunting dogs but also good family pets.

Most times, Fritz accompanied Luke when he went to visit his parents. Even Mom and Dad's barn cats tolerated the dog when he'd bound over to greet them in his happy-go-lucky manner. Sometimes, it seemed as if they actually enjoyed his company, when they'd lie down beside him on a bed of straw and take a nap.

"Do you want to play fetch?" Luke asked.

Fritz tilted his head to one side, as though understanding exactly what his master meant, and then, like a streak of lightning, he took off across the yard.

How can dogs be so smart that way—understanding what people are saying to them? Luke wondered. *Sometimes I think that critter's smarter than me.*

"Find a stick, boy!" Luke commanded, watching Fritz run around with his nose to the ground.

In no time, Fritz returned with a small branch that Luke could throw for him to retrieve. If Luke let him, the energetic dog could run for hours. Then he'd flop on the floor and sleep.

From the time Luke bought Fritz, when he was an eight-week-old puppy, he and the dog had bonded. Fritz followed Luke everywhere. He'd had an easy time training Fritz, too, and there wasn't anything the dog wouldn't do for him. So loyal and willing to please his master, Fritz would sit in anticipation, eagerly waiting for Luke's next command. Good ole Fritz was the best bird dog ever. At least Luke thought so. With hardly any training, Fritz tracked and flushed pheasant, rabbit, or grouse as well as any spaniel or retriever.

As he and Fritz played fetch, Luke looked toward the house. He and Meredith had been so excited after their home was built. Luke had beamed with satisfaction when his wife thanked him for all the hard work he had done in constructing the home. Their wedding ceremony had taken place at Meredith's childhood home, but afterward, everyone had come back here to celebrate and share the wedding meal. The fall day had been warm, so they'd set up long tables in the yard to accommodate the large crowd, as well as the variety of food and desserts that everyone enjoyed. It had been a wonderful day, starting their new life together surrounded by family and friends. Luke had felt good about their roomy two-story home that he hoped would one day be filled with their children's laughter.

"Come on, boy. That's enough for today," Luke finally called, clapping his hands after having given his dog a small workout. He wished he could spend more time with Fritz, but he had chores that needed to get done. "I see your water dish is frozen," Luke said, whacking the ice onto the ground and then refilling the bowl with fresh water.

Fritz wagged his docked tail and anxiously sniffed Luke's hand.

"*Jah*, here it is. You know I always have a treat for ya." Luke grinned as Fritz gently took the dog biscuit he offered him.

Seeing that Fritz was relaxed and content with the biscuit between his paws, Luke stepped into the barn and quickly shut the door. It was bitterly cold, and the wind howled noisily, finding its way through the cracks in the walls. He'd be glad when spring came, and he hoped he would have a job by then.

It's a good thing it's only me and Meredith right now, Luke thought as he stepped into his horse's stall. *If we had a family to feed, I'd be even more troubled than I am right now.*

Luke was glad they didn't owe any money on their house. He'd built it with the help of friends and family, and all of the building materials had been purchased by Grandpa Stoltzfus, who had since passed away. Despite the lack of a mortgage payment, property taxes still needed to be paid come spring. Taxes alone were high enough, but so far, they'd been manageable. But like nearly everything else, they were supposed to increase this year, and Luke hoped their savings account would still have enough money to cover the bill when it came due. If he could just sell a few more of the wooden things he'd made. Of course, that money would be nothing compared to the wages he'd earned at the furniture store.

Luke thought about Meredith's request to buy paint. He hated saying no to her. If he could, he wouldn't deny his wife anything. Normally, Meredith was quite understanding. For that, and many other reasons, Luke felt blessed. She wasn't the type to ask for much, and buying some paint was really no big expense—that is, until now. It may as well be the moon she was asking for. And while she only wanted to paint the room, most home projects inevitably led to more, so for now, painting or any other home improvement just wasn't a necessity.

Luke knew Meredith was concerned about their finances, too. He also knew she kept herself extra busy around the house so she wouldn't fret so much about him being out of a job. That's how Meredith had always dealt with things. She hadn't slept well since he'd been out of work, either. Many a night, he'd wake up and discover her standing in front of their bedroom window, staring out at the moon. Well, Luke was worried, too, and it was taking a toll on him. He'd become irritable and impatient, often snapping at Meredith for no reason. He owed her an apology and planned to do that as soon as he returned to the house.

Shaking his thoughts aside, Luke fed and groomed their two horses and then cleaned out their stalls. Taffy was Meredith's horse, and rightly named. The mare was the color of deep molasses taffy, with a mane and tail that was almost black. Luke's horse, Socks, was appropriately named, too. All four of the gelding's feet had white patches that looked like socks, and while pulling their buggy, it appeared as if he was showing them off with each prancing step he took.

When Luke was done with his chores in the barn, he decided to walk down the driveway to the phone shack to check for any messages.

Inside the small building it was so cold and damp that Luke's teeth began to chatter, and when he blew out, he could see his breath, heavy in the air. Blowing on his hands for some warmth, he clicked on the answering machine to listen to the first message.

"Hello, Luke. This is your uncle Amos out in Middlebury, Indiana. I was talkin' to your *daed* the other day, and your name came up. You see, I'm plannin' to retire from my headstone-engraving business, and I was wondering if you'd be interested in coming out to Indiana as soon as possible to learn how to run the business. I'm sure you'd catch on fast. And if you don't have enough money to pay for all my tools and equipment right now, you can give me half down, and the rest after you've learned the trade and have started making money. In case you're wondering, I don't expect you to move to Indiana. Just thought you could come here to learn the trade; then when you return home and the tools and supplies have been sent, you can open your own business there. There's another fellow in my area doin' this kind of work right now, so it's a good time for me to sell out, and I'd like it to be to a family member. Give me a call soon and let me know if you're coming."

Luke dropped into the folding chair inside the phone shack and listened to the message again. He wanted to make sure he wasn't hearing things. Uncle Amos had been engraving names on headstones for a good many years and was now ready to pass the trade along to a family member. Since he had no sons to take over his trade, this was a golden opportunity for Luke. Perfect timing, one might say.

"Thank You, Lord. This is surely an answer to our prayers," Luke said aloud. He knew of only one other Amish man engraving headstones in eastern Pennsylvania, but he lived clear up in Dauphin County, so Luke was sure he'd get plenty of business right here in Lancaster County, and it would be a benefit to the community.

Luke was tired of being pulled lower and lower into a valley of unanswered questions, and he wanted more than anything to stand up straight, feeling safe and secure about their future. Uncle Amos's offer was a chance for a new start, and he couldn't let it slip through his fingers. The only problem now was that Luke didn't know how he could justify to Meredith drawing money out of their savings to pay his uncle half the amount he would need to purchase the equipment. He'd just told her they couldn't afford to buy paint for the spare bedroom. How would she take the news that he wanted to withdraw money from their dwindling bank account to learn a new trade he wasn't even sure he'd be any good at? Not only that, but would Meredith be okay with him being gone for a few weeks until he learned this new skill?

CHAPTER 2

"Guess what, Merrie? I have some really good news!" Luke shouted, bursting into the kitchen with an upbeat grin.

Meredith turned from the sink, where she stood drying the dishes. The look of enthusiasm on her husband's face made him seem like a different person than the one who had abruptly walked out the door a short time ago. "What's the good news?" she asked. Luke even seemed to be standing a little taller.

"I just came from the phone shack, and there was a message from my uncle Amos. He's decided to sell his headstone-engraving business, and he wants me to buy it!" Luke's grin stretched across his face, and his turquoise eyes twinkled like they used to before he'd lost his job. "This is the answer we've been looking for, Merrie. Jah, it's an answer to our prayers!"

Meredith stood with her mouth gaping open.

"Well, what do you think? You look kind of stunned," Luke said, moving toward her. "Aren't you excited? Don't you think this is the break we've been hoping for?"

She drew in a couple of deep breaths, hating to throw cold water on his plans. "I am a bit bewildered, Luke. I'm sure your uncle means well, but doesn't he realize you don't know anything about engraving names on headstones? And we can't afford to buy his business, Luke. We don't have a lot left in savings."

"Don't worry, Merrie. At first I was shocked, too, and I had the same questions running through my mind that you have right now. But Uncle Amos is gonna teach me all that I need to know, and he said I can give him just half of the money for his equipment now and pay the rest after I get the business going. Once I'm on my feet and start bringing in an income, we should be able to pay him in no time a'tall. Uncle Amos's business has always done well, so I'm sure it'll bring in a steady income." Luke stopped talking long enough to draw in a quick breath. "It may sound kind of morbid to say this, but sad as it is, people are always dying, so this type of business isn't likely to fail."

Meredith grimaced. "You're right, that does sound morbid, and just so you know—I'm not in favor of this."

"Why not, for goodness' sake? I need a job, and the way things are now, we could use up all our money just trying to stay afloat." Luke's expression turned serious. "It's hard to face failure, Meredith, and I don't want that for us. Can't you see that I need this opportunity for a new start right now?"

"I understand all of that, but I like living near our folks, and if we had to move to Indiana I know we'd both really miss them." She clasped his arm. "Luke, this is our home."

He shook his head. "We won't have to leave. I'll be buying Uncle Amos's equipment and starting my own business right here."

"But you're a woodworker. I would think you'd want to find a job doing what you do best and what you love to do. Could you really be happy doing something other than woodworking?"

"Well, I—"

"It'll be hard to learn a new trade, and how are you going to? Is Amos going to come here to teach you?"

Luke shook his head. "He wants me to come there."

"When?"

"As soon as possible, and I thought I'd see about getting a bus ticket right away. I shouldn't be gone more than a few weeks, and I'd really like your blessing on this new venture." He gave Meredith a hug. "I need to do this for us—for our future. I can't go on like this anymore, wondering and worrying about if and when our money will run out and where the next dollar's gonna come from."

"But it's January—the middle of winter, Luke. The roads between here and Indiana are probably bad, and I doubt you could find a driver who'd be willing to take you there right now."

Luke clasped her shoulder. "Aren't you listening to me, Meredith? I don't plan to hire a driver. I'll make the trip by bus. After Uncle Amos teaches me all that I need to know, I can figure out the best way to get the equipment I'll be buying sent back to Pennsylvania." He leaned down and nuzzled her ear.

"Come on, what do you think? Are we in agreement about this? I feel like God is handing me this chance, and I can't let it go by without at least trying. Surely you understand that, don't you?"

Meredith hesitated. Then she gave a slow nod. "All right, Luke, if that's what you think is best." *Although I'm really not sure it's the right decision for us,* she silently added.

He kissed her cheek. "I'm going back out to the phone shack and give Uncle Amos a call so he'll know what we've decided. After that, I'm gonna call Mom and Dad, and give them the good news. Do you want me to call your folks, too?"

"No, that's okay. I'll let them know later today."

"I'll bet everyone from both our families will be as happy about this as we are." Luke kissed Meredith's other cheek. "There's no need to worry now. It'll all work out, you'll see. Oh, and Merrie, there's one more thing."

"What's that?" she questioned.

"I know I've been kinda hard to live with lately, and. . ." He paused and reached for her hand. *"Es dutt mir leed."*

Tears pooled in her eyes. "I've been difficult at times, too, and I'm also sorry."

Luke gave her a tender hug. "Okay, I'm goin' out to the phone shack now."

Meredith couldn't help but smile as she watched her husband hurry out the back door. He had a real spring to his step, and he definitely stood taller, with no hint of a slouch. So quickly his once-defeated expression had turned to one of hope. Despite her misgivings, Meredith truly wanted to have faith that this trip to Indiana would be the answer to their prayers.

<hr />

"I'm gonna hitch Socks to the buggy, and then I thought I'd go over to see Seth and tell him about Uncle Amos's offer," Luke informed Meredith when he returned to the kitchen after leaving a message for his parents. She was sitting at the table with her Bible open, deep in concentration, with her head bowed slightly and a wisp of strawberry-blond hair sticking out the back of her stiff white head covering. "Would you like to go along?" he asked, placing his hand on her shoulder. "You can visit with Dorine."

Meredith looked indecisive but then nodded. "It has been awhile since I spent any time with her."

"Since your folks' house isn't far from the Yoders', maybe we can drop by there after we're done visiting with Seth and Dorine," Luke suggested.

"That's a good idea. I haven't called them yet, so we can tell them in person about your uncle's message."

Luke smacked his hands. "All right, then! I'll put Fritz in his kennel and get my faithful *gaul* hitched to the buggy so we can be on our way."

❧

"This is a nice surprise," Seth said when Luke entered his barn and found him dragging a bale of hay across the floor toward the horses' stalls. "What brings you by here today?"

Luke smiled and moved closer to Seth. "I got some good news this morning and wanted to share it with my best friend."

Seth beamed. "What is it? Did you find another woodworking job?"

"Actually, I think I have found a job, but it's got nothin' to do with wood. I'm gonna be engraving headstones."

Seth's bushy brown eyebrows lifted high on his forehead. "Huh?"

Luke quickly explained about his uncle's phone message and said he'd be going to Indiana as soon as possible.

"Now that is surprising news!" Seth thumped Luke's shoulder and grinned. "Seems like our prayers have been answered."

Luke nodded. "That's how I see it, but I'm not sure Meredith agrees."

"How come?"

"She's concerned about us drawing more money out of our savings, and she's also worried about me traveling in the dead of winter."

Seth leaned against the gate on his horse's stall and raked his fingers through the ends of his chestnut-colored beard. "Guess most women would be worried about that. I know for sure that my *fraa* would be." He chuckled. *"Ich memm zu hatz alles as me; fraa saagt."*

"I take to heart all that my wife says, too," Luke said, "but sometimes she's wrong about things. I'm sure Meredith will be fine with this once I'm

19

back from Indiana and have begun making some money in my new trade," he added, feeling more confident by the minute.

"Jah, that's right, and I'll bet you will succeed if you just go for it." Seth clasped Luke's shoulder and gave it a squeeze. "Sometimes you have to give up things you thought you wanted before you reap the rewards of the things you least expected."

⁂

"It's nice to see you. Now, sit yourself down, and we'll have a cup of tea," Dorine said when Meredith entered her warm, cozy kitchen.

"*Danki*. I think that's just what I need on this chilly morning." Meredith removed her dark woolen shawl and hung it over the back of a chair. "Oh, it feels so good in here," she said, rubbing her hands together after a chill shivered through her body.

"Can you stay awhile? It's been some time since we've had a good visit." Dorine's pale blue eyes twinkled as she motioned for Meredith to sit down. "The little ones are taking their morning naps, so we can have some uninterrupted time together."

"Luke's out in the barn, talking with Seth, so we'll stay until he's ready to go." Meredith took a seat. "Yum. . .something sure smells good."

"I've had a pot of vegetable soup simmering on the stove for about an hour," Dorine said after she'd poured them both a cup of tea. "I thought it would taste good on a chilly day like this. You and Luke are more than welcome to stay and have lunch with us if you like."

"The soup sounds good, but we probably won't stay that long. We're planning to stop by my folks' place yet." Meredith sighed deeply before blowing on her tea.

"Is everything all right?" Dorine asked, pushing a stray wisp of dark hair under the side of her white head covering. "Those wrinkles I see in your forehead make me think you might be worried about something."

"Jah, just a bit." Meredith waited until Dorine had joined her at the table, and then she told her about the offer Luke had received from his uncle.

"That's good news," Dorine said. "Since Luke needs a job, it's certainly an answer to everyone's prayers."

Meredith took a sip of tea then set the cup on the table. "That's what Luke thinks, too, but I'm not so sure."

"You don't think Luke should buy his uncle's business?"

"I do have some concerns."

"But Luke needs a job, and this sounds like the solution to your financial problems."

"I know it does, but it's going to take a big chunk of our savings for him to buy his uncle's equipment—even if he only pays for part of it now and the rest once he starts making money from the business."

"He shouldn't have any trouble earning that money after he begins engraving headstones here." Dorine's tone was optimistic.

"Maybe." Meredith took another sip of tea, letting the warm liquid roll around on her tongue. She wished she could be optimistic about this like her husband and best friend seemed to be, but something deep inside her said Luke's trip to Indiana was a big mistake. If the new business didn't do well, then what? They'd still have to pay for the equipment and would be even worse off than they were right now.

"If it were me, and my husband was out of work, I'd be thrilled about the opportunity that's being offered to him," Dorine said.

"I do hope it all works out, but. . ." Meredith's voice trailed off as she struggled with her swirling emotions.

"Is there something else bothering you?" Dorine asked, placing her hand gently on Meredith's arm.

Meredith nodded. "Luke's planning to travel by bus to Indiana, and with it being the middle of winter right now, I'm worried about the weather and road conditions."

"I'm sure the roads will be fine, and even if they're not, those bus drivers are used to driving in all kinds of weather."

"I suppose you're right." Meredith paused. "It'll be hard being away from Luke, though. In the fourteen months we've been married, we've never spent even one night apart."

"Why don't you go to Indiana with him?"

"I'd like to, but I don't think we should spend the money for an extra bus ticket. Besides, Luke will be busy learning his new trade, so I think it'll be better for both of us if I stay home." Meredith was tempted to tell Dorine about her suspected pregnancy but didn't think it would be fair to say something to her friend when she hadn't even told Luke. Truth was, another reason Meredith didn't want to go was because she'd been so tired lately and didn't think she could tolerate a long bus ride.

"I know it'll be hard having Luke gone, but it shouldn't be for too long, and you can always stay with your folks."

Meredith shook her head. "Mom and Dad have enough on their hands with my seven siblings and Grandma Smucker all living under one roof."

"You're welcome to stay here with us while Luke is gone," Dorine offered, getting up to stir the soup. "Of course, our two little ones can get kind of noisy at times."

"I appreciate the offer, but I'm sure I'll be fine by myself. Besides, I'll have Fritz to keep me company, and as you said, Luke shouldn't be gone too long." Meredith smiled, feeling a little better about things. "You know the old saying 'Absence makes the heart grow fonder.' When Luke gets back, we may even have a new appreciation for each other."

CHAPTER 3

Monday afternoon, Meredith paced nervously between the living-room window and the fireplace. Pacing was a habit she'd acquired at a young age. It didn't really help anything, but it made her feel better to be doing something other than just sitting and fretting. Luke would be leaving tomorrow afternoon, and all day she'd been struggling with the urge to beg him not to go. It wasn't just the money he'd taken out of their savings that worried her, nor was it how much she would miss him. What bothered Meredith the most was the bad weather she'd heard they were having in northern Indiana. Even here in Lancaster County it was cold, and there was already some snow on the ground. How would the roads be between here and there? She'd be worried sick until Luke arrived safely at his uncle's place on Wednesday evening. *Indiana. . . Oh my, it seems so far from here,* she thought with regret.

Meredith went to the desk across the room and opened the bottom drawer, where Luke kept a map of the United States. Placing it on the desk, she studied the distance between Lancaster, Pennsylvania, and South Bend, Indiana. Looking at it this way made it not seem so far, and by bus it was only a day plus a few hours away. Maybe she was making too much of this whole thing.

I need to stop fretting and trust that God will take care of Luke, Meredith told herself as she put the map away. She stepped up to the window and focused on the beautiful red cardinals eating from the feeders in their front yard. The scene reminded her of what the Bible said in Matthew 6:26: "Behold the fowls of the air: for they sow not, neither do they reap, nor gather into barns; yet your heavenly Father feedeth them. Are ye not much better than they?"

If God takes care of the birds, then He will take care of me and Luke and help us with all our problems. I just need to believe and trust that He will.

Meredith placed one hand on her stomach. *Should I go ahead and tell Luke that I think I'm pregnant, or would it be better to wait until he gets back from Indiana?* She took a seat in the rocker near the fireplace. The rhythmic motion of the chair soothed her nerves somewhat as she thought about the situation.

She looked forward to being a mother and was sure Luke would be a good father. But if she told him now, he would probably worry about her while he was gone, and she didn't want that. If the midwife confirmed on Wednesday that she was pregnant, then she would surprise Luke with the news when he returned home. Fortunately, there hadn't been any signs of morning sickness yet, so she was sure he had no idea she might be carrying his child. Besides her missed monthlies, Meredith's only symptom was fatigue, but Luke hadn't seemed to notice that, either. Perhaps it was because he had so much else on his mind.

Meredith decided she was comfortable sticking with her decision to wait. If she was pregnant, the news would make quite a homecoming for Luke. The idea of them becoming parents made her feel somewhat giddy. By July they could possibly be a family of three.

But what if she wasn't pregnant? Maybe her fatigue and missed periods were caused from undue worry and lack of sleep. She'd heard of that happening to some people, and with the stress she'd been under since Luke lost his job, it could definitely have affected her monthly cycle.

Meredith leaned her head against the back of the chair and closed her eyes, feeling drowsy all of a sudden. It was exhausting, fretting about everything and wrestling with the fear of Luke traveling in the dead of winter, not to mention them having to spend time apart. Meredith had to keep reminding herself that this was only temporary; it was just a few weeks. Why, then, did that feel like forever to her?

I just have to get through these next few weeks, and then nothing but happiness will follow, she told herself. It sounded convincing enough. Now if only she could believe it.

She was thankful Luke had taken the time to finish up a few odd jobs that needed to be done around the house before he left. She didn't want to worry about problems with the house while he was gone. Luke was in the basement right now, fixing a leaky pipe, and Fritz was lying quietly by Meredith's feet. Maybe she had time for a short nap to ease her mind and help her relax before it was time to visit Luke's folks for supper this evening.

Poor pup, Meredith thought as Fritz grunted and changed positions. *I'll bet that dog's going to miss Luke almost as much as I do.*

⸺

When Luke finished working on the leaky pipe, he glanced around the basement to see if there was anything else that needed to be done. Last year the basement had flooded during a hard rainstorm, but Luke had taken care of that by waterproofing the walls, so he was sure it wouldn't happen again. On Saturday, he'd cleaned the debris and ice from all the gutters and chopped extra firewood, enough to last until he was back home again. The wood was stacked close to the house so Meredith wouldn't have to go far to fetch it. Luke felt good that those tasks had all been completed.

He was anxious for tomorrow to arrive so he could be on his way to Indiana. The sooner he left, the quicker he'd get back home. But he hated to leave his beautiful wife. He wished Meredith could go with him, but they'd agreed it would be best if they didn't spend the extra money for a second bus ticket. Besides, once he got to his uncle's place, he'd be so busy learning his new trade that he wouldn't be able to spend much time with her, anyway. He was sure the time would go by quickly, and he'd soon be back, ready to start his new business.

Luke had seen the sadness in his wife's eyes and knew she still had some misgivings. But she was putting up a brave front and seemed to have accepted the idea. He hoped she had, because he was almost certain that buying his uncle's business was the right thing to do. And no matter how difficult it would be in the beginning, he was determined to make a go of it. When he started earning money at his new profession, Meredith would see that, too.

Luke gathered up his tools. He needed to head outside and hitch Socks to the buggy; then he would shower and change clothes before he and Meredith went to his folks' house for supper. Mom had insisted they come, saying it would be a few weeks before they saw Luke again. She'd also reminded him to bring Fritz along. Because he was the youngest of five boys and the only son living in Lancaster County, Mom tended to hover over him a bit. Two of Luke's brothers, Daniel and David, lived with their wives and children north of Harrisburg in the small town of Gratz. John and Mark, the two oldest brothers, and their families had settled in a newly established Amish community in western New York. Luke had wondered for a while if he should move there, too—especially after he'd lost his job. He was glad he hadn't, because with this new opportunity, he and Meredith shouldn't have to worry about their finances any longer. He'd finally have what he hoped would be a secure job, and he wouldn't have to consider moving somewhere else and starting over, like some of the others in their community who'd lost their jobs had done.

Luke trudged up the basement stairs and went out the back door to get Socks out of his stall. It wouldn't be good for the horse to get lazy while he was gone, so he'd asked Seth to come by a couple of times and take the horse out for a run. Socks was a bit spirited, so Luke didn't want Meredith to take him out alone. If she needed to go somewhere, she was better off with Taffy, her easygoing mare, pulling the buggy.

<hr />

"Are you about ready to go?"

Meredith jumped at the sound of Luke's voice, followed by Fritz's excited bark. "Oh, sorry. Guess I must have dozed off." She yawned and stretched her arms over her head. "Are you done in the basement?"

He gave a nod. "I finished up with the leaky pipe some time ago. Then I went out to hitch Socks to the buggy, came back in here, and took a shower."

"I must have been sleeping so hard that I didn't hear you come in." Meredith stood and smoothed the wrinkles in her dark blue dress. "What time is it? I hope we're not running late."

"We're fine," Luke said. "Mom probably won't have supper on the table for another hour yet."

"Even so, I think we should go now, because I want to help her with the meal."

Luke pulled Meredith into his arms and kissed her gently. "You're so kind and considerate. No wonder my folks love you like their very own *dochder*."

"I love them, too, and I'm happy if they think of me as a daughter." Meredith gave him a tight squeeze then turned toward the kitchen. "I'll get my outer bonnet and shawl, along with the chocolate shoofly pie I made to take for dessert tonight, and then we can be on our way."

"Mmm. . .I hope you made an extra pie."

"I made two, and I'll take them both, so I'm sure there will be enough for you to have two pieces if you like."

He grinned. "I can hardly wait."

Meredith made a mental note to be sure she baked a chocolate shoofly pie for Luke's return home. She would also make his favorite meal of baked pork chops, mashed potatoes, creamed corn, and pickled beets.

"Did you feed Fritz?" Meredith asked when the dog barked again.

"Nope. Mom said we should bring the pup along and that she'd have something for him to eat."

"Do you hear that, pup? We're going for a ride." Meredith laughed when Fritz ran to the door, circling with excitement.

Luke leaned over to the pat the dog's head.

Meredith smiled. She was relieved that things weren't as strained between her and Luke as they had been for the last several months. The last thing she wanted was to send him off on a sour note.

CHAPTER 4

As Meredith and Luke headed down the road toward his folks' house, the only things breaking the silence were the steady rhythm of the buggy wheels and an occasional whinny from Socks. Luke was already missing Meredith, and he hadn't even left yet. He looked over at her, knowing she was probably feeling the same way. "What are you thinkin' about, Merrie?" he asked, reaching over to touch her arm.

"Oh, nothing, really. Just enjoying the ride."

From the backseat, Fritz leaned forward, poking his head between them, yapping with excitement and then panting with his tongue hanging out of his mouth.

Meredith giggled. "I'll bet if Fritz could talk, he'd be asking: 'Are we there yet?' "

Luke nodded and clicked his tongue to get Socks moving a little quicker, watching the horse's feet prance higher as if in a dance. Then he looked over his shoulder at Fritz and said, "Don't you worry, boy. We're almost there."

When Luke pulled his horse and buggy up to his folks' hitching rail a short time later, he turned to Meredith and said, "Why don't you go on up to the house while I put Socks away in my daed's barn? Fritz can come with me. I'm sure he'll want to play with the barn cats before we go in for supper."

"All right, I'll get the box with the pies."

"Don't worry about that. No need for you to lug the box while you trudge through the slippery snow. I'll bring it up when I come in."

"Danki." Meredith stepped down from the buggy, and as she made her way to the house, Luke unhitched his horse and led him into the barn while Fritz followed close behind. Dad was feeding his horse, Dobbin, in the stall closest to the door.

"*Wie geht's?*" Luke asked, leading Socks into the stall next to Dobbin's.

"With the exception of the arthritis in my knees, which always acts up during cold weather, I'm doin' pretty well," Dad replied, limping over to greet Luke and then giving Fritz a few pats before the dog explored the barn. "How are things with you?"

"I'm fine, but I'll be even better once I get back from Indiana with a new trade I can use."

The wrinkles around Dad's brown eyes lifted when he smiled. "Jah, and I'm sure that's gonna be the case."

Luke grabbed a brush from the shelf overhead and started brushing Socks. The horse had worked up a pretty good lather on the ride over here and needed to cool down.

"Sure am glad you and Meredith could come over for supper this evening." The look in Dad's eyes, peeking at Luke over the top of his metal-framed glasses, revealed the depth of his love. "Your *mamm* and I wanted the chance to say goodbye before you leave tomorrow."

"We appreciate the invite." Luke blew out his breath in one long puff of air. "I have a favor to ask of you, Dad."

"What's that?"

"I'm worried about my fraa bein' alone while I'm gone, and even though I know Fritz will be there to watch out for Merrie and keep her company, I was wondering if—"

Dad held up his hand. "Say no more. You're not to worry, Son. Your mamm and I will check on Meredith often, and I'm sure her folks will do the same."

"I appreciate that." When he finished brushing his horse, Luke leaned on the half wall between the two horses' stalls and watched as Dad groomed Dobbin. "I haven't mentioned this before, but there's been some tension between me and Meredith since I lost my job at the furniture store."

"Figured that might be the case, and your mamm's noticed it, too." Dad limped around to the other side of Dobbin and started brushing the horse's flanks. "Money—or the lack of it—can have a way of causing problems between a man and his wife."

Luke gave a nod, looking toward the commotion in the back corner of the barn and then grinning when he saw his dog and two of Dad's barn cats cavorting with each other. Fritz stood barking at one of the smaller cats that was crouched on a bale of hay, as though ready to spring. The kitten started swatting at Fritz's nose, while another cat jumped at the dog's short tail.

Turning his attention back to his dad, he said, "Things are already somewhat improved between me and Meredith, and once I get back from Uncle Amos's place and begin making some money, I'm sure they'll be even better."

Dad smiled while stroking his mostly gray beard. "I'm glad my *bruder* offered to sell his business to you, Luke. I think you'll learn the new trade quite easily 'cause you've always been able to catch on to new things. Just remember, you'll be good at whatever you do as long as you give it your best."

Luke gave a nod. "I'll probably miss not working with wood anymore, but I guess I can still make a few things on my own, even if I'm not employed at a job where I can put my carpentry skills to use. And who knows? Maybe once Uncle Amos teaches me how to engrave headstones and I start earning an income from it, I may like the new profession even better than woodworking. Whatever happens, though, I'll try to remember your words and do my best."

"I'm sure it will all work out, Son." Dad stopped grooming Dobbin long enough to give Luke's shoulder a reassuring squeeze. "It never hurts to learn another skill. Leaving is the hard part, but once you're home, you'll be glad you made the decision."

"Thanks, Dad. Talking to you always makes me feel better about things."

Dad smiled; then he put the brush away, slipped out of his horse's stall, and closed the door. "Let me give your horse some food and water, and we'll head up to the house and see if your mamm's got supper ready." He grinned at Luke. "Don't know about you, but I'm feelin' pretty *hungerich* right now. And how about you, Fritz? Are you hungry?" he asked, pointing at Luke's dog.

Woof! Woof! Fritz bounded over, forgetting all about the cats for the time being.

Luke chuckled and thumped his stomach as it growled noisily. "Guess it's pretty obvious that I'm hungry, too."

⌘

"It was nice of you to invite us over for supper this evening," Meredith said as she helped her mother-in-law, Sadie, set the table.

Sadie smiled, her hazel-colored eyes fairly twinkling. "We're glad you could come."

Luke's mother was always so cheerful. In fact, Sadie's radiant smile was contagious, and at the age of sixty-seven, she still had the cutest little dimples. Just being around her made Meredith feel at ease.

"I think Fritz was glad he was allowed to come with us. In fact, I believe the pup loves coming over here almost as much as we do." Meredith had nicknamed Luke's dog "the pup" soon after she'd married Luke.

"He sure is a good dog." Sadie grinned as she placed a pitcher of water on the table. "That first night when the puppy was brought home, Luke slept on the floor next to the box he had fixed up for Fritz. After that, they were inseparable."

"I can understand. I've gotten pretty attached to Fritz as well."

"So, tomorrow's the big day, jah?" Sadie asked.

Meredith nodded. "Luke's pretty excited about learning a new trade from his uncle."

"And well he should be. He's been without work far too long, and engraving headstones is a needed thing." Sadie's tone had become more serious. "I think it'll provide you and Luke with a good living and a job he shouldn't have to worry about losing."

"I hope so. If it were any other time of the year, I might be more comfortable with the idea of Luke traveling and being away from home. If only it was spring or summer. Then, too, I'd have more to keep me busy outside in the warmer weather, like gardening and yard work, so I could keep my mind off Luke being gone." Meredith sighed deeply. "I just wish he didn't have to travel in this cold, snowy weather."

"I'm sure he'll be fine, and you will be, too, Meredith," Sadie said with a wave of her hand. "Those bus drivers know how to handle their vehicles in all kinds of weather. You have to remember they're trained for that."

Meredith nibbled on her lower lip as she looked out the kitchen window at the snow. "That's what my friend Dorine said, too."

Sadie slipped her arm around Meredith's waist. "Just give your worries to the Lord, like the Bible says we should do."

"I'm trying to do that, Sadie." Meredith managed a weak smile. "I think I'll feel better once I know Luke has arrived safely at his uncle's place. Then

I'll just have to get through a few weeks before he comes home. There are days when I think I'll be able to handle it and then other times when I get really scared just thinking about it."

"Would you like to stay here with us while Luke is gone? You can bring Fritz along, too."

"I appreciate the offer, but I'm sure I'll be fine at home. I've already started a to-do list and plan to use the time he's away to get some things done that I've been wanting to do. Keeping busy will be my remedy for loneliness." Once Meredith found out whether she was pregnant, she planned to clean and organize the room that would become the baby's nursery. But no way was she going to share her suspicions with Luke's mom about being in a family way. Not until she'd told Luke.

"Keeping busy should help," Sadie said, pushing her glasses back in place. She lifted the lid on the pot of potatoes, poked them with a fork, and turned off the stove. "You know, in the forty-seven years Elam and I have been married we've never been apart for more than a few days."

"Really?"

"That's right, and the few times we were apart was because Elam had to go away on business when he owned the bulk food store." Sadie carried the kettle over to the sink and poured the water out. "But even during those times it wasn't so bad, because I had our *kinner* to keep me company. Of course, all the boys missed Elam, and everyone was glad when he returned home."

Meredith sighed. "I'll be glad when Luke gets back from Indiana."

"Of course you will. Elam and I will be, too. With him being our youngest son and the only one living here in Bird-in-Hand, we're kind of partial to him." Sadie chuckled. "'Course we love all five of our sons. It's just that we feel a bit closer to Luke."

"Is someone in here talkin' about me?" Luke asked as he and Elam entered the kitchen. Fritz followed close behind with his nose in the air.

Sadie gave Luke a hug. "It's a mother's right and privilege to talk about her son whenever she wants." She reached down to pet Luke's dog. "Hey there, boy. I made something special for you to eat."

Fritz's short tail wagged enthusiastically. Luke grinned and gave Meredith a wink. She was glad he had such a good relationship with his parents.

"Sure is a nice clear night," Luke said as he and Meredith walked hand in hand toward their house later that evening. In his other hand he held a battery-operated lantern to light their way. "Would you like to sit out on the porch awhile and look at the stars like we used to do when we were courting?"

"That sounds nice. I'll fix some hot chocolate for us to enjoy as we watch for falling stars."

"Sounds good to me. Would you like me to help?"

"No, that's all right, I can manage." Meredith motioned to the wooden bench that Luke had made last summer. "Just take a seat and relax. I'll be back in a few minutes."

"Okay." When Meredith went inside, Luke set the lantern on a small table, took a seat, and pulled the collar of his jacket up around his neck. It might be a clear night, but it sure was chilly. *Maybe I oughta go inside and get a blanket we can wrap up in,* he thought.

Luke was almost to the door when it opened suddenly and Meredith handed him a small quilt. "Thought we'd probably need this," she said, smiling at him.

"Guess we're thinking alike 'cause I was about to come inside and get one myself."

"I'll be back with the hot chocolate soon."

When she disappeared into the house, Luke took a seat and stared up at the sky. Ever since he was a boy he'd enjoyed watching the stars. It was fun to look for the Big Dipper and all of the other constellations. The night sky was beautiful with the bright moon and billions of twinkling stars.

Luke was also captivated seeing airplanes whiz across the sky. If he was looking in the right spot, occasionally he'd see a satellite move silently across the night sky. *I can't even imagine what it's like to be up in the sky like that, looking down at the earth,* he thought.

Early on in their courtship, Luke had told Meredith how interested he was in flying and how he'd often wished he was a bird. He'd laughed when Meredith said she was keeping both of her feet on the ground, where they belonged. Luke knew he'd probably never get the opportunity to fly because taking trips by plane wasn't allowed in their Amish community. But it gave him something to daydream about.

Interrupting Luke's musings, Meredith reappeared, this time carrying a tray with two mugs of hot chocolate.

"Oh, good, I see you didn't forget the marshmallows," Luke said, grinning at her.

"Of course not. I know how much you love marshmallows." Meredith set the tray on the table and handed Luke a mug. Then she wrapped her fingers around the second mug as she sat down beside him. "I heated the milk extra hot, so you'd better sip it slowly at first," she cautioned.

He placed the quilt across both of their laps. "Are you warm enough, Merrie?"

"I'm fine. The hot chocolate will help warm our insides, too."

They sat in quiet camaraderie, drinking their hot chocolate and watching the stars, as a hoot owl serenaded them from one of the trees in their yard.

Meredith giggled.

"What's so funny?" Luke asked, blowing at the steam rising from his mug.

"You have melted marshmallow right there." Meredith pointed to his upper lip.

Luke laughed and swiped his tongue over the sweet-tasting foam.

"I probably have some marshmallow on my face, too." Meredith snickered and licked her lips. "Wow, the stars are so vivid tonight," she said, pointing above. "Oh, look—there's a falling star, Luke."

"I'm not superstitious, but I've heard it said that a falling star is a sign of good luck and that seeing one means something good's about to happen."

"We need something good to happen, all right," Meredith said.

"Guess we'd better not stay out here too much longer, though. I'll need to pack in the morning so I'm ready to go when my driver comes in the afternoon to take me to Lancaster to catch the bus." Luke reached into his pants pocket and pulled out his gold pocket watch. *"Die zeit fer ins bett is nau."*

Meredith sighed. "I don't want it to be time to go to bed yet. Just a little while longer, Luke. I'm not quite ready for the night to end."

"I know. I'd like nothin' more than to sit out here with you, watching the stars clear into the wee hours of the morning, but unfortunately, it's not an option. Not if I want to be awake and fully functioning in the morning."

"Could we sit for a few more minutes?" she asked.

"Jah, okay, but just a few." Luke was excited about his new venture, but he felt a bit edgy about things, just as his wife probably did. Tomorrow was a new beginning, but they'd also be saying goodbye. Even just a temporary separation made the situation that much harder for him.

"Mom said she invited you to stay with them while I'm gone," Luke said as Meredith snuggled closer. "Do you think you should take her up on that offer?"

Meredith shook her head. "I'll be fine here by myself, Luke. I'll have the pup, and I don't want you to worry about me, okay?"

He nuzzled her neck with his cold nose. "I won't, if you promise not to worry about me."

She gave no reply.

"Merrie, do you promise?"

"I'll try not to worry," she finally said. "I'm going to try and do as your mamm suggested and put my trust in the Lord."

He leaned over and kissed her cheek. "Now that's the kind of talk I like to hear from my fraa."

They sat awhile longer, reminiscing about their courting days. Although tonight was special, being on the porch in the quietness of the dark, it was hard not to think about what tomorrow would bring. It was strange, but Luke felt the same sense of loneliness as he imagined the hooting owl must be feeling—listening and waiting for an answer from its mate.

CHAPTER 5

Meredith sighed as she put the last of Luke's clothes in his suitcase and closed the lid. She wished he wasn't leaving for Indiana. She wished she could talk him out of going. But all the wishing in the world wouldn't change a thing, and it was pointless to keep dwelling on it.

Wiping sweaty hands down the front of her dress, she moved over to the bedroom window. The once-clear morning sky had turned gray, with thickening clouds, a heavy mist, and temperatures hovering near freezing, which could easily cause the roads to ice up. It appeared, from what she'd read in this morning's newspaper, to be the leading edge of a storm front—perhaps a major one. Why today, of all days, when Luke would be traveling, did the weather have to turn sour? This only fueled Meredith's anxiety over him leaving. Yesterday's weather was most likely the "calm before the storm."

Dear Lord, please keep Luke safe, she prayed. *Let this trip be the right decision for our future.*

"What are you thinkin' about, Merrie? You looked like you were a million miles away," Luke said, stepping up behind Meredith and slipping his arms around her waist.

"Oh, I was just thinking how much I'm going to miss you," she admitted, leaning back into his warm embrace and resting her head on his shoulder.

"I'm gonna miss you, too, but I'll be back before you know it."

Not wanting him to know how anxious she felt, she turned and smiled when he kissed the side of her face. "I know it won't be long, and I don't want you to worry about me while you're gone."

"I won't 'cause my folks, as well as yours, will be checking up on you, and knowing that gives me comfort. Seth also said if you need anything to let him know. Oh, and don't worry about the bad *wedder*, either," he said, moving away from the window and lifting his suitcase from the bed, "because I'm sure it won't cause any problems for the bus."

Meredith gave a nod, knowing it would do no good to say anything more to Luke about the weather. She couldn't control or change it, so it was going to do whatever it did anyway. She'd just have to pray for the best, take each day as it came, and try not to worry.

Commit each day to the Lord, she reminded herself. *And trust Him in all things.*

"Do you want me to pack you something to eat for the trip in case you get hungry?" Meredith asked as she followed Luke down the stairs. "How about I make up some ham and cheese sandwiches, and if you like, I could put in a couple of those Red Delicious apples we got at the market last week."

"I appreciate the offer, but after that big breakfast you fixed me this morning, and then the hearty chicken soup and homemade bread we had for lunch, I doubt that I'll feel hungerich for the rest of the day."

Meredith gave his stomach a gentle poke. "You might be full right now, but I'm sure it won't last for your entire trip. My guess is you'll be hungry before you reach Philadelphia."

"Well, if I do get hungry, I can buy a little somethin' to eat in Phila-delphia or one of the other stops along the way." He wiggled his eyebrows playfully. "Besides, I'm so excited about this trip that I'm not even thinkin' about food. I just want to get there, learn all I can from Uncle Amos, and get back home to my beautiful fraa as soon as possible."

Meredith's cheeks warmed. She blushed way too easily—especially when Luke complimented her looks.

Just then, a horn tooted from outside. Luke went to the living-room window and looked out. "My driver's here, Merrie. It's time to go."

Meredith, wishing for a little more time with Luke, blinked against the tears threatening to escape. She wouldn't give in to them, though—at least not until after Luke had gone.

Luke pulled her into his arms and gave her a gentle kiss; then he picked up his suitcase and opened the door. "I did one more check around the house and didn't see anything that might cause you any problems," he said. "Oh, that big tree out back has a few limbs that should be taken off. They're hanging over the top of Fritz's pen, but the tree is good and healthy, and the branches aren't dead, so they should be fine till I come home. When I get back, I'll take care of trimming those branches." Luke hesitated, reaching out to gently rub Meredith's arm. "Well, it's now or never—I've gotta go."

Meredith forced a smile. Luke's concern for her needs made her cherish him all the more. Draping a shawl over her shoulders, she followed him onto the porch. "Don't forget to call me when you get there," she said, swallowing against the lump in her throat.

"I will, and remember—don't worry." Luke gave her one final hug and started across the yard.

Woof! Woof! Fritz raced back and forth, bumping his snout against the chain-link fence of his kennel. *Woof! Woof! Woof!*

That poor pup doesn't want to see his master go any more than I do, Meredith thought.

Luke stopped then walked over to the kennel. Reaching his hand through the fencing, he squatted down to bid farewell to his faithful friend. "It's okay, boy. I wasn't gonna leave without tellin' you goodbye," he said, giving Fritz's head a couple of pats. "Take good care of Meredith while I'm gone, and I'll see you in a couple of weeks."

Who says dogs aren't smart? That dog of ours sure is. Meredith smiled, despite the impending tears. Watching the way Fritz was acting, anyone could tell that he sensed Luke was leaving.

The dog continued to bark and jump at the fence as Luke turned and approached his driver's car. Just before he opened the car door, Luke looked back one more time and waved at Meredith. "Don't worry, Merrie. It'll all work out!"

She placed one hand against her stomach, while waving with the other, as the car drove away from the house. It took all her willpower not to run after Luke and beg him to stay. She stood watching as the vehicle pulled out onto the road and disappeared into the frigid mist. As she remained on the porch, looking at the spot where Luke had stood only moments ago, the fog moved in, enveloping her in its chilling mist.

Meredith wasn't ready to say goodbye yet, but then, would she ever have been ready for that? A forlorn feeling overwhelmed her, and as if walking in wet cement, her feet dragged toward the empty house.

Inside, the silence from her husband's absence nearly consumed her. It seemed as dreary and lonely in the house as it was outside with the cold, foggy mist. Grabbing the small quilt folded neatly on the couch, Meredith wrapped herself in it and went to the rocker. All she wanted to do was blot out the hollowness that penetrated her soul, seeping in little by little, surrounding her like a cocoon. It was silly to feel this way, but saying goodbye to Luke had been even more difficult than she'd imagined.

Pushing back the despair with a feeling of anticipation, Meredith thought about the new life she hoped was growing within her. She wondered once more if she should have told Luke her suspicions about carrying his child. Well, it was too late now; he was gone. If it was true, he'd learn about it once he got home. It was news that could only be shared with him face-to-face— not over the phone after he arrived at his uncle's place. Oh, how she wished Luke could be with her tomorrow when she saw the midwife.

Come on now, snap out of it, Meredith told herself, drying her eyes and swallowing past the lump in her throat. *I'm a doer, and I'm going to get through this all right.* She had known beforehand that the parting would be difficult, but now that Luke was gone, she needed to move forward and look ahead. She rubbed her hand over the front of her dress. If she was pregnant, the baby would be the link holding her close to Luke, and it would help get her through the long days until his return. Not only that, the preparations for a new baby would keep her busy. She was ambitious and organized and couldn't wait to get started once her pregnancy had been confirmed. If her calculations were correct, she was about three months along.

Meredith was excited about the prospect of being a mother. She wasn't nervous like some women were when expecting their first child. After all, she and her sister Laurie had lots of practice helping their mother when their younger brothers and sisters were born.

Meredith smiled in eagerness, knowing that when Luke returned they'd quite possibly have two things to celebrate—his new business venture and the news that she was carrying their first child.

Norristown, Pennsylvania

Staring out the window as the bus pulled out of Norristown, Luke felt as dismal as the foggy mist that seemed to envelop everything around them. At least so far the roads hadn't been icy. After hearing a few of the passengers talk about the weather, Luke knew they were headed toward the center of the storm as it came in from the west. Although the weather had been calm yesterday, it had changed overnight. But even now, it wasn't nearly as bad as the meteorologists predicted it would be.

Fidgeting on the cushioned seat to find a more comfortable position, Luke leaned in toward the window and thought about his beautiful wife. He regretted the stressful days he and Meredith had spent arguing about unimportant things and felt guilty for not letting her get the paint for the spare bedroom. What would it have hurt? After all, a few cans of paint wouldn't cost that much. Not even as much as his bus ticket had. Painting the room would have given Meredith something to do while he was gone and would have helped the time pass more quickly. Luke knew how she loved doing little projects that improved their home.

When I call Meredith after I get to Uncle Amos's place, I'm gonna tell her to go ahead and buy that paint, Luke decided. *I'm sure she'll be pleased about it, and since I'll be making money again soon, we can surely afford a few cans of paint.*

<hr>

Philadelphia

Alex Mitchell was on the run. He was hungry, cold, and in desperate need of a fix.

Crouched in an alley near the bus station, Alex peered around the Dumpster he'd been hiding behind for the last twenty minutes. With the exception of a mangy-looking cat watching him from atop the Dumpster, there was no sign of anyone or anything out of the ordinary.

Alex glared back at the cat, wondering how many more dirty critters like this there were in Philadelphia. He'd read in a newspaper not long ago that in the city of New York alone there were more than five hundred thousand stray cats. He figured there was close to that many here.

Maybe I've ditched those creeps who've been after me, he thought, forgetting about the cat and taking another look up the alley. *Better sit tight for a while longer, though, just in case they saw me run in here.*

Lately, it seemed all Alex did was look over his shoulder. He never forgot the day a certain drug dealer had said to him, "You'd better watch your back at all times, 'cause you never know who might be after you."

Who would have thought that Alex would end up on the run for what seemed like forever and a day? Alex could feel his body rebelling against the lifestyle he'd chosen, but he was powerless to do anything about it. The last time he'd looked in a mirror, he'd been shocked at the image looking back at him. Dark circles stood under his eyes, his cheeks were sunken, and his once-thick brown hair had thinned. He looked a lot older than his twenty-two years.

Alex had developed a cough recently, too, and as had been happening for so many days, another round of spasms seized his chest. Each racking cough made it hard to catch his breath, and after a while, his lungs felt as if they would explode. He coughed so loud it even scared the cat. Watching the mangy animal dart up the alley, he clamped his hand over his mouth to try to stifle the sound. If he didn't stop hacking soon, anyone looking for him would have no trouble knowing right where he was.

As Alex sat on his haunches, the coughing finally subsided. He shivered from the penetrating cold as his mind traveled through his past. He dredged up old memories of hiding like this from his drunken dad and remembered how fearful he'd been of the beating that would come if his old man discovered where he was.

Alex had shivered back then, too, but it wasn't from the cold. He would hope, and sometimes even pray, that his so-called father would grow tired of looking for him and pass out from his drunkenness before finding and beating him with a thick leather belt. Sometimes Alex got his wish. When he didn't, for days afterward he dealt with the pain of the stinging red welts left on his skin. His bum of a father needed someone to lash out at—especially after Mom ran off with some guy she'd met at the restaurant where she'd waited tables. Alex had only been ten years old when she'd split, and his older brother Steve was twelve. He had another older brother and two older sisters, as well, but as soon as they'd turned eighteen, they'd left, never to return.

It was bad enough that Alex's dad was the way he was, let alone having had a mom who hadn't stuck around to look out for him and his brother. If there was a God, which he seriously doubted, why then didn't He save Alex from this kind of life? What had he ever done to deserve all the misery he'd gone through?

Alex shifted his position as more memories flooded his mind. Back then, he'd longed for a real family—one like most of the other kids at school had. He often wondered what it would be like to have parents who'd paid attention to him and got involved in what he was doing. It was true he had two parents, Fred and Dot Mitchell, but that's where it ended. They'd held the status of being married, but really they were just two people who seemed to get some kind of enjoyment out of screaming, fighting, and making each other miserable. During the rare times when it seemed his folks might be getting along, they would often turn the tables and start yelling at Alex and Steve, ordering them around and constantly telling them what to do. To make matters worse, they seemed to get even more pleasure from reminding Alex that he never did anything right. Yes, they'd all lived under the same roof, but they were never a real family. When Alex's mother left, any hope there might have been about them becoming a true family unit vanished, just like the shabby cat that had hightailed it up the alley a few minutes ago.

Alex grimaced. School had never been fun for him, either. He remembered playing hooky each year on Parent/Teacher Day, when parents were invited to visit the classroom. Alex would leave the house as usual, making it look as if he were going to school, but halfway there, he would turn toward the woods and spend the day hidden among the trees until it was time to go home. No way was he going to invite his mom or dad into school and let them embarrass him in front of his peers. Neither was he going to sit in class being the only one who hadn't invited his folks. It was easier to avoid the whole scene altogether.

Alex avoided a lot back then, mostly to hide his bruises. He'd had one good friend for a short while, but that didn't last because Rudy moved away. After that, Alex didn't try to make friends. It was easier, because Alex trusted no one. Anyone he ever got close to left anyway, so what was the point? Even Alex's one and only pet dog had run off.

It wasn't great before Mom left, but their household turned from bad to worse afterward, and soon his brother Steve started smoking marijuana. Not long after that, Alex tried it, too. By the time he was sixteen, he was doing more drugs and had dropped out of school. Then, tired of his dad's abuse and in need of money for his addiction, he'd hightailed it out of there, landed a job, and never gone back. Alex's obsession with marijuana wasn't enough, however, and in no time, he was doing the hard stuff—cocaine, heroin, and meth.

Doing and dealing drugs had been a part of Alex's life for so many years, he didn't know any other way to live. Now he was in over his head, just barely holding on. He'd stolen money from a couple of cocaine dealers, spent it on meth, and had no way to repay it. So the dealers were after him, and if he didn't escape, when they caught him they'd make sure he was dead.

Alex's life was in a downhill spiral; he was in a hole he couldn't crawl out of. What he needed was a break, a chance for freedom, an opportunity to start over in some other place. He doubted, though, that the chance would ever come. And if it did, what kind of a life would he choose?

As a child, loneliness, heartache, and pain had been all Alex knew. Now as an adult, anger replaced the longings of a little boy. He was suspicious of everybody and trusted no one. He doubted anyone would trust him, either, especially the way he looked. Just like his soiled clothes, he felt dirty. And with the fury behind his eyes and multiple scars and needle marks on his arms, he would make anyone uneasy.

Alex slowly shook his head. *I have no one left.* He had no idea where his brother Steve had ended up, either, or if he'd ever see him again. For all he knew, his older brothers and sisters could have disappeared off the face of the earth. Long ago, he'd given up any hope of having someone care about him. At this stage of the game, he'd probably spend the rest of his life alone and on the run—that is, if he lived long enough.

CHAPTER 6

Bird-in-Hand, Pennsylvania

Meredith glanced at the clock on the kitchen wall. It was half past six, and she wasn't even hungry. It was hard to think about supper when her husband wasn't here to share the meal with her. It was hard to think about anything other than wondering how Luke was doing on his journey so far. She figured he would be in Philadelphia around eight thirty and would be there until shortly after midnight. The bus would go to Pittsburgh for another transfer and wouldn't arrive in South Bend, Indiana, until six thirty Wednesday evening. Oh, how she looked forward to Luke's phone call, letting her know he'd arrived safely.

Woof! Woof! Woof! Fritz's frantic barking pulled Meredith's thoughts aside.

She glanced out the kitchen window and saw a horse and buggy coming up the lane. As the rig drew closer, she realized it belonged to her parents.

Meredith hurried to the door and stepped onto the porch just as Dad pulled his horse and buggy up to the hitching rail.

"Wie geht's?" Mom called as she made her way through the snow and approached the house.

"I'm fine but feeling kind of lonely," Meredith admitted after Mom joined her on the porch. "Luke left for Indiana this afternoon, and I already miss him."

Mom gave Meredith a hug. "That's why your daed and I stopped by—to see if you might come home with us tonight."

"I appreciate the offer," Meredith said as they entered the house, "but I'll be fine here by myself." She pointed to the window, where Fritz was jumping at the kennel fencing while frantically barking. "Besides, I have the pup to keep me company."

Mom rolled her eyes. "Like Luke's *hund* is going to offer you any companionship out there in his dog run."

"If I get lonely, I'll bring him in. Fritz is used to being in the house in the evenings, anyhow. I believe that dog thinks he's our protector, and frankly, I'm just fine with that, especially now that Luke is gone," Meredith explained. "So how's Laurie doing with those dolls she's been making to sell at the farmers' market?" Laurie was Meredith's nineteen-year-old sister, and growing up, they had been close because they were only three years apart.

"She's doing okay, but the dolls don't seem to be selling as well as they did when she first started making them. I guess it's due to the struggling economy," Mom said with a sigh.

"Well, at least she's keeping busy making the dolls," Meredith said.

"That's true, but she spends a lot of her free time on them, and I worry that she's missing out on what should be the carefree days of her youth."

"It's good that Laurie's doing something she likes, and I'm sure she wouldn't do it if she didn't really enjoy the work." Meredith smiled. "So how would you and Dad like to join me for supper? I have some leftover soup in the refrigerator, and I'll make ham and cheese sandwiches to go with it."

"It's nice of you to invite us," Mom said, removing her shawl and black outer bonnet, "but Laurie and Kendra are cooking supper tonight, and it should be ready by the time we get home." She gave Meredith's arm a gentle squeeze. "We'd hoped you'd be coming home with us and would stay there until Luke gets home."

"I can't do that, Mom. I have things to do here. The horses need tending, and so does Fritz." Meredith sighed deeply. *Why is she bringing this up again? Doesn't she think I'm capable of staying alone?*

"Your brother can come over to feed and water the horses, and if you like, Fritz can come over to our place with you. The kinner have become attached to him since you and Luke got married—especially the younger ones." Mom smiled. "And if I know Laurie and Kendra, they'll probably fix the dog some special treats. Ole Fritzy boy will be one spoiled pooch if you stay at our house."

"I'm sure that whatever my sisters fixed would be good," Meredith said, "but Fritz and I are going to stay here while Luke is gone. I want to be available when he calls and leaves a message letting me know he got to his uncle's safely."

Just then, Dad entered the room. "Are you comin' home with us?" he asked, looking at Meredith.

She shook her head. "I appreciate the offer, but I'd prefer to stay here."

Dad looked over at Mom and said, "This daughter of ours is an eegesinnisch one, jah?"

Mom nudged his arm. "And where do you think she gets that stubborn streak from?"

Dad chuckled. Then he turned back to Meredith and said, "We accept your decision to stay home alone, but if you need anything, don't be afraid to ask."

"I appreciate that." Meredith gave her parents a hug. "Danki for stopping by. I was glad for the visit."

"It wasn't much of a visit. Least not for me," Dad said with a wink.

Meredith smiled. For a man of fifty-four years, her dad was in tip-top health. His arms were still muscular from all the farmwork he'd done over the years, and Meredith found comfort in his warm embrace. Just like when she was little, Meredith felt safe whenever Dad was around.

"Now don't you forget," Mom said, slipping her black bonnet back on her head, "just let us know if you need anything."

Meredith smiled. "I will."

Once her parents had gone, the house was quiet again, so Meredith busied herself and turned the propane stove on low to slowly heat up the soup. While that was getting warm, she decided to go upstairs and take a quick look at the spare room to see what might need to be done in preparation for a baby.

Leaning against the doorway, Meredith looked around. It was a nice-sized room, with a smaller closet than hers and Luke's, but there was plenty of room for baby furniture. *In just six short months, this could actually be our baby's room,* she thought, smiling.

Meredith's lips compressed. As eager as she was to paint this room, she didn't want to go against Luke's wishes, so if she was pregnant, the painting could wait to be done until after he got home. She was sure he'd have no objections once the news was shared with him as to why she was so eager to paint.

"I guess the first thing I need to do is go through all these boxes and take some things up to the attic," Meredith said, thinking out loud. "That way, I'll have more room in here and can plan what we'll need for the baby and where to put everything."

Continuing to look around, she could almost visualize the crib along one wall and the baby's dresser and a few other things on the other wall. Unless she found another rocking chair at an auction or sale, Meredith would use the one in the living room and maybe ask Luke to bring it up to the baby's room once the time drew closer for her to deliver. One thing was for sure: the rocker would go right by the window.

Meredith closed her eyes and could almost feel their tiny baby nestled in her arms and sleeping quietly as she rocked the precious bundle. Placing one hand over her stomach, she wondered if she might be carrying a boy or a girl. That would be the joy Luke and she would share when the baby was born. Meredith knew it was possible to find out before the baby came, whether it was a girl or a boy, but she wanted to be surprised and knew that Luke would most likely agree. As she was sure all parents felt, she didn't mind what it was as long as the baby was healthy. It seemed good to have a plan, and once she had confirmation from the midwife that she was expecting a baby, Meredith would start clearing out this room.

Back downstairs, Meredith hummed while she stirred the soup, enjoying the aroma of sweet corn and chicken broth. Meredith was getting hungry, and the hot soup would taste good.

≈

With the motion of the bus, Luke's eyes were getting heavier, and his head bobbed each time he caught himself nodding off. If he kept this up, he'd have a stiff neck by the time he got to the City of Brotherly Love. He was already missing Meredith and thinking she had probably finished supper by now.

I wonder what she made tonight, he thought. Just thinking about a home-cooked meal caused his mouth to water. The bus would be arriving in Philadelphia soon, and when it did, Luke planned to get something to eat.

Probably should have let Meredith fix me those sandwiches to bring along, he thought with regret. *Guess I oughta listen to her more often. One of those delicious ham and cheese sandwiches would sure stop my stomach from rumbling right now.*

Luke's thoughts were halted when the elderly man across from him began to snore. He sounded like an old bear growling. The fellow's snoring was louder than Luke's stomach rumbling. Even some of the other passengers on the bus turned toward the man and snickered.

Guess I can't fault him for that. According to Meredith, I snore, too. Luke smiled just thinking about it. *'Course, I don't have to listen to myself.* He tried not to laugh, but the old man's nasal rumblings sounded so funny. By now, the snoring had gone up a notch, reminding Luke of a buzz saw. *Surely,* he thought, watching the man, *my snoring can't be as bad as that. If it is, then I'm sure Meredith would have teased me about it.*

Luke removed his black felt hat and placed it in his lap. Then he leaned his head against the back of the seat and closed his eyes. He figured he may as well get a little sleep while he could, and hopefully he wouldn't snore. One snoring person on the bus was enough. Since the bus wasn't full, he was able to stretch out into the empty space beside him.

Luke couldn't quit thinking about Meredith. By now, she probably had Fritz inside with her for the night. That gave him some measure of comfort. As the bus rolled toward Philly, the last thing Luke thought about before drifting off to sleep was a prayer for Meredith's safety while he was gone.

⌖

Meredith had just finished cleaning up the kitchen and was thinking about getting ready for bed when she remembered that she'd forgotten to bring Fritz inside. She hated to go out in the dark, frigid weather, but it wouldn't be fair to let him stay out in the kennel all night, and she'd never be able to sleep, knowing he was out there in a cold doghouse, while she was warm and comfortable inside. Luke had put plenty of straw inside Fritz's shelter, but it wasn't like being in the house where it was warm and more comfortable. Meredith was mad at herself for not bringing Fritz in sooner, or even asking her dad to bring him in when he and Mom were here. But Meredith had so much on her mind, she'd forgotten all about the pup.

Bundling up in one of Luke's heavy jackets, Meredith grabbed a flashlight and went out the back door. As the cold air hit her cheeks, she breathed deeply, inhaling the scent of her husband from the coat that encompassed her. Meredith closed her eyes and could almost imagine Luke standing there holding her.

The wind had begun to blow, and it was snowing again. Meredith was sorry she hadn't thought to put on her boots. Her feet were soaking wet already and turning colder with each step she took. She shivered and made her way as quickly as possible to Fritz's dog run.

Woof! Woof! Fritz wagged his tail when Meredith approached the fence.

"Are you ready to come into the house, pup?" Meredith asked, opening the gate.

Woof! Fritz dashed out of the dog run, raced across the yard, leaped onto the porch, and started pawing at the back door.

Meredith chuckled. "I know just how you feel."

After they got inside, she kicked off her shoes and put on a dry pair of socks. Neither she nor the dog wasted any time heading into the living room. Meredith stoked up the fire then went to her rocker and picked up the Bible on the small table beside her. Fritz curled up on the braided rug next to the fireplace.

Opening her Bible to a place she had marked with a ribbon, Meredith read a verse of scripture she thought was especially meaningful and had underlined some time ago. "Thou wilt keep him in perfect peace, whose mind is stayed on thee: because he trusteth in thee." Isaiah 26:3.

Meredith smiled and felt herself relax. God's Word always had a way of speaking to her just when she needed it the most. For the moment at least, she felt sure that, despite all her worries, everything concerning her and Luke would turn out fine.

CHAPTER 7

Philadelphia

Luke was glad to be off the bus for a while. He needed the chance to walk around and stretch his legs. He'd slept most of the way and had ended up with a kink in his neck, just like he'd figured he would.

Luke felt the side of his head, amazed that there weren't any bumps. He'd hit the window so many times from his head bobbing around, it was surprising that he'd even been able to get in a few winks.

He pulled out his pocket watch to check the time. The bus he'd be transferring to in Philadelphia wouldn't be leaving the station until 12:20 a.m., which meant he had plenty of time to get a bite to eat and buy a newspaper so he'd have something to read. Luke was always interested to see what was going on in the rest of the world and wanted to check for any articles on the weather to see if the storm had reached the areas where he'd be traveling.

Before putting the watch back in his pocket, he clicked it shut, remembering what a great gift it was that Meredith had given him this past Christmas. How she'd ever found that particular pocket watch was amazing. Etched on the outer lid was a bird dog that looked just like Fritz. It was the perfect gift. Rubbing his thumb over the etching made his heart lurch. He was already homesick—for his wife, his dog, and even his horse. Luke felt like an outsider in this busy place and longed for the simple things of home.

As Luke stood on the curb looking both ways, he spotted a diner near the bus depot. The place looked inviting, and with his stomach growling and the wonderful aromas coming from the diner, he was drawn in that direction. When he stepped into the restaurant, he found a stack of newspapers on a rack near the door. He took one, paid the cashier, and then found a seat in a booth near the window, with the bus depot still in view. He noticed a tear in the vinyl seat cover, and as he looked around, Luke noticed the café was a bit run down, but the place was clean and crowded. That could only mean one thing: the food must be good.

When the waitress came, Luke ordered a ham sandwich, fries, and a glass of chocolate milk. Waiting for his food to come, he read the newspaper, while all around him, people came and went. This sure was a busy place. There was an old jukebox in the corner, and someone had chosen a tune where the singer was crooning, "You were always on my mind." Luke wasn't used to hearing that kind of music, but he couldn't help listening to the part of the song that said, "Maybe I didn't treat you quite as good as I should have." The song was kind of catchy, that was for sure, but all it did was make Luke regret even more how he'd treated Meredith recently.

Trying to block out the words in the song, he stuck his nose deeper into the paper and concentrated on what he was reading. It was hard to believe all the bad news, and he searched through several pages before he found something positive to read. A group of senior citizens had participated in a class called "Water Walking," which gave them the exercise they needed, while getting to know other people their age.

Luke smiled at the happy looks he saw on the faces of the elderly people in the picture. They obviously enjoyed being in the water, just as he did during the warm summer months. If he had an indoor pool to use, like these people did, he'd probably swim in it all year.

He also found an article on the winter storm that had already created havoc in states to the west. It sounded like his travels would be taking him right through the blizzard. Even so, his excitement about his new job opportunity outweighed any anxiety about bad weather.

Luke's thoughts turned to Meredith once again and the fact that he'd soon be able to provide a decent living for their future. Luke could never repay his uncle for the gratitude he felt for giving him a chance for a new beginning.

❧

Earlier in the evening in an act of desperation, Alex had stolen some drugs. Now he had not one, but two dealers after him. But even in his most desperate times, he still had bouts of luck. In the alley behind the bus station he'd found a five-dollar bill, so he'd ducked into the diner across the street to get something to eat. He would figure out what to do from there.

Taking a seat, he drummed his fingers nervously along the edge of the table. He was exhausted, cold, and wanted something to eat almost as much as he'd needed his last fix. He looked around while he waited, hoping he wasn't too conspicuous. The place was sure busy and bustling with people. Alex was so hungry he could eat a horse and was almost to the point where he felt faint.

"What'll it be?" the middle-aged brunette waitress asked, looking down at Alex without a hint of a smile.

"What'll five bucks get me?" he mumbled, rubbing his hands briskly over his bare arms, wishing he looked a little more decent.

"How about a burger and some chips?" she replied stiffly, making no eye contact with him.

"Yeah, that's fine."

"You want some water to wash it down?"

"Sure." Alex nearly choked, trying to hold back his irritating cough.

When the waitress went to turn in his order, Alex sat back and surveyed his surroundings. Over the years there'd been a few instances when people were nice to him, but most of the time they acted like the waitress, either looking at him with disgust or avoiding his gaze altogether. Alex didn't care anymore. There wasn't a person on this earth who meant anything to him.

Now there's a familiar scene, Alex thought when he spotted an old man slouched in a booth near the door. The guy's eyes were closed, and his mouth hung open as his head lulled against the back of the seat. *The lazy bum's probably drunk.* Alex clenched his jaw. *Reminds me of my old man when he was in one of his stupors. Sure don't need no reminders of them horrible days. Just wanna forget about my past and try to have some kind of a future. But if I don't get outa here before I get caught, that's not likely to happen.*

Directly across from Alex sat a young bearded man with blond hair, reading a newspaper. He wore dark trousers and a heavy-looking black jacket. A black felt hat lay on the table next to his plate of fries.

Alex pulled his fingers through the ends of his own bristly beard, noting that the man's beard was about the same length as his. After closer observation, he realized the guy was Amish. Alex had seen some Amish men at the farmers' market in Philly, selling their wares. Just a week ago, Alex had stolen some produce from one of their stands. The old guy had been so busy yakking with one of his customers that he hadn't noticed what Alex had done. Or if he had, he'd chosen not to say anything about it.

Alex's burger came about the time the Amish man was finishing up with his meal, and when the fellow took his wallet out to pay, Alex couldn't help but notice the wad of bills sticking out. He also noticed how nice the waitress was to the bearded man as she counted back the change he was due. *What's the point of bein' nice to people? They're all strangers anyways, and they don't care about nobody but themselves.*

Alex gave his beard a quick tug. *I'll bet that guy would be an easy target.* From what little Alex knew about the Amish, he understood them to be a peaceful bunch of folks. He figured it shouldn't be too difficult to get what he wanted from the man. He just needed the right opportunity.

CHAPTER 8

Bird-in-Hand, Pennsylvania

Meredith rolled over onto her side and bunched up her pillow. She'd been in bed nearly two hours and hadn't been able to sleep because she couldn't turn off her thoughts. She'd started nodding off while reading downstairs, but by the time she'd gone to the kitchen for a glass of milk and then climbed the stairs to her room, she was wide awake again. All Meredith could think about was how much she missed Luke. She wished he'd let her pack some sandwiches for his trip. At least he'd have something from home in his stomach right now. *I wonder where he ended up eating and what kind of food he had.*

She glanced at the battery-operated clock on the small table beside her bed and saw that it was getting close to midnight. Luke was probably in Philadelphia by now and should be boarding the next bus soon. Meredith tried to imagine everything as if it was playing out in front of her, but all she could do was guess. The trip to Indiana was long, and Luke would be glad when he got there. Being patient wasn't easy, but she'd have to wait for his call tomorrow evening to find out how his journey had gone.

Lying on the small braided rug near the foot of Meredith's bed, Fritz woke up suddenly and started to bark.

"What's the matter, pup? Do you need to go out?"

Fritz darted around to her side of the bed and put one paw on her chest. *Woof! Woof!*

"Oh, all right." Meredith pushed the covers aside and climbed out of bed. Slipping into her robe and slippers, she went downstairs and let the dog out.

"Now hurry up and do your business," Meredith called as Fritz dashed into the yard. The frigid air made her even more awake, so she quickly shut the door. Spring couldn't come too quickly. She looked forward to planting her garden and tending all the colorful flowers in their yard. She loved having the windows open and the front and back door, too. The mild spring air wafting through the house always made everything smell so fresh and clean, especially after a good rain.

Several minutes went by; then Meredith heard a—*Thump! Thump!*—on the door, followed by a loud bark. "Are you ready to come in?" she asked, opening the door.

Woof! Woof! Fritz tromped inside and raced up the stairs.

When Meredith entered the bedroom, she found Fritz sitting on the floor at the foot of her bed, whining.

"I know, pup," Meredith said, patting the dog's head. "Luke hasn't even been gone a full day, yet I miss him so much."

Then, seeing the wet paw prints on the floor, she grabbed a towel and wiped up the water.

Going around in circles until he found just the right position, Fritz grunted and finally bedded down on the floor.

Meredith crawled into bed, and as she pulled the covers up to her chin, she said a prayer on her husband's behalf. It seemed like she'd been praying for Luke a lot since he'd left this afternoon.

But that's okay, she reminded herself. *In 1 Thessalonians 5:17 we are told to pray without ceasing.*

◦≫◦

Philadelphia

Alex gulped down half of his burger and grabbed the rest of it in a napkin. Then he slapped his money on the table and followed the Amish guy out the door. When he saw the fellow enter the bus station across the street, his interest increased. He had no idea where the guy might be heading, but anyplace out of Philly would be good enough for Alex. Wanting a quick getaway, and to be far from the drug dealers he'd stolen from, he thought this might end up being a piece of cake. To have the money he needed would be an extra bonus.

Leaning into the wind, and giving in to yet another coughing fit, Alex stepped inside the bus station, grateful for the warmth. *Sure wish I had a jacket,* he thought.

Once again, his gaze went to the Amish man, who had taken a seat between two old men on the other side of the room. The lucky guy had a jacket and a hat to chase away the cold. All Alex had was a dirty old T-shirt and a pair of faded, holey jeans. If he switched clothes with this fellow, he'd finally be warm.

I'll bet the guy won't give me too much trouble, Alex thought. *If he's peaceful, like I've heard the Amish are, then he oughta do everything I ask.*

He took a seat on the bench across from the Amish man and gave a nod when the fellow glanced his way. There were too many other people in the bus station for him to make a move right now, but if he could get the guy alone, he might have a chance. Feeling a bit stronger with some food in his belly, Alex decided to finish his burger and wait the man out.

After eating, then sitting there waiting, Alex felt himself getting drowsy, but he wouldn't give in to the temptation to sleep. As more passengers departed, the bus depot started clearing out. Alex knew for sure that his luck was changing when the Amish man stood and headed for the restroom. He could make his move now. Getting to his feet, he didn't hesitate to follow, anxious to get this over with.

⁂

Luke had just finished washing his hands when the scruffy-looking bearded man he'd seen come into the bus station shortly after he had entered the restroom. He stood staring at Luke a few seconds then sidled up to him and said, "Gimme your clothes."

Luke's forehead wrinkled. "You. . .you want my clothes?"

"That's what I said. Give 'em to me right now!" The man's hand shook as he balled it into a fist. "You'd better do as I say, or you'll be sorry."

Luke was tempted to resist, but seeing the desperation on the man's face, he thought better of it. This would be a good opportunity to show his Christianity. And with nothing but a T-shirt and a pair of holey jeans, the poor man was probably cold. Luke knew he could borrow some clothes from his uncle when he got to Indiana. Besides, he'd be getting on the bus soon, and that would give him some warmth.

But the scruffy-looking fellow wasn't satisfied with just Luke's clothes.

Once they'd traded, he demanded Luke's wallet. Luke could see that the man was shaky and agitated, so he offered to buy him something to eat.

"Already ate," the man growled. "Now, don't give me no trouble! I just want some money, and I want it right now!"

Luke shook his head, determinedly. It was one thing to give up his clothes and put on the stranger's uncomfortable jeans and dirty T-shirt, which didn't smell too good. He couldn't simply hand over his wallet. He needed that money to give his uncle as a down payment for the equipment he'd need to begin his new business. He had to somehow convince this determined fellow to change his mind about the money.

"I won't give you my wallet," Luke said, holding his ground and hoping to intimidate the angry-looking man. Luke had never met anyone like this before, and he hoped the situation would be resolved peacefully but feared it wouldn't. Maybe someone would walk into the restroom, and the encounter would be over before it got any worse.

"And I say you will hand it over!" the man shouted, his eyes squinting and his face turning red.

That determined expression and rising temper caused Luke to realize he was in serious trouble. Short of a miracle, this would be anything but a nonviolent encounter.

The look of outrage in the fellow's eyes gave no hint of him wavering, either, and before Luke could protect himself, the man stepped forward and punched him in the stomach, causing Luke to double over from the pain. Unleashing his fury, and with a string of curses, the enraged man knocked Luke to the floor and began viciously kicking him everywhere, including his head and face. Over and over, Luke was beaten, until he didn't think he could take any more pain. He tried to protect himself, but everything inside of him felt like it was breaking, and he was sure his body couldn't take much more abuse.

Dear God, please help me, Luke silently prayed as another serious blow connected to his head.

Will I ever see my beautiful fraa again? he wondered. Then everything went black.

THE SILENCE OF WINTER

Blessed are they that mourn:
for they shall be comforted.

MATTHEW 5:4

CHAPTER 1

Bird-in-Hand, Pennsylvania

It was early yet, and Meredith Stoltzfus resisted coming out of the deep sleep she was in. Even though she was toasty warm under the covers, she couldn't figure out why she felt as though something was different. It wasn't the feeling of anticipation children get when they wake up on Christmas morning. It was an empty, lonely feeling.

As the cobwebs cleared, she realized it wasn't just the emptiness she felt—it was the silence and the knowledge that she was alone. Her husband, Luke, had left for Indiana yesterday afternoon, and waking up by herself gave Meredith a really odd feeling. Luke hadn't been gone twenty-four hours, and already she missed him terribly. Now she just needed to get through the rest of the days until he returned from his uncle's place, where he'd gone to learn a new trade.

After all, Meredith reminded herself, *I got through last night, and Luke will only be gone a few weeks. Now the countdown starts, and when each morning begins, it will be one day closer to Luke's return. There's plenty to do around here, so I just need to keep busy until the day he walks through our back door.*

Meredith had always been active and very organized, and she knew these traits could be used to her advantage. It was time to fill any vulnerable moments by doing something constructive.

Rolling over onto her side and snuggling deeper under the covers, she was reminded that each morning since she'd married Luke fourteen months ago had started out the same. *If Luke was here right now, I'd be waking up with him by my side.*

Just then, Fritz, Luke's German shorthaired pointer who'd been sleeping on the floor beside the bed, snorted several times, sounding like he w snoring.

Meredith giggled, suddenly realizing what else was different this morning. She missed Luke's snoring. The small simple sound seemed to start Meredith's day out right. It was a gentle noise—not the deep rumbling her dad's snoring had always been. Dad had mentioned once that even in his younger days, he'd snored really loud. He'd blamed it on his slightly crooked nose, which had been broken when he'd run into a tree while playing ball as a boy. He said he had trouble breathing out one side of his nose—especially when he was sleeping. Meredith figured that must be true, because when Dad fell asleep in his easy chair each evening after supper, his mouth hung slightly open. When Meredith still lived at home, she'd heard the rumbling snores coming from Mom and Dad's bedroom almost every single night. Sometimes it had been so loud she'd had to cover her ears with two pillows in order to get to sleep.

Poor Mom, Meredith thought. *I don't know how she gets any sleep at all. But then, maybe Mom's not bothered by Dad's snoring. Could be she's gotten used to it over the years.*

Meredith glanced at the alarm clock on the table by her bed. Rarely did it have the chance to go off, because Luke's snoring would start within minutes of when they were supposed to get up. It was amazing that Luke never snored during the night. If he did, it must be really quiet, because Meredith had never heard it, nor had it ever caused her to wake up until the morning hours.

Lying under the covers and continuing to enjoy her thoughts, she recollected how on most mornings it was hard not to laugh at the sounds Luke made. He sounded so content with each breath he took in and blew out, and she would just lie there quietly with her hand over her mouth and listen.

Luke didn't seem to mind when Meredith playfully tickled his ear to gently wake him up. That was quite evident when those turquoise eyes opened slowly and looked tenderly into hers. He'd often said that a tickle on the ear was far better than any blaring alarm.

Meredith's thoughts halted when Fritz, grunting loudly, woke himself and rose to his feet. Then he plodded over to Meredith's side of the bed, nudged her arm with his wet nose, and laid his head on the mattress, watching her intently with his big brown puppy-dog eyes. When he didn't get a response, Fritz started whimpering.

"I know," she said, clutching Luke's pillow tightly to her chest.

"You need to go out, don't you, pup?"

Woof! Woof! The dog's tail wagged at Meredith's response.

Hearing the sound of sleet pelting the bedroom window, Meredith wished she could lie in bed a few minutes longer, hugging her husband's pillow, but with Fritz needing to go outside, any more daydreaming was out of the question. Besides, she had an appointment with a midwife. It was time to get ready for what she hoped would be some really good news.

⟡

Pittsburgh, Pennsylvania

Alex Mitchell reached into his pants pocket and pulled out the gold pocket watch he'd taken from the Amish man he'd accosted in the Philadelphia bus station. It was just a few minutes past eight o'clock, he noted. He'd transferred to yet another bus thirty minutes ago, and as they headed out of the city, the bus, along with all the other traffic, was almost at a standstill. The bus he'd ridden on after leaving the station in Philly at 12:20 that morning had been a slow-go as the foggy mist had turned to black ice on the highway. Now the roads were so icy that no one could go anywhere without sliding all over the place. Motorists had no choice but to sit and wait for the salt trucks to come through in order to make travel somewhat safer.

Alex looked out the window and saw that all the other cars on the highway had pulled off to the side of the road, just as the bus had done. According to the bus schedule, they weren't supposed to arrive in South Bend, Indiana, until 6:35 that evening, but with the weather being so bad, he figured it might be midnight or even later before they pulled into the station. Well, he didn't care. He had food in his belly, a wallet full of money, and a ticket to freedom, courtesy of the Amish man, so he'd just sit back and try to relax until the bus took him to his destination. Even Alex's nagging cough was a bit better now that he wore warm clothes and had the comfort of being on the bus.

Continuing to stare out at the nasty weather and listen to sleet hit the bus windows, Alex was glad to be in a place that was warm. Thinking back to the night before, Alex was surprised that his luck had held out and he hadn't been caught—either by the drug dealers who'd been after him, or worse yet, the cops. He'd expected something to go wrong, because it usually did. But so far, nothing was out of the ordinary, and everything was going okay. The more distance Alex put between him and Philadelphia, the better he felt.

He looked down at the black felt hat in his lap and grinned. Luck had been with him once again, in that everything that had taken place at the bus station in Philly had happened late at night. Alex was sure that no one else had seen what had actually transpired between him and the young Amish man in the restroom. He felt pretty comfortable that the bus he'd boarded after the encounter had pulled out before anyone had discovered the unconscious man lying on the restroom floor where he'd left him. Of course, it wasn't uncommon for the bathroom in Philadelphia's bus depot to be void of activity so late at night. He ought to know—he'd slept in that depot a time or two when he'd been down on his luck. He'd never gotten used to the achiness that permeated his body each time he'd flaked out on an uncomfortable bench or awakened on a cold concrete floor. It was just one more thing that added to his unhappy life as a homeless drug addict.

I wonder if that guy had a dog like this one, Alex pondered, rubbing his thumb over the etching on the front of the Amish fellow's watch.

He stared at the picture of the bird dog engraved on the outer case of the pocket watch and clasped his fingers tightly around it. *That poor guy never knew what hit him.* Truth was, Alex didn't remember a whole lot about the beating, except that he'd gone berserk and started kicking and punching when the Amish fellow had refused to hand over his wallet. Once Alex had started his tirade, he'd been oblivious to everything around him and unable to stop himself. After he'd finally come to his senses, he'd taken the unconscious man's wallet, clothes, bus ticket, and pocket watch, then left him on the cold bathroom floor. After that, he'd rushed out the door, not knowing, or even caring, how badly the man might have been hurt.

If Alex was a decent sort, he would have gone back to make sure the guy wasn't dead. But Alex hadn't been decent for a good many years. Maybe he never had been. Maybe he'd always been full of hate. After the beating, all Alex had cared about was saving his own hide and getting out of there as fast as he could. Now if only this bus would get moving and put more miles between him and Philly, Alex would feel a whole lot better about things. What if the Amish guy had come to and told the police about the mugging? The police could be looking for him right now. Would they know he was on his way to Indiana, dressed in the Amish man's clothes, and using his bus ticket? Alex had never been to Indiana before, but he was anxious to get there, especially now.

Alex frowned and covered his ears. Awhile ago, some kid at the back of the bus had gotten the brainy idea to do a sing-along. Most everyone had joined in, even the adults. It was bad enough when they started singing "Oh! Susanna" and "The Wheels on the Bus" with all that swish-swishing, beep-beeping, and clink-clinking. Now it was even worse. They were singing "The Ants Go Marching." Alex thought he would go crazy if he heard one more rendition of that stupid song. It seemed to go on forever.

When that song was finally over, the kid who'd started the sing-along noticed that Alex was the only one not participating, so he got some other stupid song started about being a party pooper, and on and on it went.

Sure can't wait to get off this bus, Alex thought, twisting his body toward the window and away from the sounds of that unwanted chorus. *If I had some duct tape, I'd go back there and slap it over that kid's big mouth!*

⁂

Philadelphia, Pennsylvania

Nurse Susan Bailey had just gotten off the phone with her sister, Anne, as they finalized their plans for the evening. Anne worked at the same hospital as Susan, but Anne was a physical therapist in the rehab center, while Susan worked in the critical care unit.

Susan's morning had been busy, making rounds and tending patients. She finally found the time to take a break at eleven and couldn't believe how fast the morning had gone. She'd started her twelve-hour shift at 4:00 a.m. and had missed her early morning break, so the hunger pangs she felt now told her it was definitely past time to eat.

As Susan headed down the hall to the hospital cafeteria, she figured there wouldn't be too many people there yet, and hopefully it would be quiet. During her thirty-minute break, she planned to start a grocery list. Last night before bed, Grandma Bailey had given her a small list of things she needed from the store, as well, so all Susan had to do was add what she wanted to her grandmother's list and stop by the store on the way home. Buying groceries was just a small way of showing appreciation for all that Grandma and Grandpa had done for Susan and her sister over the years.

When Susan opened her small cooler, she frowned. *Sure wish I'd thought to pack more than yogurt and celery sticks this morning. I'll just have to make do until I meet Anne for supper this evening, because I don't want to buy a big lunch here and ruin my appetite for tonight.*

Even though Susan and her sister lived with their grandparents in Darby, just outside Philadelphia, their jobs kept them so busy they didn't see each other that much. Since they both had tonight off they'd decided to meet at a new Mexican restaurant for dinner at six thirty. Susan looked forward to biting into a zesty taco and whatever else she decided to order.

Seeing that there were only a few people in the lunchroom, Susan took a seat at one of the tables closest to the big window where she could look out at the rock garden that had been recently established by a local Boy Scout troop. This part of the cafeteria had lightly tinted glass windows that went from floor to ceiling. No matter where you sat, you could view the scene outside. The hospital had beautiful gardens all over the grounds. Different rocks of all shapes and sizes were displayed in this one, and among them sat various statues of wildlife. A squirrel statue perched on a flat rock, and a bunny rabbit sat near the edge by the grass. A family of deer gathered at the far side of the display, and a wooden wishing well sat in the center of it all. On top of the wishing well balanced a small statue of a cardinal.

Susan smiled when a real cardinal landed near the resin one then quickly flew away. It was a lovely display, and the Scouts had done a great job, but she'd heard that it wasn't quite finished. The boys were supposed to return in the spring to plant flowers among the rocks and in the bucket of the wishing well.

A little bit of color will be the perfect touch. She had just opened her container of yogurt when she was called back to the nurses' station. "Oh my! So much for my break," she murmured, putting her hand on her stomach as it growled in protest. "Guess the grocery list will have to wait, too."

She headed back to the nurses' station, where she learned that one of the CCU nurses had taken ill and left early and a new patient who'd been badly injured would be arriving on her floor soon.

At home, Susan tended to be a bit disorganized as a means of relaxing and letting down. Here at work, however, it was a totally different story. She made sure no stone was left unturned. The patients' needs were first and foremost in all that she did, and in return, the patients loved and appreciated her. Even the doctors held Susan in high regard for the dedication she displayed on the job.

Susan wanted to make sure the room was ready, and as she quickly and skillfully did her job, she sent up a prayer on the new patient's behalf.

CHAPTER 2

Bird-in-Hand

Meredith had left the midwife's office that morning feeling like she was walking on air, despite the heavy mist and icy roads that made traveling so miserable. Her suspicions had been right—she and Luke were going to be parents. She was about to burst, wanting to share the news with her folks, as well as Luke's, but it wouldn't be right to tell them without first telling Luke. She felt like pinching herself to be sure she wasn't dreaming. In July, they would be celebrating the birth of their first baby. *Oh, what a blessing from God that will be!*

After Meredith's appointment, she'd made a few stops to pick up some groceries and other things she needed. Because of the roads, she had kept her horse, Taffy, at an even, slow pace, and so far her outing had been uneventful. She hoped when Luke called from his uncle's this evening that she could hide her excitement about the baby. She wanted to wait and tell him their great news when he came home and she could do it face-to-face.

Meredith was excited to see Luke's reaction and felt sure he'd be as happy as she was. With the prospect of his new headstone-engraving business and a baby on the way, everything seemed to be falling into place at last.

In the meantime, it would be a challenge not to tell her family when she saw them next, for she knew how excited they would all be—even her sisters and brothers, whom she felt sure would enjoy having a niece or nephew to play with and dote upon. So as soon as Luke returned and had learned the news, they'd tell both of their families together.

Before Luke left for Indiana, he'd told Meredith that he thought he'd be home by the end of January, so Meredith didn't think her pregnancy would be showing that much yet. She hoped Luke wouldn't suspect any change in her looks before she had the chance to tell him.

As Meredith guided her horse and buggy down the driveway leading to their house, she sent up a prayer of thanks for getting her and Taffy safely home. The horse had done well on the slippery roads, but whenever a car passed her buggy, Meredith had clenched the reins so tightly that her fingers ached. It had been a good thing she'd been driving her docile mare and not Luke's horse, Socks. She shuddered to think of how hard it would have been to control the spirited gelding on the icy roads.

Even though Luke wasn't there, rounding the bend and having their house come into view was a welcome sight. It was a relief to be home again, where she could relax for the rest of the day. Not that she would do that. Meredith felt full of energy, and her mind swirled with so many plans. There was a lot to be done before the baby came, and she could hardly wait to get started.

First things first, she thought as her stomach rumbled noisily. Meredith had been so nervous about her appointment that she hadn't eaten much for breakfast. So after putting Taffy back in the barn and unloading the buggy, she went straight to the house to make something for lunch. Now that she knew for certain she was pregnant, she'd be sure to eat regular meals. After all, she would be eating for two from now on.

⌒⌒

Cleveland, Ohio

Alex shifted restlessly in his seat, unable to find a comfortable position. This trip was taking forever, but at least the traffic was moving again, and that annoying singing had finally stopped. Even at a slower pace, it was better than not moving at all, like they'd been forced to do earlier that morning. Their bus driver was being cautious because now the frozen mist had turned into snow. The farther west they traveled, the heavier and deeper it seemed to be getting.

The storm had really played havoc for anyone in a moving vehicle, not to mention the road crews trying to keep the roads safe enough for travel. At this rate, Alex was almost certain the bus wouldn't make it to South Bend on time this evening. But he guessed that was okay, because he really had no place else he needed to be right now. As long as the singing from the back of the bus didn't start up again, he might be able to get some sleep. The sooner he got to Indiana, the better, but at least it didn't appear the cops were after him. That gave him a measure of peace. He sure couldn't complain, as he patted his pocket and smiled to himself, knowing he had plenty of money—more than he'd had in a long time. He could lie low in a new town, not to mention buy his next fix once he found the right dealer.

Staring out the window at the falling snow, Alex noticed that the bus was slowing down as it pulled into a parking lot. He figured this must be the lunch stop he'd heard one of the passengers mention about an hour ago, and he had to admit he was starving.

As the bus pulled in, Alex realized that, according to the sign out front, the diner had a bookstore in the basement. That seemed kind of weird, but then weirdness was everywhere these days.

When the bus came to a stop, Alex noticed the singsong kid from the back of the bus had jumped up quickly, wanting to be the first one off. *Now's my chance to get back at the little runt.*

Right before the boy ran past him, Alex stuck his foot into the aisle, just enough to make the kid trip and fall.

"Oh, sorry about that." Alex gave a halfhearted apology as the boy picked himself up. *Serves you right, you little creep. Where's your parents, anyway?*

The boy didn't seem to be too bothered by it, but he got back at Alex by saying, "You got big feet, mister."

"Oh yeah? Well, you—"

"Where you headed, sir?" the elderly man across the aisle from Alex asked as they stood to get off the bus.

Glaring at the boy one last time, Alex grimaced. The last thing he wished to do was converse with anyone else, especially now that he'd have to act Amish. But it was his own fault for bringing attention to himself.

All Alex wanted to do was get something to eat, because once the bus headed back out on the road, it might not be stopping for meals again until it arrived in South Bend. Since Alex had plenty of money for a change, he planned to order something that would stick to his ribs.

"So, where you heading?" the old man asked again.

"I'm goin' to South Bend," Alex mumbled, followed by several racking coughs.

"Ah, so I'm guessin' you must live in one of the Amish communities around Middlebury or Shipshewana?" The man squinted his pale blue eyes as he looked at Alex curiously.

Alex gave a brief nod and hurried off the bus, hoping the few words he'd spoken hadn't given him away. When he entered the café, he found a seat at the lunch counter and placed an order for chicken and stuffing with mashed potatoes and a cup of black coffee. He was tempted to order a beer but thought better of it since he was dressed in Amish clothes.

"Mind if I join ya?" the old man asked, taking a seat on the stool beside Alex.

"Suit yourself; it's a free country," Alex said with a shrug. *Sure wish this guy would leave me alone. Why me, anyhow? Why doesn't he bother some other poor sucker?*

The wrinkles in the man's forehead deepened. "You know, you really don't sound like any Amish man I've ever met. Where'd you say you're from?"

"I didn't." Alex grabbed the newspaper lying beside him, hoping to put an end to this conversation.

"I'm from Mishawaka," the man said. "But I know a couple of Amish families who live in Middlebury."

Alex said nothing, just kept reading the paper.

"You goin' to Middlebury?"

Alex gritted his teeth. "I'm not sure where I'm goin' yet."

"But you said you were gettin' off the bus in South Bend. Isn't that what you said?"

Alex gave a quick nod.

"There aren't any Amish communities in South Bend, so—"

Alex was relieved when the middle-aged, slightly plump waitress came and took the old man's order. Maybe the nosy fellow would be so occupied with his food that he'd forget about asking Alex any more questions. Of course, that wouldn't happen until the waitress brought them both something to eat. In the meantime, Alex needed a break, so he hopped off his stool and headed for the restroom. He was glad when the nosy guy didn't follow.

When Alex returned to the lunch counter a short time later, the old man had moved to a booth and was slurping down a bowl of soup while leafing through a book. That was a relief!

Alex dove into the hearty meal he'd ordered and washed it down with a cup of very strong coffee. He figured it had probably been warmed over from the day before, but it didn't matter to him. The food was good, and for the first time in ages, his stomach was getting full. It felt great to have some real food in his belly for a change. Stealing bits of food here and there and sometimes gulping something down that one of the restaurants in Philly had thrown out was no way to exist. Of course, Alex hadn't done more than merely exist for too many years already. Well, that was about to change.

Grabbing the last piece of chicken and stirring it through the gravy, Alex took a quick glance around the restaurant. At the end of each table, a small bookshelf held several books.

"Would you like a refill of coffee?" the waitress asked as she took Alex's plate.

"No, I've had enough," Alex curtly answered. Then he remembered he was supposed to act Amish, which meant he should probably be a little more polite to the woman. "Uh, what's with all the books?" he questioned.

"This place started out years ago with just a few books in the cases at the end of each booth. When they saw how interested the patrons were, the store owners put shelving in the basement and started adding more books down there." The waitress smiled. "Some people just like paging through them; others want to buy them. We also do a book exchange. People can bring in a book from their home and trade it with one of ours."

That was a little more information than Alex cared to hear, but he played "Mr. Polite" and listened halfheartedly to all that she said.

In order to kill some time, after Alex paid his bill, he decided to go down in the basement to check out the bookstore for himself. As soon as he entered, the musty smell of old books hit him in the face, causing him to sneeze. He walked down each aisle of books, noticing how old some of them were. The stale odor, a combination of mildew, cigarette smoke, and mothballs, gave him the creeps, and he wondered how long these books had actually been there. Alex didn't recall if the waitress had mentioned what year they'd added the store in the basement. He did, however, recognize a few books he had read in school many years ago, so he pulled one off the shelf and flipped through the pages. Reading a page from a story he'd long forgotten until now, it unlocked unpleasant memories from his dysfunctional home and abusive father.

Back then, Alex had enjoyed reading. It had been a way to escape. Of course, whenever Alex's old man had caught him with his nose in a book, he'd made fun of Alex, saying, "Why don't you get your head outta the clouds and come back down to earth? Besides, you're too stupid to understand much about what's in them books. You'll never amount to anything, boy!"

I've had enough of this! Slamming the book shut and putting it back on the shelf, Alex hurried out of the bookstore, climbed back on the bus, and took his seat. When he spotted the nosy old man, along with several others, returning to the bus, Alex shut his eyes and pretended to be asleep. *Maybe I should have bought a book,* he thought, watching through half-opened eyes as the man took his seat across the aisle. *It might have kept my mind off my need for a fix. Oh well, it's too late for that. The best thing I can do is try to get some sleep.*

A short time later, the bus driver took his place behind the wheel, and they were back on the road.

Alex, feeling kind of shaky, turned his head toward the window and tried to focus on the weather outside, but his eyes were getting heavy, and in no time, he really was asleep.

"Look out! We're gonna be hit!" someone shouted.

Alex jerked awake and watched in horror out the front window as a gas truck, slipping all over the icy road, swerved into their lane. A terrible crash was immediately followed by an explosion.

The bus burst into flames.

CHAPTER 3

Philadelphia

The new patient's room had been ready for almost two hours. If he didn't arrive from the ER soon, Susan would have to call her sister and tell her she'd be late for supper. Her quitting time was less than an hour from now, so hopefully it would all work out. Somehow in between her duties, she'd managed to eat the yogurt she'd packed, as well as the rest of her celery. But by the time she ate supper this evening, she'd be ravenous.

It wasn't unusual for patients to be brought up from the ER later than expected, due to other emergencies that needed tending to. And that occurred more often during the winter months, when weather-caused accidents were numerous. If the patient didn't stabilize enough to be moved or had emergency surgery, that could also delay the transfer to CCU.

Back in the patient's room, she made one final check and was glad to see that everything was in order. It was after 5:00 p.m. when she finally got the official call that the new patient was being brought up.

Susan flipped on the TV to make sure it was working and turned to their local station, hoping to hear a weather report, since she'd been hearing others talk about the storm that had hit several states. The local weather was turning nasty, too, and it was comforting to know her grandparents would be safe and warm at home in Darby, instead of out on the slippery roads.

Before clicking off the remote, a special news report broke about a horrific accident that had just happened near the border of Indiana. Although she didn't hear all the details as her own patient was brought into the room, she thought about the hospital staff in Indiana who would be tending the people involved in the accident. Susan wasn't positive, but she thought she'd heard the newscaster say it involved a bus and a tanker full of gasoline.

She sent up a prayer for the accident victims, as well as the doctors and nurses who would be treating them. Susan had learned during her ER training that if there were any survivors in an accident such as this, the medical people were going to have their hands full.

❦

Bird-in-Hand

Wednesday evening, while waiting for Luke's call, Meredith sat in the rocker, enjoying the warmth of the fire and thinking about all she would need to do in preparation for their new little one. They had four bedrooms on the second floor, and she wanted the baby in the one closest to her and Luke's room because that would be most convenient. Maybe once Luke called, she'd ask him again about painting that room, even though he didn't know yet that it would be turned into a nursery. Better yet, maybe she would just go ahead with her plans and surprise him with it when he got home. Since he'd be making money soon, taking a little more money from their bank account to buy paint shouldn't be a problem. At least, she'd convinced herself of that. And if Meredith knew Luke as well as she thought, he'd be okay with the room getting painted once he knew about the baby.

Meredith tried to ignore the fact that Luke was late calling her. She had been to the phone shack several times this evening to see if he had left her a message, but there was none. Now that it was almost nine o'clock, she'd begun to worry and had to keep reminding herself that maybe he wasn't there yet because of bad weather. The bus had most likely been traveling right into the storm. And if that was the case, the bus would be running later than normal.

It had gotten even colder, and the mist had turned to a heavy, wet snow when Meredith decided to go out to the phone shack to check for messages again. Slipping into one of Luke's jackets and tying a woolen scarf around her head, she stepped into a pair of boots and hurried out the door. She was almost to the phone shack when Fritz started barking and pawing at the fence that enclosed his doghouse.

"Oh no," Meredith moaned. "I'm sorry, pup; I forgot to bring you in."

Quickly, she undid the latch on Fritz's dog run and swung open the gate.

Woof! Woof! Fritz raced across the yard, kicking up snow and frolicking like a puppy.

She grinned as he buried his nose in the snow and then jumped forward to do it again. Perhaps he'd caught the scent of a mouse or some other small critter that was under the snow. The dog sure did look funny each time his head came up and it was covered in the white fluffy flakes.

Meredith decided to let him explore a bit while she checked for messages. That might tire the dog out and make him more willing to settle down once she brought him into the house for the night.

Stepping into the phone shack and turning on the battery-operated lantern, Meredith pressed the button on the answering machine. Finding no messages, she decided it was time to make a call to Luke's uncle. Since no one was in his phone shack to answer the call, she left a message asking if Luke had arrived yet, and if he had, would he please call.

Shivering as she trudged back to the house, Meredith noticed that it was snowing even harder. Fritz seemed to have had enough frolicking, because he was lying by the back door, snow dripping off the end of his nose. He was probably as desperate to be inside as she.

Meredith hurried through the snow and slipped when her feet touched the icy porch step. She grabbed the railing. "Whew! That was close," she said, walking carefully to the door. "The last thing I need is to fall and get hurt—especially with Luke being gone right now."

⚭

Philadelphia

"I can't believe we finally made it here," Susan said to her sister, Anne, as they took seats in a booth at the Mexican restaurant that evening. "I'm glad you didn't mind us meeting for dinner a little later than we'd originally planned."

"No problem." Anne pushed a springy coffee-colored curl off her forehead and smiled, although her dark brown eyes revealed the depth of her fatigue. Anne was thirty—only two years older than Susan, who had celebrated her twenty-eighth birthday a few weeks ago. But right now, the fatigue in Anne's eyes made her appear to be much older than Susan. If not for that, they could have passed for twins, having the same hair color, olive-toned skin, and straight, white teeth. Both were slender and not real tall, and the only visible difference was Anne's naturally curly hair, while Susan's was straight.

"Rough day?" Susan asked, gently touching her sister's arm.

Anne shrugged. "It wasn't really rough, just seemed to be longer than normal. And it didn't help that I stayed up later than usual last night, reading that new novel I bought a few days ago."

"It must be a good one. What's it about?" Susan asked with interest.

"It's an Amish love story, and it's making me curious about the Amish way of life. It's one of those books that once you begin reading it, you just can't put it down."

"Maybe I can read it after you're done," Susan said. "And if you're that curious about the Amish, maybe you should take a trip to Lancaster the next time you have a day off."

Anne's lips curved into a wide smile, revealing her straight pearly white teeth. "Those are both good ideas. But I think I'll wait until we have the same day off, and then maybe we can go to Lancaster together. It's been some time since we've been there, and—"

A young dark-haired waitress came to take their order.

"Hmm. . .let's see now," Susan said, studying the menu. "I'm so hungry I think I could eat nearly everything listed here." She grinned at Anne. "I'm for sure getting tacos, because that's all I've been thinking about since we talked this morning."

"I'd like a taco, too, and I'd also like a burrito with some refried beans," Anne said to the waitress.

Susan bobbed her head. "I'd like two tacos and an enchilada with plenty of cheese. Oh, and for an appetizer, we'd like some of your jalapeno poppers."

"Would you like anything to drink besides water?" the waitress asked.

"Unsweetened iced tea for me," Anne spoke up.

"Make that two," Susan said with a nod.

After the waitress left to turn in their orders, Susan and Anne nibbled on the chips and salsa that had been placed on the table, while Susan told Anne about the patient who had been brought up from the ER that evening. "The poor guy was beat up pretty bad, and I think he must be homeless," she said, slowly shaking her head. "I heard he was found in the men's restroom of the bus depot and all he was wearing was the clothes on his back, which amounted to just a dirty T-shirt and a pair of equally dirty torn jeans. Oh, and there was no identification on him at all. The ER nurse handed me the bag containing his clothes but said she thought they were basically rags and should be thrown out."

"That's so sad." Anne's forehead wrinkled. "How badly was he hurt?"

"He sustained multiple injuries to his arms, ribs, legs, neck, and especially his head. Whoever beat him must have been on a real rampage, because he was a mess." Susan added that she'd read on the man's chart that he'd had a beard, but it had been shaved off in the ER in order to stitch up a nasty cut on his chin. "And of course his head had been shaved and bandaged, as well," she said. "I wonder what he could have done to make someone mad enough to beat him up like that."

"Did he say anything to you?" Anne asked.

"No, he was unconscious, and once I had him settled into bed and had assisted the doctor with his examination, the night nurse came in and took over, since my shift had ended. Hopefully I'll find out more tomorrow." Susan sighed. "I said a little prayer for the young man, because he certainly looked like he could use one."

CHAPTER 4

Bird-in-Hand

For the last half hour, Meredith had been lying on the sofa, with Fritz on the floor beside her, sleeping soundly. The poor dog had played himself out, and now he was even snoring.

Meredith snickered. Watching Fritz's upper lip vibrate each time he took a breath was hilarious. The poor pup probably wouldn't be too happy if he knew she was laughing at him.

Truthfully, Meredith was tired from all the trips she'd made out to the phone shack to check for messages from Luke, so she decided if she could sleep for a little while and then go back out again, there would finally be the long-awaited message from him.

She was almost asleep when a sudden knock on the front door, followed by Fritz's loud barking, brought her to her feet.

Now who would be out on a night like this, with the snow coming down as hard as it is? Meredith wondered. *And who would be knocking on my door so late in the evening?*

When Meredith went to the door, Fritz was right there with her, still barking frantically. She opened it slowly. Sheriff Tyler stood on the porch.

"How are you doing, Fritz?" the sheriff asked, looking down at the dog. But his greeting lacked the upbeat tone it usually had whenever he was in the area and had dropped by to see Luke.

"Hush, Fritz; it's okay," Meredith said, clutching Fritz's collar. Seeing the sheriff's grim expression, her heartbeat quickened. Something must be horribly wrong. Her first thought, as she invited the sheriff in out of the cold, was of her parents. Could something have happened to them? *Oh, dear Lord, please don't let it be so.*

When Sheriff Tyler motioned for Meredith to sit down, her ears began to ring. Whatever he'd come to say, it wasn't good news. Continuing to hang on to Fritz's collar, she took a seat in the rocker, while the sheriff seated himself on the sofa across from her. Fritz had stopped barking once he'd seen that it was the sheriff, but the hair on his back stood straight up as he sat by Meredith's feet, as though waiting. Even he must have sensed that something horrible had occurred.

"What is it, Sheriff Tyler?" Meredith asked, her palms growing sweaty. "Has something happened to someone in my family?"

He gave a slow nod. "I'm afraid so, Meredith. It's Luke."

Meredith sat several seconds, staring at the crackling logs in the fireplace. Slowly, what the sheriff had said registered. "Luke left yesterday afternoon on a bus trip to South Bend, Indiana," she said. "His uncle is going to teach him how to engrave headstones."

"Yes, I know. Someone in your community mentioned it when I saw them earlier today." A pained expression crossed the sheriff's face as he explained to Meredith that the bus Luke had been riding on had gotten hit by a tanker full of gas just past the Indiana border. "There's no easy way for me to say this," he said in a sympathetic tone, "but all the bodies were completely burned in the explosion. And since Luke's name was on the passenger list, they knew he was one of those on the bus."

Meredith's body went numb. How could Luke be dead? It wasn't possible. There had to be some mistake. Luke had only left yesterday afternoon, and he was supposed to arrive in Indiana this evening. She just needed to wait for his call.

"I know this must come as a shock to you," Sheriff Tyler said, leaning forward. "And I'm very sorry for your loss."

Is this what it's like when a soldier's wife is notified that her husband's been killed in combat? Everything is normal one minute, and then, all of a sudden, it's not. Meredith's thoughts were so scattered she could barely make sense of them. "No, it's not true," she whispered, letting go of Fritz's collar and slowly shaking her head. "Luke can't be dead. He'll be calling soon, saying he's made it safely to Indiana."

The sheriff left his seat and knelt on the floor in front of Meredith. "You're in shock, Meredith, and I think you need to be with your family right now.

Why don't you gather up a few things, and I'll drive you over to your folks' place to spend the night? Then I'll need to see Luke's parents and, regrettably, give them the sad news."

Meredith looked down at Fritz; the dog's head rested in her lap as though he somehow knew she needed his comfort. Tears welled in her eyes as the truth began to fully register. A sudden wave of nausea hit, and Meredith's hands went instinctively to her stomach. "Oh Luke, I should have begged you not to go," she sobbed, bending forward so that her forehead rested on top of Fritz's head. "How can I go on living without you?"

❦

"I can't believe how much colder it's gotten," Luann King said to her husband, Philip, as they headed toward home with Philip's horse, Dewy, pulling their buggy. She drew her heavy shawl tightly around her neck, but the bitter winter wind seeping into the enclosure of the buggy was hard to ignore. They'd gone to pay a call on Alma Beechy, a seventy-year-old widow in their church district, and had stayed a bit longer than planned so that Philip could do a few chores for Alma.

Alma and her husband, Abe, had never had any children, and three years ago he'd developed a rare form of cancer, which took his life very quickly. As was common in most Amish communities, people began looking out for Alma. To some, she'd become like a grandmother. She loved babysitting whenever a family had a need, and a couple of times she'd even house-sat for some people's pets. Alma was a sweet, generous person, and when she had a need, someone was always there to help out. She was an excellent cook, so to show her gratitude, she would usually treat them to a delicious meal.

"You're right about the weather," Philip said after a brief pause. "The snow's coming down much harder now, too. Guess we should have left Alma's place a little sooner than we did, but I really wanted to do a few extra chores for her—especially after eating that great-tasting supper she cooked for us."

Luann smiled and patted her husband's stomach. "*Jah.* Pot roast and cooked vegetables were sure good on a cold night like this. It was nice to visit with Alma, too, but I am a bit concerned about how things are going at home."

"What do you mean?" Philip asked.

"I just hope Laurie and Kendra have everything under control and have managed to get the younger ones put to bed," Luann said. "I'm sure they didn't expect us to be gone this long."

"Those girls of ours are pretty capable. I'll bet you anything that they're gettin' along just fine. And I'm sure, if need be, your *mamm* will step in."

Luann's mother, Doris Smucker, had been living with them since Luann's father died of a heart attack two years ago, and she'd been a big help with the children. Even so, Luann had never expected her mother to do too much.

"You're probably right, but. . ."

Philip bumped Luann's arm gently with his elbow. "Sometimes I think my *fraa* worries too much about our *kinner*."

"I know I shouldn't worry about the children, but it's hard not to when you're a *mudder*," Luann said.

"Guess I'd better get the horse moving faster then, so we can get home quickly and you can check on things."

She shook her head vigorously. "With the way the roads look tonight, I'd rather not hurry, thank you very much." Luanne didn't normally fret when they rode in their buggy, but seeing the roads get worse by the minute had given her cause to worry.

Philip chuckled and nudged her again. "I was only kidding with you. Dewy's getting quite a workout as the snow gets deeper, and he's pretty lathered up already, so I really shouldn't push him any harder. He seems to be okay going at this easy pace, though."

Dew Drop, which was their horse's real name, had been with them for seven years. He had a beautiful coat of mahogany brown and a white patch on his forehead in the shape of a dewdrop. When they'd purchased the horse from an English family who was moving out of state, one of their younger daughters, Nina, who'd been six years old at the time, had seemed quite interested as her father explained why the previous owners had given the gelding that name. Then in an excited tone, Nina had smiled up at him and said, "I think we oughta nickname our new *gaul* Dewy." The name had stuck. Dewy was a well-behaved animal and had never taken off, running out of control, like some horses did. It was as if he was born to pull a buggy, and the things that would often spook other horses didn't seem to bother him at all. It was comforting to have such an easygoing animal pulling their buggy, even if the roads were horrible.

They rode in silence for a while; then after a car went whizzing past, much too fast on the snowy road, Luann turned to Philip and said, "We're so close to Meredith's house. Would you mind stopping by there before we go home? I'd like to see how she's been doing now that Luke is gone and find out if she needs anything. Oh, and with any luck, after our visit, maybe the snow will have let up, and getting us the rest of the way home will be easier on Dewy," she quickly added.

Philip grunted. "I hope you're not going to try to convince our daughter to come home with us to spend the night."

"No, no. I respect her decision to stay alone while Luke is gone. I'd just feel better if we stopped by to see how she's doing. Is that okay with you?"

He gave a slow nod. "Sure. I guess we ought to do that."

Luann smiled. Though her husband would never admit it, he was probably a bit worried about their eldest daughter, too, and wouldn't want to pass up an opportunity to visit with her. Meredith was the first of their children to leave home and get married. It had been a difficult adjustment for Luann at first, although she'd come to accept it and was glad her daughter had married such a fine man. From the beginning of Luke and Meredith's courtship, he had fit right in with her family, and since their marriage, everyone had gotten to know and like him even more.

Philip was a good husband, too, and Luann had never regretted marrying him, although her mother had expressed some doubts about their relationship in the beginning because Philip was ten years older than Luann. That had all changed, however, when Luann's mother saw how much he cared for her. Luann had to admit Philip could be a bit stubborn and opinionated at times, but he was a hard worker, devoted to his family. The children looked up to their father, too, and usually went to him first whenever they had a problem. Even Luann's mother often sought Philip's opinion on things.

Luann just wished he didn't have to work so hard to provide for their large family. In addition to the stand he ran at the Bird-in-Hand Farmers' Market, he'd recently taken on stands at two other farmers' markets in the area in order to help with their expenses. That took up a lot of his time, so he wasn't home nearly as much as he had been before, and she and the children missed him. Feeling herself begin to relax, Luann sat quietly, watching the snow come down.

A short time later, Philip guided their horse and buggy up Luke and Meredith's driveway. When the house came into view, Luann spotted the sheriff's car parked out front.

"I wonder why Sheriff Tyler is here," Philip commented before Luann could voice the question.

"Oh, I hope nothing's wrong with Meredith." Luann clutched the folds in her dress, trying to remain patient until Philip pulled up to the hitching rail.

"Don't worry, Luann," Philip said calmly. "I'm sure the sheriff is just checking on our daughter, since he probably heard that Luke left for Indiana yesterday. News travels fast, and our sheriff, he's a good one—always checkin' on folks or just stopping by to say hello."

"I pray you're right." Luann looked toward the house as apprehension filled her senses. She had a sinking feeling that Sheriff Tyler might be there for more than just a social call.

CHAPTER 5

Meredith's heart felt like it had been torn asunder. She still couldn't believe Luke was dead, but Sheriff Tyler wouldn't have told her all of that if it wasn't true. She sniffed deeply and dried her eyes on the tissue the sheriff had just handed her, feeling dazed.

Meredith shuddered as she tried to imagine how Luke must have felt during his last moments on earth. Had he been frightened? Had he thought of her?

She swallowed against the bile rising in her throat. To be burned to death in an explosion must have been horrifying. Had Luke suffered much, or had he and the others on the bus died quickly? It was unimaginable to think that Luke had been taken from her, and in such a terrible, tragic way.

"Would you like a glass of water or something else to drink?" Sheriff Tyler asked, touching Meredith's shoulder and looking at her with concerned eyes.

"No, thanks. My throat feels so swollen, I—I don't think I could drink anything right now." And with the waves of nausea beating against Meredith's stomach, she was sure she couldn't keep anything down. Her whole body trembled, and her mind swirled with a multitude of disjointed thoughts.

"Meredith, I think we should go to your folks' house now."

Meredith remained glued to her seat as she looked past the sheriff to the corner of the room. There sat the bookcase Luke had surprised her with this past Christmas. He'd used his woodworking skills and made the beautiful oak bookcase with eight changeable shelves. Luke had mentioned to Meredith that he thought by the time they got old they'd have all the shelves full of books. Little did Meredith realize then that it would be the last Christmas she and Luke would spend together.

Her gaze went to the other side of the room, where the quilt rack Luke had given her as a wedding present sat. She'd been overwhelmed with the craftsmanship and love her husband had put into each piece of his work. It had brought tears to her eyes when he'd said that nothing was too good for his bride.

Meredith clutched the arms of the rocking chair so tightly that her fingers turned numb. There weren't many places she could look in this house and not be reminded of Luke. She'd anticipated that when he learned of her pregnancy, he would start making baby furniture right away. But that wouldn't happen now. Their firstborn would not be sleeping in a crib or rocked in a cradle that had been made by the hands of his or her daddy. Their child would never know the joy of being held in Daddy's arms, and Luke would not have the privilege of rocking his son or daughter to sleep each night.

Just then, Fritz let out a loud bark and raced into the kitchen, bringing Meredith's thoughts to a halt. A few minutes later, Mom and Dad entered the room. They'd obviously let themselves in through the back door.

"Meredith, are you all right?" Mom asked, moving quickly to stand beside the rocking chair.

"Your mamm was concerned when we saw the sheriff's car outside," Dad said, joining Mom by Meredith's side. *"Was is letz do?"* he asked.

What is wrong here? Meredith thought, unable to speak because of the lump in her throat. *Everything's wrong! How do I break the news to them when I can't comprehend it myself?*

"Meredith, was is letz do?" Dad asked again, tipping his head.

"It. . .it's Luke. He. . .he's dead." She choked on a sob then let go of the arms of the chair and clasped both hands tightly against her stomach.

Sheriff Tyler gave a slow nod and added, "I'm real sorry, Mr. and Mrs. King, but it's true."

"Wh—what happened?" Dad asked as Meredith rose from her seat and sought comfort in her mother's outstretched arms.

Sheriff Tyler gently repeated everything he'd told Meredith about the bus accident and ended by saying that he needed to see Luke's parents to tell them the sad news.

Meredith looked back at the sheriff. "No, please. I want to tell them," she said, swallowing hard as she leaned heavily against Mom for support. Her legs felt like two sticks of rubber, and her head began to pound, while the nausea increased.

"Well, you can't go alone; we'll go with you," Dad said, quickly embracing both Meredith and her mother.

Mom nodded tearfully and patted Meredith's back. "Elam and Sadie will need our support, just as you will, Daughter."

"That's fine," the sheriff agreed. "If you'd like to go there in your horse and buggy, I'll follow in my car."

"I appreciate that, but it might take us awhile," Dad said. "We shouldn't try to go very fast in this snow."

"That's okay. I don't mind going slow on a wintry night such as this," the sheriff said. "I'd just feel better following your rig and knowing you got there safely."

Fritz whined, drawing Meredith's attention to the fact that he was sitting by the front door, as though anxious to go out. "What about the pup?" she asked, still feeling as if she were in a fog.

"I'll put him in the dog run. Come on, boy." Dad opened the door, and when he stepped onto the porch, Fritz ran out behind him, bounding into the snow-covered yard.

Meredith continued to stand there, unable to think of what to do next. She felt like she was in the middle of a dream—a nightmare, really—and couldn't wake up. If only this were just a dream and she could wake from it and find everything as it had been before Luke left for Indiana. As she looked at her mother, Meredith could see the anguish hidden behind her pale blue eyes. This was not going to be easy on any of them.

As though sensing Meredith's confusion, Mom went to the utility room and returned with a heavy woolen shawl and black outer bonnet. "It's bitterly cold out tonight, so you'll need to put these on," she said, slipping the bonnet on Meredith's head and then wrapping the shawl tightly around her shoulders. It felt like years ago, when Meredith had been a little girl. Mom's motherly instinct still was to protect and comfort her.

"I know it doesn't seem like it now, but with God's help and the support of your family, you'll get through this," Mom said, leading Meredith out, while the sheriff locked the door behind them. "We all will, Daughter."

Meredith didn't see how that was possible. With or without God's help, she couldn't imagine going through the rest of her life without Luke.

❦

"So, what do you say, Mom, should we turn down the gaslights and head for *bett*?" Elam asked, setting his book down and looking at his wife as she smiled back at him.

Sadie set her mending aside and glanced at the clock above the fireplace. "Jah, it is getting late, so I suppose we ought to go to bed." It was almost ten o'clock, and they were usually asleep by now, but for some reason, they'd stayed up longer tonight, enjoying the quiet and each other's company.

"I'm not sure why," Sadie said, "but I have some words swimming around in my head. Maybe I'll try to make some sense of it all and write a little poem."

"It's been awhile since you wrote one," Elam said, looking at her affectionately while patting her arm. "I've always enjoyed hearing you read me the verses you come up with. I think the way you put them together in rhymes is a real talent."

Sadie smiled. It was nice to know her husband was so supportive and appreciated her desire to put her thoughts down on paper. "I guess I should keep a tablet and pen handy," she said. "Then whenever the words hit me, I can write them down."

Sadie had started writing poems when she was a teenager. It was just for fun, though, and only when the mood hit her. When she sat down and actually tried to write a poem, all the concentration in the world didn't help the words to come. It seemed to happen naturally, when she least expected it. The journal Sadie kept, with all of her writings, was worn and old, but she'd hoped one day a grandchild might take a similar interest, and she could hand down her journal to him or her.

"Think I'll take a pen and my journal to the bedroom with me and try to write a little poem before going to bed," she said.

Elam grinned. "Sounds like a good idea. Then you can read it to me like you've always done."

Just as Sadie and Elam rose from the sofa, a knock sounded on the front door.

"Now I wonder who that could be at this hour of the night," Elam said, pulling on his full gray beard before opening the door.

Sadie was surprised when Sheriff Tyler entered the house and even more surprised to see Meredith and her parents step in behind him.

"What's going on?" she asked, seeing the look of distress on all of their faces. Her hand went to her chest, and she had a sick feeling that something was horribly wrong.

"You'd better sit down," Sheriff Tyler said. "I'm sorry to say, and this won't be easy, but we've come here with some very bad news."

Sadie's knees went weak, but she couldn't sit down. Her hands started to shake as Elam's arm went around her waist for support. "Wh–what is it?" she asked. Noticing Meredith's tear-stained face, she said in a near whisper, "Is. . .is it Luke?"

Meredith nodded and burst into tears as she threw her arms around Sadie and hugged her tightly. "The bus Luke was on was hit by a tanker full of gas, and. . ." Meredith's voice faltered.

"The bus. . ." Sheriff Tyler slowly shook his head. "I'm sorry, but there were no survivors when the bus exploded."

"Oh, dear Lord, no," Sadie moaned, holding tightly to Meredith. "Not our boy, Luke! *Ach*, this can't be true!"

As Elam's shoulders began to shake, he embraced both Meredith and Sadie. Sadie's husband was usually a strong man and, with his deep faith in God, could take almost any news. But this was different. This was about their youngest son, and the loss was simply too much to bear.

The wrinkles on Elam's forehead deepened as Sadie clung tightly to him, unable to endure the tragic news they'd just received.

CHAPTER 6

The next three days went by in a blur, and Meredith didn't know how she'd made it through any of them—especially today's memorial service. Without Luke's body to view, it was that much harder to accept her husband's death. If only she could have looked at his face one last time and said goodbye. None of this made any sense, yet she had to force herself to acknowledge what had happened.

But would seeing his body really have helped? Meredith asked herself as she stared out her in-laws' kitchen window. *Would it have given me a sense of peace? No, probably not, but at least I'd have had some kind of closure.* She sniffed deeply, fighting for control as tears coursed down her cheeks. *I'm so lost without you, Luke. I don't know how I can go on.*

"Are you all right?" Meredith's mother asked, slipping an arm around Meredith's waist, while Dad, Sadie, and Elam remained at the table, murmuring words of consolation.

"I. . .I'm glad today is almost over," Meredith said, avoiding the question. She couldn't say she was all right, because it would be a lie. Truth was, she didn't think she'd ever be all right again. And Meredith knew if she'd admitted just how she was feeling right now, Mom would probably insist that she come home with them tonight so she'd have her family around her. Meredith wasn't up to that. She loved her two brothers and five sisters very much, but sometimes the younger ones were noisy and got on her nerves. She was sure that three-year-old Owen and six-year-old Katie wouldn't understand much about what had happened to Luke. And perhaps even Arlene, who was eight, wouldn't be able to grasp the agony Meredith felt. Only Laurie, Kendra, and Nina were old enough to really be supportive, but after a day of struggling to keep her emotions in check, Meredith needed some peace and quiet, and she really just wanted to be alone. Trying to be strong in front of everyone was taking its toll on her.

"Won't you come join us for a cup of coffee or tea?" Mom asked, motioning to the table.

Meredith shook her head. "No, thanks; you go ahead."

Without a word of argument, Mom gave Meredith a hug and returned to her seat at the table.

Meredith cringed as her stomach rolled. She may not have had any morning sickness before, but she'd been struggling with waves of nausea ever since she'd received the news of Luke's death. She didn't know whether it was because of her pregnancy or due to the intense grief she felt at the very core of her being.

Determined not to give in to the sick feeling, Meredith continued to stare out the window, focusing on the snow-covered yard, immersed in private thoughts. She'd been staying with Luke's folks since the news of his death, knowing they needed her support as much as she needed theirs. Dad had brought Fritz over to be with her, but even though the pup was back where he'd lived when he'd first come to be with Luke, the poor animal seemed as confused and forlorn as Meredith felt.

Fritz followed Meredith wherever she went, and on several occasions he'd actually tried to jump up in her lap. Perhaps the dog sensed her need for consolation, or maybe he'd become so clingy because he needed comforting, too. Did the pup realize that his master was never coming back?

Meredith had once read that animals could sense when their owners had died. Not long ago, she'd seen an article in the newspaper about a man's dog and how it had stood vigil every day over the grave site after its owner had passed away. She wished she could explain things to Fritz so he'd understand what had happened to Luke, but maybe he already knew. If only dogs could converse with humans, it would make it so much easier to communicate.

Meredith was thankful that everyone in their community had been supportive, bringing meals to Luke's parents and offering to run errands. They had taken Luke's death very hard—especially Sadie. Her usual cheerful smile and bouncy step had been replaced with deeper lines etching her forehead, slumped shoulders, and hazel-colored eyes that no longer held their sparkle. Her small frame had seemed to shrink.

The other day when they'd been talking about Luke, Sadie had tearfully told Meredith, "No parent ever expects to outlive their children. It's just not right."

That's true, Meredith acknowledged, swiping at another set of tears rolling down her cheeks. *And no wife expects her husband to be killed a year and two months after they're married.*

Many people—Amish and English—had come to Luke's memorial service, offering their support but not really knowing what to do or say. Luke had become a friend to many in the community. He'd exuded confidence, and even to strangers, he had seemed comfortable talking about most any subject. He'd been open minded and straightforward, and it was those qualities that people had liked about him. He'd had an infectious personality and had made many friends over the years because of it. Folks just gravitated toward him, and from the look Meredith had seen on so many faces during the service today, it was evident that Luke's death had hit the community quite hard.

Alma Beechy had hugged Meredith as soon as she'd seen her this morning. With tears in her eyes, she'd said she would be praying for Meredith during this time of need, and that if Meredith ever needed to talk, she should feel free to drop by her house, day or night.

Sheriff Tyler had come to the memorial service, too, dressed in his uniform. Meredith wondered if other places in Pennsylvania had law-enforcement officers as nice as theirs. Many times in the past when Luke and Sheriff Tyler had talked, it had been evident that the man took his job very seriously, wanting to assure a safe environment for the entire community. He was admired and respected by all the Amish who knew him. Over the years, Sheriff Tyler had developed a kinship with many people and usually took part in their community events. He was single, lived outside of Bird-in-Hand, and rarely turned down a good home-cooked meal when he was invited. Meredith remembered him saying once that even though there were plenty of good restaurants to eat at in the area, an invitation to one of the Amish homes was much better than sitting alone at a table in some crowded restaurant or having a microwave dinner in front of the TV at his home.

Sadie had written a poem about being a mother, which she'd shared with Meredith this morning before the service. It had almost been Meredith's undoing as she'd listened to Sadie read the poem in a quavering voice:

"A mother wants her faith to give hope to her child; stability and trust in a world gone wild. A mother's faith should be handed down; in the next generation it will be found. A mother's faith must be steadfast and sure; so her children will desire to be like her."

Meredith smoothed the wrinkles in her black mourning dress. She hoped she could be the kind of mother to her child that Sadie had been to Luke. He had respected his parents and been a good son to them. Meredith had never heard him say an unkind word about either one of his folks. In fact, he'd often commented on their kindness and wisdom in raising their children. He'd also said that when he and Meredith had children of their own, he hoped he'd be half as good a father as his dad was to him and his brothers.

Shifting her thoughts, Meredith was grateful that Luke's uncle Amos and his family had been able to hire a driver and come for the service—although seeing him had been a painful reminder of why Luke was dead. If he hadn't boarded that bus for Indiana, he would still be alive, and if Amos hadn't offered to sell Luke his business, there wouldn't have been a memorial service for him today.

Amos, full of regret, had apologized to Meredith for having asked Luke to make the trip to Indiana. "I should have waited till spring when the weather was better," Amos had said with a slow shake of his head. "Sure wish I could undo the past."

Shoulda, woulda, coulda, Meredith thought with remorse. *From the very beginning, I had a bad feeling about Luke going to Indiana.* If she could go back in time, she would tell him that she was almost sure he was going to be a father. Meredith wished she could take back all the arguments they'd had after he'd lost his job. She knew just how trivial they were now. Luke having no job at all would be better than the pain of what she was going through. Now there would be no homecoming—no surprising Luke with the news of their baby. Just like that, their dreams of raising a family and growing old together had been snatched away. Luke would never know he was going to be a father, and it was too late for regrets.

Meredith hadn't told her parents or Luke's mom and dad about the baby yet. In her grief, she'd been waiting for the right time. Now that they were all together and needed something positive to look forward to, it was probably a good time to let them know.

She turned from the window and swallowed hard, trying not to break down. She'd done enough crying to fill a bathtub these last few days—especially at night in the privacy of the room she'd been given at Elam and Sadie's. "There's something you all need to know," she said, looking first at Mom and Dad and then at Sadie and Elam.

"What is it?" Sadie asked. Her face looked drawn, and her eyes appeared sunken. It was obvious that she'd done a good deal of crying over Luke's death, too, and like Meredith, she probably hadn't slept much since they'd been given the tragic news.

Meredith placed her hand against her stomach and forced a smile as tears slipped down her cheeks. "I'm expecting a *boppli*. He or she should be born sometime in July."

Mom clapped her hands, and Sadie gasped. The men just sat with big grins on their faces.

"Praise be to the Lord; we certainly needed some good news," Sadie said, her eyes glistening with tears. "Luke's memory will live on, and we'll have the joy of knowing and loving your baby."

Philadelphia

Susan stared down at her patient, noting that there had been no change in his condition since he'd been brought to the critical care unit three days ago.

Since he had no identification, he'd been listed as a John Doe, but Susan thought that was too impersonal, so she'd decided to call him "Eddie."

"How are you doing today, Eddie?" she asked, after checking his blood pressure and other vitals.

No response. Not even an eye flutter. The poor man had been in a coma ever since he'd been admitted to the hospital, and Susan had not only been taking care of his physical needs, but she'd been praying for him often.

She thought about the day he'd been brought to her floor. When the doctor had checked the man's pupils, she'd noticed the pretty turquoise color of his eyes.

The police had come to question the patient about who'd inflicted these terrible injuries on him, but they'd been told that he was still unconscious and might never wake up. In addition to the severe trauma to his head, the young man had a crushed vocal cord, bleeding from some of his internal organs, and several broken bones, including his ribs, sternum, and collarbone. They'd been giving him medication to help dissolve the blood clot on his brain, and the patient was scheduled for surgery tomorrow.

Susan checked the man's IV and said another prayer for him. Now that he was cleaned up, he didn't look like a homeless person at all. He looked like an average young man with his head wrapped in a bandage, who needed someone to care about him.

Who are you, Eddie? Susan wondered. *Where's your family? Is anyone even looking for you?*

⌘

Bird-in-Hand

"Meredith. . . Where are you, Merrie?"

"Luke, is that you?" Meredith could hear Luke's voice just as plain as day, but she couldn't see him anywhere. He appeared to be enveloped in some kind of a fog—yet he seemed so close to her. If she just kept going, maybe she could reach him. "Luke! Luke!" she shouted, moving forward through the haze. "Oh, please, Luke, come toward me. Let me see your handsome face."

"Meredith. . ."

"Luke. . ."

"I love you, Merrie."

"I love you, too, Luke, and I always will."

"I can't stay, Merrie. I have to go. . . ."

"No! Please stay with me, Luke. Don't go away!"

"Goodbye, Merrie. Goodbye. . ."

And then there was silence.

Drenched in sweat and clutching her bedclothes, Meredith bolted upright. Where was she? Where was Luke? Why wasn't he here beside her?

She glanced around the dark room, feeling disoriented and chilled to the bone. Slowly, she became fully awake and realized that she was in the guest room at Sadie and Elam's house, where she'd spent the last few nights. Today had been Luke's memorial service, and after she'd told Mom, Dad, Sadie, and Elam that she was pregnant, she'd come down with a pounding headache and gone to bed.

"Oh, that dream seemed so real," Meredith moaned. It was as if Luke was still alive. *Is this how it's always going to be?* she wondered. *Me, dreaming about Luke then waking up feeling the pain of losing him all over again?*

She closed her eyes, hanging on to the last time she'd seen Luke alive. It was just before he'd climbed into his driver's car to take him to the bus station in Lancaster. She could still hear him yelling out to her as he turned and waved, "Don't worry, Merrie. It will all work out!"

Merrie. She'd always love the special nickname Luke had given her. It was short for Meredith, but he'd said he liked to call her that because she had such a joyful spirit.

It's not joyful now. Meredith placed one hand on her stomach and heaved a sigh. *If it weren't for this baby I'm carrying, I'd have no reason to live.*

Unable to endure the pain of her loss, Meredith buried her face in the pillow and sobbed.

CHAPTER 7

"Are you ready to go home, boy?" Meredith asked, turning and reaching over the front seat of Elam's buggy to pat the top of Fritz's head.

The dog whined and nuzzled her hand with his cold nose.

After spending nearly six weeks with Luke's folks, Meredith had decided it was time to go home and try to somehow get on with her life, however difficult it would be. It wasn't fair to expect Dad and her twelve-year-old brother, Stanley, to keep going over to her place every day to check on things, care for the horses, and do any other chores that might need to be done. While still in mourning over Luke's death, his mother seemed to be doing a little better now that she knew Meredith was expecting a baby, and at least she had something to look forward to, as did Meredith. So this morning during breakfast, Meredith had told Luke's parents that she would be going home, and Elam had agreed to take her. Sadie had argued at first, saying it was too soon, but Meredith assured her she would be okay on her own and would let them know if she needed anything.

I need to get back into a routine, she thought, turning to stare out the front of Elam's buggy. *There's so much to do before the baby comes, and maybe keeping busy will help me not think so much about losing Luke.*

Meredith wasn't sure how she was going to support herself. Half the money they'd had in the bank had been lost with Luke, and she'd have to be careful how she spent what was left. What she needed was a job—something she could do from her home. But what could it be?

I'll worry about that later, Meredith decided. *Right now I need to think about how I'm going to get through the rest of this day.* It wouldn't be easy going back to the house, knowing Luke would never walk through its doors again. Nor would it be easy to sit at the table and know that she and Luke would never share another meal together or take time out to discuss their day before going to bed. Everything around the house would remind Meredith of Luke. But even though difficult, she wanted to hold on to every single one of those special memories. No, Meredith's life would never be the same without Luke, but somehow, by the grace of God, she would have to learn how to deal with it. She had to—for her baby's sake.

◦⁂◦

Ronks, Pennsylvania

Luann had just entered her chiropractor's office when she noticed Sarah Miller sitting across the room, looking at a magazine. Sarah was a petite, small-boned woman in her midfifties who, except for her slightly graying brown hair, looked more youthful than some women half her age. Sarah and her husband, Raymond, had moved from Ohio to Lancaster County four months ago. Luann had heard they'd come to be near Sarah's aging parents. Raymond was a buggy maker, and his business had been doing quite well since he'd set up shop. There seemed to be a lot of buggy accidents due to all the increasing traffic, so more than one buggy maker was needed in the area. Since the Millers were in a different church district than the Kings and Stoltzfuses, Luann hadn't gotten to know them that well, but she and Sarah had spoken a few times at various community events.

"*Wie geht's?*" Sarah asked when Luann took a seat beside her.

Luann sighed and rubbed the back of her neck. "I'll be better once I see Dr. Warren and he works on my sore *hals*."

"What's wrong with your neck?"

"I think I may have slept on it wrong."

"I know how painful that can be. Raymond's in with the doctor right now, getting his back adjusted."

"Did he injure it somehow?"

"No, he just woke up this morning, complaining that his back hurt. He thinks the mattress we recently bought is too hard."

"It is difficult to sleep when the bed's uncomfortable." Luann released another long sigh. "To tell you the truth, I haven't slept well since my daughter Meredith's husband died. It's been so stressful with all the worrying I've done over her. I suppose that could be another reason for my neck pain."

"Jah, stress can do all kinds of things to a person's body." Sarah's eyes were full of compassion. "That was too bad about your son-in-law. I'd only met him once, when he'd come by the buggy shop while I was taking lunch to Raymond. I'm sure Luke's death has been hard on everyone in your family."

"It has been difficult, and try as I may, I just can't help but worry about Meredith. Even more so now that she's left her in-laws' house and has gone back to her home."

"Oh, when was that?" Sarah asked.

"Sadie left a message on our answering machine this morning, letting us know her husband had taken Meredith home soon after breakfast."

"I can understand your worry," Sarah said. "I fretted about my daughter when she lost her first husband, too. But now, thank the Lord, she's living in Arthur, Illinois, and is happily married to a wonderful man who's doing a fine job helping raise her two little ones."

"I know it's natural for a mother to worry about her children, and I'm praying that in time everything will be okay." Luann reached up to rub the back of her neck. "We do have some good news in our family, though."

"Oh, what's that?"

"Meredith's expecting a boppli in July. We're pleased about becoming grandparents, of course, and we plan to help out as much as we can, because it's going to be hard for Meredith to raise the baby alone."

"That's *wunderbaar*. Maybe after a suitable time, she'll get married again, like our daughter did." Sarah's emerald-green eyes shimmered as she smiled.

Luann slowly shook her head. "Meredith loved her husband very much, and she's taken his death quite hard, so I doubt she would ever marry again."

"But don't you suppose after some time has passed, if the right man came along, she might get married—for the sake of the boppli, if for no other reason?" Sarah asked.

Luann shrugged. "I suppose that could eventually happen, but it's hard to imagine. Right now, though, Meredith just needs her family's support."

"Of course she does. So how are Sadie and Elam doing?" Sarah questioned.

"They took the news of their son's death very hard—especially Sadie."

Sarah's lips compressed. "That's understandable. I don't know how I could ever deal with it if something were to happen to either of my kinner. Even though our daughter lives in Illinois and her twin brother lives in Ohio, we're all very close. It was hard for Raymond and me to leave our son and move to Pennsylvania, but we knew it was the right decision once we got here and realized how much my folks needed us."

"Families needing families; that's how it should be," Luann said, fully understanding the way Sarah felt. When Luann's mother had moved in with them, even though it meant another mouth to feed, neither Luann nor Philip had seen it as a burden.

Sarah placed her magazine on the small table to her left. "Raymond and I were pleased when we received a message from our son last night, saying he'd found a buyer for the buggy shop that he and his *daed* ran together before we moved. Now that it's sold, he plans to move here, and he and Raymond will work together again." She grinned, revealing the small dimples in her cheeks. "I'm real pleased about that, and I hope it won't be long until our son finds a nice girl and decides to get married. Then our family will be complete. Since I was only able to bear two children, I'm hoping for lots of grandchildren."

Luann didn't voice her opinion, but it sounded to her like Sarah might be trying to plan her son's future, which she didn't think was a good thing at all.

Philadelphia

"How's that young man you've been caring for these past few weeks?" Susan's grandfather asked as she sat at the kitchen table with her grandparents, drinking coffee and eating some of Grandma's warm sticky buns. Anne had already left for the hospital because she had the early morning shift, but Susan wouldn't have to leave for work until afternoon.

"Unfortunately, even after several surgeries, he's pretty much the same," Susan replied, blotting her lips on a napkin. "I've been calling him Eddie, and I talk to him all the time, but he's still unresponsive."

"That's too bad," Grandma said, reaching for her cup of coffee. "Perhaps something you say will eventually get through to him."

Susan nodded. "That's what I'm hoping for, but the longer he remains in a coma, the less his chances are of coming out of it."

"Just remember, with God all things are possible," Grandpa said, placing his hand on Susan's arm.

Susan smiled. "I know that, but I appreciate the reminder." She was thankful Grandpa and Grandma had taken her and Anne into their home and cared for them after their parents had died in a car accident when Susan and Anne were thirteen and fifteen. Grandma and Grandpa were true Christians in every sense of the word, and their gentle spirits and caring actions had proved that repeatedly. Besides offering their godly influence, Grandma and Grandpa had paid for both Susan and Anne to attend college and get the training they needed to work in the medical profession. They had flatly refused to accept any rent money from Susan and her sister after they'd begun working at the hospital. Grandma had smiled and said she enjoyed having her two special girls living in their home. She'd added with a twinkle in her eyes, "You'll both be getting married someday, so you should be saving up for that."

That's not likely to happen, Susan thought. *I'm twenty-eight and have all but given up on finding the right man, and Anne says she's married to her job. I think we're both going to end up being career women—and worse yet, old maids.*

"So have you made any plans for this coming weekend?" Grandpa questioned.

Susan shook her head. "Except for going to church on Sunday, I'll probably try to get caught up on my sleep."

"What about the Valentine's banquet our church young people are having on Saturday night?" Grandma asked. "Aren't you and Anne planning to go to that?"

"I can't speak for Anne, but I'm not going."

The wrinkles in Grandma's forehead deepened. "Why not, for goodness' sake? It would be a chance to socialize with someone other than sick and hurting patients or your crotchety old grandparents."

Susan rolled her eyes. "To me, you and Grandpa aren't old, and you're anything but crotchety."

"Be that as it may, I still think you should go to the banquet," Grandma said, handing Susan the plate of sticky buns.

"No thanks, I've had my share." She patted her flat stomach. "I need to stay fit and trim so I can keep up with my patients."

"Back to the Valentine's banquet," Grandpa said, wiggling his bushy eyebrows, "you just never know who you might meet there. Could be the man of your dreams."

Susan brushed the idea aside. "I doubt that would happen. Besides, I know all the single men at our church, and none of them interests me in the least."

The three of them sat in silence for a while, until Grandma asked Susan another question.

"Do you have any plans this morning before you leave for work, or are you just going to hang around here until it's time to go to the hospital?"

"Well, I've been thinking about making an appointment at the hair salon, because I feel like I need a change."

"What are you planning to do?"

"Maybe a perm or perhaps some highlights," Susan replied. "I'm tired of my straight brown hair. Anne was the lucky one, born with naturally curly hair," she added. "She can just wash it and go, and it always looks good."

"You know me—I'm kind of old-fashioned about the idea of changing your looks on purpose," Grandma said, patting Susan's arm affectionately. "God made us all unique. I think your hair is beautiful, and it turns under so nicely when you style it." She smiled tenderly as she touched the ends of Susan's hair. "Your hair reminds me of how I used to wear mine when I was younger, before it started turning gray."

"I hope I'm as lucky as you, Grandma, when my hair turns gray." Susan smiled. "Some people are just blessed to have gorgeous gray hair, and you are definitely one of them."

"You're right about that," Grandpa agreed. "In fact, my wife is as beautiful now as the day we got married." He leaned over and kissed Grandma's cheek.

I've always hoped that someday someone will look tenderly at me, the way Grandpa and Grandma do with each other, Susan thought. *Their deep commitment to each other and the abiding love they share are so rare. To have a relationship like that is really special. But if I don't meet someone soon, I guess that's not likely to happen.*

Grandpa bumped Susan's arm gently with his elbow, pulling her thoughts aside. "If there should be any change in Eddie's condition today, when you get home tonight, be sure to let us know, okay?"

Susan nodded. She wasn't the only person who'd been praying for Eddie, and she hoped that God would answer their prayers soon.

As if in some faraway fog, the man thought he heard voices. What were the people saying? Were they speaking to him?

He struggled to open his eyes but couldn't manage to pry them open. It felt as though something heavy rested on top of his head.

Where am I? Who am I? Why can't I wake up? Am I dreaming? Could I be dead?

He tried once more to open his eyes, but it was in vain.

I hurt everywhere, and I'm scared. Why won't someone tell me what's causing this pain? Will somebody please tell me my name?

The more the man fought to climb to the surface, the more the pain seemed to engulf him. It was like his body was sending out a warning, and the pain was telling him to stay right where he was, oblivious to everything else. Thinking was exhausting, and it made him hurt even more, yet he yearned for something—anything that was familiar. But it just wouldn't come.

As he fell back into his safe little cocoon, the pain seemed to go someplace else, and it was easy not to struggle anymore. He felt safe, insulated and protected in this little shell where he didn't have to think about anything at all. Slowly, as he gave up trying to figure out answers, the pain ebbed into some faraway place.

CHAPTER 8

Bird-in-Hand

Meredith put the mop away in the utility room and stopped to rub a sore spot on her lower back. She'd been home from Sadie and Elam's for nearly a week and had been working hard from the time she got up until she went to bed each night. She'd convinced herself that she needed to keep busy so she wouldn't have any spare time on her hands. Spare time gave way to too much thinking. Every night Meredith made a mental note of what she wanted to accomplish the next day. As long as she did that, she felt like she had a reason to get out of bed each morning. She realized that if she concentrated on her tasks and wore herself out, by the end of the day, when her head hit the pillow, she'd be out like a light. So far, she'd been able to do that. Pure exhaustion took over by nightfall, and she could barely stay awake long enough to fix herself something for supper.

She had put Fritz in his dog run this morning and would keep him there all day, because whenever he was in the house he always seemed to be underfoot. The other day, Meredith had nearly tripped on the dog when he'd been following her from room to room. As much as she enjoyed the pup's company, she couldn't have him inside all of the time, keeing her from getting things done. Besides, whenever Fritz approached something that had been Luke's— like his favorite chair—he would sit next to it and whine. This only made Meredith miss Luke even more.

To keep her thoughts at bay, she'd kept busy this morning, cleaning the house. The windows were spotless, and the woodwork in the living room and dining room glistened like polished stone. Meredith had cleaned it so well that the wood grain stood out, making it even more beautiful than it had been before. Luke would have been pleased with how nice it looked. Oh, if he could just be here to see it right now, the way he had been in the dream she'd had last night.

She'd dreamed that she'd had the baby, and the baby was giggling as Luke made funny noises and faces. He'd held the baby so tenderly, while looking lovingly at Meredith with his beautiful turquoise eyes. No wonder she'd awakened feeling rested for the first time since his death. It had been so real, like they'd truly been together. Meredith had actually giggled out loud in her sleep, and that's what had awakened her. If only it hadn't been a dream. Meredith had heard it said that time heals all wounds, but she didn't think any amount of time would heal the sorrow she felt over losing her husband.

Forcing her thoughts aside before she gave in to tears, Meredith gathered up the throw rugs in the living room and had just opened the door to shake them out when she heard Fritz carrying on from his kennel. Looking out into the yard, she spotted her friend Dorine's horse and buggy coming up the lane.

After Dorine secured her horse to the hitching rail by the barn, she hurried up to the house and gave Meredith a hug. "How are you doing?" she asked.

"I've been trying to get through this," Meredith answered truthfully, struggling not to cry. "I'm trying hard to be strong."

"You don't have to be strong," Dorine said with a shake of her head. "Your family and friends want to help, which is why I stopped by—to see if there's anything I can do for you or anything you might need."

"Seth came by a few days ago to take Luke's horse out for a run, and I don't really need anything else right now." *Except for Luke. I need my husband back in my life.* Meredith couldn't trust herself to keep talking about Luke, so she asked, "Where's the rest of your family?"

"Seth is working at the Shoe and Boot store today, and Merle and Cathy are with my mamm. I had some shopping to do, so Mom offered to take the kinner for the day so it would be a little easier." Dorine leaned on the porch railing. "I love my children, but shopping with a one-year-old and a three-year-old can be a bit daunting."

Meredith nodded. When she'd been living at home before marrying Luke, she'd taken her younger siblings shopping a few times, and it had been tiring. "I appreciate you coming by, Dorine. Sometimes, with only Fritz for company, it can get kind of lonely. I do all the talking, and the poor pup just lies around looking as sad as I feel."

"I can only imagine. If animals could talk to us and share their feelings, it might help them and us to understand things better," Dorine said, glancing at her horse, who had chosen that moment to whinny. "I'm surprised you aren't still with Luke's parents," she added, looking back at Meredith. "I would think it would help to have their support."

"In some ways it did help to be there, but it was time for me to come home and get back into a routine." Meredith opened the door and motioned for Dorine to come inside. "Let's go into the kitchen where it's warmer. We can have a cup of tea and some banana bread."

Dorine smiled. "That sounds nice."

Once Dorine had removed her shawl and outer bonnet, and they'd been seated at the table with their tea and a plate of banana bread, Meredith realized how badly she needed to take a break. She was not only tired but a bit nauseous, and the aromatic mint tea helped to settle her queasy stomach.

"This is sure good bread," Dorine said after she'd taken her first bite.

"I'm afraid I can't take the credit for it. Luke's mamm gave it to me when she dropped by yesterday."

"How's Sadie doing?"

"She's still grieving pretty hard, just as I am, but on the day of Luke's memorial service, I gave her and Elam some news and it seemed to cheer them up a bit."

"What news was that?"

"I'm expecting a boppli. It'll be born in July."

A wide smile stretched across Dorine's oval face. "Oh Meredith, I'm so happy for you! Having the baby will not only give you some comfort, but you'll be kept plenty busy as well."

Meredith nodded. "I'm really looking forward to becoming a mudder."

Dorine took a sip of tea. "My two kinner can be a handful sometimes, but I wouldn't trade motherhood for anything. Just think, my little Merle will only be a year and half when your boppli is born. I'll bet they will become good friends once they get to know each other, just like the two of us have been for so many years."

Meredith sat silently, staring into her cup, giving no acknowledgment of what her friend had just said.

"Is there something bothering you that you'd like to talk about?" Dorine asked, gently touching Meredith's arm.

Meredith sighed deeply. "There isn't a lot left in my savings account, and I need to find something to do soon that will bring in some money before taxes come due in April."

Dorine's eyes brightened. "Why don't you make women's head coverings to sell? After all, you've been making your own since we were teenagers, and you do such a good job. A lot of women don't like to make their own coverings because it's such tedious sewing, so I'm sure you'd get plenty of orders."

Meredith pondered her friend's suggestion. "Hmm. . .I might just give that a try. It probably won't bring in a lot of money, but at least it would be something to help out until the boppli comes and I'm able to look for a full-time job."

"You're right, and once you are ready to get started sewing, I'll help spread the word."

"*Danki*, I appreciate that."

Their conversation turned to the weather then and how they couldn't wait for winter to be over so they could begin planting their gardens.

"With the boppli coming in the middle of summer, I may not get as much gardening done this year as I would like," Meredith said, taking her empty cup to the sink.

"I'd be happy to come over and help out anytime you like. I'm sure my mamm would watch my little ones for me."

Meredith smiled. "Working in the garden will be a lot more fun if we can do it together." She appreciated having such a good friend.

"Changing the subject," Dorine said, "when Seth was at the buggy shop last week getting new wheels for his rig, Raymond Miller mentioned that his son, Jonah, would be moving here from Sugarcreek, Ohio, and will be working in the buggy shop with him. You don't suppose it could be the same Jonah Miller you met in Sarasota when you worked there as a teenager one summer?"

Meredith touched her cheeks. "Oh my, I haven't seen Jonah in such a long time; I'd almost forgotten that he lived in Sugarcreek."

"So you think it's him, then?"

"Jah, I sure do. In the last letter I received from Jonah, before Luke and I got married, he said he was working for his daed in his buggy shop. Until now, though, I hadn't even thought that Jonah could be Raymond and Sarah Miller's son."

"I wonder if he's married, with a family of his own," Dorine said, finishing the last of her tea.

Meredith shrugged. "I don't know. Like I said, I haven't heard from Jonah in a long while, and since I didn't know Raymond and Sarah Miller were his folks, I wouldn't have thought to ask."

"I guess we'll know soon enough, because from what I heard, Jonah was supposed to have arrived at his folks' place sometime yesterday." Dorine pushed her chair away from the table. "As nice as this has been, I really should head out now and get my shopping done before it starts snowing again." She gave Meredith a hug. "Be sure to let us know if there's anything either Seth or I can do for you."

Meredith nodded. "Jah, I will."

⸺

Jonah Miller removed the last of his clothes from his suitcase and put them away in the closet; then he placed the suitcase on the floor at the back of the closet. It was good to be unpacked. It was even better to be here now with his folks. He'd had no problem pulling up stakes and moving to Pennsylvania to partner with Dad. After all, it was just him, so making the move was a lot easier than if he had a wife and children to consider. It would be great working alongside Dad again—just like he'd done since he was a teenager, when Dad first taught him how to make and repair Amish and other types of buggies. Jonah and his dad not only had a close father-son relationship, but they were linked in a working relationship, too, and both took their work seriously. From what Dad had said, his business was growing here in Lancaster County, so Jonah figured with the two of them working together they could get a lot more done and make a good living.

For now, Jonah would live with his folks, but someday he planned to have a home of his own. He would need that if he ever found the right woman and decided to get married. He sure couldn't stay living with Mom and Dad forever, and he didn't wish to remain single indefinitely.

Jonah glanced around the bedroom he'd chosen. Just like their home in Ohio, all the rooms in Mom and Dad's new house felt homey. Maybe he'd be lucky enough to find a wife someday and have the same type of relationship that his folks had with each other. He dreamed of a spouse who would fill their home with love—a place where Jonah knew he belonged as soon as he walked through the door. His mom had a way of putting her heart into every room in her house, and anyone entering could actually feel the welcome. Even though this new home looked pretty good, he had seen a few things that ought to be done and was anxious to help Dad, not just at the buggy shop but with some of the jobs that needed to be completed here at the house.

While Jonah and his folks had been eating supper last night, he'd learned that Meredith Stoltzfus had lost her husband in a tragic accident and that she was expecting a baby. It didn't take Jonah long to realize this was the same young woman he used to know. He was stunned by the news of her sad loss, and his heart went out to her. So today, he planned to visit Meredith and offer his condolences. He hoped this would be a good time for him to drop by, because he wanted to let Meredith know how bad he felt about her situation and see if there was anything he could do to help out. After all, they'd been close friends a long time ago.

Ever since Jonah was a boy, he'd been sensitive to others, especially when they needed help in any way. He'd had an experience long ago that had embedded kindness into his soul and actually changed his attitude about people and life. Because of that, he'd helped his twin sister, Jean, as much as he could when she'd lost her first husband. Maybe he could help Meredith, as well.

Jonah thought about the friendship he and Meredith had developed when they'd worked at a restaurant in the small community of Pinecraft, in Sarasota, Florida. Meredith had been seventeen then, and he'd been eighteen. They'd quickly become friends and after returning to their homes, had stayed in touch through letters, until Meredith wrote and said she was being courted by Luke Stoltzfus and that they were planning to be married. Jonah had been disappointed at first but consoled himself with the thought that Meredith deserved to be happy. He'd been hoping she might be the girl for him but had learned to accept it as God's will when she'd fallen in love with someone else.

Meredith was slowly bringing some normalcy back into her life. At least, she was trying. She was most anxious to get things ready for the baby, which would probably keep her busy until the birth. She looked forward to her family coming over for supper this evening. It would be nice to take a break and spend time visiting with her parents and siblings—not to mention having someone to cook for other than herself. Grandma Smucker was coming, too, so they'd all be together like it had been before she and Luke got married.

Meredith was anxious to tell her family about her plan to start making head coverings. Except for the short time Dorine had been there, Meredith had been busy working around the house all morning and into the afternoon. As soon as the weather warmed, she planned to till the garden and uncover her flower beds. She would find a place to plant the bulbs Mom said she had for her. Several daffodils and tulips would add some color to her flower beds. She would also need to trim all the shrubs around the house, the way Dad had taught her to do several years ago, when she would walk around the yard helping him with spring cleanup. Those memories were probably why, to this day, she enjoyed working in the yard and around the house.

Thankfully she'd had no problems with her house except for a piece of siding that had blown off during one of the recent windy, snowy days. Dad said he would take care of that for her when they came over this evening.

Meredith planned to fix a big pot of sloppy joes for the meal, and she'd made a macaroni salad as well as a potato salad to go with it. Mom was bringing a chocolate cake—Dad's favorite—and Grandma was bringing some of Meredith's favorite ginger cookies.

Earlier, Meredith had browned the ground beef and sautéed the onions and green peppers, so all that was needed was to add the brown sugar, salt, pepper, a little mustard, ketchup, and a jar of mild chili sauce. She'd decided to prepare that in an hour or so, giving it plenty of time to simmer before supper. Until then, she thought she'd at least get a start on painting the baby's room.

She had to get the ladder from the barn and carry it upstairs, and in hindsight, she wished she had asked Dad to help her with that the last time he was here.

Well, it was only this one project, and she had consoled herself with the fact that she would get some exercise carrying the ladder up those steps. It was still early in her pregnancy, and she wasn't even showing yet, so it would be easier to do these things now, rather than when she was big and clumsy.

Meredith took her time carrying the ladder from the barn and across the yard. She had to put the ladder down a few times—first to close the barn door, and then again when she was on the porch, so she could open the back door and get the ladder inside.

"I could sure use an extra pair of hands right now," she muttered, dragging the ladder into the house.

Next was the chore of getting the ladder up the stairs, and while maneuvering it, a sharp pain streaked across her middle just as she reached the top step. It startled her, and she had to stop for a minute and catch her breath. Meredith leaned against the wall, holding her stomach until the spasm finally subsided. Slowly, she made her way to the spare room and carefully set the ladder in the corner where she wanted to begin painting.

Standing back, she tried to visualize how the room would look once it had a new coat of paint on the walls and ceiling. Meredith knew the now-drab room would transform after the color had been changed. She couldn't wait to get started.

It wasn't a real big room, so Meredith was sure she could tackle the project herself. She'd decided on a light tan color, which would be good for either a boy or a girl. And since this room was right next to Meredith's, it would be convenient for her to check on the baby.

While thinking about putting the baby's crib in her room for the first couple of weeks, she bent down to open the can of paint she'd purchased at the hardware store the day before. She'd just gotten the lid pried loose when another pain shot through her stomach. Deciding that the painting could wait for now and realizing that she was in need of a break, she headed back downstairs.

Guess I overdid it carrying that heavy ladder in by myself, she silently scolded herself.

Before sitting down to rest, she went to the kitchen and made some tea. Then she got out the kettle for simmering the sauce for the sloppy joes.

Another pain struck. She winced and stood motionless until it subsided.

Forgetting about the kettle she needed, she walked slowly to the living room to relax in her rocker with her cup of tea. She wouldn't let her brain think about what her body was warning her of right now. *I hope this goes away before my family comes over this evening. They worry about me enough as it is.*

A few minutes later, Meredith heard a knock on the door, and she slowly got up.

I wonder who that could be.

When she opened the door, she was surprised to see Jonah Miller standing on the porch. She hadn't seen him in several years, but he looked much as she remembered him from before—same curly black hair, dark brown eyes, and a small cleft in the middle of his chin. Except for being a little older, Jonah had hardly changed at all.

"Wie geht's?" Jonah asked, shifting from one foot to the other and leaning his hand on the door frame.

"Oh Jonah, it's so good to see you." Meredith opened the door wider for him to enter. "I heard you were moving to Bird-in-Hand," she said, without answering his question.

Jonah gave a slow nod. "Got here yesterday, and I wanted to stop by and say how sorry I was to hear about your husband." He paused, and Meredith could see the sympathy he felt for her in his eyes. "If there's anything I can do for you, please let me know."

"Danki, I appreciate you coming over." Meredith really wasn't up to company right now, and she was about to say so, when another cramp came—this one much worse than the last. "Oh!" she gasped, doubling over from the pain. "I think I need to see a doctor right away."

With no hesitation, Jonah scooped Meredith into his arms and placed her on the sofa. Putting one of the small decorative pillows behind her head, he calmly told her, "I'm going out to the phone shack to call 911. Don't move or try to get up. Just lie here and rest. I'll be right back."

Trembling and fighting waves of nausea, Meredith drew in a deep breath and closed her eyes. *Dear Lord,* she silently prayed, rubbing her hand over her still-flat stomach, *please don't let me lose this baby. It's all I have left of Luke.*

THE HOPE OF SPRING

Bear ye one another's burdens,
and so fulfill the law of Christ.
GALATIANS 6:2

CHAPTER 1

Ronks, Pennsylvania

"There's no need for you to fuss over me," Meredith said as her mother tucked a blanket under her chin. "I'm not having any more contractions, and I don't see why I can't go home to my own house."

Mom patted Meredith's arm affectionately. "You came close to losing the *boppli* yesterday, and the doctor said you need to rest for the next several weeks until your pregnancy is no longer at risk. I'm guessing you won't do that if you go back to your house and start looking around at things you want to do. So, since you need someone to take care of you right now, and you shouldn't be doing anything strenuous, it's best if you stay here with us for the time being."

Meredith knew Mom was right, but that didn't make it any easier to deal with. She wanted to carry the baby to full term and have a home birth in her own home in a natural way, with the midwife present.

"I'm sorry about not being able to fix supper for you and the family last night," Meredith apologized. "I was looking forward to cooking you a meal."

Mom shook her head. "Don't worry about that. There'll be plenty of other times you can make us supper. Right now, you need only be concerned about yourself and the boppli."

"I know." Meredith settled back on the sofa and tried to relax. "Did you get a chance to meet Jonah when you were at the hospital?" she asked.

"We did, but just for a few minutes, when we first got there. We're grateful he stopped by your place when he did and got the help you needed so quickly. Jonah seems like a caring young man. I'm sure he'll fit in well with our community."

"He was kind when I worked with him at the restaurant in Pinecraft, as well."

Mom's eyebrows lifted. "Is he the same young man who wrote letters to you for a few years after you returned from Florida?"

"*Jah*." Meredith sighed. "I don't know what I would have done if he hadn't stopped by when he did. With the way I was hurting, and then having to trudge through the snow, I might not have made it to the phone shack in time to call for help."

Mom clicked her tongue. "Which is exactly why you shouldn't be alone."

Tears seeped out from under Meredith's lashes and splashed onto her cheeks. "I appreciate you letting me stay here, Mom, but you really don't need one more person to take care of right now."

"It's not a problem," Mom said, smiling at Meredith. "Around here everyone has a job to do, and right now, my job is looking after you."

"But I have responsibilities at home, and now I have a hospital bill to pay, so I really need to get busy and make some head coverings to sell. Then there's that spare room next to mine. I want to get it painted and fixed up before the boppli comes."

"Since the baby isn't due until July, there's plenty of time for that. Your *daed* can do the painting as soon as he finds the time, and Stanley will take care of your horses, get the mail, and check for phone messages after school every day." Mom gave Meredith's shoulder a gentle squeeze. "Your daed is over at your place right now, checking on things. I believe he was planning to fix the piece of siding that broke off your house."

"I should have told Dad to get the sloppy joes, potato salad, and macaroni salad out of my refrigerator and bring everything back here so we could have them for supper. That way, you won't have to cook anything tonight."

"That's okay. We can get your *bruder* to go after the food if your daed doesn't think of it. Now I want you to relax and quit worrying about things."

In hindsight, Meredith knew she should have taken better care and not done anything too strenuous yesterday. It had been foolish to carry the ladder from the barn up to the second-floor bedroom. Now her body needed time to rest and heal. She really had no choice but to stay here right now, so she might as well try to relax and enjoy the pampering.

I've lost Luke, Meredith thought as her eyes drifted shut, *and I won't take the chance of losing our baby.*

≈

Bird-in-Hand, Pennsylvania

Jonah had just finished working at the buggy shop for the day, so he decided to go over to Meredith's house. She was supposed to get out of the hospital this afternoon, and he wanted to see how she was doing.

Jonah borrowed his dad's horse and buggy, but he couldn't seem to get the horse, Knickers, to move along very fast. No matter where he went with the horse and buggy, Jonah usually enjoyed taking in the scenery, but not today. He barely noticed the snow in the fields, and the blue jays squawking overhead seemed more of an annoyance to him.

Finally, he was there, and after securing Knickers to the hitching rail near the barn, he headed for the house. Jonah had just stepped onto the porch, when another horse and buggy pulled into the yard. After the driver got out and secured the horse, Jonah realized it was Meredith's dad, whom he'd met at the hospital. Jonah waved and waited for Philip to join him on the porch.

"If you're lookin' for Meredith, she's not here," Philip said.

"Is she still in the hospital?" Jonah asked.

"Nope. She was released this afternoon, and she'll be staying at our place for a while."

Jonah nodded. "Guess that makes sense. It's probably not a good idea for her to be here alone, trying to do things by herself."

"It sure isn't—especially now that she's expecting a boppli. Losing Luke has been hard on Meredith. She loved him a lot. But having a baby will help keep his memory alive." Philip leaned against the porch railing. "It'll be hard for her to raise the baby alone, so we're gonna help out as much as we can, despite her objections."

"Will Meredith sell her house and move in with you permanently?" Jonah questioned.

Philip shrugged. "I'm not sure about that. My daughter can be stubborn sometimes, and I know she wants to make it on her own. But there are bills and taxes to pay, and with no money comin' in, she may be forced to sell."

"That'd be a shame," Jonah said, wishing there was something he could do to help out. "Won't some folks in this community give Meredith money?"

"There will probably be a benefit auction to help with her medical expenses." Philip glanced toward the barn. "But I'm thinkin' she ought to sell Luke's horse, because she doesn't need him anymore, and I'm sure the gelding would go for a fairly good price."

"I'd be interested in buying it," Jonah said. "The horse I had in Ohio was getting old, so I sold him before I moved here, and now I need a new one."

Philip reached under his hat and scratched his head. "That should work out well for Meredith, but I'll have to discuss it with her first, of course."

"Since she's staying over at your place, why don't I follow you home? Then I can ask her about buying Luke's horse."

Philip shook his head. "I think it's better if I talk to her first. Why don't you drop by our place sometime tomorrow?"

"All right then, I'll come over after work tomorrow afternoon," Jonah agreed, although he was disappointed he wouldn't be seeing Meredith until then.

Out back, an energetic German shorthair pointer barked frantically from his kennel. "Guess I'd better get ole Fritzy boy and take him home with me," Philip said. "Poor mutt probably can't figure out what's goin' on. Luke is gone, and now the dog's most likely wondering where Meredith is."

Jonah extended his hand. "It was nice to see you again, Philip. I'll take a look at the horse before I go so I'll have a better idea of how much I should offer for him."

⚬⚬⚬

Ronks

Meredith had been resting on the sofa most of the day and was bored. Lying here gave her too much time to think about Luke and how much she missed him. Her mind drifted back to the day they'd said goodbye and the sincere expression she'd seen on his face. If she had known it would be the last time she'd ever see her beloved husband, she would have said so many things.

Tears welled in Meredith's eyes and trickled down her cheeks. *Oh Luke, I love you so much.* The thought that she would never see his handsome, smiling face again was almost too much to comprehend.

Forcing herself to think about something else, Meredith began to fret because she couldn't be at home doing the things she'd planned in preparation for the baby. If only there was something she could do while she rested—anything that would keep her mind off the troubles she faced and help her focus on something else. She'd always been the type to keep her hands busy, and doing nothing was so frustrating.

"Would you like a cup of tea?" Meredith's grandmother asked as she entered the living room with a tray in her hands.

Meredith nodded appreciatively. "That'd be nice."

Grandma Smucker set the tray on the coffee table, poured each of them a cup of tea, and took a seat in the rocker across from Meredith. "How are you feeling, dear one?"

Meredith managed a weak smile. "Better than yesterday. I overdid it, and because of my stupidity, I almost lost the boppli."

Grandma slowly shook her head. "Don't be so hard on yourself, Meredith. We all make mistakes."

"I guess I'm full of *hochmut*, or I would have asked for help painting the baby's room."

"You should never be too proud to ask. That's what families are for, you know." Grandma took a sip of tea and winked at Meredith. "You're a lot like me, though. It was hard to move in with your folks after your grandpa died, and I still feel bad about them having to support me. But I know they're doing it because they love me, and for that, I'm grateful." She sighed as she set her cup on the coffee table. "It's sad to say, but some folks, like Alma Beechy, don't have any family around to help."

"I appreciate my family and friends," Meredith said, taking a sip of tea and savoring the delicious flavor of ginger, which soothed her upset stomach almost immediately. "My friend Dorine Yoder suggested that I make head coverings to sell. I was planning to start doing that right away, but now I guess it'll have to wait awhile."

"I've made a few coverings in my day," Grandma said, "so I'd be happy to help when you're feeling up to doing some sewing."

"*Danki*, I would like that."

"How are you doing?" Dad asked as he and Mom entered the room.

"I'm okay. Just tired of lying around doing nothing but worrying about things—including my finances," she answered honestly.

"First things, first. I have a surprise for you." Dad grinned at Meredith and went out to the back porch. When he returned, he had Fritz. The dog spied Meredith and raced over to her, resting his head gently on her lap as though sensing that he needed to take it easy with her. His stub of a tail, however, flopped back and forth on the floor, beating a rhythm of happiness. Meredith laughed at how funny he looked. It felt good to find something to laugh about.

"Hey, pup," she said, patting the top of his head. "How are you doin', boy?"

Fritz slurped Meredith's hand in response.

"I bet you were lonely last night, weren't you, pup? I'm sorry I had to leave you alone in your kennel all night." Meredith felt her nerves begin to relax as she continued to pet Fritz, and he alternated between licking and nuzzling her hand.

"I think I may have an answer that could help you. At least, it will help out with your finances," Dad said.

"Oh, what's that?" Meredith asked as she pampered Fritz with soothing murmurs.

"I ran into Jonah Miller at your place today, and he's interested in buying Luke's *gaul*."

"What was Jonah doing at my house, and why does he need a horse? Doesn't he have one of his own?" Meredith questioned.

"He went over there to check on you. And *jah*, he did have a horse when he was in Ohio, but he sold it before he moved here, so he needs a new one. Said his other horse was gettin' too old."

Mom's eyebrows pulled tightly together. "I wish we were better off financially so we could buy the horse."

"First off, we don't need another horse, and second, I don't need the reminder of how bad off we are financially." Dad rubbed the side of his slightly crooked nose and frowned. "When you say things like that, Luann, it makes me feel like a failure—like I can't provide well enough for our family."

Mom shook her head. "I didn't mean that at all, Philip. I know how hard you work to keep your stands at three farmers' markets going, and I hope you're not thinking of taking on any more."

"I had given it some consideration," he said. "Thought maybe I could get a stand going at the Crossroads Farmers' Market in Gratz."

"But that's clear up in Dauphin County." Mom planted both hands on her hips and looked at him with a determined expression. "Besides the expense of hiring a driver to take you there every week, it would mean you'd be gone from home even more than you are already."

"I don't like being away from the family, either," he said with a slow shake of his head, "but I need to make sure we have enough money coming in to provide for everyone's needs."

Mom clenched her teeth. "I'm sorry I even mentioned our financial situation. Please, Philip, let's pray about this before you decide to take on another stand."

"Yep. I'll definitely be doin' that. In the meantime, though," he said, looking back at Meredith, "what do you think about sellin' Luke's gaul?"

She swallowed hard as tears pricked the backs of her eyes. If she sold Luke's horse, she'd be letting go of something that had been important to him. But if she kept the gelding, she'd never use him for pulling the buggy because Socks was too spirited for her to handle.

"It would be hard to let the horse go, knowing how much Luke liked him," Meredith said. "Can I think about it for a day or two before I give Jonah an answer?"

Dad nodded. "Sure, take all the time you need. In the meantime, though, I also brought something else back with me."

"More surprises, Dad?" Meredith asked.

"Not exactly. I saw a bag of hamburger rolls on your kitchen table, so I took a peek in the refrigerator and spotted two delicious-looking salads and some ground beef you'd browned for sloppy joes. Figured we may as well eat it here tonight so it won't go to waste." Dad grinned and thumped his stomach. "So now it'll go to my waist instead."

"I'm glad you thought to look in the refrigerator. Now Mom won't have to do much cooking for supper tonight." Meredith looked at her mother. "The ground beef has sautéed peppers and onions mixed in, and the only thing you'll have to do is add a little brown sugar, salt, pepper, a bit of mustard, and some mild chili sauce if you have some."

"I'll get that simmering right away," Mom said. "It'll be a nice treat having an evening off from cooking a big meal."

Meredith wished she could have had her family to her house for supper, but this was the next best thing. At least they could all be together, and she thanked the Lord one more time for her caring family, and most of all, that she hadn't lost the baby.

CHAPTER 2

Philadelphia, Pennsylvania

"I sure wish all this snow would go away. I'm more than ready for spring," Nurse Susan Bailey said to her sister, Anne, as they rode in Anne's compact car out of the city toward their grandparents' house in Darby.

"I wholeheartedly agree," Anne said, turning her blinker on to move to another lane. "The sooner the weather warms up, the sooner I can start jogging in the park again."

Susan smiled. Her thirty-year-old sister had always liked to be outdoors and enjoyed exercising, which was probably why she was so fit and trim. Of course, Susan had never had a problem with her weight either, but she wasn't into exercise. She figured she got enough of a workout on the job, although so did Anne, since she was a physical therapist. Anne might be extra motivated to stay in tip-top shape, so she'd be able to perform her duties without injuring herself and would be a good role model to her patients, who often needed encouragement.

Today had been one of those rare occasions when Susan's and Anne's work schedules coincided, and they'd been able to ride to and from the hospital together. The drive to work was only about ten minutes, but it was still nice to have someone to chat with along the route.

"Just think, spring's less than a month away, so we don't have too much longer to wait," Anne said, breaking into Susan's thoughts.

"I know, and as soon as the weather warms up, I'll be sticking my hands in the dirt and helping Grandpa putter around in his garden."

"You definitely inherited your desire to work in the garden from him." Anne flipped a curly tendril away from her face. "I'd rather read a good book than play in the dirt."

"I like to read, too," Susan agreed, "but not as much in the warmer weather, since I can do other things. You know how it is with me." She held up her hands. "I like to see results from something I've worked on with my hands—especially if it takes me outside."

Susan's thoughts drifted as she glanced at her polished fingernails and thought about the vegetables she and Grandpa would plant this year. Her nails wouldn't look this good once she started working the soil for their garden, but that was okay. She'd rather have dirt under her nails than give up something that brought her so much pleasure and satisfaction. Susan could almost smell the earthy aroma of the damp soil as she worked it through her fingers. Better yet, she could just about taste those delicious BLTs they would make with the juicy beefsteak tomatoes they'd pick. What wasn't there to like about biting into a sandwich made with fresh, homegrown tomatoes? Even better was sharing a meal at the picnic table Grandma and Grandpa had in the corner of their backyard, under the shade of the maple tree.

They rode in silence for a while, until they passed a homeless man holding up a sign saying he was out of work and needed money. Seeing him made Susan think about one of her patients who'd been admitted to ICU a little over a month ago. Anne must have been thinking of him, too, because she glanced over at Susan and said, "How's that John Doe of yours doing?"

"About the same. The poor guy had surgery to repair the damage that had been done to his spleen, but unfortunately he's still in a coma."

"That's too bad. Has there been any sign of him waking up?"

Susan shook her head. "He flutters his eyes and jerks his hands once in a while, but he hasn't responded to any verbal stimulation. Along with the trauma to his spleen and his vocal cords, he suffered a serious injury to his brain tissue, which resulted in a blood clot. The doctor's still giving him medicine to dissolve the clot. His other injuries included several broken ribs, a cracked sternum, and a fractured collarbone. They're healing okay on their own and won't require surgery, but I fear he may never wake up. And if he does, he may not be as he once was. We still don't know his name, so I call him Eddie." She sighed. "Even though I know he might not hear me, I talk to him about all sorts of things, and I also pray for him—sometimes out loud."

"It's good that you're doing that," Anne said. "Doctors always encourage nurses to talk to their patients, even though they don't seem to hear what you're saying. That will keep his brain stimulated, just hearing your voice. And of course," she added, "prayer is important, too."

Susan smiled. "Well, if Eddie does hear what I'm saying, he probably thinks I'm a bit of a motormouth."

"I doubt it. Your positive attitude and compassion are the best medicine that young man can get right now." Anne switched lanes again. "I'm happy to say that most of my patients aren't in as bad a shape as your Eddie. It's easier to work with them when they're conscious and able to communicate. Hopefully, by the time Eddie is stable enough to be moved to rehab, he'll have woken up from his coma."

⁂

Bird-in-Hand

"How long will it be till supper?" Jonah asked when he entered the kitchen and found his mother in front of the sink, peeling potatoes.

She turned and smiled, her green eyes twinkling. "You're home early today, and since I'm just getting started on the potatoes and carrots that will go with the roast we're having for supper, it won't be ready for at least another hour yet."

"Can you keep something warm for me in case I don't make it back before then?" Jonah asked as Mom handed him a piece of raw potato.

He went to the table and sprinkled a little salt on the potato before popping it into his mouth.

Mom grinned. "I see you still like eating raw potatoes."

"Some things never change," Jonah answered, enjoying the uncooked morsel. "I'll take another chunk if you don't mind."

"So, where are you going?" Mom asked, handing him one more piece.

"Over to the Kings' place to speak with Meredith. Remember, I told you last night that I planned to go over there after Dad and I finished up at the buggy shop today. I want to see about buying her husband's gaul."

Mom thumped the side of her head, pushing her covering slightly askew, and exposing the light brown bun at the back of her head. "I'd forgotten about that," she said, readjusting the covering. "I assume you'll be taking your daed's horse and buggy?"

"Yep, that's right."

"You're welcome to ride over to the Kings' on my scooter." Mom grinned, reminding Jonah of a young schoolgirl. Truth was, his fifty-six-year-old mother was so thin and petite she could almost pass for a teenage girl if it weren't for the few wrinkles on her forehead. Dad often teased her, saying she was his child-bride.

"Think I'll stick to Dad's horse and buggy," Jonah replied with a chuckle. "It'll take me less time, and won't be as hard on my legs as a scooter."

"That's true," Mom agreed, "but at least with my scooter you won't have an unruly horse to deal with on the road." She looked past Jonah toward the door. "Where's your daed?"

"Out in the barn. Said to tell you he'll be in soon." Jonah stepped up to Mom and gave her a hug. "I'm going to wash up and change into some clean clothes, then I'll be heading over to see Meredith." He snatched a raw carrot before heading out of the room, and smiled when he heard Mom crunch one, too.

◈

Ronks

Meredith had been resting on the sofa most of the afternoon, and her youngest siblings, Owen and Katie, were getting on her nerves. They were either fussing at each other or running through the house, hollering at the top of their lungs. Owen, who'd turned three last November, had started walking by the time he was ten months old and never had any trouble keeping up with six-year-old Katie. Mom had been trying to keep the little ones quiet today, but every time she got them interested in doing something in another room, they'd end up back in the living room. With Meredith's teenage sisters, Laurie and Kendra, both working at the farmers' market today, and thirteen-year-old Nina visiting a friend after school, Mom was shorthanded this evening.

"You'd better give me that!" Katie shouted as she raced past Meredith, chasing after Owen, who had taken her doll.

Meredith grimaced. *I wonder if I'll feel this way when my own baby is born and starts fussing or being too loud. I hope not, because I don't want to be an impatient mother.*

Meredith loved her family, but she wished she could go back to the quiet of her own house. She didn't remember that the antics of her younger brothers and sisters bothered her before she got married like they did now. Maybe that was because, for over a year, it had just been her, Luke, and Fritz, with no energetic little ones underfoot.

Adding to Meredith's frustration were all the things she wanted to get done at home, and the preparations she wanted to make for the baby. But there was nothing more important than the safety of her unborn child, and most of her aggravation was from not doing anything except lying around. Hopefully, she could get started on making those head coverings soon.

She glanced around the room. Not much had changed in the large home where her family lived. From the looks of the furniture, one would never know that seven children were still being raised in this house. Most of the pieces were still original and had been here when Meredith was growing up. Mom had a knack for taking good care of things and teaching her children to do the same. With a little sanding and some varnish, Mom had brought new life to some of the old pieces of furniture she and Dad had purchased at auctions a long time ago. Meredith had been told that some of the pieces in this room had been handed down to Mom and Dad from their parents. She remembered Dad saying once, "If you take care of what you have, it'll last a long time."

Looking around, the proof was here, right down to the large oak table and chairs in the dining room. A lot of celebrations had been held around that table, and many great memories were made with family and friends.

I hope I can be a good role model for my child, like my parents still are with all of us, Meredith thought. She closed her eyes, breathing in the wonderful aromas coming from the kitchen. Was that fried chicken she smelled? She hoped so. Mom's fried chicken was the best.

"I'm sorry if the little ones are disturbing you," Mom said, dashing into the living room, hoisting Owen onto her hip, and taking hold of Katie's hand. "Your grandma and I have been busy fixing supper, and we figured either Stanley or Arlene would keep an eye on the little ones, but things didn't quite go as planned."

"Where are my little bruder *un schweschder?*" Meredith asked.

"Stanley's in the barn doing some chores, and Arlene's resting upstairs in her room. She came home from school this afternoon complaining of a *koppweh*."

Meredith sighed. "Arlene's not the only one with a headache. My head's pounding so hard I can barely think."

"Why don't you go to your room and lie down?" Mom suggested. "I'll call you when supper's ready."

"Maybe I will." Meredith swung her legs over the side of the sofa, and had just started across the room when a knock sounded on the door. "I'll get that," she said, looking at Mom. "You've got your hands full right now."

Mom nodded and hurried into the kitchen, with the two little ones in tow.

When Meredith opened the front door, she was surprised to see Jonah Miller.

"*Wie geht's?*" he asked with a smile.

"I'm doing okay," Meredith replied, making no mention of her headache. "Come in out of the cold," she said, opening the door wider.

"*Danki.*"

When Jonah stepped in, Meredith motioned for him to take a seat in the rocker, and she returned to the sofa.

"I want to thank you for calling 911 for me." Meredith looked at Jonah, feeling shy all of a sudden. "Your timing was perfect."

"You're welcome, and I'd have to say that it was God's timing, not mine, that brought me to your house. I'm glad you're doing better and were able to come here to stay with your folks." Jonah removed his straw hat and raked his fingers through the ends of his dark, curly hair. "Uh. . .the reason I'm here is to talk to you about your husband's gaul."

She nodded. "My daed said you were interested in buying the horse, but there's something you need to know."

"What's that?"

"Socks can be a bit spirited, so he may not be what you need. Luke seemed to be the only one who could handle the horse effectively."

Jonah smiled. "I've had spirited horses before, so I'm not worried about that."

Meredith sucked in her lower lip as she mulled things over. Jonah was probably right about handling Luke's horse. It was just the thought of giving Socks up that made her feel like crying. Unfortunately, it was another reminder that the love of her life was gone and would never be back.

At least she had warned Jonah about Socks being feisty. The rest would be in Jonah's hands if he ended up buying the horse. "How much would you be willing to pay for the horse?" Meredith questioned.

"Does two thousand dollars sound okay?"

"Oh no," Meredith said with a shake of her head. "That's way too much money."

Jonah leaned forward, looking at Meredith with a most sincere expression. "I checked the horse over before I left your place yesterday, and I think Socks is worth every bit of that."

Meredith sat for several seconds, then finally nodded. She needed the money. She just wished she didn't have to part with Luke's horse. If only he hadn't been killed on that bus. If he'd just stayed home like she'd wanted him to do, instead of heading for Indiana to buy his uncle's business. Would she ever stop regretting that she hadn't tried harder to convince Luke not to go?

Oh Luke, she thought, fighting back tears, *I don't think I'll ever get over losing you.*

CHAPTER 3

As Meredith headed down the hall from her room, she yawned and stretched her arms over her head. It was the second Monday of March, and she was more than ready to go home. Not only were her younger siblings still getting on her nerves, but she missed her own surroundings and the things that reminded her of Luke. She was feeling stronger, with no more contractions, so she didn't see any reason to keep staying with her folks. Now she just needed to convince Mom of that.

When Meredith entered the kitchen, she found Mom in front of the stove, stirring a kettle of oatmeal. *"Guder mariye,"* Meredith said, moving across the room.

Mom turned and smiled. "Good morning. Besides me, you're the first one up. Did you sleep well last night?"

Meredith shook her head. "Not really. Between Dad's snoring, the wind howling and rattling my bedroom window, and then Owen crying out several times during the night, I had a hard time staying asleep."

"I'm sorry about that," Mom apologized. "I've grown used to your daed's snoring, so it doesn't bother me that much, but I'll ask him to be sure he wears one of those nose strips he bought awhile ago. And I think things will be better with Owen once he gets over his cold." Mom sighed. "I'm not sure about the window, though. The March winds are picking up, and for as long as I can remember, that window's been making a racket. I'll ask your daed to look at it. Maybe there's something he can do to make the window tighter so it won't rattle so much."

"You don't have to worry about any of those things, because I'm ready to go home," Meredith blurted out. "It's quieter there, and since I'm feeling better now, I'm sure I can manage fine on my own."

Mom's lips pursed. "It's not a good idea for you to be alone, Meredith. I shudder to think what would have happened if Jonah Miller hadn't dropped by to see you the day you started having contractions."

"I'm glad he was there, but if I had been alone when the pains got bad, I would have somehow made my way out to the phone shack and called for help," Meredith said in her own defense. She could see by the look on Mom's face that she wasn't convinced. Truthfully, Meredith knew she might not have made it, and she was thankful that Jonah had showed up when he did.

"If it's too noisy for you here, then we can talk to Luke's folks and see if you can stay with them, like you did for a few weeks after Luke died."

"Sadie and Elam are getting up in years, and they don't need me to look after."

"I'm sure it wouldn't be an imposition. They'd probably love having you there for a while again."

Meredith shook her head. "I don't need to stay with anyone, Mom."

"What if someone stays with you at your house? Would you be okay with that?"

"Who?"

"I was thinking of your sister Laurie. I'm almost sure she'd be willing, and I know she would be a big help to you."

"But Laurie has her stand at the farmers' market, so she'd be gone most of the day," Meredith pointed out. "How would that help me?"

"But the market's only open on Fridays and Saturdays through April. And in May, it's just three days a week. It's not until July that it goes to four. On the days Laurie's working, we can ask someone else to come and stay with you." Mom's eyes brightened, and she snapped her fingers. "I know. We can see if Alma Beechy would go to your house whenever Laurie's at the market."

Meredith's jaw clenched. She didn't want anyone babysitting her, but if she didn't agree, Mom would insist that she stay with the family.

"Okay," she said with a slow nod. "If Laurie's agreeable, then she can move in with me for now, and if Alma's willing, she can come during the hours Laurie's not there."

Mom's face relaxed a bit, and she gave Meredith a hug. "I know you think it's not necessary, but it'll make me feel a little more at ease." She patted Meredith's growing stomach. "It's nice to see that you're starting to show. It makes me even more excited about becoming a *groossmudder*."

"I'm excited about being a *mudder*, too," Meredith said.

"Just wait until your child is born," Mom added. "No matter what age he or she should be, you'll still worry, same as I do now."

Mom was right. Even though she was only four-and-a-half months pregnant, Meredith already worried about her baby.

⟨⟨⟩⟩

Darby, Pennsylvania

"Would you please pass the syrup?" Susan's grandfather asked after she'd handed him the platter of fresh buttermilk pancakes Grandma had made for breakfast.

Susan smiled, and after she'd passed him the maple syrup, she bit into one of the pancakes on her plate and wiped the sticky, warm syrup from her lips. "Yum! Grandma, this is delicious. You're such a good cook."

Grandma laughed, her cheeks turning pink. "You say that at nearly every one of our meals."

"That's because it's true," Anne agreed from her place across the table. "I doubt that I'll ever be able to fix a meal as tasty as any of yours."

Grandpa leaned over and kissed Grandma's cheek. "Now you know why I've stayed married to her all these years."

Grandma playfully swatted his arm. "Oh Henry, you're such a big tease."

Susan smiled. She loved watching the camaraderie between her grandparents and felt blessed to have them both in her life. Many people didn't have a close relationship with their grandparents, and some didn't know them at all. Susan couldn't imagine that, and it made her all the more thankful for what she and Anne had.

"Not to change the subject or anything," Anne said, "but Susan, I was wondering if you're still interested in reading that Amish novel I told you about."

Susan nodded. "Yes, I sure am."

"Great. I'll get it from my room as soon as we're done with breakfast."

"The Amish are quite an unusual group of people," Grandpa said. "I admire their commitment to keeping true to their heritage."

"Yes," Grandma agreed. "Unfortunately, for many people, there isn't much commitment to anything in this day and age, and if there is, it seems to be short-lived."

"Speaking of the Amish," Anne said, "I still want to visit Lancaster soon, to look around some of the shops where they sell Amish-made products."

"Are you looking for anything in particular?" Grandma asked, finishing the last bite of her pancake as she took her plate to the sink.

Anne shook her head. "I think I'll know it when I see it, though." She looked over at Susan and grinned. "As soon as we both know our work schedules for April, let's plan a day when we can go to Lancaster like we talked about doing before."

"I suppose we could," Susan agreed. "It would be something different to do, at least."

Grandma nodded, testing the water in her sink before starting the dishes. "As hard as you two work, you deserve to do something fun on your day off."

"Maybe you and Grandpa would like to go, too," Anne suggested.

Grandma looked at Grandpa. "What do you think about that, Henry?"

He shrugged his shoulders. "I don't know, Norma. Guess we'll just have to wait and see how it goes."

⌘

Bird-in-Hand

"Where are you headed, Son?" Jonah's mother asked when he slipped into his jacket and put his straw hat on his head.

"Since today's my day off, I plan to run a few errands, and I thought it'd be good to take my new gaul out for a run," he answered, stopping near the back door. "In case you're wondering, I should be home in plenty of time to help with the chores before supper."

Dad looked up from reading the newspaper and frowned. "I still can't figure out why you bought that gelding. The horse is too spirited, if you ask me."

Jonah bobbed his head. "You're right about that. Meredith warned me about his friskiness before I bought him. But I think with some work and a little time, Socks will settle down and be a good horse for me."

"I've seen the way he acts around our *hund*," Mom said, "and I don't like it one little bit. Why, the other day when Socks was waiting at the hitching rail, he nearly kicked poor Herbie in the head."

"That's probably because the dog was pestering him," Jonah said.

Mom shook her head vigorously. "Herbie's an easygoing animal, and it's not like him to bother any of our livestock. I think that new horse is just plain mean." Her eyebrows furrowed. "I'll bet the March winds we've been having will spook that critter of yours, too."

Jonah didn't argue. He figured there was no point. Once Mom made up her mind about something, it practically took a miracle to change it. Well, maybe after Socks became adjusted to his new surroundings, he'd prove to Mom that she was wrong.

"Speaking of Herbie, I've been wondering where he came from," Jonah said, wanting to change the subject.

"Guess you could say that Herbie found us," Dad replied. "A few weeks before you moved here, the dog showed up on our doorstep, and he's been with us ever since." He went on to explain how he'd posted DOG FOUND signs all over the community, on telephone poles, and in local grocery stores, as well as passing the word to folks when they came into his buggy shop. Since no one knew about any lost dog or who the border collie belonged to, as time went by, Herbie became one of the family.

"Ah, I see. And how'd you come up with his name?" Jonah inquired.

"That's another thing that just seemed to happen," Mom said. "When Herbie first showed up, we started saying 'here boy' whenever we took food out to him or when we didn't know where he was. Then when it looked like the dog was here to stay, I decided to give him a name."

"We never kept him tied or penned up, thinking that one day he might try to find his way home," Dad put in, "but he seemed to like it here, and since he always responded to 'here boy,' your *mamm* came up with the name 'Herbie,' since it sort of sounded like 'here boy.'" He chuckled. "Herbie seemed to like it, too, so that's how the name stuck."

"When we're with him, Herbie watches, like he's waiting for us to tell him to do something." Mom glanced out the kitchen window, where Herbie lay in front of the buggy shop. "Just look at him out there. I'll bet he's waiting for someone to show up."

"That's right," Dad agreed. "And the dog always lets us know when someone's coming by giving a few loud barks." He grinned. "Herbie's friendly with most people, though. Whenever I'm in the shop and a customer comes in, Herbie greets them with a wag of his tail, and does he ever like the attention when someone stops to pet him."

"It sounds like Herbie's found himself a good home," Jonah said.

"Jah, and we're glad he's here with us. Oh, by the way, Jonah, where all are you going today?" Mom asked as Jonah's hand touched the doorknob.

"For one thing, I'll be stopping by the Shoe and Boot store," Jonah replied. He wished he didn't have to answer to Mom; it made him feel like a schoolboy.

"That shouldn't take all day," she said. "Are there some other places you'll be stopping, as well?"

"Stop badgering the boy, Sarah," Dad said, flapping the end of his newspaper at Mom. "It shouldn't matter where he's going."

Mom's lips compressed. "I wasn't badgering him, Raymond. Just was curious to know why he said he'd be home in time for the evening chores." Mom glanced at the clock on the far wall, and then at Jonah. "It's not even noon yet, and if you're just going to the Shoe and Boot store, I wouldn't think you'd be gone more than a few hours at the most."

Jonah tapped his foot impatiently. This inquisition was getting worse. "If you must know, I'm planning to stop by the Kings' place to see how Meredith is doing."

Deep wrinkles formed across Mom's forehead. "Do you think that's a good idea?"

"Why wouldn't it be?" Jonah asked. He had an inkling of what she was going to say next but hoped she wouldn't.

"Well, some folks might get the wrong idea."

"The wrong idea about what?" Dad questioned.

"Meredith's husband hasn't even been gone two months yet, and some might think our son has taken an interest in her." Mom tapped her fingers along the edge of the table. "That's not the case, is it, Jonah?"

" 'Course not," Jonah was quick to say. "Meredith is just a good friend, and I'm doing what the Bible says in Galatians 6:2: 'Bear ye one another's burdens, and so fulfil the law of Christ.'"

"I know what the Bible says." Mom flapped her hand. "But Meredith is the friend you had an interest in after you came back from Sarasota with stars in your eyes."

"Well, you two enjoy your day," Jonah said, giving no reply to Mom's last comment. "Looks like we might get some rain," he called over his shoulder as he headed out the door, needing to sidestep this conversation. He wasn't about to say anything more, but deep down, he hoped that someday, after Meredith had recovered from her husband's death, she might take an interest in him.

CHAPTER 4

Stepping onto the porch, Jonah realized it was raining. That was pretty typical for this time of the year, and it was a lot better than snow, but he really preferred sunshine to rain. He looked forward to nicer weather so he could get out Mom and Dad's grill and cook some steaks, burgers, or chicken. He was sure Mom would appreciate not having to cook once he started grilling, too.

By the time Jonah got his buggy out of the barn and Socks hitched to it, he was pretty wet. He grabbed the towel he kept on the floor of the backseat for such occasions, lifted his straw hat, and wiped his face and head. Hopefully the rain would let up soon, or he'd probably be drenched by the time he finished running all his errands.

Socks bulked a bit when Jonah tried to back him away from the hitching rail, but once he got the horse turned and headed down the driveway, things went okay. Socks liked to trot at a fairly good pace, so Jonah had to keep a firm grip on the reins. If he gave the horse too much slack, he'd take off like a shot. And on a busy stretch of road such as this, that would not be a good thing.

Jonah's first stop was at the Shoe and Boot store, where Seth Yoder helped him find a good pair of work boots. As he left the store, a strong wind nearly blew his hat off. At least it had stopped raining. He glanced at the sky, still heavy with gray clouds. Now if only the wind would quit sending chills down the back of his neck.

Socks pawed at the ground, while chewing on the hitching rail. Talk about an impatient animal! "You can relax now, Socks," Jonah said soothingly as he released the horse's lines from the rail. "We'll soon be on our way again."

As they traveled down the road toward the Kings' place, Socks started tossing his head from side to side, especially when a gust of wind blew clusters of old wet leaves across the road in front of them. A couple of times the horse acted like he was going to rear up, but Jonah quickly brought him under control. As they neared the furniture store where Meredith's husband used to work, Socks bolted right into the parking lot, nearly running into the fence along the side of the road. Was this overly zealous horse looking for his master? Jonah wondered. Did Socks miss his previous owner? Could that be why he was acting up? Of course, it didn't help that the roads were still wet, but Jonah had a feeling there was more to it than that. Socks might be a one-man horse; however Jonah had always had a way with horses, and he was determined to win this one over.

"Easy now," he said, turning the horse back onto the road. "Your master's not here anymore. I'm your new owner."

A car whizzed by, and Socks whinnied. "It's okay, boy," Jonah called. "There's nothing to worry about."

As soon as Jonah spoke, he realized his words weren't exactly true. Horse and buggies were vulnerable on the roads. As a buggy maker, he knew all too well how devastating an accident could be to a buggy, its passengers, and even the horse if it was hit by a car, or worse a big truck or bus. And there were lots of tour buses in Lancaster County.

Jonah grimaced, remembering a time when a speeding pickup truck had crested a hill near the small town of Charm, Ohio, and smashed into the back of a buggy. Another time, the driver of a car in Sugarcreek swerved to avoid hitting a buggy and ended up ramming into another buggy going in the opposite direction.

Other vehicles weren't the only thing that caused buggy accidents, though. Horses sometimes spooked and ran out of control because of water splashing from passing vehicles, loud noises, or uneven roadways. Jonah had seen many buggies in such bad condition that they were beyond repair. That meant the owner had the expense of buying a new one, which could cost anywhere from two thousand to five thousand dollars.

All of Jonah's knowledge about buggy accidents made him work even harder to keep Socks under control. Finally, the Kings' house came into view, and Jonah was glad when the horse turned easily up the driveway. No doubt Socks had brought Meredith and Luke here a good many times, so he probably felt comfortable in his surroundings.

After Jonah had Socks secured at the hitching rail, he sprinted for the house. He was about to knock on the door, when it swung open, and a freckle-faced boy, who looked to be around ten or eleven years old, stepped onto the porch. "Can I help ya?" the little fellow asked.

Jonah nodded. "I'm Jonah Miller, and I'm here to see Meredith."

The boy squinted his blue eyes as he stared up at Jonah. "So you're the buggy maker's son, huh?"

"That's right, and I'm also a buggy maker."

The boy nodded. "My *naame* is Stanley."

Jonah held out his hand. "It's nice to meet you, Stanley. I'm guessing you're Meredith's little bruder."

Stanley squared his shoulders and stretched to his full height. "I ain't her *little* brother. Owen's the little one. He's three, but I'm twelve."

Jonah bit back a chuckle. "When your sister and I were teenagers, she mentioned you in one of her letters, but you were her only little bruder back then."

Stanley flicked a blob of white cat hair off his trousers and grinned. "Guess that was true enough."

"So is it okay if I come in?" Jonah asked, hoping he'd won the boy over. "I'd like to see how Meredith's doing."

Stanley shook his head. "She ain't here."

"She ain't? I mean, she's not?"

"Huh-uh. Meredith went back to her own house this mornin' 'cause the little ones were gettin' on her nerves." Stanley snickered. "Oh, and Dad's snorin' was keepin' her awake at night, too."

Jonah smiled. "So I assume if she went home that she must be feeling better?"

Stanley shrugged. "Don't know for sure, but I do know that our sister Laurie went with her, 'cause Mom said she had to."

Before Jonah could comment, Meredith's mother stuck her head through the open doorway. "Wie geht's?" she asked, smiling at Jonah.

"I'm doing fine. I came by to see how Meredith's doing, but Stanley said she went home."

"That's right, and Laurie will be staying with her most of the time. When Laurie's working at the farmers' market, Alma Beechy will be with Meredith." Deep wrinkles formed across Luann's forehead. "I'd be a nervous wreck if Meredith was home by herself right now. She came close to losing the boppli, and might have, too, if you hadn't been there to call for help." Her face relaxed some. "I believe the Lord must have sent you to my daughter's house that day."

"I think you might be right about that." Jonah shuffled his feet a few times. "Do you think Meredith would mind if I stopped over to see her right now? I want to make sure she's doing all right and see if there's anything she might need."

Luann smiled. "That's nice of you, and since you're going that way, would you mind taking something to Meredith for me? I was going to send it with her this morning, but things got hectic around here and I forgot."

"I don't mind at all. What have you got?" Jonah asked.

"A bunch of posies," Stanley spoke up, motioning to the two pots of primroses sitting on one end of the porch. "Meredith likes *blumme*."

"I'd be happy to take the flowers to her," Jonah said. "There's more than enough room in the back of my buggy."

Luann glanced across the yard. "How's Luke's horse doing for you? Has he given you any trouble?"

Jonah wasn't about to admit that Socks had acted up on the way over because he didn't want Meredith to hear about it and feel guilty for selling him the horse.

"Socks and I are still getting to know each other," he said, carefully choosing his words. "And I'm sure after a while we'll get along just fine."

Stanley frowned. "I don't like that gaul. He tried to bite me once when I was hitchin' him to the rail for Luke."

Jonah didn't like the sound of that. If Socks had been unruly even when his master was around, maybe he'd never get him trained. Well, he'd just have to keep trying.

"Stanley, why don't you help Jonah by carrying one of those pots out to his buggy?" Luann said. "Just be sure you stay away from the horse."

"Okay, Mom." The boy bent down, picked up a pot, and tromped off across the yard.

"Is there anything else you'd like me to take Meredith?" Jonah asked as he picked up the second pot of flowers.

Luann nodded. "As a matter of fact, there is. My mamm made some of Meredith's favorite ginger *kichlin* this morning, and I'm sure she'd enjoy having some."

"No problem. I'd be happy to take the cookies to Meredith." *Is it too much to hope that Meredith might offer me a few of those cookies?* Jonah thought as his stomach rumbled.

⌘

"What would you like for lunch today?" Laurie asked Meredith as they sat on the sofa in the living room, drinking hot chocolate while they visited.

Meredith shrugged. "It really doesn't matter. But you don't have to wait on me, because I can fix my own lunch."

"If I don't take good care of you, I'll never hear the end of it," Laurie said. "In case you didn't know, Mom's really worried about you."

"I realize that, but she doesn't need to worry. I'm feeling fine right now." *Except for missing Luke,* she thought. *I don't know if I'll ever recover from that.*

Laurie patted Meredith's arm, the way Mom often did. "That's great, and we want to keep you feeling fine."

Meredith smiled. Laurie reminded her in many ways of their mother. She had the same blond hair and pale blue eyes. She even had Mom's light complexion and oval face. Meredith figured the way Laurie looked right now was probably how Mom must have looked when she was nineteen.

"Sure wish I could get the boppli's room painted," Meredith said, redirecting her thoughts. "There's so much left that needs to be done before the baby comes."

"I know, but with the help of your friends and family, it'll get done."

Meredith sighed. "I hate asking for help all the time, but now I feel like I have no other choice."

Laurie set her cup of hot chocolate on the coffee table, and turned to face Meredith. "You need to let others help. Remember, as Grandma Smucker always says: 'Next to the gift of Jesus Christ, the greatest gifts in life are family and friends.'"

Laurie was right, but that didn't make it any easier to accept help. Meredith was about to suggest that they go to the kitchen to see about fixing their lunch, when she heard the *clip-clop* of horse's hooves coming up the driveway.

"Someone's here," Laurie said, jumping up from her chair. "Maybe it's Mom or Dad."

Meredith watched as her sister went to the door. Several minutes later, Laurie returned to the living room with Jonah at her side. He smiled and held a paper sack out to Meredith. "Your mamm asked me to bring these ginger cookies to you, and there are some primroses on the porch."

"Oh, you saw Mom today?"

He nodded. "I stopped by your folks' house to see how you were doing, and your mamm said you were here."

"That's right, and I'm happy to say that I'm doing much better now and was more than ready to come home."

"I'm glad to hear that, but you need to take it easy and not try to do too much," he warned.

Meredith stiffened. First Mom, then Laurie, and now Jonah? Why did everyone think they needed to tell her what to do?

"Would you like me to plant the flowers for you?" Jonah asked. "Today's my day off, and I have nothing better to do."

"We'd appreciate that," Laurie said before Meredith could respond. "And when you're done, you can join us for lunch, and we'll have the ginger kichlin for dessert." She glanced quickly at Meredith. "Isn't that right, Sister?"

Meredith nodded. What else could she do? With Jonah offering to plant the flowers, she couldn't very well say no to him joining them for lunch.

"That sounds good," Jonah said with a grin. "But don't go to any trouble on my account."

"It'll just be soup and sandwiches, and I'll start fixing our lunch right now." Laurie flashed Jonah a wide smile and hurried from the room.

Meredith didn't know why, but she felt kind of awkward and shy around Jonah. She was relieved when he said he was going to plant the flowers and went out the door.

Rising from the sofa, she headed for the kitchen to see what she could do to help Laurie with lunch.

"What are you doing in here?" Laurie asked, turning from the stove, where she was stirring a kettle of leftover vegetable soup.

"I came to help."

Laurie shook her head. "I can manage just fine. Besides, you're supposed to be resting."

Meredith's fingers dug into the palms of her hands. "I'm not an invalid, Laurie, but if it would make you feel better, I'll sit at the table while I make the sandwiches."

"I guess that would be okay. Sorry if I seem so bossy." Laurie handed Meredith the sandwich fixings, along with some plates and a knife. "I'm just trying to do as Mom asked and take care of things so you can rest."

Meredith took a seat and relaxed against her chair. "I appreciate that, and I promise not to do anything strenuous."

"That's good to hear." Laurie stepped away from the stove and glanced out the window. "Looks like Jonah has gotten one bunch of primroses planted already. He sure is a nice man. Makes me wonder why he's not married."

Meredith shrugged. "I don't know. I guess he hasn't found the right woman yet."

"Jah, maybe so." Laurie remained at the window a few more seconds, then returned to her job at the stove.

I wonder if my sister is interested in Jonah, Meredith thought. *I suppose the two of them might get together someday, but Laurie doesn't really seem like Jonah's type.* Meredith opened the bread wrapper and took out several slices. *But then, I guess that's really none of my business. I just need to concentrate on getting ready for the birth of my baby.*

CHAPTER 5

"This is sure a *gut middaagesse*. Danki for inviting me to stay for the meal," Jonah said after he'd eaten a few spoonfuls of soup.

Laurie smiled at him from across the table. "I'm glad you think the lunch is good. With the weather warming more every day, it won't be long before we'll want something cold to eat."

"That's probably true for most," Jonah agreed, "but I like soup just about any time of the year. It's a hearty meal that sticks with you. Least it does for me. And by the way, don't let this weather fool you. Winter can remind us that it's not letting go just yet. I know the wind isn't slowing up any."

Meredith sat quietly eating as her sister and Jonah continued chatting.

"Do you ever get tired of working on buggies?" Laurie asked, placing a sandwich on her plate, while looking at Jonah with an eager expression.

Jonah shook his head. "I like what I do, and since I've also started making other types of buggies that aren't for the Amish, it's created some new and interesting challenges for me."

Meredith stared at her half-eaten bowl of soup, barely listening to the conversation going on around her. She felt tired all of a sudden and really had no appetite. However, for the baby's sake, she needed to eat regular meals, so she forced herself to finish the soup and eat half a sandwich.

"You're awfully quiet," Jonah said, lightly touching Meredith's arm. "Am I boring you with all this talk about my job?"

Meredith jumped at his unexpected touch. "Uh, no. Guess I just don't have much to say." She quickly reached for a napkin and blotted her lips. "I'm feeling kind of tired, so if you two don't mind, I think I'll go back to the living room and rest awhile."

"Go right ahead," Laurie was quick to say. "Plenty of rest is what you need right now."

Wordlessly, Meredith cleared her dishes and placed them in the sink. She was almost to the kitchen door, when Jonah called, "Meredith, is there anything else you might need me to do?"

She turned, and was about to say no, when Laurie spoke up. "Actually, there is something. Meredith is planning to use one of the spare bedrooms upstairs for the boppli's room, and it needs to be painted."

Meredith's face heated as her lips tightened. *How could Laurie embarrass me like this?* She looked at Jonah and forced a smile. "I'm sorry my sister brought that up. I certainly don't expect you to do any painting. My daed will get it done whenever he finds the time. And if he can't do it, then. . ."

Jonah held up his hand. "I don't mind painting. In fact, I'd be happy to do it, and I have the time right now."

"That'd be great." Laurie smiled at Jonah. "Why don't we go upstairs, and I'll show you which room? The paint's sitting out, and the ladder's up there already, so everything's all set to go."

Jonah looked at Meredith, as though seeking her approval.

"It's fine with me, if you're sure," she said quietly. It was hard enough to accept help from her family and close friends, and it made her feel funny to have Jonah, whom she really didn't know that well anymore, here at the house doing chores for her—chores she'd once planned to do herself.

Jonah gave her a lopsided grin. "I'm definitely ready to begin."

"Before I forget," Meredith added, "danki for planting those flowers for me."

"You're welcome. The soil was good and wet from the rain we had earlier, so they were easy to put in the ground."

Meredith stood awkwardly, looking at the floor, unsure of what else to say. She was glad when Laurie turned to Jonah and said, "Okay then. I'll lead the way." She paused a moment and smiled at Meredith. "I'll do the dishes as soon as I show Jonah the room."

Meredith nodded and started for the living room. She was certain her sister was interested in Jonah. The whole time they'd been eating lunch, Laurie could hardly take her eyes off him, and the slight blush on Laurie's cheeks made it apparent that she felt attracted to him. Meredith wondered if Jonah noticed Laurie's interest. Could he be attracted to her, too? If so, Mom would be pleased, because she was always saying she wished Laurie had more of a social life.

But it's none of my business, Meredith reminded herself as she wandered over to the living-room window and looked out. Luke's horse was moving about in the corral. A lump formed in her throat. Seeing Socks there made her feel guilty for selling him, and worse than that, it caused her to think about Luke. If he hadn't been killed, he would have been painting their baby's room, not Jonah. If Luke were still alive, she wouldn't need her sister's help, either. If Luke were here, they'd be making plans for when the baby came and taking childbirth classes together at the midwife's clinic.

She closed her eyes and tried to imagine that Luke was right there. She could almost see him helping her paint the baby's room, going to childbirth classes with her, and holding their baby. It was so clear and real, it was nearly a shock when Laurie came down the stairs and announced that Jonah needed some rags.

Meredith quickly wiped away the tears that had crept from her eyes. "You'll find a box of *lumpe* in the utility room."

When Laurie left the room, Meredith moved away from the window and curled up on the sofa. *No amount of wishing will bring Luke back,* she told herself, squeezing her eyes tightly shut. *Dear Lord, will it ever stop hurting so much?*

⌘

When Jonah left Meredith's house later that day, he was tired, sweaty, and speckled with beige paint. For once, the persistent breezes actually felt good after painting all afternoon in the stuffy room. Jonah hadn't wanted to make the upstairs too chilly for Meredith, so he'd opened the window in the room he'd painted, just a little, for ventilation. He would never have admitted it to Meredith, but painting walls was not really his thing. He was glad he'd been able to help her, though. She had seemed a bit hesitant at first, but when she'd seen the finished room she'd smiled and said he had done a good job and that she appreciated all his hard work. Jonah planned to check on Meredith as often as he could, and if there were other things that needed to be done, he'd gladly do them. He just hoped she'd be willing to accept his help.

Jonah gripped the reins a bit tighter as Socks shook his head and started to trot. "Whoa there, steady, boy. What's your rush, anyways?"

The horse had been in no hurry when they'd first left Meredith's place.

In fact, Socks had balked like a stubborn mule when Jonah tried backing him away from the hitching rail. He figured the horse was familiar with his surroundings and didn't want to leave. Then, too, maybe Socks thought Luke was coming back. Either way, it had taken some coaxing to get the horse down the driveway and onto the main road, and now the unpredictable animal wanted to run at lightning speed. Of course, it hadn't helped when Meredith's dog started barking and running back and forth in his kennel.

Jonah felt the relentless wind rushing against his still-perspiring skin. A chill went through him, and he pulled his jacket tighter around his neck. March was the month when everyone celebrated spring's arrival, but it could be a real teaser. Jonah felt good whenever he could get outside and use all that pent-up energy he'd been storing through the winter to get something done. Then days later, it could be just the opposite, reminding him that winter was still hanging on and he'd have to wait a bit for more of those spring-fever days. It was always nice when the winds were behind them and April came rushing in.

One thing's for sure, Jonah thought. *This horse of mine will keep me on my toes. I'll have to remember not to let my guard down no matter where I am or what the weather is like.*

Jonah's thoughts went to Meredith again. He could tell she was struggling with depression over losing Luke. It was understandable, though. Who wouldn't be despondent after they'd lost a loved one—especially when they'd thought they had their whole future together? Jonah knew from seeing all that his sister Jean had gone through that grieving for a loved one was an ongoing process that required continued help and support. But Jean had made it through the rough times after losing Abe, so he felt sure that Meredith would, too. She just needed time to heal, and support from friends and family would surely help.

By the time Jonah turned his horse and buggy up the lane leading to his folks' house, he was exhausted. He'd had to fight for control of Socks almost the whole way. He'd just gotten Socks unhitched from the buggy when Herbie came running around the side of the house, barking and wagging his tail.

"Stay back!" Jonah shouted, but it was too late. The dog was already nipping at the horse's feet.

When Jonah loosened his grip slightly on the lead rope, Socks jerked free and took off after the dog.

Woof! Woof! Herbie raced around the yard, with Socks kicking his feet in the air, hot on the dog's tail. The next thing Jonah knew, Herbie took a flying leap and landed in a pile of manure on the side of the barn.

Jonah groaned. "Phew! What a *schtinke!*"

Mom rushed out of the house. "What's going on out here? What is all the commotion about?" Then she spotted Herbie yelping and rolling around in the grass. "Oh no," she moaned, pointing to the dog. "How in the world did that happen?"

Jonah explained what had transpired and ended with an apology. "Guess I should have kept a better hold on Socks. Just never expected Herbie to start nipping at him like that."

Mom's brows furrowed. "That gaul's been nothing but trouble since you bought him from Meredith. I know she needed the money and all, but you should have thought twice before bringing that unpredictable animal home."

"It wasn't the horse's fault that Herbie started nipping at his feet."

"That may be so," Mom replied, "but it is his fault that he chased after the dog, and now Herbie smells so bad he's going to need a bath."

"I'll do it," Jonah said, knowing it was probably the best way to get back in Mom's good graces. "Just give me a minute to get Socks put away in his stall, and then I'll fill one of the galvanized tubs for Herbie's bath."

"Just be sure you add some hot water to the tub. The weather's not warm enough to give the poor dog a cold-water bath." She studied Jonah a few seconds. "Looks like you could use a bath yourself. What have you been up to today?"

"I ran a few errands, and then I stopped by the Kings' place to see Meredith. But when I got there, I learned that she'd gone home and one of her sisters would be staying with her. So I went to Meredith's house to see how she was doing." Jonah motioned to the paint splatters on his arms. "Ended up planting some flowers and painting a room, but all in all, it was a pretty fair day." He looked at Herbie, still wallowing around the yard, and grimaced. "At least it was, until I came home."

Philadelphia

Susan's shift was just about done for the day, but before she left the floor, she wanted to check on her John Doe patient one last time. A few days ago, he'd taken a turn for the worse and had begun having seizures. The doctor had prescribed medication for the convulsions, and she hoped and prayed it was doing the job. This poor man had been through enough and deserved a chance to be well again.

"I'm going home now, Eddie, but I'll see you tomorrow," Susan said as she entered the patient's room and checked his vitals, ventilator, and feeding tube one last time. "Nurse Pamela will be here with you tonight, so you'll be in good hands."

No response. Not even the flutter of an eyelid.

Sometimes Susan felt foolish talking to her patient when he was in a coma, but there was a chance he could hear her, even if he wasn't able to respond. She couldn't imagine what it would be like to be trapped within one's own body. But then again, maybe the mind went someplace else— somewhere safe until the person eventually woke up.

Susan stopped at the foot of his bed. "Heavenly Father," she prayed out loud, "whoever this young man is, You must have a purpose for keeping him here on earth, so please touch his body as only You can."

CHAPTER 6

Bird-in-Hand

By the first of April, Meredith felt much better physically, and with Grandma Smucker helping her sometimes, she'd begun making head coverings to sell. She had been warned by the doctor, as well as her midwife, not to do anything strenuous and to let others help with the things she couldn't or shouldn't be doing. Meredith spent much of her time sewing on the coverings, and even though she sat to do it, she felt good to be actively doing something again. Sewing was relaxing, and it gave her plenty of time to plan and think about her new role as a mother.

Meredith also enjoyed going to the childbirth classes at the midwife's clinic a few miles up the road. Laurie went with her because she had agreed to be Meredith's coach. During the sessions, they learned the Bradley Method. Meredith was all in favor of using a more relaxed approach to childbirth, which this method emphasized. By practicing deep breathing and having Laurie's support as labor coach, Meredith would be able to deliver her baby without using drugs or going through surgery, unless she experienced a problem during labor. She also appreciated the emphasis on having a healthy baby and what she could do to eat right and stay in shape.

Meredith was glad she was no longer housebound and looked forward to going to the farmers' market with Alma in a week. Today was Friday, and Alma was baking bread, while Meredith sat at her Grandma King's old treadle sewing machine, making another head covering. Some women in their community used converted machines, run by a battery, but she preferred the old-fashioned kind. There was a sense of satisfaction that came from pumping her feet up and down to get the needle moving. Sitting at this older machine made Meredith think of all the things Grandma had made for her family over the years. Grandma and Grandpa King lived in a rural area of Kentucky, with Dad's brother Peter and his family, so Meredith didn't see them that often. Before they'd moved there four years ago, Grandma had given Meredith her old sewing machine, saying her fingers were stiff from arthritis, and she couldn't sew anymore.

Meredith glanced toward the kitchen door, listening to Alma hum while kneading her bread dough. Alma didn't have any children or grandchildren to pass things down to, but she'd been generous in sharing some personal items with those in their community. Just this morning, when Alma came over a few minutes before Laurie left for the market, she'd brought Meredith an old wooden cradle that had been hers when she was a baby. Meredith appreciated the gift but felt bad that Alma hadn't been able to use the heirloom for her own babies. If Luke were still here, their firstborn's cradle would have been made by him.

But she couldn't let her what-could-have-been thinking take over her life, and when thoughts like that entered her mind, she'd just have to let them go. She had to be positive. This cradle would be special, too, because it was from Alma. She could feel Alma's love and encouragement, and appreciated all that the woman did to help out.

Meredith's gaze went to the cradle sitting in one corner of the living room. Tears sprang to her eyes. In just three short months her own baby would be lying in that cradle, and she could hardly wait. She hadn't told anyone, but she secretly hoped it would be a boy with his father's blond hair and beautiful turquoise eyes. Of course, if she had a little girl with strawberry-blond hair like hers, she would love her just as much. The fact that the child would be a part of Luke brought Meredith some measure of comfort.

"Are you ready to stop for lunch?" Alma asked when she ambled into the living room sometime later. "I've heated the leftover stew from last night, and we can have some fresh bread to go with it."

"That sounds *wunderbaar*." Meredith stopped sewing and patted her protruding stomach. "I didn't even realize I was *hungerich* until you mentioned food. That bread sure smells good. Now my belly won't stop growling."

Alma grinned and pushed a wisp of gray hair back under her covering. "I'll see you in the kitchen then, because just smelling the bread baking, along with that savory stew on the stove, has made my stomach rumble, too."

Meredith smiled as Alma headed back to the kitchen. She was glad Alma had remembered to turn her hearing aids on today so they could communicate easily. More times than not, Meredith ended up with a strained voice from talking loud enough for Alma to hear. But she never said anything about it, for Alma was such a sweet, caring person.

The slightly plump, rosy-cheeked woman was in her early seventies, and her cooking and baking skills made Meredith feel her own paled in comparison. But it wasn't Alma's cooking Meredith admired the most; it was her sweet, gentle spirit and knowledge of the scriptures. Some folks—both Amish and English—didn't read their Bibles often enough, and therefore didn't always know when God was speaking to them. Alma, on the other hand, read her Bible faithfully and liked to talk about some of the verses she'd memorized. This morning when she'd first arrived, she'd quoted Matthew 5:4 to Meredith and talked about how God blessed and comforted those who mourn, and how that comfort often comes from family and friends who surround the grieving one with their love and support.

I needed that reminder today, Meredith thought as she pushed her chair away from the sewing machine and stood. Even though at first she hadn't wanted Laurie or Alma to stay with her, now she was glad to have their help, as well as their company. She especially appreciated listening to Alma talk about when she was a girl and how the Lord had given her a heart for other people's children when she'd found out she couldn't have any of her own. Alma was a remarkable woman, who had not only learned to accept the fact that she was barren, but had also relied heavily on the Lord, as well as her friends, after her husband's sudden death.

Meredith started toward the kitchen, but stopped for a minute and closed her eyes. *ThankYou, heavenly Father, for bringing Alma into my home, and for the knowledge that You know my pain and will see me through this time of grief.*

Philadelphia

"I can't wait to see the look on their faces when we surprise Grandma and Grandpa tonight," Anne told Susan as they ate lunch. It was one of those rare times when they had the same schedule and could actually meet in the hospital cafeteria at noon.

Susan smiled as she sprinkled a little salt on her hard-boiled egg. "It's not often we get to do anything special for them, so I hope everything works out as we've planned."

"I'm sure it will," Anne said in a confident tone, scraping the container of her tuna salad. "I mean, what could go wrong?"

"Nothing, I hope." Tonight was their grandparents' fifty-fourth wedding anniversary, and Susan and Anne had planned a surprise dinner in their honor at Keya Graves, a lovely seafood and steakhouse in Darby. They'd invited Grandma and Grandpa's closest friends, and told their grandparents to meet them there at seven o'clock this evening. Grandma and Grandpa had no idea that family and friends would arrive half an hour early and be waiting to surprise them when the hostess ushered them into the restaurant's banquet room.

"I'm thrilled that everyone we invited is coming," Anne added. "Usually with an event like this, a few people can't make it."

"You're right, and it's an indication of how well Grandma and Grandpa are liked," Susan added. "Everything should be perfect, right down to the old-fashioned anniversary cake we ordered."

"Any change with your Eddie fellow?" Anne asked.

"He's stopped having seizures, so that's one positive thing."

Anne smiled and took a bite of her apple. "It sure is. Do you think he'll be moved to rehab soon?"

"I don't know. Guess it all depends on whether he continues to progress."

Deep lines formed across Anne's forehead as she slowly shook her head. "I wonder if we'll ever know who's responsible for that young man's injuries."

Susan shrugged. "I'm still hoping and praying, but only the Lord knows what lies ahead for poor Eddie."

❧

Bird-in-Hand

"I know Mom's not back from her dental appointment yet, but when she gets here, would you let her know that I might be a little late for supper?" Jonah asked his dad as they finished up their work in the buggy shop.

Dad's bushy eyebrows furrowed. "Are ya goin' someplace?"

"Thought I'd hitch up my horse and take a ride over to Meredith's house. I haven't seen her for a few days, and I'd like to know how she's doing and see if she needs my help with anything else."

Dad tapped his foot as he stared at Jonah. "You've been goin' over there a lot lately. Aren't ya worried about what others will say?"

Jonah tipped his head. "What is it you think they might say?"

Dad cleared his throat real loud. "Do I need to remind you that Meredith's a young widow, and she's expecting a boppli besides?"

A rush of heat spread across Jonah's face. "Exactly what are you saying, Dad?" he asked.

"I just feel you oughta be concerned about what others may think. Some folks could get the idea that you have it in mind to make Meredith your wife."

Oh great, Jonah thought. *Now I'm in for one of Dad's long lectures. I'd better put an end to this before it gets started.*

"Look, Dad," Jonah said, talking slowly and deliberately, "I'm helping Meredith because she's a friend, and after seeing what Jean went through when she lost Abe, I want to do whatever I can to help Meredith during this difficult time. That's all there is to it, and I don't care what anyone thinks." Before Dad could say anything more, Jonah slapped his straw hat on his head and rushed out the door.

A short time later, after he'd washed up and changed his clothes, Jonah headed down the road with his horse and buggy. He didn't know if it was because Socks was getting used to him, or just pure luck, but for the first time since he'd acquired the horse, Socks was actually behaving himself.

Jonah looked out at the freshly planted fields and figured as long as they didn't get any flooding, the corn and other crops would do well with the spring rain they'd been having. The last couple of days had been rainy and raw, but the sun had come out around noon today, causing everything to smell clean and fresh. The harsh winds had finally died down, making room for milder days. Seeing the grass green up and the trees and flowers bloom, gave Jonah a sense of joy and anticipation for the future. He hoped Meredith sensed that, too, for she certainly needed the hope of spring—something positive to look forward to.

As Jonah approached Meredith's house, Socks picked up speed, and when he turned the horse up the driveway, Socks ran all the way to the barn.

Jonah chuckled. "This is home to you, isn't it, boy?"

Socks whinnied as if in response.

Woof! Woof! Fritz barked out a greeting from his kennel. As soon as Jonah had the horse secured to the hitching rail, he strode across the yard to greet the dog.

"You're smart, just like Herbie, aren't ya, boy?" Jonah reached his hand through the wire fencing and stroked Fritz's silky head.

Plink! Plink! A few drops of water landed on his hand. He looked up and noticed that the canvas tarp, held up by four poles over part of Fritz's dog run, was full of rainwater.

"All that water needs to come off," Jonah said, giving Fritz another pat. "Otherwise the tarp might break, and you'll end up with a bath you probably don't want."

Fritz looked up at Jonah and whined. Did the animal understand what he'd said?

Jonah unlatched the gate and let Fritz out. "Go on now, boy! Go up to the house."

Fritz hesitated a minute, then tore across the yard and leaped onto the porch.

Jonah looked around for something he could use to drain the water from the tarp. He spotted a broken tree limb lying just outside the kennel, so he picked it up. Standing directly under the tarp, he gave it a good push. A quick burst of water rolled off one end, but most of it remained in the middle.

Jonah pushed against the tarp once more, this time jiggling the limb around a bit.

R-r-i-i-p! W-o-o-sh! The canvas tore down the middle, and a blast of chilling water poured out on Jonah's head, drenching his shirt and trousers, and finding its way into his boots.

"Oh great," Jonah moaned. "Now what have I done?"

CHAPTER 7

Meredith set her sewing aside and glanced at the clock on the wall above the fireplace. It was a quarter after six, and soon it would be time to eat supper. She was surprised Laurie wasn't back from the farmers' market yet. The market closed at five thirty, and Laurie's driver usually had her home by six.

Try not to worry, she told herself. *They probably got caught up in traffic, which is normal for a Friday evening.*

Meredith was about to head for the kitchen to see if Alma needed any help, when a knock sounded on the door. She hadn't heard a vehicle or horse and buggy come up the driveway, but then she'd been engrossed in her work.

Meredith opened the front door. Jonah stood there, soaking wet. Fritz sat beside him, perfectly dry. "*Ach,* Jonah, what happened?"

"I—I tried to get the water off the tarp co–covering Fritz's dog house," Jonah explained through chattering teeth. "And I–I'm afraid in my eagerness to do a good job, I ended up t–tearing a hole in the canvas, so all the w–water spilled out on me." Jonah leaned away from Meredith and shook water from his hair. "It's not that chilly outside today, but the water was c–cold as ice."

Meredith stifled a giggle. Poor Jonah looked so miserable, but he also looked funny with his thick, curly hair sticking out in all directions and water dripping down his face. "I'm so sorry that happened," she said. "You'd better come inside and get warm." Meredith hesitated a moment, then added, "My husband was about the same size as you, so you can borrow some of his clothes."

Jonah gave her a sheepish grin. "I appreciate that. If I t–tried to go home like this, I'd not only get the inside of my b–buggy all wet, but I'd probably lose my grip on the reins. My hands are almost numb."

When Meredith opened the door wider, Jonah stepped in and stood on the small braided entrance rug. "It's okay, pup," she said looking down at

Fritz. "You can come in, too." She smiled as the dog went over and flopped down in his usual spot near her rocking chair. "If you'll wait right here, I'll go upstairs and get you some clothes," she said to Jonah. "And it looks like you'll need a towel as well."

Jonah, looking more than a little grateful as well as a bit embarrassed, nodded. While he waited in the entryway, Meredith went upstairs to get the clothes. She hadn't given away any of Luke's things, because she couldn't part with them, even though they'd go to good use if she gave them to the local thrift shop. Maybe someday she'd be ready to give his things up, but not yet. She wanted to save a few articles of clothing, anyway, to show their baby when he was old enough to be told about his father.

Meredith opened the dresser and took out a pair of Luke's black trousers and the pale blue shirt she had made for his last birthday. Just holding them made her tear up.

Out of impulse, she bent her head into the material of his shirt and inhaled deeply. It was freshly laundered, but she could still smell the fragrance of Luke. Or maybe it was just the idea of touching something Luke had worn that made her feel so gloomy all of a sudden.

Struggling to keep her emotions in check, Meredith went downstairs and handed the clothes to Jonah. "You can change in there," she said, pointing to the bathroom down the hall. "You'll find some towels in the closet behind the door."

Jonah hesitated a minute, looking at Meredith with obvious compassion. Did he know how hard it was for her to let him wear Luke's clothes?

"Go ahead. I'll wait for you in the living room," she said.

"Danki." Jonah went quietly down the hall.

Meredith returned to the living room, and as she seated herself in the rocking chair and reached down to pet Fritz's head, the baby kicked. The joy of feeling that movement drove her tears away, and she smiled, placing both hands against her stomach. It was so amazing, feeling life within her belly. Sometimes it felt light, like a butterfly fluttering around. Other times, such as now, she felt a good solid kick or two. If the baby turned out to be a boy, she might name him after his father. If it was a girl, she'd have to come up with a name she liked.

When Jonah returned to the living room a short time later, tears sprang to Meredith's eyes once again. Seeing him dressed in Luke's shirt and trousers was almost her undoing.

"I tossed my wet clothes out on the porch, and I'll bring your husband's clothes back tomorrow after work," Jonah said, shifting from one foot to the other. Did he feel as uneasy as she did right now?

"I'll get you a plastic sack." Meredith stood, but before she could take a step, Alma entered the room.

"Oh, it's you, Jonah. Thought I heard voices out here. Did you come to join us for supper?" Alma asked.

He shook his head. "Just dropped by to see how Meredith was doing and ask if she needed me to do anything."

Alma's gaze went to Meredith. "So, do you have anything for this nice young man to do?"

Meredith, feeling more flustered by the minute, could only shake her head. It was strange how she felt when Jonah was around. Years ago, when they'd become friends in Florida, she was as comfortable with him as with any of her other friends. But now, for some reason, she felt somewhat uneasy around Jonah, and even a little guilty, wondering how others would feel about their friendship given that she was a widow.

"Well, since you're here, Jonah, and I have supper ready, I think you ought to join us," Alma practically insisted. "There's plenty to eat, and one more at the table won't make any difference."

Before Jonah could respond, the back door opened, and Laurie joined them.

"Hello, Jonah," she said, her lips curving into a wide smile. "I knew that was your horse and buggy out there because I recognized Socks. It's nice to see you again."

He nodded in response. "Same here."

There it is again, Meredith thought, walking into the kitchen to get Jonah a bag for his wet clothes. *That special look on Laurie's face whenever she sees Jonah. I wonder if I should talk to her about it—warn her that Jonah might already have a girlfriend in Ohio, or that she's being too forward. Or maybe it's best if I don't say anything. She might not appreciate it, and what if I'm wrong about things, and it's just my imagination?*

"Guess I'd better get going," Jonah said when Meredith came back, handing him the plastic sack.

He was almost out the door when Laurie hollered, "Aren't you gonna join us for supper?" She sniffed the air. "From that delicious aroma, I'm sure Alma's made something special."

"I appreciate the invite, but my mamm's probably holding supper for me right now, so I'd better go." Jonah gave a quick smile and hurried out the door.

Meredith turned to Laurie. "How come you're so late?"

Laurie's face flamed. "What's the matter, Meredith, don't you trust me?"

"Of course I do," Meredith replied. "Why would you even ask such a question?"

"Well, you looked upset when you asked why I was late, and I thought maybe. . ."

Meredith held up her hand. "I was only concerned because you're not usually late. And since this is Friday night, when traffic is usually worse, I couldn't help but worry."

"Sorry about that, but I stayed awhile to help one of the other vendors put some things away in his booth. And you're right—there was a lot of traffic."

"That's okay, you're here now, so let's eat," Alma said, motioning to the kitchen.

Meredith didn't know why, but she had a funny feeling her sister wasn't being completely honest. Of course, she saw no reason for Laurie to lie, so she was probably imagining that, as well.

⬥

Ronks

Sitting around the kitchen table with her family that evening, Luann smiled at her youngest son, Owen, as he chomped away on a juicy drumstick. Grandma Smucker had made fried chicken for supper, and everyone seemed to be enjoying it.

"This chicken is *appenditlich*, Grandma," eight-year-old Arlene said, licking her fingers.

Luann's mother smiled. "I'm glad you think it's delicious."

Luann's sixteen-year-old daughter, Kendra, wrinkled her nose and glared at Arlene. "It's not polite to lick your fingers, Sister."

"Maybe not," Luann's husband, Philip, put in, "but this chicken is finger-lickin' good." He swiped his tongue over his fingers and grinned at Luann's mother, who gave him a wide smile in return.

"Not to change the subject or anything," Luann said, "but Meredith's birthday is coming up in two weeks, so I think it would be nice if we did something special to celebrate."

"That's a good idea." Nina, who was fourteen, nodded her head. "That will let Meredith know how much we love her."

"I don't think Meredith will be up to a big party," Grandma said. "Maybe a nice, small family gathering is all that she needs."

"Just a little celebration among us," Luann agreed. "I can make her favorite cake and decorate it the way I used to when she was little. I'll even make it a three-tiered cake and use the pretty glass cake dish you used for my birthday when I was growing up," she added, looking at her mother.

"That all sounds good to me—especially the cake," Philip said with a wink.

"Let's make it a surprise, though, because if we tell Meredith we want to have a get-together for her birthday, she'll probably say not to bother or that she doesn't feel like celebrating this year," Luann said. "We'll tell Laurie and Alma about it, of course. Maybe Alma can take Meredith someplace that afternoon, and while they're gone, I'll go over to Meredith's house and get things ready. I'll make sure to tell Alma not to bring Meredith home until six o'clock. By then, we'll all be there, ready to surprise Meredith when they get back."

"What about our horses and buggies?" Stanley asked as he pulled the fried coating from his piece of chicken and ate that first. "Won't Meredith see 'em out in the yard and know we're there?"

"We can put the horses in the barn and hide the buggies around back," Philip responded.

Stanley grinned. "That's a good idea, Dad."

"I think so, too, and I'm gonna make Meredith a pretty birthday card with birds on it," Arlene grinned. "Meredith likes feeding the birds in her yard."

"Should we invite Luke's folks, as well as Meredith's friend Dorine and

her family, too?" Luann asked Philip.

He nodded. "I think they'd feel left out if we didn't."

"All right then, I'll start working out the details tomorrow morning." Luann looked at her mother. "Would you like to help me plan things, Mom?"

A big smile formed on the elderly woman's face. "Of course I would."

❦

Darby

"This is really a nice place," Susan said as she and Anne entered the restaurant. Several of Grandma and Grandpa's closest friends had already arrived, and they'd been taken to the banquet room, where tables had been set up with a few anniversary decorations. The cake had been safely delivered; the guests were all there; all they needed now was Grandma and Grandpa.

While everyone visited, Susan kept checking her watch. Forty minutes later, when they still hadn't arrived, Susan turned to Anne and said, "Grandma and Grandpa should have been here by now. Think I'd better give them a call."

"That's a good idea," Anne agreed. "Maybe we shouldn't order our meals until they get here."

Susan pulled out her cell phone and called Grandma's cell number. All she got was her voice mail. She left a message, then dialed the home number, but only got the answering machine there. The later it got, the more she worried. *Now where could they be? The weather's not bad or anything. It just doesn't make sense.*

"Do you think they forgot?" Susan asked Anne.

Anne shrugged. "They could have, I guess. Either that or they got lost, which would make no sense since the restaurant isn't all that far from their home." She motioned to one of the tables where several elderly couples sat. "It's getting late, and I'm sure everyone's hungry, so I think we should go ahead and let these good people order their meals. If Grandpa and Grandma haven't arrived by the time everyone's done eating, we'll head for home and hope that they're there."

"Okay," Susan agreed. "I pray that Grandma and Grandpa are all right.

⟨∞⟩

Upper Darby, Pennsylvania

"I don't see any sign of Susan or Anne," Norma Bailey said to her husband, Henry, when they entered the Italian restaurant where they were supposed to meet their granddaughters.

"They probably got waylaid at the hospital," Henry said. "You know how that can be when things get busy."

Norma nodded as she took her seat at the table their hostess had shown them. "I think I'll give the girls a call and let them know we're here." She reached into her purse for her cell phone. "Oh, oh."

"What's wrong?"

"No cell phone. I must have left it at home."

Henry frowned. "Never did have much use for those little gadgets. They're so small, no wonder you forgot it. Probably wouldn't have seen it if it'd been right under your nose."

She laughed and elbowed his arm. "Are you saying my eyesight is failing?"

"No, I'm saying most of those cell phones are way too small." He glanced at his watch. "Do you think maybe the reason the girls aren't here is because we have the wrong night?"

"I suppose that's possible, but I'm almost certain they said they'd meet us here tonight." Norma glanced across the room. "Say, isn't that Mary and Ben Hagen, the new couple from church?"

Henry's gaze followed hers. "I believe it is."

"Maybe we should ask them to join us."

His eyebrows furrowed. "What about Susan and Anne?"

"What about them?"

"Won't they be upset when they get here and see that we've invited someone to join our little party?"

Norma shook her head. "Our granddaughters are both very social. I'm sure they won't mind a few extra people at our table. Besides, we should make the Hagens feel welcome, so why don't you go over there and invite them to join us?"

Henry's eyebrows furrowed. "Why me? It was your idea, Norma."

She clicked her tongue. "All right then, I'll invite them."

A few minutes later, Norma returned with Mary and Ben. They all ordered their meals and got busy talking. When the couple mentioned that their twenty-seven-year-old grandson, Brian, who was single, would be visiting during the summer, Norma perked right up, saying they'd have to make sure that he met Susan, who was close to his age.

When their meal was over, the Baileys decided to go home. Susan and Anne were obviously not coming.

When they entered their house sometime later, Norma was surprised to discover their granddaughters sitting in the kitchen with an anniversary cake.

"Where have you been?" Susan asked, jumping up from the table. "We've been crazy with worry about you."

"That's right," Anne agreed. "How come you didn't meet us at the restaurant?"

Henry's eyebrows pulled together. "What do you mean? We were there. Where were you two girls?"

"We were there with some of your good friends waiting for you." Susan tipped her head and looked at Henry with a peculiar expression. "What restaurant did you and Grandma go to?"

"Pica's Italian Restaurant in Upper Darby. Isn't that where we were supposed to meet?"

"No, it was Keya Graves, the seafood and steakhouse here in Darby." Susan looked at Anne, and they both burst out laughing. When they finally quit, Susan explained that she'd tried to call but had only gotten voice mail and that they'd ended up eating at the restaurant with Grandma and Grandpa's friends and had brought the cake home.

Norma chuckled and then told the girls how they'd met Mary and Ben and eaten supper with them.

Henry pointed to the cake. "Well, we may not have celebrated our anniversary dinner with you two, but we can sure eat this tasty-looking cake right now."

"Good idea." Susan jumped up and got out the plates, forks, and napkins, then cut the cake.

"This tastes just like the buttermilk cake we had on our wedding day." Norma smiled at the girls after she'd taken her first bite.

"It is," Anne said. "We found a bakery that makes vintage cakes, and couldn't believe it when we described your wedding cake and were told that they could make one just like it."

As they ate, they visited and laughed some more about the crazy evening and how it had turned out. Although not together, at least they'd all had a good meal.

"It's good to see you laughing," Norma said, patting Susan's arm. "You've been much too serious lately—probably due to all the stresses at work and worrying about your John Doe patient."

Susan smiled as she started clearing the dishes. "You're right, and this has been a fun evening, even if you didn't get to celebrate your anniversary with all your closest friends."

"We celebrated with our family," Norma said, "and that's what's important. But I'm sure we're going to be in for a lot of ribbing when we see some of those friends at church on Sunday."

"Especially when they find out we went to the wrong restaurant." Henry released a noisy yawn and stood. "Guess I'd better head for bed."

"Me, too," Norma agreed, rising to her feet. "It's been a long day and, I might add, an exciting evening."

"Before you leave the kitchen, there's something I wanted to say," Anne spoke up as she got the sponge to wipe a few crumbs off the table.

"What's that?" Henry asked, turning around.

"I wanted to remind you that Susan and I will be going to Lancaster County on Saturday, and you're more than welcome to join us."

"That's nice of you," Norma said, "but your grandpa and I already have plans."

He looked at her and quirked an eyebrow. "We do?"

She nodded. "We're getting together with Mary and Ben, remember?" She placed her hand on Susan's shoulder. "You two should go and have fun. If your grandpa and I went along, we'd only slow you down."

"I don't think so, Grandma," Susan said, giving Norma a hug. "But if you've made other plans, we understand."

"Well, good night then." Norma was glad Henry hadn't mentioned anything about Mary and Ben's grandson, because that would probably put Susan on the defensive. Norma had tried playing matchmaker with both

Susan and Anne a few times, and it hadn't been well received.

Maybe I won't have to play matchmaker, she told herself. *I'll just keep praying that God will bring the right men into my granddaughters' lives. After all, He knows better than I do who Susan and Anne both need, and if it's meant to happen, it will be in His time.*

CHAPTER 8

Bird-in-Hand

"This day is turning out to be so much fun," Anne said to Susan as they pulled into the parking lot at the farmers' market on Saturday afternoon.

"Oh, I know," Susan agreed. "The homemade rootbeer and soft pretzel we had at that roadside stand awhile ago were sure good. I'm glad we bought a gallon of rootbeer to take home so Grandma and Grandpa can enjoy it, too."

"Yes, and it's a good thing you thought to bring the cooler along." Anne parked the car and turned off the ignition. "Maybe we'll find some other tasty morsels inside the market."

Susan chuckled. "If we eat anything else, we'll probably be too full for supper."

"I don't care if I am," Anne said. "I've waited a long time for this trip, and I'm going to enjoy every minute of it—including the food. By the way, Susan, did I mention how much I like that cute pink blouse you're wearing today?"

"Glad you like it. On a whim, I stopped at the clothing store near the hospital the other day and found this on the bargain table." Susan held the market door open. "Now let's go see what we can find to eat!"

When they entered the building, Susan inhaled deeply, enjoying the delicious aromas coming from the various food vendors. At a booth near the door stood a man making fried corn fritters. The smell of coffee brewing was in the air, as well as the sweet aroma of baked goods coming from the stand across the aisle. From where she stood, Susan could see they had whoopie pies, apple fritters, homemade bread, cookies, and an assortment of delicious-looking pies. It would be hard to get past that booth without taking something home for dessert.

Susan glanced in one direction and then another, unable to take everything in. All the seats were filled in the eating area, and she noticed several people enjoying sandwiches and hot dogs.

"Let's start over here," Anne suggested, pointing to her right.

As they walked up and down the aisles, they stopped to sample some pickled vegetables, then moved on to taste a few homemade pretzels and chips with several dipping sauces.

"Look at this," Susan exclaimed as they approached a stand with unique wooden art. "Imagine taking an old shutter and turning it into something that beautiful."

"The artist must be very talented." Anne ran her hand over the smooth piece of shutter that had a deer scene carved into the wood. "I wonder if Grandpa would like something like this to hang on the living-room wall."

"I think he might. We'll get it for him before we leave," Susan said. "It'll make a nice belated anniversary gift to surprise him with."

"I'm thirsty now," Anne said as they continued browsing. She pointed to a vendor selling freshly squeezed lemonade. "Let's get something to drink."

Susan followed Anne over to the stand, and as they stood drinking their lemonade, she noticed a young, blond-haired Amish woman across the aisle selling faceless Amish dolls. "I think I'll go over there and see how much those dolls cost," she told Anne.

"Seriously? Are you thinking of buying one?"

Susan nodded. "I've always been fascinated with the Amish culture, and a doll like that would look cute on my bed."

"I'm fascinated, too, but I think I may buy a quilted wall hanging or table runner to give Grandma," Anne said. "We might find something else for Grandpa before we're done, as well."

Susan smiled. "Since the party we planned for them didn't work out, the least we can do is get each of them something nice."

"I think so, too," Anne agreed.

"I wonder if Grandpa would like one of those straw hats they're selling over there?" Susan pointed in the direction of the hats. "He could wear it when he's working in the yard, and it'll keep the sun off his head."

"That's a good idea. Let's get that for Grandpa, too," Anne said with a nod.

When they approached the stand where the Amish dolls were being sold, the young woman looked up at them and smiled. "Can I help you with something?"

"Yes, I'd like to know the price of your faceless dolls," Susan said.

"The smaller ones are thirty dollars, and the larger dolls are forty dollars."

"I think I'd like one of the larger dolls." Susan looked at Anne. "Should I get one with blond, brown, or auburn hair?"

Anne touched Susan's straight bob. "Well, since you're a brunette, why don't you get a doll with brown hair?"

Susan pursed her lips as she studied the dolls on display. "Come to think of it, I may get a boy doll and a girl doll—both with blond hair like Eddie's."

A crease formed across Anne's nose as she frowned. "This is our day off, and you're not supposed to be thinking about your patients."

"I know, but seeing the color of these dolls' hair made me think of him, that's all." She picked up one of the girl dolls and studied the detail of its clothes—a dark blue dress, white apron, and a little white cap. On the back of its cloth body was a tag that read: *Handmade by Laurie King.*

Susan smiled at the Amish woman. "Is your name Laurie? Did you make these dolls?"

"Jah. I mean, yes," Laurie replied. "I enjoy sewing, and I've been making dolls like these since I was fifteen."

"You don't look much more than that now," Anne interjected.

A pink blush erupted on the young woman's cheeks. "I'm nineteen," she said, dropping her gaze to the dolls.

"You do a nice job of sewing, and as soon as I make up my mind, I'm definitely going to buy at least one."

<hr />

"It feels good to be here at the market," Meredith said as she and Alma walked past Groff's candy stand, where delectable-looking fudge, peanut brittle, nuts, and dried fruits beckoned people. "I just wish we'd gotten here a bit sooner, because everything will close down in an hour or so."

"I know, but I think we still have plenty of time to see what we want." Alma made a sweeping gesture of the booths nearby. "Even though there are bigger farmers' markets in the area, I like coming here because it's close to my home, and it's a much smaller market than some."

"That's true," Meredith agreed. "The Green Dragon and Roots Markets are a lot larger, but it's really hard to see everything; although I have enjoyed visiting those markets many times before."

They strolled past several other stands, and as they approached Sue's Sandwich Shoppe, Meredith halted. "Should we get some subs to take home for supper? That way we won't have to cook anything tonight."

"Uh. . .I'm not really in the mood for a sub sandwich."

"How about some other kind of sandwich or a pretzel dog?"

Alma shook her head. "You need a more substantial meal than that." She slipped her arm around Meredith's waist. "I'll fix us a hearty meal as soon as we get home."

Meredith didn't argue. If there was one thing she'd learned about Alma, it was that once she'd made her mind up about something, there was no changing it. And the truth was, her home-cooked meals were delicious, so Meredith figured whatever Alma fixed would be a treat.

"If you're really hungry and can't wait for supper, why don't we snack on a few samples?" Alma suggested.

"Okay." Meredith led the way to her dad's stand, where he sold kettle corn. They visited with him awhile and tasted a few of the little cups he had setting out for people to try.

"Your kettle corn is as good as ever," Meredith said, leaning on the edge of his table.

"I've always enjoyed making it, and it sells really fast. Especially today, with the good crowd that's here." He grinned at Meredith. "By the way. . .*hallich gebottsdaag*. I heard you were coming here to celebrate your birthday."

She smiled and motioned to Alma. "It was her idea."

"And a good one it is," he said, winking at Alma.

Several people came up to Dad's stand then, so Meredith told him goodbye.

"Your mamm and I will see you tomorrow at church," Dad called as Meredith and Alma moved on.

Their next stop was the Kitchen Kettle Village booth, where they sampled some pepper jam and chow-chow. Eating the chow-chow made Meredith think of Luke, because his mother made it often and Luke had always said that no one could make chow-chow quite like his mom.

Knowing she needed to focus on something else, Meredith suggested they go over to Laurie's stand and see how she was doing. When they arrived, she saw two young English women talking to Laurie, and one of them was buying two blond-haired dolls—a boy and a girl. Even the sight of the dolls caused Meredith to think about Luke, as their hair color was almost the same as his.

I've got to stop doing this, she told herself. *I can't dwell on how much I miss Luke every time I see something that reminds me of him.*

As Meredith and Alma stepped up to Laurie's table, she heard the English woman who wore blue jeans and a pink blouse say something about being a nurse. Then the other woman, also wearing jeans with a matching jacket, turned to Meredith and smiled. "These are beautiful dolls, aren't they?"

Meredith nodded. "My sister makes them."

"Oh, so Laurie King is your sister?"

"That's right." Meredith nodded as she smiled at Laurie.

"I'm glad you're here," Laurie said. "Could you and Alma give me a ride home?"

"We can, but I thought your driver would be picking you up."

"I'll explain in a few minutes," Laurie said. "I just need to make change for this customer and put her dolls in a box." Her forehead wrinkled as she studied Meredith. "You look tired. Why don't you take a seat behind my stand, and we can talk as soon as I'm done."

Meredith really wasn't that tired, but she quietly slipped behind the table and took a seat in one of the folding chairs. She figured Alma would do the same. Instead, Alma started up a conversation with the dark-haired women, who seemed to be full of questions about the Amish way of life. Finally, they thanked Laurie for the dolls and went on their way.

Meredith figured Laurie would say what was on her mind. Instead, she leaned across the table and whispered something to Alma.

"What are you two talking about?" Meredith asked, rising from her seat.

"Just discussing what we'll have for supper," Alma said, looking red-faced and a little flustered.

Meredith's lips compressed. She had a feeling there was more going on than just a discussion about what they'd be having for supper. Were they planning some kind of a birthday surprise behind her back? Meredith had thought Mom would invite her to their place for supper tonight, but she hadn't heard a word from Mom since earlier this week. It made her more than a little suspicious.

⁂

"Could you please hurry and get the dining-room table set?" Luann asked her daughter Kendra as they scurried around Meredith's kitchen, getting the final preparations for supper finished.

"Sure, Mom." Kendra removed a stack of plates from the cupboard and took them to the other room.

"I'm glad your daed could close up his stand and come home early to help out," Luann mentioned. "He's going to take care of hiding the horses and buggies when the Yoders and Luke's folks arrive."

"I heard Dad say that he sold out of kettle corn early today, so it was a good reason for him to leave the market before closing time," Kendra put in.

"He also told me that Meredith and Alma stopped by his booth, but he was able to sneak out soon after they headed to Laurie's stand." Luann chuckled as she gently stirred the fresh fruit salad. "So far, everything is working out." She smiled at her mother, who sat at the kitchen table making a tossed green salad. "When I stopped by the farmers' market this morning to see Laurie, she said she and Alma had planned it so that Alma and Meredith would go to the market this afternoon, and then she would ask them for a ride home."

"I think Meredith will be very surprised," her mother said. Then she grinned at Arlene, Katie, and Owen as they stood staring at the beautiful cake she'd decorated earlier. "You kids can look at the cake, but don't touch."

"I won't," Arlene said with a quick shake of her head. "And I'll make sure my little bruder and schweschder don't touch it, neither."

Luann smiled. Arlene always did like bossing the two younger ones around. "I hope Laurie doesn't give our surprise party away," she said. "She's never been very good at keeping secrets, you know."

"I'm sure it'll all work out," her mother said in a positive tone.

Luann glanced nervously out the window. "I wonder where Seth, Dorine, and Luke's folks are? I figured they'd be here by now."

"Don't you start fretting. I'm sure everything will work out fine."

"I just want everything to be perfect. Meredith deserves to have a happy time tonight."

"You're right. She does." Luann's mother went to the refrigerator to get a bottle of salad dressing. She'd no more than returned to the table when Luann heard the rumble of buggy wheels outside. She glanced out the window again and smiled. "Oh good, Sadie and Elam are here, and I see the Yoders' buggy coming in right behind them."

"I brought a potato salad and some deviled eggs," Sadie said when she and Dorine entered the house with Dorine's two little ones in tow. "Elam and Seth are putting the horses in the barn, and Philip's hiding the buggies."

Dorine glanced around. "Meredith's not here yet, I hope."

Luann shook her head. "I expect she, Alma, and Laurie will arrive soon, though."

The women visited while they continued with the supper preparations, and a few minutes after the men came in, another horse and buggy rumbled up the driveway.

"It's Meredith," Philip announced, peering out the window. "If we're gonna surprise her, then we'd better all hide."

<hr />

Meredith was a little disappointed when she guided her horse up to the hitching rail and didn't see any other buggies parked in the yard. Maybe she'd been wrong about her family planning a party for her.

"I'll put the horse away," Laurie was quick to say. "Just wait right here in the buggy until I get done."

"Now why would I do that? I'm perfectly capable of putting Taffy away in her stall." Meredith started to get out, but Alma, who sat in the backseat of the buggy, put her hand on Meredith's shoulder and said, "We did a lot of walking this afternoon, and I'm sure you're tired, so why not let your sister put the horse away?"

"Okay," Meredith relented, "but there's no reason for us to wait here until she's done. We should go in the house and get supper started."

Laurie had already led Taffy to the barn, but Alma just sat there, staring straight ahead.

"Alma, did you hear what I said?" Meredith questioned.

Alma tipped her head. "What was that?"

"We should go inside and fix something to eat."

"Did you say something about your feet?"

Meredith shook her head. "I said, eat, not feet. Alma, are your hearing aids turned on?"

Again, Alma said nothing.

Feeling a little perplexed, Meredith climbed down from the buggy and extended her hand to Alma. A few moments ago, Alma seemed to hear what she'd said, and now suddenly she couldn't? What was going on here anyway?

"I'm not so old that I can't get out of the buggy by myself," Alma said. "It just takes me a little longer than some."

A little longer? Meredith thought. She'd never seen anyone be so slow about getting out of a buggy. At least Alma seemed to be hearing better again.

By the time Alma had finally climbed down, Laurie came out of the barn. "I'm sure hungerich," she said. "Let's get up to the house so we can fix something to eat."

"What about the buggy?" Meredith questioned. "It needs to be put in the buggy shed."

"I'll do it after supper." Laurie stepped between Meredith and Alma, placing her hands in the crook of their arms.

As they walked slowly to the house, Meredith wondered once again if something might be amiss. She opened the door and entered the house.

"Surprise! Hallich gebottsdaag, Meredith!" hollered a chorus of voices.

Tears welled in Meredith's eyes. It felt good to know her family loved her so much, and it would be a lot easier to put on a happy face this evening because they were here. But her heart still ached, for she missed Luke and wished he were also here to help celebrate her birthday. Somehow, she must learn to accept her loss, because no matter how much she wanted it, Luke wasn't coming back.

Meredith looked at each of her family members, as well as Alma, Sadie, Elam, Dorine, Seth, and their children. She couldn't have felt more loved and knew without a doubt how very blessed she was.

⊰⊱

Philadelphia

Voices. . .Voices. . . Somewhere in a faraway place there were voices. What were they saying? Were they talking about him? Were they talking to him?

I feel like I'm suffocating and the darkness is swallowing me up. I need to open my eyes. I want to wake up.

Someone touched his arm. More voices—something about his blood pressure and pulse. He winced, feeling pain radiating from different parts of his body.

Pulling from somewhere deep inside, the man willed his eyes to open. He squinted against the bright light invading his senses and tried to focus on the faces before him. Who were these people, and why were they staring at him? He stared back, blinking several times, trying to make his eyes focus. A woman with blond hair smiled at him.

"Look, Doctor," she said, turning to the man who stood beside her. "I think our John Doe is finally awake."

THE PIECES OF SUMMER

Peace I leave with you, my peace I give unto you:
not as the world giveth, give I unto you.
Let not your heart be troubled, neither let it be afraid.

JOHN 14:27

CHAPTER 1

Philadelphia, Pennsylvania

When Susan returned to work on Monday morning, she was surprised, as well as pleased, to learn that her John Doe patient had woken up from his coma.

"He's still groggy from all the medication," Nurse Pamela told her as they sat at the nurses' station going over the patients' charts. "But at least he's conscious."

"That's really great news. The poor man has been here since January, and here it is April already. I was beginning to wonder if he'd ever wake up."

"We've all been wondering that," Pamela said with a brief nod. "It's always good to see a patient improve, and hopefully this man you call Eddie will recuperate fully."

"Was he able to say anything? Maybe tell you his name or how he got injured?"

Pamela shook her blond head. "He responded with eye blinks when we questioned him on how he was feeling, but he was unable to talk. Most likely, it's due to the injury his vocal cords sustained."

"Hopefully, there's no permanent damage, and he'll be able to talk once he starts using his voice again. We need to find out who he is so we can notify his family." Susan stepped out from behind the nurses' station. "I'm going to his room right now to check on him."

When Susan entered the patient's room, she was disappointed to see that his eyes were closed. Was he sleeping, or had he fallen back into a coma?

She took his blood pressure and checked the rest of his vitals. Since there was no cause for alarm, she seated herself in the chair beside his bed. "Are you awake, Eddie? I heard that you opened your eyes on Saturday."

Susan watched closely, but there was no response. Not even a flutter of his eyelids.

Susan placed her hand on his shoulder. "Heavenly Father, I believe You want this young man to be well, so please continue to touch and heal his body."

&

Bird-in-Hand, Pennsylvania

Meredith pushed her chair away from the sewing machine and stood. She'd received an order for several more head coverings and had been working on them all morning, so she really needed a break. Her eyes were tired, and her body ached from sitting so long. She felt like she could use a change of scenery and a breath of fresh air.

"Think I'll go outside and check the mailbox," Meredith called down the stairs to Alma, who was in the basement, washing clothes.

There was no reply. Meredith figured Alma probably had her hearing aids turned off again. Either that or she couldn't hear because of the noise coming from the gas-powered washing machine.

Meredith knew it wouldn't take her long to walk to the end of the driveway to get the mail, so she slipped out the back door, figuring Alma probably wouldn't even know she was gone. A little exercise and some fresh air would be good for her. Being outside always seemed to help, both physically and mentally.

As Meredith approached Fritz's dog run where he was sleeping near the gate, he awoke and started barking and jumping at the fence. "I know, pup," she said, unlatching the gate. "You want to take a walk with me, don't ya, boy?"

Woof! Woof! Fritz licked Meredith's hand and wagged his stubby tail as he romped in circles around her with his lips parted, as though he was grinning.

"Come on then, let's go get the mail!" Meredith clapped her hands and watched as Fritz ran ahead of her. *That dog sure is* schmaert. *He always seems to know just what I'm saying to him.*

Meredith had just reached the mailbox when Sheriff Tyler's car pulled in. As soon as he stepped out of the vehicle, Fritz greeted him with a *yip*, and pranced up beside him.

The sheriff chuckled and bent down to pet Fritz's head. "You're always glad to see me, aren't ya, boy?"

Fritz responded with a wag of his tail.

"Are you getting along okay?" Sheriff Tyler asked, looking back at Meredith.

She nodded.

"You're not staying here alone, I hope."

"Oh no. Alma Beechy's going to be with me all week while my sister Laurie takes a little holiday to Sarasota, Florida, with her friend Barbara, who's celebrating her birthday this week. They're renting a small house in the village of Pinecraft, where many Amish go for vacation."

"I see. Well, I'm glad you're not alone, because over the weekend we've had some break-ins in the area, which is part of the reason I stopped by. Besides checking to see how you're doing, I wanted to warn you about these incidents and suggest that you keep your doors locked, even when you're at home. Just to be on the safe side," he quickly added.

Meredith, already feeling a bit apprehensive, shivered and said, "I hadn't heard anything about this before. Have many homes been affected?"

"Just a few, and so far they've all been homes owned by Englishers, but I'm warning everyone in the area, just in case."

"Do you think it's only one person doing these things, or could there be more?" Meredith wasn't sure she wanted to know the answer to that question, but she had to ask. Just the thought of a stranger breaking into her home, let alone several, was frightening enough.

"Wish I could tell you the answer to that," the sheriff replied. "Some of the victims have had more things stolen than others, and it looks like the thieves are after anything that's valuable and could be sold."

Meredith gulped. "It's hard to hear about things like that going on in other places, but you never think it could happen in your own neighborhood. Thanks for letting me know. I appreciate you stopping by."

"Be sure and call my office if you hear or see anything suspicious," he said before getting back in his car and rolling down his window. "It might be a good idea to keep the number for my office in your phone shack. Oh, and please pass the word along to others you may talk to, because I might not be able to get around to everyone today."

"I will, and thank you again, Sheriff Tyler." Meredith waved as he pulled his vehicle back onto the road. Then she quickly took out the mail and headed back to the house. She could see that Fritz was already waiting for her by the back door.

Meredith was glad Alma would be staying with her all week, because knowing there had been some robberies in the area, she'd be even more nervous if she were here all alone.

Her mind was already at work, thinking of ways to make it safer around her home. She was in the habit of locking her doors, especially since Luke had passed away. But even though the weather was getting nicer, Meredith decided that from now on, until the thief had been caught, the pup would be staying in the house with her more, and definitely during the night. She figured Fritz was the best burglar alarm she could possibly have.

Meredith had just stepped onto the porch when a horse and buggy came up the driveway. She turned to look as Fritz barked. Recognizing the horse as Socks, she knew her guest must be Jonah.

"*Wie geht's?*" Jonah asked when he joined her on the porch.

"I'm doing all right," she replied with a smile. "If you came to see Laurie, she's not here. In fact, she'll be gone all week."

Jonah gave his left earlobe a tug. "I'm not here to see Laurie. Came to find out how you're doing, and to give you this." He held out a paper sack. "Happy belated birthday."

Meredith's face heated. "How'd you know I had a birthday?" she asked, feeling a bit hesitant to take the sack.

Fritz sat expectantly looking up at Jonah, probably hoping there was something in the sack for him, because whenever Jonah stopped by he usually had a treat for the dog.

"Back when we were teenagers you mentioned your birthday in one of your letters." He took a step closer, still holding out the sack. "I would have brought this by on your birthday, but things were busy at the buggy shop all day, and I figured you'd be celebrating with your family that evening, so I didn't think it'd be right to come by and interrupt."

Not wishing to be impolite, Meredith took the paper sack, reached inside, and removed several dahlia tubers. "I'm sure these will look nice in my garden when they bloom in the fall," she said. "*Danki*, Jonah."

"Today's my day off, so I have time to plant them for you right now. That is, if you want me to," Jonah said with a wide smile.

Meredith grinned, too, noticing that Fritz had lost interest and run into the yard to chase after a squirrel.

"I appreciate the offer, but I can put them in the ground myself," she said, bringing her gaze back to Jonah.

Jonah's smile disappeared. "Okay, if that's what you'd prefer." He leaned on the porch railing, as though needing it for support. "Umm. . . Is there something else you'd like me to do?"

She shook her head. "I can't think of anything right now, but I do appreciate your willingness to help."

Fritz leaped back onto the porch and pawed at Jonah's pant leg. Jonah's smile returned as he bent to pet the dog. "You sure like attention, don't ya, boy? Sorry I forgot to bring you a treat, but I'll remember the next time I come over."

Fritz responded with a wag of his tail.

"My folks' dog, Herbie, is the same way," Jonah said, looking at Meredith. "He just can't seem to get enough attention."

"I guess most pets are like that."

Just then, Alma, carrying a wicker basket full of laundry, came around the side of house where the outside basement entrance was.

"Here, let me help you with that," Jonah said, extending his hands.

Alma smiled appreciatively. "Danki, Jonah, that's real nice of you. Would you mind carrying it over to the clothesline for me?"

"Not at all." Jonah took the basket and headed across the yard.

Alma turned to Meredith and smiled. "Jonah is one of the nicest young men I've ever met."

"That's what Laurie says, too," Meredith said. "To tell you the truth, I think she might have a crush on Jonah."

Alma's eyes widened. "You really think so?"

"*Jah*. Haven't you seen the way she acts when he's around—all smiles and full of so many questions?"

"I hadn't really noticed." Alma rubbed her chin thoughtfully. "But I have seen the way Jonah lights up whenever he looks at you."

Meredith's face heated again, and she knew without question that her cheeks must be bright pink. If Jonah was interested in her, she wasn't sure what to do about it. Luke had only been gone a few months, and it was too soon for her to even be thinking about a relationship with another man. Surely Jonah must realize that, too. Maybe he had no desire to be anything more to her than a good friend. Maybe Alma was just imagining things.

And what about Laurie? Meredith thought. *If she is interested in Jonah, which I'm quite sure she is, she'd be hurt if she thought Jonah was after me.*

"Please don't say anything to anyone about your suspicions," Meredith said to Alma.

Alma squeezed Meredith's arm gently. "I won't say a thing. But mark my words: eventually that man's gonna ask you to marry him."

❧

Philadelphia

Where am I? the man wondered as he opened his eyes. He was conscious of voices, but none of them sounded familiar. Were they discussing him? If so, why? Was he sick or injured? There must be something terribly wrong, because it hurt when he breathed, and he couldn't talk.

He tried to raise his head, but he couldn't do that, either. Why did he feel so strange?

"It's okay, Eddie. Just lie still and relax." A young woman with dark hair and dark eyes stood a short distance away, smiling down at him.

Why did she call me, Eddie? Where am I? he silently screamed, but he couldn't form the words.

"You're in the hospital," the woman said, as though sensing what he wanted to know.

How many days have I been here? How bad am I hurt? Was I in an accident or something? So many questions swam around in his brain it made his head hurt even more trying to think things through. All he wanted to do was sleep and escape the pain.

"It's okay," the woman said, placing her hand on his arm. "You've been through a lot. What you need more than anything is lots of rest. When your throat heals sufficiently and you can talk, we hope you'll be able to tell us who you are and what happened to you."

I've been through a lot? What does she mean? I wish I knew what happened to me, the man thought as he closed his eyes and succumbed to sleep.

❦

Bird-in-Hand

That evening as Meredith lay sleeping, she was awakened by a strange noise. Fritz must have heard it, too, for he began to growl.

Thinking maybe Alma had gotten out of bed and bumped into something in the guest room, Meredith grabbed the flashlight on her nightstand and got up. After slipping into her robe, she tiptoed across the hall to Alma's room.

The elderly woman lay curled on her side, snoring softly. Meredith noticed that Alma's hearing aids were lying on the dresser, which explained why the strange noise hadn't awakened her.

With Fritz still growling and walking at her side, Meredith stepped back into the hall and listened. There it was again—a noisy clatter. Slowly, Meredith made her way down the stairs, with Fritz plodding right beside her, ears perked and head cocked, as though ready for action.

When Meredith's feet touched the bottom step, she heard the noise again—this time much louder. She was sure it was coming from the basement.

A sense of panic welled in her chest. There was definitely someone down there. What if whoever had been breaking into people's houses had somehow gotten into her cellar? *But how could that be?* she reasoned. *I was careful to keep all the doors locked today.*

Then a thought popped into Meredith's head. When Alma had done the laundry this morning, maybe she'd forgotten to lock the outside basement door. Meredith wished Luke was with her right now, because she was really scared. She was sure Luke would have known what to do. Alma was no help, either, since she was sleeping, and Meredith hated to wake her. Besides, if there was someone in the basement, what could two helpless women—one heavy with child, and one quite elderly—do to prevent a robbery?

One thing Meredith knew for sure—she wasn't going to the basement to check on that noise! Who knew what kind of person could be down there?

183

From the sound of things, whoever it was must be rummaging through everything. In her basement were several metal storage cabinets, where Luke had kept a few extra tools that he'd used occasionally around the house. There were also some paint cans, and shelves with household supplies, such as paper towels, napkins, and garbage bags, but nothing Meredith could think of that would be of interest to a robber to steal—unless, of course, he was after the tools.

She quickly grabbed a kitchen chair and propped it against the door, making sure the top of it was securely under the doorknob. Then, grabbing her jacket, and telling Fritz to come with her, she hurried out the back door. She needed to get to the phone shack right away and call the sheriff. She just hoped that chair would keep the intruder from entering the main part of the house, because poor Alma was still upstairs by herself.

CHAPTER 2

Meredith's hand shook as she reached for the phone to dial the sheriff's number. Thankfully, she'd done as Sheriff Tyler suggested and tacked the number for his office to the wall inside the shack. She assumed he wouldn't be in his office at this hour, but surely someone would be there to answer the phone. Or maybe it would be better just to call 911, because she was sure whomever she talked to would send help.

Woof! Woof! Woof! Fritz barked frantically from outside the phone shack, and Meredith cringed. *Maybe I should have left him in the house to protect Alma. But if I'd done that, his barking might have woken Alma, and she wouldn't have understood what was going on.*

Meredith felt so rattled, she could barely think straight, much less make a phone call. *If Luke was here with me right now, I wouldn't feel so afraid and confused.*

With trembling fingers, Meredith made the 911 phone call. After she'd told the dispatcher there was an intruder in her basement, she was warned not to go back in the house but to wait in the phone shack for help to arrive.

Meredith didn't want to go back to the house, but the thought of leaving Alma there all alone made her nervous.

Remain calm, a voice in her head seemed to say. *Remain calm and stay put like you were told to do.*

She thought about the verse of scripture she'd read the other day: *"Peace I leave with you, my peace I give unto you: not as the world giveth, give I unto you. Let not your heart be troubled, neither let it be afraid" John 14:27.*

Feeling a bit more relaxed, Meredith paused to offer a prayer. "Heavenly Father, please keep Alma and me safe, and send us some help real soon."

Meredith opened the door and let Fritz into the phone shack with her. It should keep him from barking and help her remain calmer, too. She didn't want Fritz's yapping to alert whoever was in the basement any more than it might already have.

It seemed like an eternity before she saw the sheriff's car pull into the yard. She was glad it was him and not some other officer she didn't know very well.

"We were on patrol and received word that you'd called about an intruder," Sheriff Tyler said when he and his deputy, Earl Graves, got out of the car.

Meredith nodded, relieved that help was finally there. "The intruder's in the basement. I wedged a chair in front of the basement door, so hopefully he won't get into the main part of the house."

The sheriff gave her a nod. "Good thinking. Did you get a look at him, or did he say anything to you?"

"No, but I know someone's in the basement because of all the noise I heard coming from down there. It sounded like they were rummaging through everything, although I don't know why, because there's nothing really valuable down there."

"Well, you'd better stay out here and let us handle the situation." Sheriff Tyler looked at his deputy. "Let's go, Earl."

With the door of the phone shack partially open, Meredith watched as the two men entered her house. "*Ach*, my. . .I hope Alma's all right."

Meredith prayed as she waited, but when she heard someone scream, she couldn't wait any longer. She had to know if Alma was okay.

With Fritz on her heels, Meredith, cradling her stomach with her hands, ran as fast as she could to the house. She'd just entered through the back door, and lit a gas lantern, when she heard the sheriff holler, "Get that feisty fellow, Earl! See if you can trap him in one of those empty boxes."

Meredith's forehead wrinkled. Who in the world was in her basement? Only a child could fit in a box. Was it possible that one of her neighbors' children had gotten into her basement? But it was the middle of the night, so that made no sense.

Meredith crept closer to the basement door, keeping a firm grip on Fritz's collar, but jumped back when she heard a loud crash. She was glad she hadn't gone into the basement when she'd first heard the noise. Whoever was down there must be putting up a fight.

"You okay, Sheriff?" Earl yelled.

"Yeah. Just tripped over some boxes and fell on the floor. Sure wish there was a light I could turn on down here. Can't see much with just our flashlights."

"Did ya trap him, Sheriff?"

"Nope. He got away from me again. Oops. . .there he is now. . . Open the basement door and we'll see if we can chase him out."

Meredith wasn't sure whether the sheriff was referring to the outside basement door or the one that led to the kitchen. But the next thing she knew, Earl let out a yelp, and the inside basement door swung open. A few seconds later, a fat little raccoon darted into the kitchen, with Earl right behind it.

"What are you doin' in here?" he shouted, nearly bumping into Meredith. "Thought the sheriff told ya to wait outside."

Meredith answered the deputy's question, but her voice was drowned out when Fritz started yapping and chasing after the raccoon. Round and round the room they went, bumping into the table, the cupboards, and even the stove. The animal with the masklike eyes skirted past Fritz and jumped on the countertop, knocking over a canister of flour. Talk about Fritz being in the wrong place at the wrong time! The flour not only spilled onto the countertop but cascaded down onto the dog's head and body, just as he ran under the falling powdery white stuff.

Yip! Yip! Yip! Fritz now looked more like a white Dalmatian than the German shorthaired pointer he truly was, with only a few spots of brown color showing from his coat.

Fritz sneezed, sending puffs of flour from his nostrils, and tried to gain traction on the slippery white mess as he pursued the bandit-looking creature with determination. Sheriff Tyler and Deputy Earl were hot on the chase, slipping and sliding where Fritz had just been, while Meredith stood back, watching the whole thing as she struggled not to laugh. It was really quite a comical scene, and she felt relief, knowing the intruder was just an animal and not a robber after all.

Finally, with Fritz nipping at its bushy ringed tail, the varmint darted out the open back door and into the yard.

"Whew! That's a relief," Sheriff Tyler said, quickly shutting the door. "Don't know how that critter got in your basement, but he sure gave us a merry chase."

"What's going on in here?" Alma asked, yawning as she stepped into the room. "I woke up to use the bathroom, and as soon as I put my hearing aids in, I heard a ruckus down here in the kitchen."

Seeing Alma look around in obvious disbelief at the mess in the kitchen, Meredith quickly explained what had happened. Flour dust was still in the air, but it slowly settled, leaving a film on all the surfaces. Everyone burst out laughing when Deputy Earl removed his glasses that were also coated with flour particles.

When their laughter subsided, the sheriff smiled and said, "When I responded to this call I knew it couldn't have been the fellows who'd done the robberies in the area, because they were caught a few hours after I stopped by your place to warn you about them. I was a bit concerned, however, thinking we might have another thief in the area."

"In a way, there was." Deputy Earl motioned to the floor, where a hunk of carrot lay. "I think that critter was all set to raid the root vegetables you've been storin' in your cellar," he said, looking at Meredith.

Alma slipped her arm gently around Meredith's waist. "The next time Jonah drops by, I'll ask him to check for any places in the basement where an animal might get in and fix it so that nothing like this happens again."

Meredith shook her head. "Let's not bother Jonah with that. I can ask my *daed* or Dorine's husband, Seth, to do it. Right now," she said, looking around at the mess, "I have a kitchen to clean up and a disgruntled dog to bathe."

⌁

Darby, Pennsylvania

"I sure like this straw hat you got for me at the farmers' market," Susan's grandfather said as the two of them worked together in the garden early Tuesday morning. "It helps to keep the sun out of my eyes."

"I'm glad you're pleased with it, Grandpa." Susan stabbed her shovel into the ground and pulled up another clump of weeds. It felt good to be outdoors in the fresh spring air, with her hands in the dirt. Gardening was kind of a hobby for her, and she found a sense of satisfaction in it. Grandpa obviously felt the same way, because ever since the weather had turned nice, he'd been spending several hours each day outside in the yard. Susan didn't have the luxury of gardening that often, though. Most of the time when she got home from the hospital, she was either too tired to work in the yard or it was late and already dark. Today, her shift wouldn't begin until noon, so she'd taken advantage of the early morning hours to help Grandpa get some weeding done.

"Eww. . .look at this." Susan wrinkled her nose as she watched a lengthy, plump earthworm wiggling from the dirt, still clinging to the bottom of the weed in her gloved hand.

"Now that's a good one." Grandpa bobbed his head. "If I had plans to go fishing soon, I'd suggest puttin' the wiggler in my bait box. But for now, you can just throw him in one of your grandma's flower beds. It'll be good for the soil."

Susan did as Grandpa suggested. "Oops! I missed the flower bed," she said, watching as the worm landed in the grass.

"Don't worry about it," Grandpa said. "The ground's damp over there, and I'm sure it'll worm its way under the grass and into the dirt."

Susan was just getting ready to pull another weed when she noticed movement out of the corner of her eye. She pointed in the direction where Grandpa was already looking, watching a robin gobble up the worm she'd just tossed onto the grass.

"See what fun your sister is missing?" Grandpa chuckled as Susan made a face. "I tried to talk Anne into joining us out here," he said, "but she turned me down flat. Guess she'd rather put on her jogging clothes and run all over the neighborhood, working up a sweat, than dig in the dirt with us."

Susan laughed and wiped the perspiration from her forehead. "And what do you think we're doing out here, if not sweating?"

He grinned and yanked up another weed. "This is different. At least when we work up a sweat, we have somethin' to show for our troubles. The only thing Anne has to show for all that jogging she does every day is a skinny body, without an ounce of flab."

"Well, you know my sister. . . She does like to keep fit and trim, which I'm sure helps her as a physical therapist."

Grandpa grunted. "She could get fit and trim pullin' weeds, I'll bet."

"Not everyone likes gardening the way we do," Susan reminded him. "Grandma doesn't like it that much, and it doesn't seem to bother you any."

"Well, she might not like to pull weeds, but she does cook all the produce we grow." Grandpa jiggled his eyebrows playfully. "Yes indeed, my wife's a mighty good cook."

Susan smiled. "I can't argue with that."

They worked in silence for a while, until Grandpa set his shovel aside and said, "Think we got most of the weeds out now, don't you?"

"Yes, but a few days from now, there will probably be more." Susan motioned to the picnic table under the leafy maple tree in the corner of the yard. "Should we sit awhile and visit before it's time for me to get ready for work?" she asked.

"Sounds good to me."

After they'd both taken a seat on the picnic bench, Susan turned to Grandpa and said, "When I got home from the hospital last night, you and Grandma were already in bed, so I didn't get the chance to tell you that Eddie finally woke up."

Grandpa's thick eyebrows lifted high on his forehead. "That John Doe patient of yours?"

She nodded. "I guess he came out of the coma on Saturday while Anne and I were in Lancaster County. One of the nurses told me about it when I got to work yesterday."

"That's good news, Susan. Did you get to talk to the young man?"

She shook her head. "Unfortunately, he slept through most of my shift, and due to the injury to his vocal cords, even when he was awake, he was unable to talk. I'm hoping it won't be long before he can communicate. I'm really anxious to find out who he is and how he got injured."

CHAPTER 3

Bird-in-Hand

"Did you have a nice time in Florida?" Meredith asked when Laurie showed up at her house the following Monday morning.

Laurie nodded enthusiastically, her face fairly glowing. "Oh, jah. It was a lot of fun spending time on the beach. No wonder you stayed in Sarasota a whole summer when you were eighteen. I think I could live there, too."

"You're nice and brown, so it looks like you got plenty of sun," Meredith said, making no comment about the time she'd spent in Florida. Sometimes she wished she could return to those carefree teenage days, when all she had to worry about was being courteous to the customers at the restaurant where she'd worked and enjoying her free time at the beach.

"I sure did get some sun." Laurie held out her arms. "With my fair skin, I had to be careful not to burn, so I used plenty of sunscreen. It must have helped, because I look more tan than burned."

"What else did you do besides go to the beach?" Meredith asked, glancing at her own arms, which were as pale as ever.

"Oh, we. . ." Laurie stopped talking and dropped her gaze to the floor. "So, have you seen Jonah lately?" she asked, abruptly changing the subject.

"He's dropped by a few times. Why do you ask?"

"Oh, just curious, is all."

"Do you like him?" Meredith questioned, curious at how quickly Laurie had changed the subject.

"Who?" Laurie dropped into a seat on the sofa.

"Jonah."

"Of course I do." Laurie smiled. "He's a very nice man."

Meredith hesitated a minute, wondering how best to express her

191

thoughts. "I know you are interested in him, but I don't think it's good for you to be so obvious about it," she said, taking a seat beside her sister.

Laurie's forehead wrinkled. "What are you talking about, Meredith? I've never said I was interested in Jonah."

"Maybe not in so many words, but whenever he comes around, you smile at him and seem to be hanging on his every word."

Laurie's cheeks flamed. "I'm not the least bit interested in Jonah. I just know he's a good friend of yours, and since he might end up to be my brother-in-law someday, I thought I should be nice to him."

Meredith's mouth dropped open. "Wh—where did you come up with that idea?"

"I've seen the way he looks at you, Meredith. It's obvious that he's smitten."

"You can tell that just by how he looks at me?"

Laurie shrugged. "That's only part of it. I don't think Jonah would come over here so often, wanting to help out, if he wasn't interested in you."

Meredith shook her head. "That's ridiculous! Jonah's just a friend, and he knows I'm still mourning Luke's death."

"That doesn't mean he's not interested in having a relationship with you whenever you're ready."

Meredith stared straight ahead. "I don't think I'll ever be ready for that. I love Luke, and I always will."

Laurie placed her hand on Meredith's arm. "Of course you will, but it doesn't mean you can never love another man. Luke wouldn't want you to grieve for him forever. He'd want you to be happy and find love again."

"How do you know what Luke would want?" The pitch of Meredith's voice raised a notch. "You can't speak for him."

"I realize that," Laurie said, "but I know Luke loved you very much, and I'm sure he would want you to move on with your life and, most of all, be happy again."

"That's easy for you to say." Meredith instinctively looked around the living room at all the things that reminded her of Luke. "You don't understand what it's like for me."

"No, I don't, but I do know how it feels to be in love." Laurie clamped her hand over her mouth. "I—I. . . What I meant to say was. . ."

"You said a few minutes ago that you're not interested in Jonah, so if not him, then who?" Meredith questioned, bringing her focus back on her sister.

"I—I'd rather not say," Laurie mumbled.

"If you've come to care about someone, then why not just admit it? What have you got to hide?"

"Do you promise not to tell?"

"Tell who? Mom and Dad?"

Laurie nodded. "If they knew who I've been seeing secretly, they'd be *umgerennt.*"

"Why would they be upset? Who is it, Laurie? Who have you been seeing that Mom and Dad wouldn't approve of?"

"Kevin Byler," Laurie said in a near whisper.

"But Kevin's not Amish, Laurie. You know what that would mean if you married him?"

"It would mean I wouldn't join the Amish church like I'd planned to do this fall. But at least I'd be going to Kevin's Mennonite church, and they preach God's Word there, too."

Meredith sighed. She knew how much their folks, and especially Mom, were looking forward to seeing Laurie baptized into the Amish faith. She also knew, or at least hoped, that their folks would show some understanding if Laurie and Kevin decided to get married.

Meredith gave her sister a hug. "I won't tell Mom and Dad that you've been seeing Kevin, but if you two are getting serious, then you need to tell them yourself, and soon, before they hear about it from someone else. News travels fast in our community, and if anyone's seen you and Kevin together, there is bound to be talk."

Tears welled in Laurie's eyes. "I know you're right. Kevin has a stand at the farmers' market, too, and we've sometimes taken our lunches together, but we've always gone somewhere outside the market, where Dad and the others who work there couldn't see."

Meredith looked her sister straight in the eyes. "Was Kevin with you in Florida last week?"

Laurie sniffed deeply as she gave a slow nod. "We weren't alone, though. Three other couples were with us. Oh, and the girls stayed together in one of the places we rented, and the guys stayed in another," she quickly added.

Meredith couldn't believe her sister had been so deceitful, but then she didn't think it was her place to judge Laurie. "From one sister to another, I'd like to give you some advice," she said, giving Laurie's shoulder a gentle squeeze.

"What's that?"

"Go to Mom and Dad as soon as possible and tell them the way you feel about Kevin. They may not like it at first, but at least this secret won't be between you anymore, and you'll feel better once you've apologized and stopped sneaking around. It never does anyone any good to be deceitful. Besides, you know it would hurt Mom and Dad deeply if they heard about this from anyone other than you."

"I know," Laurie said tearfully. "I feel better already, just having told you." She leaned forward and gave Meredith a hug.

Jonah whistled as he guided his horse and buggy down the road toward Meredith's house. He was in good spirits this morning—partly because it was such a beautiful spring day, but mostly because his horse was behaving so well. Jonah had figured when he'd first bought Socks from Meredith that it was just a matter of time before the frisky animal got to know and trust him, and he'd been right. Each time he took the gelding out on the road, things had gone better than the time before. Now Socks obeyed all of Jonah's commands and didn't try to run when he wasn't supposed to. Apparently all the horse needed was time to adjust to his original owner being gone. And Jonah's persistence in trying to win the horse over had no doubt played a role in the animal's improved behavior, too.

When Jonah arrived at Meredith's, he was surprised to see her out working in the garden. After nearly losing the baby a few months ago, he was under the impression that she would need to take it easy right up until the baby was born.

Once Jonah had Socks secured at the hitching rail, he hurried across the yard to the garden, where Meredith was pulling up weeds.

"Should you be doing that?" he asked after he'd said hello. "It might be a little too strenuous for you."

Her lips pursed as she stared up at him, the sun making the sides of her strawberry-blond tresses look like golden threads. It was all Jonah could do to keep from reaching under her head covering and touching her hair.

"I'm not overdoing," Meredith was quick to say. "The exercise is good for me, and if I don't get these weeds pulled, I won't have a garden."

"*Ungraut rope aus em gaarde is ken gschpass,*" Jonah said, kneeling on the grass beside her.

Her face relaxed a bit. "I guess you're right. Weeding a garden would be more fun if I wasn't doing it alone. Laurie's back from Florida now, and she was going to help me, but she's busy washing clothes at the moment."

"It's not a problem, because I'm here now, and I'm more than willing to help." Jonah dug his fingers into the dirt and snatched up a weed.

Meredith wrinkled her nose. "Don't you want a shovel or a spade to do that? It's much easier on your fingers and nails."

Jonah chuckled. "Working on buggies the way I do with my daed is harder on my hands than pullin' weeds. But if you have another hand shovel I can use, that might make it easier to dig out the roots of these nasty ungraut."

Meredith motioned to the small shed near the barn. "You'll find several sizes of shovels in there."

"Great. I'll go get one." Jonah rose and strode across the yard to the shed.

"My sister and Alma think you're really a nice man," Meredith said when he returned with a small shovel and started pulling weeds.

"What about you, Meredith? Do you think I'm a nice man, too?" he asked, glancing over at her.

Meredith's cheeks warmed. "Of course I do. I've always thought you were nice. You've been more than helpful to me since Luke died, and I appreciate it very much."

Jonah smiled. "Guess it's just in my nature to be that way. Least that's how it's been ever since a kid I didn't even know cared enough to save me from drowning when I was just a boy. Since that time, I've had a new appreciation for life, and whenever I see someone who has a need, I try to help them as much as I can."

Meredith returned his smile. "That's a good way to be, because it's what the Bible teaches us to do."

He nodded as he shook the dirt loose from the clump of weeds he'd just pulled out from between some pea plants. "Jah, that's so true."

They worked for a while in companionable silence, until the *clip-clop* of horse's hooves interrupted their quiet. Meredith shielded her eyes from the glare of the sun, gazing across the yard to see whose buggy it was.

A few seconds later, Luke's mother, Sadie, stepped down from the buggy and secured her horse at the hitching rail. A frown creased her brow as she approached the garden. Was she upset about something? Had she come with bad news?

"Wie geht's?" Meredith asked.

"I'm fine," Sadie said curtly. "I just came by to see how you're doing." She glanced at Jonah, frowned slightly, and then quickly looked away.

Meredith thought Sadie's behavior was a bit strange; she was usually quite warm and friendly.

"I'm doing okay," Meredith said. "Jonah stopped by awhile ago, and he's helping me pull some weeds."

"I can certainly see that." Sadie motioned to her buggy. "I brought you some of Luke's baby clothes, thinking you could use them when the *boppli* gets here. Should I take the box inside?"

"I'll get it for you," Jonah offered, rising to his feet. Before Sadie could respond, he'd sprinted to her buggy. While Jonah hauled the box to the house, Meredith and Sadie visited.

"Isn't Alma here with you today?" Sadie questioned.

"No, Laurie's here today. She's in the basement, washing clothes."

As if on cue, Laurie came around the house, carrying a basket full of laundry. She smiled at Sadie as she walked by. "It's nice to see you."

Sadie smiled in return. "Same here."

"Do you need my help hanging the laundry?" Meredith asked.

"No, that's okay, I can manage. Just enjoy your time visiting with Sadie." Laurie hurried away and began clipping the clothes to the line.

When Jonah came out of the house, Sadie turned to Meredith and said, "Should we go inside and look through the box of baby things now?"

"That'd be fine," Meredith replied, "but I may not be able to use all of Luke's baby clothes."

Sadie's eyebrows furrowed. "Why not?"

Meredith placed her hands against her bulging stomach. "I don't know yet if the boppli's a *bu* or a *maedel*."

Sadie nodded. "That's true, but many of the sleepers and blankets are in neutral colors, so you should be able to use those for either a boy or a girl."

"I'll pull the rest of these weeds while you two go look at the clothes," Jonah called as Meredith and Sadie headed toward the house.

Meredith stopped walking and turned to face him. "There isn't too much left to do, and I appreciate all the help you've already given me, so you really don't have to finish the job. I can do it later."

Jonah shook his head with a determined expression. "There's no need for that. It'll only take me a short time, and then I'll be on my way home."

"Danki, Jonah." Meredith smiled; then she followed her mother-in-law into the house.

When they entered the living room, Sadie turned to Meredith with a deep frown wrinkling her forehead. "How often has Jonah been coming around here? He seems awfully familiar with you."

Meredith stiffened. "What are you getting at, Sadie?"

"I just don't think it's right for him to be here—especially when you're a young widow, expecting a boppli."

Meredith sighed deeply. "Jonah is just a good friend, and all he wants to do is help out. I'm sorry if you don't think he should be here, but I won't hurt his feelings by telling him not to come over anymore."

Sadie opened her mouth, but then she snapped it closed and folded her arms.

"Let's look at Luke's baby clothes now," Meredith suggested. "I appreciate you bringing them over."

❧

When Sadie arrived home later that morning, she found her husband, Elam, sitting on the front porch with a glass of lemonade.

"How was your visit with Meredith?" he asked, taking a sip of the refreshing drink. "Was she glad to get the baby clothes?"

"I think so," Sadie replied, "but that buggy-maker's son, Jonah, was there."

Elam quirked an eyebrow. "Oh?"

"Jah, and I don't think it's right that he's been hanging around there so much. I'm afraid he's trying to take Luke's place, and it's way too soon for

Meredith to be seeing another man." She placed her hand on Elam's shoulder. "I think you should do something about it, and the sooner the better."

"What do you want me to do, Sadie?" Elam asked, shrugging his shoulders. "Am I supposed to barge into the buggy shop and demand that Jonah stay away from Meredith?"

"That might not be a bad idea," she said with a nod.

Elam looked at her and frowned as he slowly shook his head. "If Jonah and Meredith are meant to be together, there's nothing either one of us can do about it."

Sadie's lips compressed while she tapped her foot. "We'll just have to see about that."

CHAPTER 4

As the cooler days of spring turned into warmer days of summer, Meredith grew weary of everyone doing things for her. It was the middle of June, and her stomach had grown much bigger. She missed the physical work she could no longer do because she was so top-heavy. This morning, she felt almost worthless, wishing she could do more than sit and sew.

She moved from the kitchen to stand in front of the screen door and drew in a deep breath. The sweet smelling scent of the lilacs blooming along the property line wafted up to her nose. The butterflies obviously liked them, too, she noticed, as they glided from one bloom to the next.

Meredith smiled, watching the birds in her yard flitting from the trees to the feeders she kept filled for her enjoyment as much as providing for the birds. Jonah had come by a few weeks ago and repaired a couple of the feeders that had been damaged during a strong wind they'd had in the middle of May.

Jonah had been so kind to her and helped out in many ways. Mom had her hands full, taking care of the children still living at home. Dad kept busy with his stands at the markets, not to mention the chores he had to do at home, so he didn't have much free time at all. Luke's folks helped out sometimes, too, but they were getting up in their years, and Meredith didn't feel right about asking either of them to do a lot—especially with some of the heavier things that needed to be done. So with Jonah helping Meredith, she didn't have to call on anyone else too often.

Meredith enjoyed Jonah coming by; he was easy to talk to. She felt more comfortable in his presence than she had at first. He listened and seemed to understand the way she felt about things. At first, she'd been a bit uneasy about him doing things around the place to help out, but that was getting less awkward, especially as she grew in her pregnancy. Jonah had shared some things with her about his twin sister, Jean, and how it had been for her when she'd lost her first husband. He had tried to help her as much as possible and had been there to listen and offer support whenever she'd needed a shoulder to cry on. It seemed obvious to Meredith that Jonah was not only a good brother but also a friend she could count on.

Meredith's one concern, which was never far from her thoughts, was her financial situation. Her home-based business of making head coverings for Amish women was helping some, but it was hard to stretch her budget every month, even with the money her parents and Luke's folks sometimes insisted that she take. There had also been a charity auction in their community last month, and she'd been given some of the money from that to help with expenses. Every little bit helped, but how long would it last? Others in the community needed help, too, and Meredith wanted to be able to make it on her own.

She was glad Dad hadn't taken on another stand at the Crossroads market, like he'd talked about doing a few months ago. He worked hard enough as it was, and it was difficult for the family to have him gone so much. It was important for a father to spend time with his wife and children, not only for the family's sake but for his own, as well.

Thinking about fathers and their children caused Meredith to choke up. Her precious baby would never know his father. But she would make sure the little one knew all about Luke and what a wonderful husband he had been, and how she'd loved him so much. Meredith tried not to dwell on the past or reflect too much about the future. She didn't even want to think about how she would make it through the days ahead. It was best just to take one day at a time and trust the Lord to meet all of her needs.

Meredith's thoughts shifted to her sister Laurie. She'd been back from Florida for almost two months and still hadn't told their parents about Kevin. Meredith kept reminding Laurie that the longer she put it off, the harder it was going to be, and Laurie kept promising she would say something soon.

What is she waiting for? Meredith wondered. *It will be a lot worse if our folks hear the news from someone else.*

"Why don't we go outside and enjoy the sunshine for a bit?" Alma asked, joining Meredith at the screen door and interrupting her thoughts.

"I really should be at the sewing machine right now," Meredith replied, "but I guess I can do that after we've enjoyed the warmth of the sun for a while."

⌾

Philadelphia

As Susan made her rounds in ICU that morning, she felt a keen sense of disappointment. Eddie, her John Doe patient, had been moved to rehab two weeks ago, and she missed seeing him every day. As luck would have it, though, her sister, Anne, had been assigned as Eddie's physical therapist, so she saw him several times a week and always gave Susan a full report on how he was progressing. During supper last night, she'd told Susan that she'd been working with Eddie to regain the strength in his legs. He'd been confined to his bed for so many months, and even though they'd exercised his legs when he was in a coma, he'd been left unable to walk on his own.

Another therapist worked with Eddie vocally. Serious damage to his vocal cords had left him unable to speak for a time, but he was now talking again—although his voice sounded gravelly and hoarse and would probably always be that way. He was also receiving memory-training therapy, but so far Eddie's mind remained a blank.

I think I'll stop by the rehab center when I get off work today, Susan told herself. *I'd like to see for myself how Eddie is doing and let him know that I'm still praying for him.*

⌾

Eddie groaned and clicked the button to change the channel on the TV above his bed. One of the nurses had shown him how to work the remote, because he'd had a hard time trying to figure it out. The programs seemed strange to him, too—like he'd never seen them before. *Maybe I didn't have a TV,* he thought. *Or is that just another thing I've forgotten about?*

Susan, the nurse he'd had before they moved him for therapy, had said he'd been found in the bathroom of the bus depot in Philadelphia, wearing nothing but a pair of dirty blue jeans and a holey T-shirt. She'd also told him that he'd been beaten up pretty badly and might have died if he hadn't been found in time.

Eddie. The nurses all call me that, but they say it's not my real name. Who am I, really, and how did I end up in the hospital in such bad condition?

Eddie didn't remember anything at all about his life before waking up in the hospital. It was frustrating to have so many unanswered questions swimming around in his head, as if he'd just been born, knowing nothing at all.

What was I doing in the bus station? Was I traveling somewhere? he wondered. *Who beat me up, and why?* There was so much to figure out, and he didn't know how to piece any of it together. His head hurt when he tried to think. *If I could just remember who I am and what my life was like before coming here. Did I have a job in the city? If so, what did I do for a living? Was I married? Did I have children? Or was I some poor man on the street with no home or family of my own?*

"I'm hungry," Eddie murmured, breaking free from his troubling thoughts. He pushed his call button, but no one responded. He waited awhile and pushed it again. Still no reply.

He frowned. *Guess I'll get up and head down to the nurses' station.*

Holding on to the side rail, Eddie crawled out of bed. As soon as his feet hit the floor, a wave of dizziness and nausea washed over him. He'd been told that due to the severe head injury he'd sustained, he might have trouble with headaches and wooziness for quite some time. He stood still until his head quit swimming then took a step forward. The room started spinning again, and everything visible whirled into one. The TV blended in with the window, and then the window merged into the picture hanging on the wall. He closed his eyes to try to regain his balance, but his legs felt like rubber. Try as he might, Eddie couldn't walk on his own. Instead, he wobbled and dropped to the floor with a groan.

❧

Bird-in-Hand

I'm glad Elam's visiting his friend Joe today, Sadie thought as she hitched her horse, Daisy, to the buggy. *If he knew I was going over to confront Jonah about seeing Meredith, he'd probably tell me I shouldn't go and that it's none of my business what Jonah does.*

Sadie had wanted to pay a call on Jonah sooner but hadn't had the chance until today. The last week of April, she and Elam had gone to watch their granddaughter Mary Beth's end-of-the-year school program in Gratz. From there they'd made a trip to Wisconsin to see Elam's brother Sam, who had been in the hospital after suffering a stroke. They'd stayed until he was out of the hospital and had returned home only two days ago. After running into Meredith's mother at the grocery store yesterday and hearing that Jonah had continued going over to Meredith's on a regular basis, Sadie decided it was time to pay him a visit.

As Sadie headed down the road with her horse and buggy, she rehearsed what she would say to Jonah. She wouldn't beat around the bush or make light of the situation. She'd get right to the point and tell him in no uncertain words how she felt about things.

When Sadie arrived at the Millers' place, she stopped at the buggy shop, thinking Jonah would be working there. But then seeing a CLOSED sign in the shop window, she headed straight for the house.

Jonah's mother, Sarah, answered the door. "It's nice to see you, Sadie. Can I help you with something, or did you just drop by for a visit?" she asked.

"I came to see Jonah," Sadie replied stiffly. "I need to speak with him about something."

"Today is Jonah's day off, and he's out in the barn getting his horse ready because he'll be going fishing soon."

"Oh, I see. I'll go out there and speak to him then." Without waiting for Sarah's response, Sadie turned and hurried off toward the barn. She found Jonah about to lead his horse out of the stall.

"I need to speak with you," Sadie said, boldly stepping up to Jonah.

"About what?" he asked with a curious expression.

"I don't think it's right for you to be going over to Meredith's so much. It's only been a little over five months since our son Luke died, and Meredith is still quite vulnerable."

Jonah smiled, although it appeared to be forced. "I assure you, Sadie, Meredith and I are only friends, and actually, I'd be there for anyone who needed my help, not just your daughter-in-law."

"It's good to be helpful, but I think it would be best if you stop seeing Meredith."

Jonah's dark eyebrows pulled together. "Unless Meredith asks me to stop going over to her place, I'll continue to help out."

Sadie frowned deeply. She was not the least bit happy about this, but she didn't say anything more. She knew it wasn't right to hope that Meredith would continue struggling financially, but maybe once the baby came and Meredith was too busy to make head coverings, she'd be willing to move in with Sadie and Elam. She could either sell her house or put it up for rent. If Meredith was living with them, Sadie could help out with the baby, and then she'd be certain that Jonah wouldn't be coming around any longer.

⬥

As Jonah meandered along the stream a few miles from his folks' place, he thought about his unexpected visit with Sadie Stoltzfus. He couldn't figure out why she was so upset that he'd been helping Meredith. Couldn't she see that they were just friends?

But I wish it could be more, he admitted to himself. *I wish I could make her my wife. When enough time has passed, I'll tell Meredith how I feel. Maybe she'll come to care for me as much as I do her. I just don't want to rush her, that's all.*

Jonah hadn't told anyone yet, not even Dad, that he loved Meredith. Truth was, he'd fallen in love with her during the time they'd known each other in Florida. Maybe if he hadn't been too timid to tell her back then, she might not have married Luke. Jonah had lived with his mistake for many years. Working hard and keeping busy had helped, but it wasn't like coming home each evening to someone he loved—a wife who shared her life with him.

"Guess there's no point in thinkin' about the past," Jonah mumbled as he stopped beside a tall birch tree that was leaning slightly over the stream. He noticed half the roots from the tree were suspended out over the water, as if reaching for something to cling to. An empty space under the tree had washed out when the water was flowing high.

Jonah pushed against the tree, wondering how long it would stay upright. He figured someday it would end up lying across the stream, creating a natural bridge.

Purdy. . .purdy. . .purdy. . . Jonah looked up and spotted a cardinal sitting on a branch overhead. The music of the bird's singing blended with the gentle sound of green leaves blowing in the warm summer breeze.

Jonah hadn't felt like fishing, after all, so he'd left his pole in the buggy. He had secured Socks to a tree some distance away, and before they headed home, he would bring the horse down to the stream for a good long drink. For now, though, Jonah just wanted to relax and enjoy the beauty of nature. There was no doubt about it—God had created a beautiful world for man to enjoy. It was a shame some people took it for granted and never noticed what was right in front of them, free for their enjoyment.

Wanting to get more comfortable in the warm air, Jonah untucked his shirt to let it hang loosely and rolled up his sleeves. He then took a small box of raisins from his pocket. They tasted good and eased his hunger pangs just a bit.

He threw a few raisins into the water and watched as several minnows came from nowhere to nibble on the morsels as they slowly sank to the bottom of the stream. Jonah tossed in a few more raisins, drawing a huge cluster of the small silvery fish swimming around like they were waiting for another handout.

Leaning against the tree again, Jonah spotted a water snake slithering along and then going under the water's surface where all the fish were gathered.

The tree's roots suddenly gave way, and the tree fell toward the water. Jonah wasn't quick enough to catch himself, and as the tree crashed, his foot became wedged between two of the big roots. He struggled to free it, as the snake swam toward him.

Dear Lord, Jonah prayed, *help me to get out of here fast!*

CHAPTER 5

Philadelphia

When Anne entered the rehab floor and headed for Eddie's room, she whispered a prayer. "Dear Lord, I pray that things will go well with Eddie's therapy today, and help me to be an encouragement to him."

As soon as Anne stepped in her patient's room, she spotted him lying on the floor beside his bed. Relieved to see that he was conscious, although struggling to get up, she quickly squatted down beside him. "Eddie, what happened? Did you try to get out of bed by yourself?"

He nodded, offering her a guilty-looking grin. "I was hungry and thought I could walk down to the nurses' station and ask for something to eat. But the room started spinning, and the next thing I knew, I was flat on the floor."

Anne slipped her arms around his waist and helped him to stand. "You should have punched the call button for help," she said, assisting him back into the bed.

He frowned. "I tried that, but no one came."

"Well, you should have kept trying." She pulled the sheet up and tucked it under his chin. "I'll go see if I can get you something to snack on, and then we need to begin your therapy session."

Eddie's nose wrinkled as he raked his fingers through the ends of his white-blond hair. "What's the point in me learning how to walk on my own when I don't even know who I am? I'm pretty much worthless, and if I ever do get to leave this hospital, I'll probably have to go beg on the streets 'cause I don't even know what I can do to earn a living." He groaned. "Since I have no identification, who'd hire me anyways?"

"Let's take these issues one at a time," Anne said. "I'll be back in a few minutes with some food." She tapped him gently on the arm. "So please stay put."

Anne wasn't sure what else to say. If they knew who Eddie was, and he had a family to take care of him, he could begin life anew. But with no evidence of his identity and not even a glimpse of his lost memory, the poor man was like a ship without any water to stay afloat.

I wonder when Eddie's well enough to leave the hospital, if Grandma and Grandpa might consider taking him in, Anne thought. *They have a big house, with five bedrooms, two of which are vacant, so maybe they'd be charitable enough to let Eddie live there in exchange for him doing some chores around the place. Guess I'll wait to mention that until he's stronger and getting closer to being released.*

As Anne continued down the hall toward the nurses' station, she spotted Susan heading her way.

"I came to visit Eddie," Susan said eagerly. "I wanted to see how he's doing today."

"Well, he was determined enough to get some food that he tried to get out of bed by himself." Anne smiled, despite the seriousness of the situation. "That determination is what's going to help him get well—at least physically. I don't know what it's going to take to bring his memory back."

"Perhaps someone will say or do something that will jog his memory," Susan said with a hopeful expression. "And of course, I'll continue to pray for his full recovery."

Anne nodded. "Same here."

⁕

Strasburg, Pennsylvania

Luann King had been out shopping all morning and decided to stop at a sandwich shop for a bite of lunch before going home. Her mother was watching the little ones today, and sixteen-year-old Kendra was there to help out. Laurie and Philip were working at the Bird-in-Hand farmers' market in Bird-in-Hand today, so everyone in the family had something to do.

Luann smiled as she entered the restaurant. It was kind of nice to be out on her own for a while. She didn't get the opportunity to shop by herself that often, much less go out to lunch.

As Luann looked for a place to sit, she spotted a young couple seated at a table with their backs to her. They sat close to each other, with their heads almost touching, as though they were courting. The woman was dressed in Amish clothes, but the young man wore blue jeans and a white T-shirt. Luann figured he could be Amish and going through his time of *rumschpringe*. Or maybe he was English. If that was the case, it would no doubt sadden the young woman's family. Most Amish parents wanted their daughters to be courted by men who wouldn't sway them to leave their Amish way of life.

Luann slipped into a booth across the room, and as she turned to look for a waitress, her mouth dropped open. The young woman at the table across from her was Laurie!

Laurie looked at Luann at about the same time, and her jaw dropped slightly as her eyes widened. "Mom, wh—what are you doing here?" she asked, her face turning red with obvious embarrassment.

Luann rose to her feet and moved over to stand beside Laurie's table. "More to the point, what are *you* doing here? I thought you were supposed to be selling dolls at the farmers' market today."

"Well, I—" Laurie moistened her lips with the tip of her tongue. "I'm on my lunch break right now." She turned to the young man sitting beside her. "Uh, Mom, this is Kevin Byler."

Luann studied Kevin a few seconds then slowly nodded. She hadn't recognized him at first, but now she realized his folks lived just a mile or so down the road from them.

"It's nice to see you, Mrs. King." Kevin smiled and extended his hand.

Luann shook it briefly; then she turned to Laurie and said, "I'm going to the ladies' room. I'd like you to come with me."

Laurie hesitated but finally nodded. She smiled at Kevin and said, "I'll be back soon."

When they entered the restroom, Luann didn't mince any words. "Are you and Kevin seeing each other socially, Laurie?"

"Jah." Laurie dropped her gaze to the floor. "We've been going out for a few months."

"Why didn't you tell your daed and me about this?"

"I—I didn't want to hurt you."

Luann's lips tightened. "Oh, and you don't think I'm hurt right now, finding this out after the fact?"

Laurie placed her hand on Luann's arm. "I'm sorry, Mom. I know I should have said something sooner, but—"

"But you thought it'd be better to sneak around behind our backs?"

Laurie shook her head. "I knew you wouldn't approve, and I was going to tell you, but I just couldn't seem to find the right time, or the right way to say it. I wasn't sure how to explain things to you because I knew you'd be upset."

Luann narrowed her eyes. "Just how serious are you about Kevin?"

Laurie leaned on the counter by the sinks and drew in a quick breath. "I—I love him, Mom. He asked me to marry him, and I said I would."

Luann held her hands stiffly at her sides, fingers clenched until they dug into her palms. "We'll talk more about this at home, after your sisters and brothers have gone to bed."

∽⳩∾

Bird-in-Hand

Sweat beaded on Jonah's forehead as he struggled to get his foot free from the roots of the tree. Keeping his eye on the water snake, he felt relief when it swam off in the opposite direction, in pursuit of an unsuspecting minnow. The last thing he needed was to be eye-to-eye with a snake!

Jonah's ankle throbbed something awful, and he wondered if it might be broken. One thing he knew for sure: he needed to get his foot unstuck so he could take a look at it and find out how badly he'd been hurt.

Suddenly, an idea popped into his head. If he untied his boot he might be able to slip his foot out, and then he'd be free. It was shocking to Jonah to discover just how deep this particular spot was in the stream, because the water was now well over his chest. Standing on the bank earlier, he'd never imagined the water being more than a few feet deep.

"Talk about bad luck," Jonah mumbled, wondering how he had managed to get into this predicament. He leaned over and reached down until his fingers touched the laces on his boot. The water was very cold, not yet warmed since the return of summer. He could feel, but not see, his boot.

Jonah had never learned to swim that well, and he didn't like to put his face under water, but it would be much easier to see what he was doing if he got closer to the boot. He dreaded it, but realizing he had no other choice, Jonah knew he'd need to go into a sitting position. Taking in a deep breath, he let his body sink to the water's depth of five or so feet. Being under water brought back memories of the day he'd nearly drowned when he was a boy, and he almost panicked. Pinching his nose shut would have helped, but Jonah needed both hands to untie the wet laces. Feeling the cold water seep into his ears, he just wanted to get this over with.

The water had been clear before the tree fell, but now it was murky with sediment that had been kicked up from the stream's bottom. Under water, peering through the murkiness, Jonah could see parts of the tree root that held his foot securely, but he could barely make out his bootlaces.

Too bad that brave kid's not here to rescue me now, Jonah thought as he fumbled with his laces. He came up once for a breath of air then ducked his head under the muddy-colored water again. This time he was successful in getting his laces untied, and after wiggling his foot around a bit, he was finally able to pull it free from the boot.

Jonah hobbled onto the bank and winced when he tried to put weight on his bootless left foot. It was either broken or he'd sprained it pretty bad. He stood on his uninjured foot for a moment, shaking his head to one side, trying to get the water out that had clogged his right ear. Finally, after several attempts, he felt the now-warm liquid trickle down over his earlobe.

Using a broken tree limb as a sort of crutch, Jonah hobbled over to the tree where he'd secured his horse. After untying Socks, he climbed into the buggy and took up the reins. Once he got out to the highway, Socks took off like a shot. It was almost as if he knew Jonah needed to get help, and this was one time Jonah didn't care if the spirited horse wanted to run, because he had to get home as soon as he could!

<hr>

"Did Jonah say what time he'd be home?" Sarah asked her husband, Raymond, as they sat down at the kitchen table for lunch.

Raymond shrugged his shoulders. "Just said he was going fishin', so guess it all depends on how well things go. I'm sure he'll be home before supper, though."

They bowed their heads for silent prayer, and then Sarah passed Raymond the potato salad she'd made. "Sadie Stoltzfus came by here this morning. Said she wanted to speak with Jonah."

"Oh, really? What about?"

"I don't know. Whatever it was, it must have been serious, because she looked quite agitated." Sarah took a tuna sandwich then handed the plate to Raymond. "You don't suppose it had anything to do with Meredith, do you?"

He reached for a sandwich and took a bite. "Beats me. What makes you think that, anyways?" he asked.

"Well, our son has been helping Meredith quite a bit lately, and since Meredith's husband was Sadie's son, she might not like it."

"Why would she care who helps Meredith?"

"She might be worried that Jonah has a personal interest in Meredith." Sadie took a few potato chips from the bowl in front of her then passed it on to Raymond.

"Would that be so terrible?" he questioned, his eyebrows lifting slightly.

"I don't think so, but Sadie might. She may not have come to terms with Luke's death yet. The idea of Jonah or any other man taking her son's place in Meredith's life might be too painful for her."

Raymond rubbed the bridge of his nose, looking at her with a thoughtful expression. "I suppose you might be right about that. Even so, it's Meredith's life, not Sadie's or anyone else's, so she ought to be free to begin her life again with the man of her choice, when the time is right."

Sarah nodded. "I totally agree."

Just then, the back door swung open, and Jonah, soaking wet and dripping water all over the floor, hobbled into the kitchen, wearing only one boot.

"What happened to you?" Sarah gasped, jumping out of her chair.

"A tree fell into the stream, and I got my left foot caught in its roots." Jonah grabbed the back of a chair for support and groaned. "My ankle's really swollen, and I either broke it or sprained it badly."

"You'd best get out of those wet clothes," Sarah said, heading to get the clothes basket. "And while you're daed's helping you with that, I'll go out to the phone shack and call the doctor—the one in the area who makes house calls to the Amish." She paused at the back door and pointed to a spot on Jonah's chest where his shirt hung open. "Ach, Jonah! Is that a leech?"

CHAPTER 6

"I don't like being laid up like this and unable to help with things," Jonah mumbled as he hobbled across the kitchen to the breakfast table. It had been two weeks since he'd broken his ankle, and even though he wore a walking cast, he couldn't do many things. Helping Dad paint the barn was out of the question right now. And he hadn't been able to go over to Meredith's and help with any chores. He missed their visits and the good food they shared whenever he'd been invited to stay for a meal. He longed to see Meredith's pretty face and enjoy their conversation.

"Don't be so impatient, Son." Mom gave Jonah's arm a tender squeeze. "You just need to stay off that foot as much as you can and give your ankle a chance to heal."

Dad bobbed his head. "Your *mamm*'s right. I can either paint the barn later this summer or I'll ask someone else to help me get it done."

"Who are you gonna ask?" Jonah reached for a piece of toast and slathered it with Mom's tasty homemade strawberry jam.

Dad shrugged. "Don't know yet. Guess I could ask my friend Harvey if his sons, Mahlon and Amos, might be available to help."

Jonah shook his head while he used his finger to wipe up some jam that had dripped onto his plate. "I think you should wait till I can help you." He paused to lick the jam from his finger and smacked his lips. "Those two boys probably don't know much about painting. They're farmers, Dad."

Dad took a drink of coffee. "Maybe you're right. We can wait and paint the barn sometime in August."

"If you want to do it now, maybe I could sit on something and at least help to paint the bottom part of the barn," Jonah said. "I'd be off my feet, but I'd have something meaningful to do."

"I know how bad you want to help out around here, but it's probably best if you just keep resting that foot. There's nothin' critical that needs to be done, and the barn can wait a few more weeks," Dad assured him.

"Well, one thing I know for sure," Jonah said, reaching for his cup of coffee, "I'm going to sit on a stool and barbecue some steaks for supper this evening."

Mom grinned widely. "That sounds *wunderbaar*, Jonah. I'll make cucumber and pasta salads to go with the meat. There's nothing like nice cold salads for a meal during the hot summer months."

"And for dessert, I'll make a batch of homemade ice cream," Dad put in. "Is there any particular flavor you'd like?" he asked, looking at Jonah.

"Anything but orange," Jonah said, shaking his head. "Don't think I could tolerate that."

Mom chuckled. "You've always had an aversion to orange. Even when you were a boppli and I tried giving you orange juice, you'd make a face and spit the juice right out."

Dad chuckled. "I remember once when you and Jean were toddlers, you snitched her little pink sippy-cup, probably thinking it had milk it in, and boy, did you get a surprise when you took a drink."

"It wasn't so funny when he spit the juice all over Jean's new dress, and we ended up being late for church because I had to take the time out to change her clothes." Mom looked at Jonah and wrinkled her nose. "After that, you smelled everything you ate and drank to be sure it wasn't flavored with orange."

Jonah chuckled, despite his melancholy mood. It felt good to be living here in Pennsylvania with his folks, where they could enjoy being together and reminisce about the past. But he still wished he hadn't injured his ankle so he could do more to help them. *Meredith, too,* he thought once again. *I can't wait till I'm able to pay her another visit and offer to do some needed chores.*

⬥

"I'm sorry Jonah Miller broke his ankle," Sadie said to Elam as he sat at the table, reading the latest issue of *The Connection* magazine, while she cleared the breakfast dishes. "One good thing came out of it, though."

He looked up. "And what would that be?"

"Jonah's not going over to see Meredith right now."

"No, and you've made sure that we checked on her often, so that ought to make you happy."

Sadie poured Elam a second cup of coffee. "I'm always happy to see Meredith, but are you trying to make some particular point?"

He placed the magazine on the table and looked directly at her. "I just think you're overly *bekimmere* about Meredith."

"I have every right to be concerned. She's our daughter-in-law, for goodness' sake."

"That's true, but she's not our flesh and blood *dechder*, and as hard as this is to say, she's not married to our son any longer." Elam leveled Sadie with a stern look. "I think it's time you realize that Meredith has her own life to live, and you're not in control of her destiny."

Sadie recoiled. "I'm not trying to control her destiny. I just think Jonah, who isn't even part of the family, should not be doing things for her that we, as well as Meredith's family, ought to be doing."

"It's not our place to decide who should or shouldn't help Meredith. We should be grateful that not all the burden falls on just one person and that Jonah's willing to help her out."

Sadie set the coffeepot down and thumped the table. "You might think otherwise if Meredith ends up marrying Jonah."

Elam turned his hands palms-up. "If she does, she does. That will be her choice, not ours."

"So are you saying that you'd be okay with it if Meredith should marry Jonah?"

Elam gave a quick nod; then he pushed his chair away from the table, grabbed his straw hat from the wall peg across the room, and headed out the door.

Tears welled in Sadie's eyes. *I just can't bear the thought of Meredith becoming the wife of another man. Oh, I hope it doesn't come to that.*

⁂

"It sure is a hot, humid day," Meredith commented to Laurie as they sat on the porch, drinking iced tea with lemon. They'd just gotten home from her eighth and final childbirth class. All the other sessions had been easy to get through: learning the breathing exercises and discovering each month how big the baby was as it grew inside of her; techniques for coping with pain; and how the partner could help during labor. This final class was the most intense and explained the birth in detail. Meredith didn't want to let on, but it made her a bit nervous to think about the pain she would experience and how long her labor might last. She knew that some women, like her friend Dorine, experienced a long labor with their first child.

I won't dwell on it, Meredith told herself. *I'll just wait and see how it all goes.*

She raised the drink to her face, enjoying the cool moisture of the glass as it touched her flushed cheek. "Thank goodness it was air-conditioned at the midwife's clinic," she said to her sister.

"That's for sure." Laurie lifted her dark apron and fanned her face with the edge of it. "It's times like this when I wish we had air-conditioning like Kevin has in his car."

"Speaking of Kevin, have Dad and Mom said anything more about you going out with him?"

Laurie nodded. "I think they've finally accepted it, but I know they were hoping I'd fall in love with an Amish man and join the church." She sighed. "Since Kevin and his parents attend a more modern Mennonite church and don't use horses and buggies for transportation, Mom and Dad are concerned that I'll succumb to worldly ways."

"Has Kevin considered joining the Amish church?" Meredith questioned.

"No. If he did that, he wouldn't be able to drive his car anymore, and I'm sure he'd have a hard time giving that up."

"But if he loves you enough, he should be willing to give up anything." Meredith's thoughts went quickly to Luke. He'd owned a car during his running-around years but had gladly given it up when it was time to join the church and later get married.

"It's not just his car he'd have to give up," Laurie said. "Kevin wants to become a missionary, and I want that, too. I think it'd be a real adventure, not to mention an opportunity to help others and tell them about the Lord."

Meredith's eyes widened. "You mean move away to some foreign country?"

Laurie nodded. "Kevin has gone on some work-and-witness trips with a group from his church, and he feels that mission work is what God's calling him to do."

"Do Mom and Dad know about this?" Meredith asked.

"Jah. I told them last evening when I stopped by the house to get some clean clothes before I came here to spend the night."

"What'd they say?"

"Mom was pretty upset, but Dad took it fairly well. Said I should pray about it—make sure I felt the same call on my life as Kevin does before I commit to marrying him."

Meredith nodded. "I think that was sound advice." She placed her hands against her ever-growing stomach and smiled. "I've already begun praying for my boppli's future—that he or she will make wise choices and someday find the right spouse."

"Your little one will be making an appearance sometime soon." Laurie reached over and placed her hand next to Meredith's. "Are you feeling *naerfich* about giving birth?"

"I'm a little nervous," Meredith admitted. "The childbirth classes we've taken have been a big help in preparing me for what to do and what to expect. And I must say, I'm glad this morning was the last session, because it means my time is getting close." She sighed deeply. "I just wish my boppli's daed could be here to witness the birth of our child."

The babe kicked, as if in response to what Meredith had just said. "Feel this," she said, taking hold of Laurie's hand and placing it against her stomach. "I do believe my little one's as anxious to make his appearance as I am for him to get here."

⁂

Philadelphia

"It's a warm day, isn't it, Eddie?" Anne asked as the two of them sat on a bench on the hospital grounds.

He gave a slow nod. "But it feels good to be outside in the fresh air."

Anne smiled. "Since part of your therapy is getting you back on your feet, walking and spending time outdoors is a good thing."

Eddie glanced around and breathed in deeply. Humid as it was, the air smelled so refreshing—not like it was inside the facility. Oh, it was nice and comfortable in the rehab center, and so clean you could probably eat off the floors, but he didn't enjoy the medicinal odors in some parts of the hospital.

Outside where they sat, flowers and bushes were in full bloom, and a small pond a short distance away reflected the beauty of their surroundings. Eddie could see several goldfish swimming around in the shaded part of the pond, and he wished he could join them in the nice cool water. It would be better than sitting here doing nothing at all and knowing that he didn't have anything to look forward to when they went back inside. It was lonely in his room, and he felt frustrated seeing other patients in rehab receiving visits from family members. Eddie had no family to encourage him, but he was thankful for Anne and her sister, Susan, who continually offered their support. He enjoyed Susan's chatter when she came to visit, which wasn't often enough to suit him. Of course, Eddie realized that she kept busy with her nursing duties, but he wished she could come to see him every day. Anne was nice, too, but she didn't talk to him as much as Susan did, and she seemed a little older and more serious about life than her sister.

"See that birdhouse over there?" Anne said, pointing.

Eddie nodded.

"A pair of bluebirds raised their babies in it last summer, and I've been watching to see if they'd return to their little home again this year."

Eddie just kept staring at the fish. They really had no place to go, except around and around the circumference of the pond. *Kind of like me,* he thought regrettably. *I have nowhere to go but here.*

"Well, would you look at those two?" Anne giggled.

Eddie looked toward a big rock that was nestled in one of the flower beds. Two wrens in front of the rock were taking turns trying to snatch a scrap of food away from each other. It looked like they'd found a piece of bread crust, and it was too big for either one of the birds to fly away with it. One of the birds would steal it from the other and run a few feet away from the one competing. Then the other wren did the same, with neither of them wanting to give up the precious morsel they'd found. This rivalry between the two little birds went on for several minutes until the scrap of bread was small enough for one bird to fly away with it. Not far behind, was the other wren, flying close to its competitor's tail.

Eddie smiled, until another thought popped into his mind. "Who's gonna pay for all my hospital bills?" he asked, turning to look at Anne. "I have no money."

Anne placed her hand gently on his arm. "You don't need to worry about that, Eddie. The hospital will absorb your expenses, just like they do with others in your situation."

Eddie sat, trying to digest that piece of information. It didn't seem right for him not to pay. If he knew who he was, maybe there'd be a relative who'd be willing to help out with his expenses. If he could just remember something—anything at all, it would be better than the way things were right now. All he had was a big blank hole in his life that might never be filled with memories from the past. His future looked pretty bleak and frightening.

CHAPTER 7

Bird-in-Hand

It was the first Monday of July, and as Meredith took a seat in the hickory rocker on her front porch, she looked up at the gray clouds overhead and yawned. She'd had a hard time sleeping last night, and tonight would probably be the same, because the air was warm and thick with moisture. In this kind of weather, a person didn't have to do much of anything to break out in a sweat.

Alma was inside, taking a nap, and would be here with Meredith until Laurie got home this evening. Meredith had gotten used to having either her sister or Alma staying with her. She appreciated their help, and it was nice to have someone other than Fritz to talk to. Eventually, though, that would come to an end. Laurie would no doubt marry Kevin, and Alma was getting up in years. Besides, Meredith wanted to be on her own once the baby came; although there would be some chores she'd still need help with.

Maybe Jonah will continue to help out once he gets his cast off, Meredith thought. Between Jonah, Dad, and Luke's father coming by to do the outside chores, Meredith was sure she could manage the inside things on her own.

She glanced at the garden, overflowing with produce. *I really should pick some tomatoes and cucumbers.* It would be nice to have them along with the fried chicken and pasta salad Alma said she would fix for supper.

Meredith bent to pick up the wicker basket on the porch and winced when a sharp pain shot through her back. She stood, drawing in a deep breath and releasing it slowly. It would be a relief when the baby came and she could do things easily again. Based on what she'd learned about the final weeks of pregnancy at the childbirth classes, it wouldn't be long now.

When the pain subsided, Meredith headed for the garden. She was tempted to get on her knees to pick the beans but was afraid she might not be able get back up on her own. Placing the basket on the ground, she leaned over the best she could and started picking.

Meredith had only pulled a few beans from the vine when her friend Dorine Yoder rode in on her scooter.

"Wie geht's?" Dorine asked, parking the scooter near the porch.

"I'm doing okay," Meredith replied, making no mention of her painful back. There was no point in complaining about it. "What brings you by on this hot afternoon, and where are your *kinner?*"

"Merle and Cathy are with my mamm." Dorine smiled. "And since the children are well occupied, I decided to come over here and see how you're doing."

"I'd be better if this weather would cool down some," Meredith said. "Even standing still makes me sweat."

Dorine wiped the perspiration from her forehead. "I know what you mean. Unfortunately, we still have over two months until fall's officially here, and we could have hot, humid weather even into September."

"I know." Meredith blew out a puff of air. "The heat probably won't bother me so much once the boppli is born. All this heat is beginning to get to me, though. I think the dog days of summer are definitely upon us."

"Which is why you shouldn't be out here in the hot sun." Dorine picked up the basket of beans and motioned to the porch. "Now go sit and rest while I finish picking these for you."

Meredith didn't argue. She was more than ready to return to her seat on the porch. "Danki for being willing to help," she said, giving Dorine a hug.

Dorine gently patted Meredith's back. "That's what friends are for, you know."

As Meredith made her way back to the porch, she thanked God for the wonderful friendship she and Dorine shared. They'd been close for several years, and Meredith had always enjoyed Dorine's easygoing ways and pleasant company.

Philadelphia

"How'd things go with Eddie today?" Susan asked her sister as they rode home from the hospital that afternoon.

"He's progressing," Anne replied. "What he seems to enjoy most is the therapy walks outside, getting fresh air, and especially sitting at the nature gardens. I think sometime within the next few weeks he might be strong enough to be seen as an outpatient. Of course, that will be up to his attending physician."

Susan felt immediate concern. "Where will Eddie go? He doesn't have a house, a job, or any family to go home to. The poor man doesn't even know who he is."

"You've formed an attachment to him, haven't you?" Anne asked, glancing over at Susan.

"I'm concerned, if that's what you mean."

"I think it goes deeper than that." Anne tapped the steering wheel a couple of times. "I believe you've formed an emotional attachment to Eddie."

Susan sat a few seconds; then she finally nodded. "Okay, yeah; I guess maybe I have. He seems like a really nice person, and it saddens me to think he may never know who his family is or be able to contact them. It's hard not being able to be there for him as much as I'd like to."

"I understand. It saddens me as well that he's in such a predicament." Anne turned her blinker on to change lanes. "What would you think about us asking Grandpa and Grandma if they'd be willing to take Eddie into their home in exchange for him doing some work around the place?"

"Are you kidding me? That would be great, if they're willing. But how would Eddie get to and from the hospital for his therapy sessions?" Susan questioned.

"If any of the sessions should fall on your day off, maybe you could take him to the hospital, or we could see if Grandpa would be willing."

Susan smiled. "I like that idea, and if I know Grandma and Grandpa, they'll be happy to take Eddie in. I can already imagine Grandma's eagerness. You know how she is. The more people she can cook for, the better she likes it."

"Great. We can talk to them about it as soon as we get home."

❧

Darby

Norma Bailey hummed as she sliced a hefty beefsteak tomato for the BLTs they would have for supper. It was a warm summer evening—too hot to heat up the kitchen with the oven. Anne and Susan would be getting home from work soon, and then they'd eat outside under the shade of the maple tree while they visited about their day and made plans for the weekend.

Norma had talked to her friend, Mary Hagen, today, and she was looking forward to following through on the invitation they'd been given to visit the Hagens' home for a meal after church this coming Sunday. The best part was that Mary and Ben's grandson Brian would be there. Norma had been hoping Susan would get the chance to meet Brian while he was visiting his grandparents this summer, and this looked like the perfect opportunity.

She smiled and set the plate of tomatoes aside. If the young couple should hit it off, maybe Brian would decide to stay in the area permanently. *And maybe,* Norma thought, feeling hope well in her chest, *at least one of our granddaughters will get married and give Henry and me some great-grandchildren.*

"Is there anything I can do to help you, Norma?" Henry asked when he entered the kitchen a few minutes later. "I got the picnic table wiped off, so that much is done." He chuckled. "And you should have heard George out there, chattering away at me. I think he knows we'll be eating outside this evening."

George was a squirrel that for the last couple of years had become almost tame around Norma and Henry. They'd noticed how every time they were in the backyard working or eating at the picnic table, this curious little squirrel would appear and patiently sit and watch until they went back inside. Norma and Henry had started talking to the squirrel and tried not to pose a threat to it. Of course, it helped that Henry always had some sort of a snack in his pocket that he used, hoping to entice the little gray critter each time he went outside. One day the squirrel walked right up to Henry and took the morsel gently out of his hand. From that time on, little George became their outdoor pet.

"Yes, I'm sure George will be waiting nearby for a handout," Norma said, smiling. Then she motioned to the toaster. "If you'd like to toast the bread for the sandwiches, I'll start frying the bacon. Oh, would you also open that new loaf of bread? There's only a few slices left in the other package, and we'll share those with George."

"Sure, I can do that." Henry reached around Norma, snatched a tomato slice, and popped it into his mouth. "Mmm. . .my garden has been producing some delicious tomatoes this year, don't ya think? Look how meaty these are," he said, pausing to wipe the juice dripping down his chin. "And there are hardly any seeds in them, either."

She nodded. "But if you keep eating the tomato slices, I'll have to cut up some more."

He chuckled. "That's okay. There's plenty more where these babies came from."

"I know that." Norma paused, using a napkin to dab at the spot where some tomato juice had dribbled onto her husband's shirt. "I'd just like to have everything ready when the girls get home."

"What else are we having besides BLTs?" he asked.

"I made a macaroni salad and added some shrimp and a little crabmeat."

He smacked his lips. "Always did like a good seafood salad."

As Henry took care of toasting the bread and Norma fried the bacon, they discussed the garden, the weather, and their friends from church.

"I sure hope Susan and Anne will join us at the Hagens' for dinner on Sunday," Norma said, turning off the stove after the bacon was nice and crispy.

"I'm sure they will if they haven't made other plans," Henry said.

Sponging up some of the bacon grease that had splattered on the stove, Norma was about to bring up the topic of Susan meeting Brian, but she changed her mind. Henry would probably accuse her of trying to play match-maker again, and she didn't want any lectures from him. She'd just have to wait and see how things went. She'd like nothing more than to see her grand-daughters find someone special to spend the rest of their lives with. Norma knew, deep down, that it wasn't up to her, but she couldn't help hoping Susan and Anne would one day have a wonderful marriage like she and Henry had. *Well,* Norma reasoned, *it doesn't hurt for me to hope.*

Anne and Susan arrived home just as Norma finished putting the sand-wiches together. "Oh good, you're right on time, because supper's ready," Norma said, turning to smile at her granddaughters. "And we're going to eat our meal in the backyard this evening."

Susan grinned. "That's good, 'cause I'm more than ready to eat."

"Me, too," Anne agreed as she and Susan washed up at the kitchen sink. "I'm really glad we're eating outside. After being cooped up in rehab all day, I'm in need of some fresh air and sunshine. The only time I get to go outside is during my short breaks or when I'm walking with Eddie for his therapy."

"Well, let's get started then," Norma said. "If you two would like to carry the macaroni salad and pitcher of lemonade out to the picnic table, I'll bring the tray with paper plates, silverware, and sandwiches."

"I'll grab a bag of chips and the pieces of bread for little George," Henry said, winking at the girls.

When they were all seated around the picnic table, Henry led in prayer. "Dear heavenly Father," he said, "we thank You for the delicious meal set before us and for the hands that prepared it. We also want to give thanks for the beautiful warm weather we've had so far this summer, and for the many blessings You've bestowed upon us. Amen." He opened his eyes and smiled. Grabbing a sandwich, he announced with a twinkle in his eyes, "Let's dig in!"

As they ate in their pleasant backyard, a chorus of birds sang overhead, and several butterflies flitted from one flower to another. The conversation was mostly centered around Anne and Susan, and how things had gone for them at the hospital that day.

"It was even busier than usual in ICU," Susan said. "A couple of new patients were brought in this morning, and we were shorthanded besides, with one nurse out sick and another on vacation."

"Things were pretty crazy in rehab, too," Anne interjected.

"How's that Eddie fellow doing?" Henry asked.

"He's making some headway with everything except his memory," Anne replied, before taking a drink of lemonade.

"Speaking of Eddie," Susan quickly said, "if he keeps progressing, he should be well enough to be released from the hospital in a few weeks. Only trouble is, he has no place to go, so he'll probably have to stay on, like so many other patients do when they have no home or family."

Henry slowly shook his head. "I read an article awhile back about that very thing. Guess the hospitals can't simply throw someone out in the street when they're well and have no place to go. So they often keep them there until some other arrangements can be made. Of course, that means the hospital must absorb the cost of the patient's care."

"That's too bad," Norma said. "It's a shame to think about all the people right here in our state who are homeless."

"Susan and I were talking about Eddie on the way home." Anne looked first at Henry and then Norma. "We were wondering if you two might consider letting him stay here in exchange for whatever work you might want to have done."

Henry sat, rubbing his chin, but it wasn't long before Norma tapped his arm and said, "I think that's an excellent idea. Maybe Eddie can help you paint the outside of the house."

"I don't think he should do anything too strenuous," Anne was quick to say. "At least not until he's a bit stronger."

"Oh, you're right, of course. Maybe at first he could just do some light chores—or help with some yard work." Norma nudged Henry's arm again. "What do you think? Should we let Eddie stay with us—at least until he gets his memory back and is able to move out on his own?"

Henry sat quietly for several more seconds then finally nodded. "If it doesn't work out, though, we'll have to find him a place at the homeless shelter."

CHAPTER 8

Bird-in-Hand

Meredith shifted on the backless wooden bench where she'd taken a seat almost three hours ago in Deacon Raber's barn. Her back hurt something awful, and no matter how hard she tried, she couldn't seem to find a comfortable position. She glanced over at Laurie, sitting straight on the bench beside her, with her hands clasped in her lap. She didn't look uncomfortable at all.

I wonder how many more times I'll get to sit beside my sister like this in church? Meredith wondered. *If Laurie marries Kevin Byler and they move to some foreign country, I may never see her again.*

A cramping sensation gripped Meredith's stomach, causing her thoughts to redirect. *Maybe I should have stayed home from church this morning.* Due to the back pain and a few stomach cramps that had finally gone away last night, she hadn't slept well. She'd had another dream about Luke, too, which had woken her around four o'clock this morning. It was hard to believe he'd been gone nearly six months already, yet there were times when it seemed like only yesterday that they'd said their goodbyes on the porch.

Will the pain of losing Luke lessen or increase after the boppli is born? Meredith asked herself as she reached around and placed her hands on the lower part of her back. One thing for sure: she'd be glad when the baby arrived, for the heat and humidity of summer was really getting to her. That, coupled with her top-heavy stomach and inability to do many things, made her feel cross at times.

When Mom had dropped by for a visit the other day, she had told Meredith that she'd felt irritable and unproductive with each of her pregnancies that had occurred during the heat of summer. While Mom was there, she'd also lectured Meredith on the importance of getting plenty of rest and staying hydrated. Meredith was drinking lots of water, but it was hard to rest when she felt so miserable and couldn't find a comfortable position. If this unrelenting backache didn't ease by evening, she might have to consider sleeping in one of the recliners in her living room.

Meredith shifted on the bench once more and glanced across the room to where the men and boys sat. She spotted Jonah and noticed that he seemed to be staring at her. Hoping no one else had seen, she gave him a brief nod then quickly looked away. It was one thing for Jonah to drop by her house on occasion, to do a few chores, but she didn't want anyone here to get the idea that she might be interested in him.

Am I interested? she asked herself. *If Jonah were to ask me to marry him after my year of mourning is up, what would I say? I enjoy his company, and I'm sure he'd be a good daed to my boppli, but is that enough? Could I ever feel the kind of love in my heart for Jonah that I've felt for Luke ever since we first became serious about each other and got engaged? Down the road things might change, but right now, I'm thinking probably not.*

❧

When their church service concluded, Jonah was tempted to seek Meredith out but thought better of it. From the way she looked during the service, she didn't feel very well. She appeared to be tired and seemed fidgety, like she couldn't find a comfortable position on the bench. A couple of times he'd noticed Meredith placing her hands against her lower back, as if to support it. He could only imagine how uncomfortable that hard wooden bench must be for a woman so far along in her pregnancy—especially sitting there for three whole hours.

If he saw a chance to speak to her when nobody else was around, he would take it. Otherwise, to avoid scrutiny, visiting with Meredith would have to wait until he could stop by her house again. It didn't help that he still had his foot in the immobility boot and couldn't do much to help with any chores, but he would be getting the boot off soon and would be glad to get back to doing things again.

Jonah was thankful he'd been blessed with loving, understanding parents. Not everyone, Amish or English, could say the same.

After the noon meal, Jonah noticed Meredith and her sister head for their buggy. They were obviously going home, and he resigned himself to the fact that he wouldn't get the chance to speak with her today.

Sure wish it was me taking Meredith home instead of Laurie, he thought ruefully. *I wonder if I'll ever be able to tell Meredith how I feel about her. If I did, what would she say?*

❦

Philadelphia

As Susan headed down the hall toward Eddie's room in the rehab wing of the hospital, she thought about everything the poor man had been through over the past six months. From what Anne had told her, Eddie worked hard in therapy, consistently striving to improve his physical abilities. She credited his progress to a positive attitude and persistence, whereas many patients would have given up by now.

Anxious to talk with Eddie on her day off about the possibility of moving to Grandma and Grandpa's, she'd decided to visit right after church. Besides, she'd learned that Brian, the Hagens' grandson, would be at lunch this afternoon, which made her suspect that Grandma was up to her old matchmaking tricks.

Susan wasn't having any of that, so as soon as the service had ended, she'd told Grandma that she was going to the hospital to see Eddie. She could tell by Grandma's frown that she wasn't happy about it, but at least she hadn't put up a fuss. Maybe she'd changed her strategy and had decided that Anne and Brian would make a better match, because she seemed quite happy when Anne said she'd be pleased to join them at the Hagens' house for lunch. Either way, Susan was glad she'd had an excuse to duck out.

When Susan got to Eddie's room, he wasn't there. She checked at the nurses' station and was told that Eddie had taken a walk. Thinking he might be in the garden area outside, Susan headed in that direction.

When she stepped into the courtyard, she spotted Eddie sitting on a bench, with a fluffy white kitten in his lap. He looked like a cute little boy, content and relaxed as he gently stroked the kitten's head.

"I see you've made a new friend," Susan said, taking a seat beside Eddie.

His beautiful turquoise eyes sparkled as he grinned. "I heard some meowing in the bushes, and when I went to take a look, she leaped right out and started pawing at my leg, like she wanted me to pick her up. So I did."

Susan smiled. It was refreshing to meet a man with such a tender spirit. She wondered if he'd ever had any pets of his own. If he had, he'd probably treated them with the same gentleness he was using on this kitten right now, as it purred and rubbed its small head against Eddie's hand. The kitten was definitely content lying there in his lap.

They visited about the warm, sticky weather; then Eddie told Susan about his latest physical therapy session in a jetted spa tub. He mentioned that he enjoyed being in the water and felt like he was getting stronger every day.

"I'm glad. I know it's taken a long time and lots of patience, but it's been worth the effort, don't you think?"

He nodded. "I'm hoping that as my body becomes stronger my brain will heal, as well. If I could just figure out who I am, I could leave this hospital soon."

"Has Anne said anything to you about moving to our grandparents' home?" Susan asked.

"Yes, she did, and I'm glad they're agreeable, but now that I've had some time to think about it, I'm not sure it's such a good idea."

"How come?"

"For one thing, I have no money and wouldn't be able to pay them any room and board."

"You'll earn your keep by helping out with some chores."

"But why would they want to take a total stranger into their home? For all they know, I might be a terrible person."

"Do you think you're a terrible person, Eddie?" Susan questioned.

He shook his head. "I don't feel like I am, but since I can't remember anything about my past, guess I could have done some terrible things."

"I doubt it," she said, reaching over to stroke the kitten's head. "You're kind and gentle, even with this little stray kitten, so I'm thinking you've always been like that."

Eddie sat quietly for several minutes, then he released a soft moan.

"What's wrong? Are you in pain?" she asked, feeling concern.

"Not here," he said, touching his head. "But here." He placed his hand over his heart. "I've been having nightmares lately where I see a woman holding her arms out to me, but she has no face." He looked at Susan, and his beautiful turquoise eyes seemed to penetrate her soul. "I know it wasn't you I was dreaming about, 'cause if it had been, I'm sure I'd have seen your pretty face."

A rush of heat spread over Susan's cheeks. Was Eddie flirting with her? Did she want him to? "Thanks for the compliment," she murmured. Knowing she needed to get back to the subject of where he would stay, she quickly said, "You know, Eddie, if you take a room at my grandparents' place, we'll see each other more, because Anne and I live there, too."

Eddie's face brightened. "You do?"

She nodded. "We've been with Grandma and Grandpa ever since our folks were killed in a car crash when we were girls."

Deep wrinkles formed across his forehead. "I'm sorry to hear about your folks, but I think your grandpa and grandma must have done a good job raising you 'cause you and your sister are the nicest women I've ever known." He dropped his gaze, and his shoulders slumped. "Course, I'm not sure how many women I've known before."

She gave his shoulder a gentle squeeze. "So, how about it, Eddie? Are you willing to stay at my grandparents' house when the doctor releases you as an outpatient?"

He nodded slowly, while stroking the kitten's head. "If your grandparents are anything like you and Anne, then I'm sure I'll like it there."

<hr />

Bird-in-Hand

"Are you okay?" Laurie asked Meredith as they rode in the buggy toward Meredith's home. "You look downright miserable today."

"My back hurts really bad, and I've been having twinges all morning." Meredith touched her stomach. "I'll sure be glad when the boppli is born."

Laurie's eyes widened as she turned to look at Meredith. "You're not in labor, I hope."

Meredith shook her head and flinched when the buggy hit a bump in the road. "At least, I don't think I am."

"How bad is the pain? Should we turn around and head back so you can talk to Mom about this?"

"No, I don't think it's anything to worry about. I'm not due for a couple more weeks, and most first-time mothers that I know have been late, not early, giving birth."

"But everyone's different," Laurie said, clucking to the horse to get him moving faster. "Remember what they said at the last childbirth class? Those back pains you're having could be labor pains, after all."

"I suppose, but—" Meredith grimaced. "Oh, oh."

"What's wrong Meredith?" Laurie's voice held a note of panic.

"My water just broke, and. . ." Meredith winced. "I—I think the boppli wants to be born today, not two weeks from now."

"Hang on while I look for the nearest phone shack so I can call for help."

Another pain came, this one harder than the last. "You'd better pull over, Laurie. I can't believe it, but it's happening so fast." Meredith clenched her fingers until they dug into her palms. "I think I may have been in labor during the night and didn't even realize it."

"Well, you can't have the boppli until we get you some help, 'cause I can't help you birth the baby." Laurie's voice shook, and so did her hands.

"Jah, you can," Meredith said, working to keep her own voice calm. She tried to think of that verse of scripture she'd memorized awhile back. It was something about God giving peace, and not being afraid.

Oh yes, now I remember. John 14:27. "Peace I leave with you, my peace I give unto you: not as the world giveth, give I unto you. Let not your heart be troubled, neither let it be afraid." If she kept her focus on that, she wouldn't feel so frightened.

She turned to Laurie and quoted the verse aloud. Then she said, "You've gone with me to all the birthing classes, and the last one we attended was all about the birth, so you know what to do. Just try not to be afraid." She took her sister's hand and gave it a squeeze. "We can get through this together."

Laurie shook her head vigorously, as though she hadn't heard a word Meredith said. "No, I don't want to do it, Meredith. I'm terribly frightened I'll do something to mess up. All I know is how to help you through the birthing process by reminding you how to breathe and coaching you along. I can't deliver the boppli, Meredith. I'd be too naerfich."

Another pain came, harder than the last, and Meredith shouted, "Pull over, Laurie—right now!" Breathing deeply, she held on to the edge of her seat. "This boppli is coming, whether you like it or not!"

A REVELATION IN AUTUMN

In thee, O Lord, do I put my trust:
let me never be put to confusion.
PSALM 71:1

CHAPTER 1

Bird-in-Hand, Pennsylvania

"Don't push, Meredith! Don't push!" Laurie shouted as she directed her horse and buggy to a clearing along the side of the road next to an open field. The closest farm was some distance away, and Meredith didn't think there was enough time for them to get there.

A slight breeze picked up, and Meredith caught a glimpse of some fuzzy-looking dandelion seeds drifting through the air like little parachutes. The once-yellow meadow, where they'd pulled over, was now white with the globe-shaped seed bundles. One particular cycle of life was slowly coming to an end, while another's life was soon to begin.

Meredith ground her teeth together as another contraction came quickly, pulling her focus away from the dandelions. The pains were closer together, and she knew she shouldn't fight them, but it was hard to remember to breathe, like she'd been taught to do in the childbirth classes. Was it supposed to hurt this much? This certainly was not how she'd planned for her baby to be born. She'd imagined herself having plenty of warning and giving birth under the direction of the midwife at the clinic, not here in a buggy with her panicked sister, whom she was now forced to count on to help deliver this baby.

Meredith tried to remember what the instructor had told them during one of the classes, about what to do if the baby came unexpectedly at home. *"First and foremost, stay calm. Put the breathing techniques you've learned into play. Don't push prematurely. Keep your body relaxed, and work with nature."*

Struggling to deal with the pain, Meredith felt what seemed like a million emotions swirl through her brain. Her life was about to change in enormous ways. She had thought about this moment so many times, and now within minutes of this baby being born, it worried her even more. *Will I be able to do all of this on my own as I take on the role of being both mother and father? Can I provide for my baby?*

Meredith would have given anything if Luke could have been here right now, holding her hand and guiding her through each contraction. She was sure he would have remained calm and helped bring their baby into the world. Luke would have been a wonderful father. But this baby would never experience the joy of having Luke as his or her daddy.

She straightened her shoulders and drew in a deep breath. Well, Luke wasn't here, and with God's help, she would be guided along the way. First things first, though. She and Laurie would have to do this birth on their own, no matter how frightened either of them felt.

" 'In thee, O Lord, do I put my trust: let me never be put to confusion,' " Meredith quoted from Psalm 71:1. She clasped Laurie's hand tightly. "First and foremost, we need to pray and ask God to settle our nerves and guide us through this procedure."

"You're right." Laurie bowed her head. "Heavenly Father," she prayed aloud, "please give me the courage and wisdom to help Meredith bring this precious new life into the world. And I ask that You protect Meredith and the baby. In Jesus' name, amen."

"We need to gather some things," Meredith said, opening her eyes and focusing on what had to be done.

"What kind of things?" Laurie questioned, looking anxiously at Meredith. "I don't have much in my buggy and certainly nothing to help deliver a *boppli*."

"Do you have some clean newspaper?"

Laurie shook her head.

"How about a blanket or quilt?"

"There's a blanket in the backseat that Kevin and I used when we went on a picnic a few weeks ago. Oh, and there's also a large towel that I covered the picnic basket with."

"That's good. Get them, and place the blanket under me," Meredith said as she positioned herself with her back leaning against the buggy door for support.

She would have given anything to have a comfortable mattress beneath her instead of this narrow buggy seat. But during the childbirth classes, she'd learned there were far more unusual places some babies had chosen to be born. One day in the future, this would be some exciting story to share with her child.

"There's a bottle of hand sanitizer in my purse. You can use some of that to clean your hands and arms really good," Meredith told Laurie, taking control. "Since there isn't much room on the buggy seat, you'll need to stand outside with the door open so you can help this boppli make his or her appearance."

With her face looking a little less tense and a bit calmer, Laurie did as she was asked, and then she took her place outside of the buggy, in front of Meredith. "Try to pant, and only push very gently with each contraction," she said.

"I know. I know. But *danki* for reminding me," Meredith answered, willing herself to concentrate as another contraction came. Feeling a little less panicky herself, she was glad her sister sounded more in control. Hopefully between the two of them, they'd keep their wits and get through this without too much difficulty. Besides, there was no time to dwell on how apprehensive she felt. The baby was coming, and it was happening now!

⌘

Jonah stayed around Deacon Raber's place for a while after church, visiting with some of the men. However, when his ankle started throbbing, he knew he'd been on his feet too long, so he decided it was time to go home and rest for the remainder of the day. He needed to prop up his foot because his walking cast seemed tighter. Jonah could only assume his ankle was swelling, and the sooner he got home and off his feet, the better it would be.

Mom and Dad had come to church in their own buggy, and seeing that they were occupied with friends, he figured he probably wouldn't be missed. Besides, Jonah looked forward to spending some time alone, where he could think about his future—a future he hoped to spend with Meredith and her baby.

"Would ya like me to get your *gaul* and hitch him up to your buggy?" Meredith's twelve-year-old brother, Stanley, asked when Jonah headed for the corral where he'd left his horse.

"I appreciate the offer," Jonah said, smiling at the boy, "but Socks is a bit spirited, so he might be hard to catch."

"That's okay. I'm sure I can manage." The child grinned up at him, looking full of confidence. "Besides, with your foot still in that walkin' cast, it'd probably be hard for you to catch him."

"You might be right about that." Jonah smiled. "So if you feel up to the challenge, go right ahead."

Stanley hurried off toward the corral, while Jonah stood near his buggy. To his surprise, the boy showed up a few minutes later, holding Socks's lead rope in one hand, while the horse followed obediently behind.

"Here ya go," Stanley announced. "I got him for ya, just like I said I would."

Well, would ya look at that? Jonah thought. "I appreciate your efforts. Did he give you any trouble?"

Stanley shook his head. "After I showed him a lump of sugar, he followed me like a *hund*. I remember Luke sayin' how that always worked for him."

Jonah chuckled. Over the last few months, Socks had tamed down quite a bit. He seemed to have accepted Jonah as his new master, but the horse had never followed him like a dog. "Guess I'll have to get some sugar cubes and carry them in my pocket," he said, taking the lead rope from Stanley.

"Want me to hitch him to your buggy?" the boy asked, seeming eager to please.

Jonah was on the verge of telling Stanley not to bother, when he remembered what the bishop had said during his message. The sermon had been about servanthood and how folks should not only help others when they saw a need but be willing to accept help, too. "If we don't accept help when it's offered to us, we're being prideful," the bishop had said. "We also steal that person's blessing if we reject their help, for it is truly more blessed to give than receive."

"*Jah*, sure, go ahead and hitch Socks up," Jonah said. "I'll just wait inside the buggy till you have him ready to go."

Stanley flashed him a wide smile and led Socks around to the front of the buggy. While he worked at getting the horse hitched, Jonah limped around to the right side of the buggy and climbed into the driver's seat, yearning to get the weight off his feet.

Someday, when I have kinner of my own, I'll be teaching them to do things like this, he thought, watching to be sure Stanley did everything just right.

An image of Meredith flashed into his head. *If I'm ever fortunate enough to make Meredith my wife, I wonder how many children we'll have and if they'll have my dark curly hair or be blessed with Meredith's beautiful strawberry-blond hair. Would our daughters have Meredith's sweet personality? Would the boys want to learn the trade of buggy making from me?*

It was foolish to daydream like this, but he couldn't seem to help himself. He'd fallen hopelessly in love with Meredith and wanted nothing more than to make her his wife. Realistically, though, it was too soon for him to even hint at such a thing to Meredith. Her husband had been gone nearly six months, but she was still in mourning. If Jonah expressed his feelings to her, and she reciprocated, they'd have to wait to be married until she set her black mourning clothes aside after Luke had been gone a year.

Guess that's really not so long, Jonah told himself. *It's just a little over six months from now, so I'll take one day at a time and try to be patient. I'll keep helping Meredith whenever I can, and wait to see what develops between us.* The friendship Jonah and Meredith shared had been special when they were in Florida years ago, but for him, at least, recently their friendship had grown even deeper. Meredith was precious to Jonah, and for now, difficult as it was, loving her secretly was enough. Someday, he hoped, she would love him equally.

"Socks is ready to go!" Stanley called, disrupting Jonah's thoughts.

"Danki. You did good." Jonah waved and directed Socks up the driveway and onto the main road. Looking back, he saw Stanley's smile spread from ear to ear, making him glad he'd let the young boy help him.

Riding down the road, Jonah relaxed and let Socks take the lead. As they passed a field, he noticed how the dandelions had gone to seed and realized that the season was approaching an end. He thought about how he'd always liked the months during springtime and how ever since he could remember, his mother would pick tender dandelion sprouts every March. After washing them several times, she'd mix them with a little onion and cooking oil. Jonah usually ate so much his mouth would turn dry, but he didn't care. For a couple of weeks each year, Jonah's family enjoyed this special springtime salad. Sometimes, Mom cooked the dandelions and drizzled bacon-flavored dressing over them. But as far as Jonah was concerned, there was nothing like eating it freshly picked. It not only tasted good, but as Mom had often told him, the dandelion weed was full of healthy vitamins.

Jonah had only made it halfway home when he spotted a horse and buggy along the side of the road. After a second look, he realized the rig belonged to Meredith's sister Laurie, so he pulled over next to the field to see if there might be a problem.

I wonder what's going on. Jonah didn't see anyone at first, and then he spotted Laurie standing outside the buggy with the door open.

He tied Socks to a nearby tree then reached up to scratch where a dandelion seed had tickled his nose as it slowly wafted by in the breeze. Seeing that Laurie's horse hadn't been tied, he secured it, too. Then, hobbling toward the buggy, he called, "Is everything all right in there?"

Laurie turned to him with a panicked expression. "Meredith's boppli is about to be born. Could you get us some help?"

Jonah stood a few seconds, letting her words sink in; realizing the seriousness of the situation, he said, "I'll find the nearest phone shack and call 911."

Untying his horse and stepping back into his buggy, Jonah got Socks moving at a fast trot as he headed for the next Amish farm down the road. He barely took notice that his cast felt even tighter, making his ankle throb all the more. *Dear Lord,* he silently prayed, *please be with Meredith right now, and if help doesn't arrive before the boppli is born, let the birth go smoothly for both the mother and her child.*

<hr>

"Oh Meredith," Laurie said with a catch in her voice, "I don't think this boppli's gonna wait until help arrives. I can see the baby's head already!"

Meredith felt a mixture of excitement and trepidation. As anxious as she was to hold her baby, she feared something might go wrong during the delivery. Neither she nor Laurie had ever delivered a baby before, but they had the knowledge of what to expect and had witnessed puppies and kittens being born. But that wasn't the same as delivering a baby on the front seat of an Amish buggy instead of in a sterile delivery room.

"Put your hands in front of the boppli's head, and let it come out nice and slow," Meredith instructed, trying to keep her voice calm and reassuring, even though she was anything but relaxed.

"I know. The baby's supposed to slide out slowly, in waves, as your uterus contracts." Laurie sounded more confident, as though remembering the things they'd been taught in the classes. "Don't push too hard, Meredith; just pant and push gently until the baby's head is fully out. You're doing great so far."

Meredith did as her sister told her to do. "You're doing pretty good yourself, Laurie," she said, hoping to offer encouragement. Trying to control her breathing as another contraction knifed through her, Meredith bit down on her lip, ignoring the metallic taste of blood, knowing that soon she'd be holding her precious baby.

"The baby's head is out now," Laurie said, her voice rising with a sense of excitement. "I'll use one of my clean handkerchiefs to wipe away the fluid from the baby's airway."

"Whatever you do, don't pull on the baby," Meredith coached. "Just guide its shoulders out. Once that happens, the boppli will slip right through the birth canal, so hold on tight."

"The boppli is out, Meredith! And guess what? It's a *bu!*"

"Thank the Lord!" Tears welled in Mere-dith's eyes as Laurie placed the baby facedown across her stomach, and she was able to look upon her precious son for the very first time. "Make certain his airway is cleared, and then cover him with the towel. Oh, and be sure you leave his face uncovered so he can breathe."

Laurie did everything Meredith said, and when the baby started to cry, both women did, too. It was one of the most emotional moments Meredith had ever experienced, and she felt euphoric.

"I'm going to name him Levi Luke," Meredith murmured once she was able to speak without sobbing. "He'll never get to meet his father or great-grandfather, but I want him to have both of their names."

"That's so special," Laurie said, wiping the perspiration from Meredith's forehead. "I know Luke and Grandpa Smucker would be real pleased."

The birth of a baby was one of the most natural things in the world, but to Meredith, it was a miracle—her and Luke's special gift to the world. Already, she could feel the power of love between mother and child. It was a bond like no other—one she would protect for the rest of her life.

CHAPTER 2

Meredith smiled as she gazed at her son, lying in his cradle next to the rocking chair in her living room. It was sweet of Alma to have given Meredith the cradle, and now, after months of picturing her baby lying in it, at last he was here, nestled all cozy and warm.

It had been three days since Levi's birth on the front seat of Laurie's buggy, and Meredith was grateful everything had gone as well as it had. Not long after the baby made his appearance, and thanks to Jonah's unexpected arrival, the paramedics had come and taken Meredith and Levi to the hospital, where both were pronounced in good condition and sent home the following day. Meredith's mother had insisted on coming over to help out for a few days, so Laurie would be staying at home to help Grandma care for the children. Alma Beechy had offered to stay with Meredith, too, but she'd come down with a cold and thought it would be best not to expose the baby. Mom had let it be known that she looked forward to helping out and spending time with Meredith and the baby, so Meredith figured everything had worked out for the best.

"I've never seen a more beautiful boppli," Mom said, stepping up to the cradle beside Meredith and staring down at Levi.

"Maybe that's because he's your first grandchild, and you're feeling a little prejudiced."

Mom laughed, her eyes gleaming with tears. "That could very well be. And just look at how attentive Fritz is with your son. Why, I don't think he's left that spot since you put Levi in the cradle."

"Jah, the pup sure seems to like being close to the boppli." Meredith reached down to pet the dog's head. "You've seen how he barks as soon as Levi wakes up. The least little noise the baby makes, Fritz comes to me and starts whimpering." She laughed. "I think he wants to make sure I know whenever the boppli's awake or needs my attention."

"Some dogs get jealous when a baby comes along, but it doesn't seem like Fritz is that way at all," Mom added. "It's kind of nice having a dog like that. It never hurts to have an extra guardian around, watching over you and the boppli."

"I know what you mean," Meredith agreed. "I haven't been keeping Fritz in the kennel much anymore. I feel more comfortable with him being inside—especially now that he's been with the baby these first few days and has adjusted so well." She smiled as she continued to admire her sleeping son. Levi had his father's white-blond hair; although it was still very thin. Would this child have Luke's adventurous personality, too? Or would he take after his mother, who tended to be a little more cautious about things?

Meredith's heart swelled with love as she bent to stroke the baby's soft cheek. All she wanted to do was stay close to Levi and take in everything about him—from his long, doelike eyelashes lying delicately on his cheeks to the way he held his thumbs, each hand encircling a thumb with his tiny fingers. Every day since Levi's birth, she had made little discoveries that made her cherish him even more.

Watching her son in his peaceful slumber, Meredith thought once again of how this precious little boy would depend solely on her. Could she make enough money selling head coverings to support them both? Should she seek employment outside the home once she was strong enough and felt that she could leave Levi with someone else during the days she'd be working? Meredith had thought at first that she would look for a job, but she didn't like the idea of being away from Levi several hours each day. There were so many unanswered questions. She'd just have to keep trusting in the Lord and take one day at a time.

"Would you like me to start supper now?" Mom asked, touching Meredith's arm.

Meredith smiled and nodded, aware of just how much her mother was enjoying this new role as a grandmother. "I think while you're doing that, I'll lie down and take a nap."

"That's a good idea. You need all the rest you can get." Mom gave Meredith a hug and hurried off to the kitchen.

Meredith was still a bit exhausted from giving birth, yet she felt full of excitement. But she knew she should take it slow and easy and try not to rush things, so she lay on the sofa, settled herself against one of the throw pillows, and tried to relax.

She'd only been lying down a few minutes when she heard a horse and buggy coming up the driveway. She figured whoever it was would probably go to the back door and that Mom would let them in, so she remained on the sofa.

A bit later, Luke's parents entered the room, wearing eager expressions.

"I hope it's not too soon for us to pay you a visit," Sadie said, "but we've been anxious to see the boppli and couldn't wait any longer."

Meredith smiled and motioned to the baby's cradle. "He's right over there, sound asleep." She lifted herself from the sofa and followed Sadie and Elam across the room. Then they all stood staring down at the baby.

"*Ach*, my," Sadie whispered, clasping her hands together. "Just look at him. He looks like his *daed* when he was a boppli." Tears welled in her eyes as she turned to Luke's father. "Don't you think so, Elam?"

He bobbed his head. "Sure is a tiny fella. Don't remember any of our kinner being so small."

"That's because it's been so long since our five boys were born." Sadie turned to look at Meredith. "Have you chosen a *naame* for the baby yet?"

"Jah. His name is Levi Luke—after his father and great-grandfather."

Sadie smiled, and Meredith knew that despite the tears on her mother-in-law's cheeks, she was pleased with the name.

"Would either of you like to hold him?" Meredith asked, figuring Sadie was eagerly waiting and ready to hold Levi.

"We'd better not. He might wake up," Elam was quick to say.

"He's a pretty sound sleeper, so he probably won't," Meredith replied. "And even if he does wake up, it's okay, because I'm sure it won't take much to put him right back to sleep."

"I'd like to hold him," Sadie said, taking a seat in the rocking chair and extending her arms.

Meredith lifted the baby from the cradle and placed him in Sadie's arms. *How sad that Luke can't be here to share in this moment,* she thought as Sadie started humming to her new grandson.

⁓

Jonah whistled as he guided Socks toward Meredith's house. It had been three days since she'd given birth, and he couldn't wait any longer to pay a call on her.

When Jonah turned his horse and buggy up Meredith's driveway, he spotted two other rigs parked near the barn, so he knew she had company.

Should I stop? he wondered. *If her family is here, she might not appreciate me dropping by.*

Jonah's head told him to turn around and go back home, because he didn't want to overwhelm Meredith with too much company. But his heart said otherwise. He'd only seen the baby briefly on Sunday afternoon, when the paramedics came to take Meredith and the infant to the hospital. Now that she'd been home a couple of days, he was anxious to get a good look at her son, and if Meredith didn't mind, maybe he could even hold the little guy. Jonah loved kids and couldn't wait until he had some children of his own.

I'm here now, so I may as well go inside, he decided. *I won't stay long; just enough time to say hello and hold the baby.*

When Jonah knocked on the door a few minutes later, he was greeted by Meredith's mother, Luann. "It's nice to see you, Jonah. Come inside," she said politely.

Jonah smiled and stepped into the kitchen, which was filled with the aroma of savory stew. Luann was a friendly woman, and he appreciated her welcoming spirit. "How are Meredith and the boppli doing?" he asked.

"Quite well, but why don't you go in and see for yourself?" Luann gestured toward the door leading to the living room.

"I don't want to intrude, but I would like to say hello," Jonah said.

"I'm sure Meredith will be pleased to see you. She's grateful you came along when you did and were able to call 911."

"I believe it must have been God's timing that led me there at just the right moment." He smiled. "Laurie did a good job helping Meredith deliver the boppli. God was with them, too."

"He certainly was," Luann agreed. She motioned to Jonah's left foot, still encased in the walking cast. "How are you getting along these days?"

"Okay, but I'll sure be glad to get this off my foot so I can start helping my daed more in the buggy shop. I've been able to do some things while sitting down, but I can't be on my foot too long or it starts to swell."

"Well, go on into the living room and take a seat."

"Danki, I will."

When Jonah entered the living room he halted. Sadie Stoltzfus sat in the rocking chair, holding the baby, while Meredith and Elam were seated on the sofa. Knowing that Sadie didn't care much for him, Jonah was tempted to turn around and head out the door. But before he could take a step, Meredith smiled and said, "It's good to see you, Jonah. I'm glad you stopped by. I wanted to thank you for getting us the help we needed when the baby came."

Jonah shook his head. "No thanks is necessary. I'm just glad I happened along when I did." He glanced over at Elam. "It's nice to see you."

"Same here," Elam replied.

Jonah turned to Sadie then. "It looks like you're enjoying holding your grandchild."

She nodded her agreement but said nothing.

Jonah moved slowly across the room and stared down at the baby. "I think he looks like you, Meredith," he said, looking back at her.

"He looks just like Luke," Sadie was quick to say.

Jonah squirmed. Since he'd never met Luke, he couldn't say whether the baby looked like his father or not. But he wasn't about to argue with Sadie. It was obvious from the icy-cold look on her face that she wasn't happy to see Jonah there, so he didn't dare ask if he could hold the baby.

How long will Sadie's hostility toward me continue? he wondered. *Will her dislike of me make it harder to win Meredith over? I wonder just how much influence Sadie has with her daughter-in-law.*

Jonah took one last look at the baby then moved across the room to where Meredith sat. "He's a nice-looking boppli. Have you chosen a name for him yet?"

She smiled. "Levi Luke."

"That's a nice name," Jonah said. "I'm sure if his daed were here, he'd be real pleased."

Tears pooled in Meredith's blue eyes. "I know he would."

"Well, I'd best be going. Just wanted to come by and see how you're doing and take a peek at the baby." Jonah started for the door but turned back around. "I should be getting my walking cast off sometime in the next two weeks, so as soon as I'm able, I'll come by to help with any chores you may need to have done."

"Don't concern yourself with that," Sadie curtly replied. "Elam and Meredith's daed will take care of any chores that Meredith might need to have done."

Hesitantly, Jonah glanced at Meredith to see her reaction and was pleased when she smiled and said, "I appreciate you coming by today, and I'll let you know if I need anything."

At least she hasn't shut me out, Jonah thought as he hobbled from the room. *I just need to make sure that the next time I drop by Sadie isn't here.*

∽

Philadelphia, Pennsylvania

Eddie stood looking out the window of his room for one last time. He'd gotten used to the scene before him, and during his stay here in rehab, he had enjoyed watching the bluebirds come and go as they busily fed their babies inside the birdhouse. Toward the end of spring, he'd even watched as the babies left their nest, all gathering at the entrance of their little house. Then one by one, they'd taken flight, landing in the nearby shrubs. The poor parents had been frantic, flitting from one chick to the next, trying to keep them all in sight.

Redirecting his thoughts, Eddie glanced down at the pale yellow shirt and denim jeans he now wore. Susan had stopped by yesterday to give him some clothes to wear on the day of his release. She said they were a gift from her grandparents. From what Eddie had been told, he hadn't had much when he'd come to the hospital—only the clothes on his back, which he'd later learned had been so tattered they were thrown away. He shook his head slowly, wondering once more if anybody had been searching for him.

Susan and Anne's grandparents must be really nice folks. Imagine, letting a complete stranger stay with them, let alone buying me clothes, Eddie thought. The jeans and shirt fit pretty well, although for some reason he felt funny wearing them. He couldn't figure it out, but the pullover shirt felt a bit constricting, even though it fit good and wasn't tight. And the jeans, although they fit around his waist, seemed somewhat snug against his skin.

Eddie left the window and looked in the mirror across the room. Who was this person staring back at him? Even though he was dressed in normal clothes, nothing sparked a memory or a small glimpse of his past.

"Wow, just look at you! Those clothes my grandma bought for you fit

247

quite well," Susan said, stepping into the room. "Anne and I tried to guess your size, and it seems like it was a pretty good guess."

Eddie smiled. "I appreciate the clothes, but I'll never be able to repay your grandparents for letting me stay in their home."

"They're happy to do it." Susan motioned to the door. "Are you ready to head out?"

He nodded and grabbed the satchel the hospital had provided with his comb, toothbrush, and other toiletry items. Eddie didn't admit it to Susan, but he was a bit nervous about meeting her grandparents. What if they didn't like him? What if things didn't work out for him to stay in their home? Where would he go then?

Feeling as though he was leaving the only home he'd ever really known, Eddie squared his shoulders, ready to start another phase of his life. Maybe by being in new surroundings, his memory would come back to him.

CHAPTER 3

Bird-in-Hand

"I can't believe Jonah had the nerve to show up at Meredith's this evening," Sadie fumed as she and Elam headed for home in their buggy.

"Guess he wanted to see the boppli, same as you and me," Elam responded, holding tightly to the reins as they passed the horse farm not far from their place.

Dobbin nickered but didn't slow down when a few of the horses ran to the fence, watching as they rode by.

"But Jonah's not part of our family, and he's pushing his way in as though he is," Sadie said with a huff.

Elam grunted warily. "You need to mind your own business. We've been over this before, and it's time you realized that Meredith has her own life to live. If her future includes Jonah someday, then you'll just have to accept it." He clucked to the horse, while nudging Sadie's arm. "See there," he said, pointing to the west. "That's what you should be enjoying instead of fretting about things beyond your control."

Sadie glanced at the sky, ablaze from the beautiful sunset. The deep orange near the horizon blended with the hues of pink and purple, making Dobbin's auburn coat glow even more. As lovely as it was, it didn't remove the worry she felt deep in her heart. Elam might be able to deal with it, but she wasn't sure she could ever accept the idea of another man taking her son's place in Meredith's life. Sadie didn't know what she was most afraid of— Jonah stepping in, or Meredith pushing them out of her and little Levi's lives. What if Meredith fell in love with Jonah and they got married? What if they decided to move away? It would be a hard pill to swallow if she never got to know her new grandson well. She was sure Meredith's mother wouldn't like it either.

"How'd your visit with Meredith go?" Jonah's mother asked as they ate supper that evening. "Are she and the boppli doing okay?"

Jonah nodded. "He's a cute little fellow, and they both seem to be healthy enough, but I wish I hadn't gone over there today."

"How come?" Dad asked, reaching for the basket of bread.

"I should have realized her family would be there. Besides Meredith's *mamm*, Sadie and Elam were there, too." Jonah solemnly grimaced. "I got a cold reception from Sadie, which made me very uncomfortable. I don't think she wanted me anywhere near Meredith or the boppli."

Mom handed Jonah a bowl of green beans. "Why not? You didn't go over there with a bad cold or anything contagious."

"I think she's still upset about me seeing Meredith," Jonah replied. "Remember when I said she'd talked to me about it?"

Mom frowned. "I was hoping she'd get over that."

Jonah shook his head. "Apparently not. She made me feel like I didn't belong there, so I only stayed a few minutes."

"How'd Meredith react to you dropping by?" Mom asked.

"She seemed okay with it; although she didn't say a lot, except that she appreciated me coming by and would let me know if she needed anything."

"Well, there ya go!" Dad grabbed a drumstick from the platter of fried chicken. "Don't think she would have said that if she didn't want you comin' over."

Jonah smiled. "Guess you're right. I'll just have to make sure that the next time I go, Sadie's not there."

"That's probably a good idea." Mom patted Jonah's arm affectionately. "As time goes by and Sadie comes to grips with her son's death, I'm sure she'll warm up to you. After all, it's not like you and Meredith are courting or planning to get married."

Jonah shoved the beans around on his plate, debating whether he should tell his folks how much he cared for Meredith. Throwing caution to the wind, he blurted out, "I'm in love with Meredith, but I won't express my feelings to her until I think she's ready."

❦

Philadelphia

"Whew! It sure is hot this evening. I'll be glad when fall gets here and the weather turns cooler," Susan said as she pulled her compact car out of the hospital parking lot.

Eddie gave a brief bob of his head.

"Autumn's my favorite time of the year," she continued. "I love all the pretty colored leaves, but the season's colors don't last long enough for me."

Still no response from Eddie. Maybe he seemed pensive because he didn't remember the colored leaves from autumn. Or perhaps he was deep in thought and didn't hear what she'd said. "October is my favorite month; although it goes too quickly for me." Susan tried once more to engage him in conversation.

"Hmm. . ." Eddie quietly responded as he watched out the side window.

Changing the subject, Susan informed Eddie that traffic would be thinning out once they got off the expressway and headed toward Darby. "If traffic is bad, it could take us half an hour to get home, but most times it only takes ten to fifteen minutes to get to my grandparents' house." She scowled, watching as the guy who'd just passed her in a sports car cut over in her lane, way too close. "Boy, you sure have to watch people like a hawk. Just look at the way that man is weaving in and out of traffic, like he owns the road."

Eddie released a heavy sigh—almost a groan. "I still can't get over the fact that your grandparents would be willing to take me in when we've never met."

She smiled, realizing that Eddie hadn't even noticed the crazy driver whose sports car was now nearly out of sight.

Relaxing a little after they got farther away from Philly, Susan pushed the button to close the windows and turned on the air-conditioning. The cool air felt wonderful, and having the windows closed drowned out the road noise as well. Hearing that alone could frazzle one's nerves. "After you get to know Grandpa and Grandma, you'll understand," she said, glancing over at Eddie with a smile. "They're the most loving couple, and they always try to follow God's principles, while showing others what it's like to be a Christian by their actions."

Eddie squinted and rubbed his forehead. "I have no memory about whether I'm a Christian or not. But I have seen from the way you and your sister have treated me, as well as the scriptures you've read and the prayers you've said on my behalf, what it's like to show your beliefs and not just talk about them."

Susan nodded. "The Bible tells us in John 13:35: 'By this shall all men know that ye are my disciples, if ye have love one to another.' "

"Hmm. . .guess that makes sense," he said, thoughtfully tapping his chin.

Susan was tempted to say more but decided to let him think about the verse of scripture she'd quoted as they got off the exit ramp and onto the road toward Darby. She was sure that Eddie would be hearing plenty of verses in the days ahead, not to mention seeing for himself what a fine example of Christianity her grandparents lived.

⁂

Darby, Pennsylvania

When Susan pulled her car into the driveway of a large, two-story house a short time later, Eddie was impressed with the two huge maple trees in front. He was sure he couldn't reach his arms around them, their trunks were so huge. He figured the trees probably made good homes for a lot of birds, and they looked like they'd be fun to climb, too—that is, if he were still a kid. *I wonder if I used to climb trees when I was a boy.*

"Well, this is it," Susan said, turning off her ignition. "This is where my grandparents have lived since they were married. You'd never know it from the looks of all the well-maintained homes in the area, but this is actually one of the older, original neighborhoods of Darby. Their house isn't as new as some of the homes we passed along the way, but it has lots of room, and I believe you're going to like it here. Grandma and Grandpa are pretty active for their age, but I think they'll appreciate your help with some of things they're not able to do anymore."

"I'll be happy to help out," Eddie said, staring at the stately old home. "It's the least I can do in exchange for them letting me stay here."

"I'm sure they'll appreciate that. Grandpa and Grandma do a lot of charity work, and they give to others at church, too. So it'll be nice for them to be on the receiving end for a change." Susan's cheeks turned pink. "Well, just listen to me chattering away like a monkey begging to be fed. Guess we'd better go in." She opened the car door.

Just as they were getting out, an elderly couple came out of the house and met them on the sidewalk.

"Grandma and Grandpa," Susan said, gesturing to Eddie, "this is Eddie." She motioned to her grandparents. "I'd like you to meet my grandpa, Henry, and my grandma, Norma."

Henry shook Eddie's hand firmly.

Eddie smiled. *For an older man, he sure has a strong, firm handshake. I'll bet he's still pretty capable of doing a lot of the work around here himself.*

When Eddie reached for Norma's hand, she offered a welcoming handshake. Even though he'd been a little nervous about meeting Susan's grandparents, Eddie found himself instantly comfortable with these two friendly people.

"Come in. Come in." Norma offered Eddie a warm smile as she stepped onto the porch and opened the front door. "We hope the traffic wasn't too bad coming out of Philly this evening. It can get pretty snarled on that interstate sometimes."

"Other than some guy in a little sports car cutting me off, coming out of the city wasn't too bad," Susan said as they stepped into the hallway.

Once inside, a wonderful aroma hit Eddie's nostrils, and it was all he could do not to head straight for the room it was coming from.

"It's almost suppertime, and as soon as Anne gets home from the errands she's running, we'll be ready to eat," Norma said. "I have a pot of homemade vegetable soup simmering on the stove, and we also fried up some ham to have for sandwiches."

Henry bobbed his head. "My wife made some of her famous coconut cookies for dessert, too."

Susan leaned close to Eddie's ear. "You'll never be able to eat just one of those cookies, either. Grandma's coconut dreams, as I like to call them, are so chewy and soft you'll automatically reach for more. Not only that," she added, smiling at her grandmother, "but Grandma's cookies have won many blue ribbons at the church bazaar each year."

A blotch of red erupted on Norma's cheeks. "Now there's no need to brag on my cookies, dear. After supper we'll let Eddie be the judge of how good they are."

"Don't let my wife fool ya. She's a real fine cook." Henry grinned at Norma. "I'm gonna show Eddie around the house now."

"That's good. I'll help Grandma set the table while you do that," Susan said. "Eddie, you can set your satchel over there by the stairway, while Grandpa shows you around down here."

Eddie followed Susan's grandfather to the kitchen and looked when Henry pointed to a desk in the corner. "There's a laptop computer right there, in case you ever want to use it."

Eddie scratched the side of his head. "I can't remember if I even know how to use a computer."

Henry chuckled. "Don't worry about it, son. I don't use the computer either. Susan and Anne have both tried to teach me, but that kind of technology is way over my head."

Eddie tagged along with Henry as they went from room to room and then headed up a flight of stairs. He noticed that though the house was neat and tidy, it also had a cozy, lived-in feeling.

"This will be your room," Henry said, after they'd entered the first door on the right. He opened the closet door. "As you can see, Norma got you a few more items of clothing." He motioned to the outfit Eddie was wearing. "The shirt and jeans she sent to the hospital with Susan seem to fit you quite nicely."

Eddie nodded. "Yes, and I appreciate it." Even though the clothes felt a bit uncomfortable to him, he didn't want to sound ungrateful, so he kept that thought to himself.

"There are a few things in the dresser drawers you may find useful as well," Henry said. "Oh, and feel free to open or close the curtains whenever you want. Your room gets the morning sun, but I'm sure the birds will wake you before it's fully daylight." He chuckled. "They like to roost in the trees around here, and it's a bit of a chorus every morning when they start chirping away. We rarely set an alarm clock anymore, 'cause we're usually up with the birds at the crack of dawn. But don't feel that you have to get up early," he quickly added. "You can sleep however late you want."

Eddie couldn't remember how early or late he'd ever gotten up before his stay in the hospital. He didn't remember setting an alarm clock either. But he did look forward to hearing those birds chirping and waking him every morning, instead of all the hospital sounds he'd grown accustomed to over the last several months. He didn't think he'd miss hearing the constant voices out in the hall and at mealtime or the food carts with their squeaky wheels and rattling dishes as the nurse's aides pushed them into each room. Although the hospital food wasn't too bad, it didn't compare to that delicious smell coming from the kitchen downstairs.

Wonder where I lived before all of this. Did I wake up with the sun or when the birds started singing each morning?

"Anne's home now, and supper's ready!" Norma called up the stairs.

"The bathroom's right down the hall." Henry motioned in that direction. "Guess we oughta get washed up before we eat, or Norma might not let us sit at her kitchen table."

Eddie grinned. *These folks are sure nice. Whatever my life was before all of this, I'm pretty lucky to be here right now. Sure hope I don't do anything to mess up. I wouldn't want them to ask me to leave and then end up having to sleep somewhere on the streets.* Wherever Eddie's real home was, he hoped there was a sense of belonging like he felt here.

CHAPTER 4

Bird-in-Hand

"I can't believe your boppli is a month old already," Meredith's friend Dorine said as the two of them sat on Meredith's front porch one hot Monday morning in early August.

Meredith smiled and stroked the top of her son's silky head. "I know, and he's growing as fast as the weeds in my garden."

"I can't do anything about how fast Levi's growing, because that's what babies do," Dorine said, motioning to her own son and daughter playing on the other end of the porch. "But I can do something about those weeds in your garden."

"There's no need for you to do that," Meredith responded quickly. "Laurie said she'd pull them later this week. Today, I just want us to sit and visit. Between you taking care of Merle and Cathy, and me balancing my time between caring for Levi and making head coverings, we don't get to see each other that often."

"That's true." Dorine sighed. "Things were much easier when we were girls playing on the swings in your folks' backyard or riding around my parents' field in my pony cart." Dorine settled against her porch chair with hands clasped behind her head. "Just listen to those cicadas. When I was younger, hearing them always reminded me that school was about to start."

"Jah, it's funny how hearing certain things sparks memories." Meredith chuckled. "I'll never forget the time your daed bought that new pony and we took him out before he'd had a chance to get to know you very well. Little Rosie wouldn't pull the cart for us at all."

Dorine giggled. "That stubborn pony waited till we got out of the cart, and then she took off across Dad's field like a shot. My brother Thomas wasn't too happy when he had to chase after Rosie and bring her back to the barn." She gestured to her two little ones again. "Makes me wonder what kinds of things Seth and I will have to handle with our own kinner."

"Guess it's good that we don't know what the future holds." Meredith leaned over and kissed Levi's little nose. "If we did, it might be too hard to bear." She moaned. "When I fell in love with Luke, never in a million years did I think I'd lose him the way I did."

Dorine reached over and clasped Meredith's hand, giving her fingers a gentle squeeze. "That's why it's best to take one day at a time, asking God to give us the strength and courage to deal with things as they come."

Meredith nodded slowly. She knew her friend's words were true, but living them out was a tall order sometimes.

"On a lighter note," Dorine said with an eager expression, "how would you feel about the two of us hiring a driver and taking our kinner to the Elmwood Park Zoo the first week of September? By then the weather should be cooler. We can stop in Paoli on the way there and see the hot air balloons."

"That sounds like fun," Meredith said. "But Levi's so young yet. He wouldn't get much out of going to the zoo."

"True, but since you're nursing, you probably wouldn't want to leave him with anyone for the day."

"You're right about that, and if I go, I'll take the boppli along." Meredith's thoughts went to Jonah. The last time he'd stopped by to visit, he'd mentioned something about visiting the zoo sometime in the future. Meredith was tempted to invite him along but thought better of it. She didn't want anyone to think they were a courting couple. Besides, she and Dorine hadn't done anything together for a long time, so this day would be just for them and their children.

❧

Darby

"What would you like me to do this morning?" Eddie asked as he and Henry got up from the breakfast table.

"Why don't you take the day off and laze around the yard?" Henry draped his arm across Eddie's shoulders. "Between your therapy sessions at the hospital and all the odd jobs we've found for you to do around here these past four weeks, I think you deserve some time off."

Eddie shook his head vigorously. "I wouldn't feel right about doin' nothing all day. You and your wife have been so kind to take me in. The least I can do to pay you back is to keep doing chores." He was glad when Henry nodded his agreement.

Eddie had settled in nicely after moving to the Baileys' house a month ago. Right from the start, Norma and Henry had gone out of their way to make him feel at home. When he'd first arrived, it hadn't taken him long to realize that he'd been worried for nothing. Anne and Susan's grandparents made sure he didn't want for a thing.

Thinking back on getting familiar with the room he'd been given that first day, Eddie couldn't believe how considerate this couple had been—especially when he had looked in the dresser drawers and found all the items Henry and Norma had gotten for him. These kind folks had gone to the store and bought him underwear, socks, T-shirts in various colors, two pairs of jeans, two sets of pullover sweatshirts with matching sweatpants for the upcoming autumn weather, some dressy slacks and shirts to wear when they went to church, and a pair of pajamas. In the closet, he'd found a jacket for colder weather, and a lighter-weight hooded sweatshirt, as well. On the closet door hung a red baseball cap, which he'd immediately put on his head. It fit him quite well, and except for meals and sleeping at night, he wore it most of the time. On top of the dresser, he'd noticed a man's hairbrush, comb, a razor, and shaving cream. He still couldn't believe they'd thought of everything he might need.

Even after a month's time, it almost brought tears to Eddie's eyes, thinking about the kindness Susan, Anne, and their grandparents had shown him. Before he'd come here, Susan had mentioned that she'd told her grandparents about his amnesia and said she hoped he didn't mind. That didn't bother Eddie at all. He wasn't ashamed of his situation, just frustrated by it.

Almost from the start, Eddie had started healing—physically, that is. He enjoyed helping Henry with his garden, pulling weeds and seeing what vegetables were ready to pick. Overnight, the cucumbers seemed to double in size, and the warm weather was making the tomatoes turn a brilliant red. The

Baileys even had a small patch of sweet corn, and just this week the ears had become ripe for picking. Norma had told Eddie that August was "produce month," and she was right about that.

Last evening, they'd all sat around the picnic table in the backyard, enjoying their first kettle of steaming corn on the cob. Eddie couldn't seem to get enough of it. Everyone laughed when George, the squirrel, ran up the tree with a cob of corn Henry had given him. Norma had also made what she called "cucumber delights," which consisted of slices of cucumber on a small piece of pumpernickel bread that had been spread with cream cheese. On top of the cucumber, she'd sprinkled some lemon pepper. Eddie couldn't believe how good they were.

The Baileys' yard was so inviting, and Eddie could understand why they liked to spend time outdoors. He liked all the trees in their neighborhood, too. They were so big along the property line that he couldn't even see the house next door. All the homes in the neighborhood weren't real far apart, but they were just close enough to run to in case of an emergency. Eddie couldn't get over how close-knit everyone seemed to be. He'd even gotten used to seeing certain neighbors waving to him as they took their daily walk down the tree-lined street.

Henry and Norma were not only hospitable in sharing their home with Eddie, but they were easy to talk to, as well, just like their granddaughters. Eddie found himself laughing more times than not as the Baileys shared some of their special memories from the past. He had to admit it felt good to find something to laugh about these days.

Norma, who'd been standing at the sink doing dishes, lifted a soapy hand and shook her finger at Eddie, bringing him out of his daydreaming. "Now you listen to my husband, young man. He's right about needing to take it easy sometimes. In fact, I insist that you take two days off every week for as long as you're staying with us. Sunday is one of them, of course, because the Lord commands us to rest on the Sabbath." Two dimples dotted Norma's cheeks when she smiled. "But you can choose which of the other days you'd rather not work, and it doesn't have to be the same day every week."

Eddie lifted his hands in defeat. "Guess I have no other choice."

Henry thumped him lightly on the back. "Now that we have that all settled, why don't the two of us head out to the backyard and relax on the porch glider for a while? Anyways, George is probably anxious to see if we have a treat for him today. When we get tired of sitting, we can take a walk around the neighborhood."

Eddie nodded agreeably. That cute little squirrel sure was entertaining, and he liked the fact that George had begun to eat from his hand, just like he did with Norma and Henry. For the first time in a long while, Eddie felt lighthearted. Although he was unsure how long it would last, he had a feeling of belonging and looked forward to each new day. It was nice to see Susan and Anne more often, too. It was almost like having a family of his own.

Eddie had energy inside that had been pent up way too long and was just itching to be used. It wouldn't be easy to sit around today and do nothing, but if it made Henry and Norma happy, then he'd do it.

Philadelphia

"I can't believe how warm and humid it is today," Susan said to Anne as they visited during their morning break, sitting on a bench outside the hospital grounds. Today was one of the few times they had the same schedule, and Susan was glad for the opportunity to visit awhile with her sister.

"I know what you mean." Anne fanned her face with her hand while blowing out, which lifted her curly bangs off her forehead.

Susan giggled. "Did you see how Eddie enjoyed the corn on the cob we had for supper last night?"

"Yes." Anne grinned. "I have to say, I think I enjoyed it as much as he did. Corn always tastes better when it's fresh from the stalk. And it was so tender and sweet."

Susan bobbed her head in agreement. "How'd Eddie's therapy session go yesterday?" she asked.

"Real well. He's gained back most of his mobility, but as you know, none of his memory has returned. I hate to say this, but maybe it never will."

Susan sighed, remembering how last night after supper she and Eddie had taken a walk to a nearby park. They'd visited, laughed, and strolled hand in hand. Susan felt like a teenage girl when Eddie pushed her on one of the swings. She was beginning to form a strong attachment to him and thought he might be starting to care for her, too. But nothing could come of it unless he regained his memory. He might be married, and until she knew for sure that he was single, she couldn't allow herself to fantasize too much about having a permanent relationship with Eddie.

"Say, I have an idea," Anne said, nudging Susan's arm.

"What's that?"

"Why don't the two of us take Eddie on a little outing to see the hot air balloons in Paoli?" Anne suggested.

Susan shook her head. "It's too warm out for that. Besides, we won't have the same days off until the first week of September."

"That's okay. I was thinking early September. It'll be better if we go when the weather's a bit cooler."

Susan considered the proposal then said, "I think that might be a good idea. It'll be fun for all three of us."

CHAPTER 5

Bird-in-Hand

"*Harebscht* is definitely upon us," Jonah said, blowing warmth into his hands as he and his dad worked together in the buggy shop on the first Saturday of September. "Can't ya just feel the chill in the air?"

"Jah, fall is one of my favorite times of year, and the heat from the woodstove sure makes the shop feel good this morning," Dad said, reaching for a safety triangle to apply to the back of the Amish buggy they'd just repaired. The rig had been in an accident a few weeks ago, but they'd made it look good as new. Fortunately, the Amish family who'd been in the buggy when it had been hit by a car hadn't been seriously hurt. Many Amish involved in buggy accidents weren't so lucky.

Jonah was happy to be working with his dad again—especially since they were a bit behind. He'd only been able to help in the shop a little during the time his ankle had been broken. It wasn't fun being laid up, but they were catching up with things now. Last week, he'd been able to begin work on an antique carriage for an Englishman who lived in the area, and that task had been keeping him busy as well. The only downside was that he hadn't been able to spend as much time with Meredith and the baby lately. He'd seen them at church last Sunday, though, and noticed that little Levi was growing like a weed. It was hard to believe he was two months old already.

When Jonah had stopped to see Meredith a few weeks ago, the baby, while lying in Meredith's arms, had actually looked up at him and smiled. Jonah's heart had melted when the little guy did that, and he knew it would be hard to hide the mounting attachment he felt each time he saw Meredith and Levi. There was no stopping the images in his mind of Meredith and her son becoming a part of his family one day. Those thoughts were close to the surface almost every waking hour, not to mention the recurring dream that had recently filled his nights with hopes of the future.

Levi's going to need a daed, Jonah thought. *And Meredith needs a husband to love, nurture, and take care of her. I don't know how much longer I can wait before expressing my feelings to her.*

⟨∾⟩

Darby

Eddie woke to the fresh smell of coffee and bacon. As he hurried to get dressed, he grinned, thinking if he stayed with the Baileys too much longer, he'd probably gain weight from Norma's good cooking.

That's okay, though, he thought, patting his flat stomach. *It probably wouldn't hurt for me to put on a few extra pounds.* As he bent his arm and made a fist, Eddie decided that he liked the larger muscles he'd recently noticed. It was wonderful to be healing and feeling better every day. Likewise, it was satisfying for Eddie to have a routine, even though things weren't altogether perfect. Until he regained his memory, he would enjoy each day as it came. This feeling of contentment was something new for him. Or maybe he'd never experienced it before.

He yawned and stretched his arms over his head, already missing the comfort of his warm bed. If not for the aroma of breakfast pulling him from his slumber, he'd probably still be cuddled down under the cozy blankets. He'd slept so soundly last night that the chirping of birds outside his bedroom window hadn't wakened him like it usually did.

Guess I needed the extra sleep, he thought, *'cause today's gonna be an exciting day.* Susan would be taking him to see the hot air balloons in Paoli. Anne was supposed to go along, but she'd come down with a bad cold and thought it would be best if she stayed home and rested. Henry and Norma had been invited to go, too, but they had a church bazaar to attend. So it would just be Eddie and Susan, but that was okay with him. Susan was a lot of fun to be with, and he looked forward to spending the day together, just the two of them. It was good to feel so lighthearted and full of anticipation. He was having more and more of those kinds of days lately, and he liked it.

Halting his thoughts, Eddie pulled open the curtains to let the morning sunlight in. The room immediately transformed, draped in the day's golden warmth, not just from the sun but also from the trees right outside the window. The autumn brilliance from their yellow leaves made his bedroom glow. Before too long, the trees would be bare, and he'd be raking up the leaves. But he looked forward to that. He enjoyed doing anything in the fresh air.

I wonder if I liked being outside before I lost my memory. Did I have a job working outdoors, or was I just a bum living on the streets?

Eddie hated the fact that he still had no memory of his past, and each day that came and went without a glimmer of his memory returning made him feel more discouraged that it might never return. If not for the warm welcome he'd received from the Baileys, he'd probably have fallen victim to depression.

Eddie's stomach growled, interrupting his thoughts. He needed to get some breakfast, and soon after that, he and Susan would head out for the day. He'd probably have so much fun he wouldn't even think about his memory loss.

❧

Bird-in-Hand

"Are you ready for a little outing?" Meredith leaned over Levi's crib, wrapped a blanket around his squirming body, and picked him up. "We're going to see some animals at the zoo, precious baby."

Levi nuzzled her neck while she gently patted his back. He was such a good baby and a comfort to her, as well. Meredith knew it would be difficult to raise him alone, but she was determined to do it. She'd been managing financially so far, but real estate taxes would be due next spring, and that worried her. She was making enough money selling head coverings to pay for food and their basic expenses, but she wasn't sure how she could put enough extra in the bank to pay taxes.

As much as Meredith dreaded doing it, she might have to rent the house out and move in with her folks. Selling the place would be her last resort, because if she did that, she'd have no place to come back to if she found a way to make more money. Meredith didn't want to look for work outside the home until Levi had been weaned, so renting out the house might be her only option if things got any worse.

A horn honked outside, interrupting Meredith's thoughts. Dorine and her driver were there, so it was time to head for the zoo.

Meredith grabbed her lightweight jacket along with Levi's diaper bag and headed out the door.

"Are you ready for a fun day?" Dorine asked as Meredith climbed into Marsha Hubert's van.

Meredith nodded. "I don't think Levi will get much out of it, but I'm sure looking forward to this time we can be together."

Dorine gestured to Merle and Cathy. "My two kinner are excited about seeing the animals at the zoo, and I'm also looking forward to watching the hot air balloons in Paoli."

"You're not planning to take a ride in one of them, are you?" Meredith questioned.

Dorine shook her head vigorously. "Ach, no! I just want to watch awhile, and then we can be on our way to the zoo."

"I've been to these hot air balloon displays before," Marsha told them. "Some of the rides you can take float you from one place to a totally new location. But if you just want to experience what it's like to go up in one, then I recommend taking a tethered ride."

"What's that?" Meredith and Dorine asked in unison.

"It's a ride that takes you up high in the balloon, but you don't really go anywhere. There's a rope that's tied from the ground up to the balloon, securing it in place," their driver explained. "I can tell you from personal experience that the view up there is breathtaking."

"That sounds exciting, but I think I'll just observe," Dorine said. "I'd be too scared to go way up there."

"I agree. All I want to do is watch." Meredith buckled Levi into a car seat then settled back for the one-hour drive.

⁂

Paoli, Pennsylvania

"Would ya just look at all those colorful balloons?" Eddie pointed upward with the exuberant look of a child opening gifts on Christmas morning.

Susan smiled. "Would you like to take a ride in one of them?"

Eddie's turquoise eyes widened. "Would that be possible? I think it'd be expensive."

"We can buy a ticket for one of the tethered rides. Those don't cost as much."

"But I don't have any money," he said.

"I'll buy your ticket. And then I'll take your picture when you go up in the balloon."

"I can't let you do that."

"Why not?"

"I wouldn't feel right about you paying, but if you're gonna buy a ticket, then you should be the one takin' the balloon ride."

Susan shook her head. "Not me. I'm keeping both of my feet planted firmly on the ground."

"Then I won't go either." Eddie tipped his head and stared up at the balloons. "I've always wondered what it'd be like to fly. Least, I think I have. I can't remember actually saying that, but way down deep inside I feel like I have."

Susan touched his arm. "Then I insist that you take a balloon ride. It might spark some special memory for you."

"You really think so?"

"It's worth a try, don't you think?"

He bobbed his head, grinning from ear to ear. "You're a nice person, Susan, and I'll always be grateful for everything you've done to help me." He reached for her hand and gave her fingers a gentle squeeze.

Heat flooded Susan's cheeks. It was great being with Eddie like this—away from the hospital and away from the house for a few hours. It was almost like they were on a date—just the two of them having fun and getting to know each other better.

***

"*Guck emol dutt!* Have you ever seen so many balloons all in one place?" Dorine asked when they stepped out of the van in Paoli.

Meredith shielded her eyes from the glare of the morning sun. "I am looking at that, and I see so many beautiful colors it's hard to believe!" Some of the balloons were checkered with bright yellows and reds. Others were solid, brilliant colors. But seeing them all together made it look like a rainbow of shades.

Dorine laughed as she motioned to her children, who were busy pointing and giggling. "Cathy and Merle seem to like them, too."

"I'll bet they'd like to take a ride."

"Maybe someday," Dorine said, "but right now they're too little for something like that."

"I have no desire to soar up in the air like a bird." A lump formed in Meredith's throat. "But I remember how Luke said many times that he wished he could fly."

It seemed like only yesterday that Luke had grinned and pointed skyward when a plane flew over. Meredith had always smiled at his boyish reaction. Luke had also gotten excited during geese migration. He'd mentioned many times that he wondered what it would be like to fly with those birds, as they'd watched them depart every autumn in their V-formation, heading south for the winter. Meredith, enjoying springtime like she did, became excited as she heard the distant honking, signaling the geese's return. But she had no desire to be up there flying with them.

Dorine slipped her arm around Meredith's waist, bringing her back to the present. "You still miss him something awful, don't you?"

Meredith nodded as she stroked the top of Levi's head. "But I'm thankful for this little guy who reminds me so much of his *daadi*."

Dorine smiled. "He definitely has his daddy's white-blond hair, but he gets his pale blue eyes from you, Meredith."

Meredith was about to respond, when a young woman with straight dark hair walked up to them. "Didn't I meet you at the Bird-in-Hand Farmers' Market in the spring?" she asked, smiling at Meredith.

Meredith tipped her head and studied the woman. "I–I'm not sure. My sister sells her homemade faceless dolls there. Could you have met her?"

"Is her name Laurie King?" the woman asked.

Meredith nodded. "So you've met her?"

"Yes. I bought one of her dolls, and while we were talking, you and an older woman came by the stand. I was with my sister, and we spoke to you for a few minutes."

267

Meredith smiled. "Oh yes, now I remember. You were asking some questions about our Amish way of life."

"That's right." The young woman extended her hand. "My name's Susan Bailey."

"I'm Meredith, and this is my son, Levi." Meredith kissed the top of the baby's head.

"He's a beautiful boy."

"Thank you."

"I'll bet he's the apple of his daddy's eye."

Meredith blinked to keep tears from spilling over. "My husband passed away in January."

"I'm sorry to hear that," Susan said sincerely. Then she glanced up and said, "Are you here to take a balloon ride?"

"Oh no," Meredith was quick to say. "My friend Dorine and I are taking our children to the Elmwood Park Zoo in Norristown today, and we decided to stop by on our way to see all the colorful hot air balloons."

"I'm with a friend today, too." Susan pointed to a red-and-blue balloon that was tethered to the ground and had just lifted off. "See that young man wearing the red ball cap and sunglasses, leaning over the edge of the basket, waving to everyone?"

"I—I think so," Meredith said. "But the balloon's getting higher, and it's hard to see the people inside."

"Well, my friend Eddie is taking what I believe is his first hot air balloon ride." Susan smiled and snapped a picture with the camera she held. "I'm pretty sure he's having a wonderful time."

Meredith stood watching the balloon lift higher and saw Susan's friend waving to the people on the ground. She could only imagine what it must feel like to be up there so high. That man sure looked like he was having fun. For a split second, she thought about taking a ride, too. After all, that particular balloon was somewhat stationary, being tethered safely to the ground. From up there, it would surely give a beautiful view of Lancaster County. But the baby started to cry, so she dismissed her thoughts.

"I think Levi is hungry, so we'd better go," Meredith whispered to Dorine.

"That's fine with me, if you're sure you've seen enough," her friend replied.

"Yes, I believe so." Meredith turned to Susan and said, "It was nice seeing you again. I hope you and your friend will enjoy the rest of your day."

"You, too," Susan said, before taking another picture of her friend in the balloon. She certainly seemed excited about seeing him up there.

Meredith turned and followed Dorine back to the van, where their driver sat slurping on the last of the milk shake she'd bought from a nearby vendor. Meredith looked back one last time and giggled when the man in the balloon, slowly drifting to its highest point, waved again. She realized he'd been waving to everyone, and he probably wasn't even looking at her, but she waved back anyway. She wished she could stay and watch the balloons a few more minutes, but Levi, who'd started crying even louder, couldn't wait any longer to eat. Besides, they really needed to be on their way to the zoo.

<hr />

Eddie leaned over the edge of the basket, grinning like a child. He couldn't believe how high he was. It felt like he could see for miles and miles. The countryside was so beautiful, and the trees were awesome in their autumn glory. If Norma had come, she'd probably say that God had painted this perfect picture.

Looking out over the vibrant reds, blazing oranges, and sensational yellows that stood in contrast to the green grass and wheat-colored fields made it look as if a colorful quilt were blanketing the earth.

When the tether got to its highest point, the balloon just floated where it stopped. It seemed to Eddie as if everything else had disappeared. He could hear the other people who'd ridden up with him in the basket talking, but it was like hearing voices that were far away. At this very moment, up there in the bird's atmosphere, he felt free.

Eddie inhaled deeply. The air felt so pure; it smelled like the wind. He felt alive and at the same time incredibly grateful that he'd had the opportunity to take this ride. This seemed like a dream come true, only he couldn't remember ever wanting to do it before.

He closed his eyes briefly, thanking God for this special day, which he knew he'd remember for a long time to come.

"So what do you think, son?" the middle-aged balloon pilot asked, clasping Eddie's shoulder.

"I—I think it's great being up here so high." Eddie looked down. He could see several cars and trucks on the roads below, winding through all that color. "Everything seems so small from way up here," he murmured. "It's pretty amazing."

"You're right about that." The pilot pointed to the ground. "Everyone down there looks like tiny specks."

Eddie nodded. The people reminded him of the little ants he'd seen scurrying back and forth across the Baileys' porch steps.

At first, when the balloon ventured higher and higher, Eddie had shouted and waved to those on the ground. Now, though, he felt humbled and could hardly talk. He didn't want this moment to end. It was as if he was somehow fulfilling a dream.

CHAPTER 6

Darby

As Eddie walked through the Baileys' living room on a Monday morning in early October, he spotted an old shutter that had been refinished and painted with an unusual design. He reached out his hand and rubbed the glossy finish, amazed at how smooth it felt.

"Ah, I see you're admiring my piece of art," Henry said, strolling into the room, wearing a straw hat with a wide brim.

Eddie nodded. "Did you make it?"

Henry shook his head. "Not hardly. Susan and Anne bought it for me at a farmers' market some time ago."

"This is the first time I've seen it here," Eddie said. "Think I would have noticed something this nice before."

Henry chuckled. "It was in our bedroom, but Norma said it was too nice to keep where only we could enjoy it, so this morning I brought it out here."

"It's sure smooth." Eddie pursed his lips. "Whoever made it did a fine job of sanding, that's for sure."

Henry's bushy eyebrows lifted high. "You sound like you know a little something about that. Do you think you might have done some type of carpentry work before your accident?"

Eddie shrugged. "I don't know. Wish I did, but try as I might, I still can't remember anything about my life before I woke up in the hospital." He dropped his gaze to the floor. "I'm beginning to think I'll never get my memory back."

Henry clasped Eddie's shoulder and gave it a reassuring squeeze. "Just give it some time, son, and try to relax. My guess is if you try to force yourself to remember, that may do more harm than good. Why, I'll bet when you aren't even thinking about it, one day"—he snapped his fingers—"memories from your past will just pop into your head."

Eddie wished Henry was right, but did he dare hope for such a miracle?

"Just remember," Henry added, looking Eddie straight in the eyes, "Norma, the girls, and I are praying for you."

"I appreciate that." Eddie had gone to church with the Baileys every Sunday since he'd moved into their home, and he'd heard the pastor talk about prayer. He didn't remember ever going to church before moving here, but for some reason, a few of the scriptures the pastor had read seemed familiar to him. However, the worship service wasn't familiar at all. In fact, the first Sunday Eddie had gone to the Baileys' church, he'd felt kind of odd—like he didn't belong inside such a fancy building. Was it because he'd been a bum living on the streets before he'd been brought to the hospital all those months ago?

Henry gave Eddie's back a light thump. "So what do you say? Should we head out back and rake up those leaves? After that wind last night, most of them are off the trees. The day looks like it's gonna be a beaut."

"Sure, no problem." Eddie followed Henry out the door. Once outside, he grabbed a rake and started to tackle the leaves. Inhaling a deep breath, he noticed the scent of decaying leaves as he raked them into piles. A slight breeze still blew but nothing like the howling wind they'd had overnight. The grass was green yet, like it had been over summer, but with the recent frost they'd had, it was no longer growing so fast. Soon, the days of mowing would come to an end, and not long after, as Henry had mentioned the other day, it'd be time to get the snow shovels out.

Henry was right about this day being beautiful, Eddie thought as he paused to lean on the rake handle. Looking up into the crystal sky, the color was so blue it almost hurt his eyes. This was a far cry from the last couple of mornings, when the fog had been heavy and the grass wet with dew.

"I always hate to see autumn come to an end," Henry said, raking his own pile of leaves. "It comes and goes too quickly for me." He looked over at Eddie and smiled. "What's your favorite season?"

Eddie shrugged. "I don't really know." He looked up at the sky once more as a helicopter flew overhead and listened as the whirl of the propeller grew fainter. He thought then about the hot air balloon ride he'd taken just a month ago. It had sure been fun to be up there so high, looking down on the people below. *I wonder if I'll ever have the chance to ride in another balloon again. Or better yet, maybe an airplane.*

As Eddie raked the piles of leaves into one big mound, he stopped to look at it and thought how inviting it looked. *I wonder what Henry would think if I took a flying leap right into the middle of those leaves.*

Dismissing that thought as being too childish, Eddie reflected on how much fun he and Susan had had that day at the balloon festival. He enjoyed being with Susan so much and wished he felt free to begin a relationship with her. If he could just get his memory back, maybe he and Susan could start dating. Until then, however, he couldn't let her know how he felt, not to mention the voice inside that nagged at him relentlessly. As much as Eddie tried to ignore it, the voice kept warning: *Hold off; just wait. Don't make any hasty decisions.*

⁂

Ronks, Pennsylvania

Breakfast was over, and everyone in the King household was going about their normal routine. Nina, Stanley, Arlene, and Katie had left over an hour ago for school. Kendra was downstairs, helping Mom sort the laundry, and Laurie could hear her three-year-old brother, Owen, who was also in the basement, laughing out loud. No doubt he was amusing himself with the empty boxes stacked in the corner. Owen loved crawling inside them. Sometimes he would put several of the boxes together, like he was playing house. Once he'd even fallen asleep inside one.

Laurie's dad had left at sunup to pick up his friend Richard Zook for a ride over to Gordonville, where they'd be looking at some Rhode Island Reds to buy. Laurie had already cleaned up the kitchen and had just stepped into the living room to join Grandma Smucker, who sat in the rocking chair, crocheting a bed covering for her great-grandson, Levi.

"How's that blanket coming along?" Laurie asked, picking up a pencil and tablet and taking a seat on the sofa across from Grandma.

Grandma smiled. "Pretty well. It should be done by the time the temperatures dip." She held up the covering for Laurie to see. "It'll be an extra coverlet for Meredith to put over little Levi when winter's upon us."

"I'm sure it'll be nice and warm for him," Laurie commented, focusing on the list she'd started.

"Looks like a nice day out there," Grandma said, glancing toward the window. "Fall is surely upon us. Did you ever see so many leaves in the yard?"

"Hmm. . ." Laurie chewed on the end of her pencil, trying to think of what all she wanted to add to her list. She and Kevin were planning to be married the first week of December, and a lot remained to get done in the coming weeks. It wasn't just the wedding either. A month after that, Laurie would be accompanying Kevin on a work-and-witness trip to Mississippi, where they'd be working in a Native American community. Her future husband had been on several missionary trips before. He'd even gone out of the country a few times. But since this would be Laurie's introduction to missionary work, Kevin had signed them up for work in the United States.

Little by little, Kevin had been orienting Laurie on what they'd be doing once they got to Mississippi. Things like taking the children to local events at a nearby church, preparing food, and helping to celebrate the children's birthdays, which were a festive occasion among the Native Americans. At times the mission also provided transportation for the elderly to doctor and dental appointments, as well as trips to town for other things.

Laurie's life was about to change, but she was excited about it. She'd be working side by side with the man she loved. She only wished everyone in her family was as exuberant as she was.

"Ah-hem."

"Sorry, Grandma. Did you say something?" Laurie's face heated as she looked up from the tablet.

"I asked how your list was coming along."

"Oh, I don't know. There's so much to do yet before the wedding, not to mention the work-and-witness trip Kevin and I will be taking."

"Maybe you should think more about this decision you've made," Grandma said. "It might not hurt to give yourself a little more time to make sure you're doing the right thing and choosing the right direction for your future."

"There's nothing for me to think about, Grandma. I love Kevin. He's a kind, caring person, and the things I've learned from him about missionary work make me love him even more. I think everyone in our family just needs to give him a chance." Laurie sighed. "I wouldn't be doing this if I didn't feel it was right. I know Kevin will be good to me, and I'll be good to him, too."

"But it seems like this is all happening rather quickly," Grandma rationalized, placing her crocheting in her lap. "Your parents had hopes of you remaining in the Amish faith."

"I know that, but—"

"Please, hear me out." Grandma's glasses had fallen to the middle of her nose, and she paused to push them back in place. "I wanted to add that the important thing is that Amish and Mennonite Christian beliefs are very much the same except for some differences in how we view the outside world. Only you can decide if becoming a missionary is the path you wish to take."

"Oh, it is, Grandma," Laurie was quick to say. "I want to spend the rest of my life with Kevin, helping others who are less fortunate and teaching them about Jesus. I know in my heart that this is the right thing for me, because I have a personal relationship with Jesus, and I feel called to work alongside Kevin in sharing the Gospel."

Grandma smiled. "I understand. Just give us all some time to adjust to this new change. It's not easy to let go—especially knowing at times you'll be far from home."

"But I'll never forget you," Laurie said with a shake of her head. "I'll never forget any of my family."

⌘

Bird-in-Hand

Holding Levi firmly in her arms, Meredith shuffled through the fallen leaves in her backyard, enjoying the crackling sound beneath her feet. It was a lovely fall day, and she took pleasure in being outside. She thought the baby must like it, too, for he seemed so alert, making gurgling noises and turning his little head in the direction of the birds chirping and soaring overhead.

Meredith hugged her son even closer. This little guy had brought so much joy to her, as well as to the rest of her family. The other day, when Mom had come by with Owen and Katie, Meredith had laughed when Owen crawled inside an empty cardboard box in her utility room. In another few months, Levi would probably be crawling, and he might be looking for boxes to play in, too.

Meredith smiled. She couldn't imagine life now, without her precious son.

As a bird swooped down to get a drink from the birdbath, Meredith thought about the hot air balloons she and Dorine had seen in Paoli last month. *Oh, how Luke would have enjoyed taking a ride in one of those,* she thought.

Meredith could still remember the group of people she'd seen in the tethered balloon. One of them—the nurse's friend, wearing a red ball cap and sunglasses—had seemed the most excited of all, waving and shouting to the people below. It sure looked like he was having the time of his life. As the balloon rose as far as it could go, the people in the basket had looked so small she couldn't make out any of their faces. She figured from their perspective the people on the ground probably looked even smaller.

Meredith wished now that she'd taken a ride in the balloon, just to see what it was like way up there. She'd never been an adventurous person, but maybe it was time to step out of her comfort zone and start taking some chances. What those chances would be, she didn't know yet, but she'd be ready when the opportunities arose. Being afraid all the time and cautious of everything was no fun at all.

Her thoughts shifted again, thinking about Laurie and the new adventure she and Kevin would take on once they were married. Mom and Dad weren't happy about Laurie not joining the Amish faith, but they were trying to be understanding. Sometimes when grown children made a decision to do something their parents didn't agree with, they just had to let go and accept things as they were.

When Jonah pulled his horse and buggy into Meredith's yard, he spotted her walking through a pile of leaves, holding the baby in her arms. Just the sight of her caused his heart to pound. Oh, how he longed to make her his wife.

He pulled Socks up to the hitching rail, and as soon as he had him secured, he sprinted across the yard toward Meredith. *"Wie geht's?"* he called as she waved and headed toward the house.

"I'm doing okay," she said when he joined her on the porch. "How are you?"

I'm fine now that I'm here with you. "Doin' good," he replied, keeping his thoughts to himself. "Just came by to check on you and extend an invitation."

"Oh?" She tipped her head and looked up at him with questioning eyes.

"My folks and I are planning a little barbecue on Saturday night, and I was wondering if you and Levi would like to come." Jonah reached out and stroked the baby's head.

"Sure, that sounds real nice." Meredith smiled. "Can I bring anything?"

Jonah shook his head. "Just a hearty appetite, 'cause between my barbecued burgers and all the food Mom will fix, there'll be more than enough to eat." He shuffled his feet a few times, feeling like a bashful schoolboy. "Would it be okay if I came by and picked you up around four o'clock?"

"Oh, you don't have to do that. Your folks' place isn't too far from here, and I can ride over with my own horse and buggy."

"I'm sure you can, but I thought it'd be easier for you and the baby if I gave you a ride."

Meredith didn't say anything for several seconds, but then she slowly nodded. "All right then, Levi and I will be ready for you to pick us up by four o'clock."

Jonah grinned. If everything went well on Saturday evening and his nerves didn't take over, he planned to ask Meredith if he could court her.

CHAPTER 7

Bird-in-Hand

Jonah whistled as he flipped hamburgers on the grill. It was great having Meredith and little Levi with them tonight. He glanced up at the porch where Meredith sat on the glider, holding the baby in her arms. Mom was seated nearby in a wicker chair, with Herbie lying on the porch next to her feet. It looked as if the women were deep in conversation, and he was curious to know what they were talking about.

Maybe Mom's putting in a good word for me, Jonah thought. He'd confided in her the other day that he planned to ask Meredith if he could start courting her. Mom had smiled and said she hoped it worked out.

Tonight's the night, Jonah thought. *I just can't wait any longer.*

"Ya better watch it, Son, or you'll burn those burgers," Dad said, stepping up to Jonah and pointing at the grill. "They look pretty done to me."

"Oh, right." Jonah quickly pulled his thoughts aside and scooped the burgers onto the serving tray Mom had provided. The last thing he wanted to do was serve scorched burgers to Meredith. Tonight he wanted everything to be perfect. "Guess I had my mind on something else."

"And it doesn't take a genius to know who." Dad chuckled, nodding toward the house.

Jonah's face heated. Although he hadn't told him of his intentions tonight, he had a feeling Dad already knew. With him going over to Meredith's place so often these days, it was fairly obvious.

Dad thumped Jonah's shoulder. "Well, let's get the ladies and tell 'em it's time to eat. I can't speak for anyone else, but I'm *hungerich.*"

Jonah smiled. Smelling the meat as it cooked had made him hungry, too. Soon they were all seated around the picnic table. Mom and Dad sat on one side and Meredith and Jonah on the other. Levi, sound asleep in his little carrier, was close to his mother. Taking a quick look around, Jonah almost felt as if Meredith and the baby were part of his family.

After their silent prayer, Mom passed around the coleslaw and potato salad she'd made earlier, and Jonah put a burger and bun on everyone's plate. There were also potato chips, some of Mom's homemade dill pickles, and Jonah's favorite—pickled eggs and red beets. It was a little chilly, but the grown-ups wore jackets, and baby Levi was bundled in a cozy-looking blanket Meredith said her grandma had made.

"Sure is a pleasant evening for a barbecue," Mom said after she'd poured everyone a cup of warm apple cider. "Right now it's pleasant because there's hardly any bugs this time of year, but it won't be long before the days will be too cold for eating outside."

"That's okay." Jonah grinned. "I can still barbecue, and we'll eat inside."

"You won't barbecue when there's snow on the ground, I hope," Meredith said, wrinkling her nose.

He shrugged his shoulders. "Probably not; although I could put the grill on the porch."

Dad shook his head. "What would be the point in you standin' outside in the cold when your mamm can cook supper in her kitchen where it's warm and toasty? You can save the barbecuing for the months with nicer weather and leave the wintertime cooking to her."

Mom looked over at Meredith with furrowed brows. "You don't have much on your plate. Don't you care for either of the salads I made?"

"Oh, it's not that. I'm just not very hungry tonight," Meredith replied.

"Jonah will probably eat your share then," Dad said, reaching for some ketchup to put on his bun. "He always eats at least two burgers."

Meredith smiled, but her face looked a bit strained. Jonah wondered if she wished she hadn't come. "Is everything all right?" he asked with concern. Jonah wasn't so sure he'd be able to eat two burgers like he usually did. All of a sudden, he wasn't real hungry either.

"I haven't been sleeping well the last few nights, and I think it's affected my appetite," Meredith explained.

"Is the boppli keeping you awake?" Mom asked, motioning to Levi, who was still asleep.

"That's only part of it," Meredith murmured. "I've been worried about my finances and wondering if I ought to put my house up for rent."

"Where would you go if you did that?" Jonah asked, wishing he could solve her problems right now.

Meredith shrugged. "Probably back home with my folks. I'm sure Luke's parents would take Levi and me in, but I'd rather not impose on them."

Jonah drew in a long breath. If he and Meredith were already courting, he'd ask her to marry him right now so she wouldn't have to worry about her finances. But now wasn't the time to speak of marriage. In just a few more months, her year of mourning would be over. In the meantime, he needed to take things slow and not rush her. But if his folks hadn't been sitting there, he'd ask Meredith if he could court her right now.

⁂

"I think we should go inside now," Jonah's mother, Sarah, said after they'd finished eating. "The sun's going down, and it's getting too chilly for the boppli to be out here."

"You're right," Meredith agreed. "I'm thinking maybe it's time for Levi and me to go home." She glanced over at Jonah.

"But we haven't had our dessert yet," Jonah said. "Mom made a couple of apple pies."

"That's right," Sarah agreed. "So why don't I take the boppli inside, and you and Meredith can sit out here awhile and watch as the sun goes down and the stars come out. After you've seen enough, you can join us in the kitchen for a piece of pie."

"That sounds nice," Meredith replied, "but I have to change Levi first. Come to think of it, I haven't taken the time to watch the stars come out in a long while." *Not since Luke died,* she thought with regret.

"I'll help clear away the dishes," Jonah said, jumping up from the table. "Then I'll grab a blanket from the house in case we get cold."

Meredith smiled. She was sure the look of pleasure on Sarah's face meant that she appreciated her son's willingness to help out.

"I'll move the grill back to the shed," Jonah's dad, Raymond, said.

"Better make sure it's cooled off good before you put it away," Jonah

280

commented. "Remember what happened a few years ago when the Bontragers' barn burned down?"

Dad nodded. "Who could forget that? It was unfortunate that a day of celebrating turned to tragedy when Ethan Bontrager wheeled their grill into the barn when it wasn't cooled off yet."

Jonah's forehead wrinkled as he reflected on that evening. The Bontragers had been his folks' best friends when they lived in Ohio. They'd been celebrating one of their children's birthdays by having a big cookout. Everything had been going well, until a sudden thunderstorm blew in; then chaos broke loose. Everyone ran, grabbing what they could. The grill, which had still been hot, was wheeled into the barn, and they ended up continuing the party inside the house. In the end, they lost their barn and all its contents, including tools, buggies, two horses, and a milking cow, all because they hadn't let the grill cool.

Goose bumps erupted on Jonah's arm, imagining such a disaster happening to his folks. Thankfully, no one in the Bontrager family had been hurt that night, but having seen what had taken years to acquire go up in smoke because of a careless decision, Jonah knew the little reminder he'd given his dad could do no harm.

"It's all good," Dad said, as he pulled the grill toward the shed. "There's no heat left at all."

While Jonah's dad headed for the shed, Meredith, carrying Levi's infant seat, followed Jonah and Sarah up to the house. Once inside, Meredith fed the baby and changed his diaper. When she was done, she set his carrier in the living room, where Sarah and Jonah had gone after the dishes were done. Raymond joined them a few minutes later.

"Should we go outside now?" Jonah asked, lightly touching Meredith's arm.

Meredith looked at Sarah. "Are you sure you don't mind keeping an eye on Levi?"

Sarah shook her head. "Not at all."

Meredith, feeling a bit apprehensive about leaving the baby, said, "If he starts fussing and you can't get him settled down, just come and get me."

"I'm sure he'll be fine. If he does wake up, it'll give me a good excuse to hold him." Sarah motioned to the door. "Now you and Jonah go out and enjoy watching the stars."

Jonah grabbed a crocheted afghan from the back of the sofa and held the door for Meredith. When they stepped onto the porch, Meredith's breath caught in her throat. Glowing splashes of color—pink, orange, and red— spread across the sky as the sun sank slowly into the west. She stood on the porch, watching until the sun and its glorious shine disappeared. Suddenly, a multitude of stars peeked out under the dark night sky.

"Sure is a beautiful night, isn't it?" Jonah whispered, leaning close to Meredith.

"Jah." She shivered, not knowing if the chill she felt was from the cool evening breeze or from Jonah's breath blowing softly against her ear.

"Should we stay here on the porch or walk out to the picnic table to watch for falling stars?" Jonah asked, draping the afghan across her shoulders.

"Let's go out to the picnic table. I think we'll be able to see the stars better from there."

Jonah led the way, and once they were seated on the picnic bench, Meredith turned to face him. "Luke and I used to sit outside and watch for falling stars. It was a special thing we liked to do. We did some stargazing our last night together."

Jonah placed his hand gently on her arm. "You still miss him, don't you?"

She nodded. "I wake up some mornings and expect to see Luke lying there beside me. Sometimes I dream that I look out the window and see him walking up the driveway. But just as he nears the house, he suddenly disappears."

"It's hard to lose someone you love," Jonah said. "I know Luke's memory will always be with you, but do you think you might ever find room in your heart to love again?"

Meredith sat several seconds before she replied. "I don't know—maybe."

"I care for you, Meredith," Jonah murmured. "And I—well, I was wondering if you'd be willing to let me court you."

Meredith wasn't sure what to say. She cared for Jonah, too. He was a good friend, but could she ever love him the way she had Luke? If Luke could reach down from heaven and tell her what to do, would he give his approval for her to be courted again?

She looked up at the starry sky, and when she spotted a falling star, a lump formed in her throat. Could this be a sign from Luke that it was okay for her to move on without him and perhaps take the next step to continue her life—a new life with Jonah?

"Meredith, have I said too much? Is it too soon for me to be talking about us courting?" Jonah asked.

After seeing the falling star, Meredith drew in a deep breath and released it slowly. "No, Jonah, it's not too soon. I'd be honored to have you court me."

Jonah reached for her hand, surprised at how warm it felt. "I'm the one who's honored."

⌘

Darby

"Did you ever see such a beautiful night sky?" Susan asked as she took a seat beside Eddie on the lawn swing in the Baileys' backyard. Norma, Henry, and Anne had already gone to bed, but Susan had said she wasn't tired, and when Eddie said he wasn't either, she'd suggested they go outside and gaze at the stars.

"You're right," he said, tilting his head back to look at the sky. "Some of the stars are so bright it seems like you could almost reach out and touch 'em."

"Ever since Anne and I were little girls, we've enjoyed watching the stars. It's fun to search for the Big and Little Dippers and all the other constellations. But it's not only that. Watching the stars this time of the year holds a special place in my heart."

"What do you mean?" Eddie asked, his curiosity piqued.

"Well, as far back as I can remember, sitting outside on a cool October night is something my family did every year. That is, up until our parents were killed. Anne and I were teenagers when it happened." Susan paused, and her voice faltered. "But before their deaths, every fall we'd pick a night such as this and call it our 'make a wish night.' At sunset, Dad would put a log on to burn in the barbecue pit in our backyard, and we'd wait until the coals turned to embers. By then the sky was totally dark, like it is now. Mom made hot chocolate, and we'd sit side by side and watch the sky, holding our

283

mugs with fingers sticky from the marshmallows we'd roasted." She paused again, her voice growing lower. "All year long I'd think of one special wish, and I'd save it for that special night. Then, when I'd see a falling star, I'd make my wish. Of course, even back then I knew making wishes was just for fun. From the time we were little, Dad and Mom taught Anne and me about the importance of prayer and how we should ask God to meet our needs."

"And has He?" Eddie asked.

She nodded slowly. "Even though Mom and Dad were taken from us, Anne and I have never done without. Grandma and Grandpa make sure of that, and we're grateful to them."

Eddie reached for Susan's hand as they stared up at the velvety blackness above. Suddenly, out of the darkness, a shooting star streaked across the sky, causing him to shiver. A strange feeling came over him; he felt like he'd done this before with someone else—a young woman, perhaps. He felt goose bumps rising on his arms. Was it the strange feeling of having stargazed with someone before, or was it because Susan's soft hand rested securely in his?

"Did you see that shooting star, Merrie?" he murmured.

Susan's hand slipped away from his. "Merrie? Who's Merrie, Eddie?"

"I don't know." He shook his head slowly, feeling even more confused. "I don't know why, but I feel like that shooting star has something to do with my past. If I could only remember who I'd seen it with, it might give me a clue as to who I am."

CHAPTER 8

Ronks

"Ach, Meredith, what a surprise! I didn't expect to see you this morning," Luann said when she opened the door and found Meredith on the porch with Levi in her arms.

Meredith smiled. "I've been meaning to come by and tell you my news, but Levi's been fussy all week, and I didn't want to take him out."

"What news is that?" Luann asked, reaching out to stroke the baby's soft cheek.

"Jonah and I are going to start courting."

Luann gasped. "When was this decided?"

"Last Saturday Levi and I were invited to the Millers' for a barbecue, and later that evening Jonah asked if he could begin courting me."

Luann sucked in her breath. "Ach, Meredith, are you sure about this? I mean, do you love Jonah?"

"Not in the same way I did Luke, but Jonah's a wonderful man, and I'll get to know him even better when we start courting. If we should end up getting married someday, I'm sure he'll be a good daed to Levi."

Luann stood a few seconds, unsure of what to say. She knew Jonah and Meredith were friends and that he'd gone over to her place many times to help out, but she hadn't realized things were getting serious between them.

"You're awfully quiet, Mom. What do you think about this?"

"Well, you took me by surprise. I hadn't realized your relationship with Jonah was anything more than friendship, but if being courted by him will make you happy, then you have my blessing." Luann paused, and her forehead wrinkled. "I hope you won't agree to marry him too soon, though, or that your decision will be based on your financial needs."

Meredith shook her head. "I know Jonah would be a good provider, but that's not the reason I agreed to let him court me. I care very much for Jonah, and he's good with the boppli."

"So have you made this decision more for the baby than yourself?"

"Not more; it's just one of the reasons."

"Do Sadie and Elam know about this?" Luann questioned.

"No, not yet. It'll be hard telling Luke's folks that Jonah and I will be courting, but I know I have to. I wouldn't want them to hear about it from someone else. It would hurt them deeply."

❦

Gordonville, Pennsylvania

"Wie geht's?" Sadie asked when she stepped into the bookstore and spotted Sarah Miller browsing through a stack of cookbooks.

Sarah smiled. "I'm doing well. How are you?"

"Doin' as well as can be expected, I guess."

"Have you heard Meredith and Jonah's news?" Sarah asked.

Sadie's eyebrows arched. "What news is that?"

"They're going to start courting."

Sadie's mouth dropped open, and her heart pounded so hard she felt like her chest might explode. "W—when was this decided?"

"Last Saturday Jonah asked Meredith if he could court her." Sarah smiled widely. "Raymond and I think the world of Meredith, and we're happy Jonah's found such a wonderful woman. If they were to marry someday, it would mean so much to have someone as special as Meredith for our daughter-in-law."

Sadie gripped the edge of the bookshelf for support. Learning that Meredith and Jonah were planning to court was surprising enough, but the fact that Meredith hadn't said anything to her and Elam about it was disappointing and hurtful. Didn't their daughter-in-law think they had the right to know? How long was she planning to keep this news from them?

Sadie looked at Sarah, unable to form any words. Did Sarah expect her to be happy about Jonah and Meredith courting? She knew what a wonderful daughter-in-law the Millers would be getting if Meredith ended up marrying their son. But it didn't seem fair. Meredith was Sadie's daughter-in-law, and Levi was *her* grandson. This year had been difficult enough for her and Elam with the loss of their son. Sadie had been hoping the family's support would be enough for Meredith and that she would give herself more time before agreeing to let someone court her. *Time, though, for who?* she wondered. *Would I be happy about anyone courting Meredith, or is it just Jonah I don't approve of?*

Jonah seemed like a nice enough man, and he would probably be good to Meredith and Levi. But if Meredith should marry him, things would be different, and she might end up pulling away from Sadie and Elam. That would hurt so much—especially if they didn't get to see Levi very often.

"Sadie, I'm so sorry," Sarah said with a look of pity in her eyes. "I wasn't thinking, blurting that out. I should have let Meredith tell you."

Sadie squared her shoulders, determined not to let Sarah know how she really felt. "It's okay," she murmured. "I'm glad you told me."

Sarah looked like she might say something more, but Sadie turned and hurried from the bookstore before the tears welling in her eyes spilled onto her cheeks.

<hr />

Bird-in-Hand

Jonah and his dad had been working hard in the buggy shop all morning, and at noontime, Jonah was more than ready to take a break.

"Let's get this wheel put on Aaron Raber's buggy, and then we can go up to the house for lunch," Dad said.

"That's fine. Guess my stomach can wait a few more minutes," Jonah said with a grin.

As they worked together, Jonah told his dad about a house he was interested in buying. "It's only a few miles from here," he said. "So if I get the place, I can probably ride my scooter on nice days to get to work."

"Are you thinking of puttin' an offer on it now, or will you wait to see how things work out between you and Meredith?" Dad asked.

"I think I ought to buy it now 'cause it might not be there in a few months," Jonah replied. "Besides, if I get the place now, then I'll have some time to fix it up. I want things to work out for me and Meredith, probably more than you realize. But even if it doesn't, I'd still like to buy a place of my own. Maybe someday I'll have a wife and family, like I've always hoped for."

"That's good thinking, Son." Dad gave Jonah's shoulder a tight squeeze. He headed across the room to his workbench. "Think I'd better look for a bigger wrench." He'd no sooner reached for the wrench when he let out a yelp. "Yikes! I think something bit my hand."

Jonah set the wheel on the floor and hurried across the room. "Better let me take a look at that."

"I think it was a spider," Dad said, looking toward the tool he'd dropped, while rubbing his hand. "I've been meaning to spray the shop after seeing several webs but haven't gotten around to it yet. It's warm in here with the woodstove burning, and since it's getting cooler outside, I've noticed more webs showing up in the shop."

"You might be right, but don't worry about that right now." Jonah took hold of his dad's hand. "Let's hope it wasn't a black widow." Taking a closer look, he noticed how quickly the area of the bite had begun to redden and swell. "You'd better get inside and put some ice on that bite while I go to the phone shack and call our driver. The sooner you see a doctor, the better it'll be." Jonah knew that, while usually not deadly, the bite from a black widow spider could be serious.

The wrench still lay on the workbench where Dad had dropped it, and sure enough, on a post right by the table, a shiny black spider was repairing its damaged web.

A quick look around revealed numerous webs up in the rafters and some spun between several unused tools. Jonah picked up a hammer and stood watching, taking in the spider's details. Just as the eight-legged menace came out of its web and crawled across the tabletop surface, Jonah smacked it with the hammer.

Dashing from the shop to the phone shack, he mentally pictured the red, hourglass shape on the spider's belly. He was positive that Dad had been bitten by a black widow spider.

Darby

"Sure will be glad when we get this done," Henry said as he and Eddie chopped a stack of firewood.

Eddie stopped long enough to wipe his sweaty forehead. "Guess we can be glad it's not hot and humid like it was this summer."

Henry grinned. "Always did like the fall for that very reason."

Eddie went back to chopping, while Henry stacked the wood into a pile under a lean-to near the shed. When they were halfway done, Henry removed the straw hat on his head and waved it in front of his face. "Don't know about you, but I'm hungry. Let's go inside and see if Norma has lunch ready yet."

"Sounds good to me." Eddie set his axe aside and followed Henry toward the house.

They found Norma in the kitchen, stirring a pot of soup. Eddie sniffed the air. "That sure smells good. What kind of soup did you make?"

"It's lentil with chunks of ham, potatoes, carrots, and onions." Norma smiled. "The vegetables are from Henry's garden, of course."

"Is the soup about ready to eat?" Henry asked, moving over to the sink to wash his hands.

"Yes it is, and as soon as you hang up your hat, we can eat."

Eddie joined Henry at the sink and watched as the older man moved slowly across the room to hang his straw hat on a wall peg near the back door. Eddie had seen Henry wear that hat many times before, but for some reason, seeing it now made him think he might have seen a hat like that before.

Shaking the idea aside, he thought about how he and Henry had been working hard all morning and how Henry's muscles were probably sore. Eddie, on the other hand, felt pretty good. He figured all the physical therapy, plus working around there, had built up his muscles. He'd noticed the other morning when he looked in the mirror that his arms were really toning up. If things kept going as well as they had, he'd be done with therapy in the next few weeks. Now if he could just get his memory back, he'd be good as new.

Guess I'd better accept the fact that my memory may never return, he thought as he finished washing his hands. *And if that's the case, then I'll need to come up with some way to support myself. Can't stay here with the Baileys forever.*

"Come on, Eddie. Take a seat." Henry pulled out a chair at the table.

After everyone was seated, Henry led in prayer. "Heavenly Father, we thank You for this good-smelling soup my wife prepared and for the beautiful fall weather. I also want to thank You for bringing Eddie into our home, and we appreciate all the help he's given us. Be with Anne and Susan at the hospital today, and give them the strength they need to do their jobs. In Jesus' name we ask, amen."

A lump formed in Eddie's throat. These kind people felt like family. Even with all that had happened to him, he was truly blessed.

"Here you go," Norma said, handing Eddie a bowl of soup.

"Thanks. If it looks as good as it smells, then I'm in for a treat."

"Oh, I can guarantee it'll be good," Henry said, smacking his lips. "My wife's lentil soup is the best there is."

Norma smiled and gave Eddie the basket of crackers, followed by a tray full of sliced turkey and cheddar cheese. "Oh my, I forgot to get out the apples I had sliced. Those always go so well with cheese." Going to the refrigerator, Norma laughed when she paused to glance out the kitchen window. "I see George out there. He's hopping all over your stack of firewood, Henry. Why, I'll bet that little critter is looking for something to eat."

"You're probably right," Henry agreed.

"We'll have to save him a treat from our lunch." Eddie smiled. Even that little squirrel had become special to him.

As they ate they talked about the church social coming up, and Norma described some of the craft items she was making that would be auctioned off. "The money our women's missionary society makes from the benefit auction will go to help some of our missionaries in Africa."

"Maybe there's something I could make to donate," Eddie said. "I'm just not sure what it could be."

"How about helpin' me make some wooden birdhouses?" Henry suggested. "I usually make several whenever we have a benefit auction, and they've always gone for a pretty good price."

"If you'll show me what to do, I'll be glad to help. Maybe if I get good enough, I can make a feeder for little George."

Henry grinned. "Don't think it'll take much to show you. From what I've seen, you've caught on pretty fast to everything I've asked you to do since you moved here."

"That's right," Norma chimed in. "You're not only a hard worker, but you're smart."

Eddie's face heated. It was nice to be appreciated, but it embarrassed him, too.

"What time will Susan be home today?" he asked, needing to change the subject.

"She left at the crack of dawn," Norma said. "So she'll probably be here around three."

"Susan mentioned the two of us going over to the park so we could walk through the fallen leaves," Eddie said.

"That's my Susan." Norma smiled. "Always did like to tromp around in the leaves during the fall."

Henry reached for a piece of cheese and put it between two crackers. "I remember one year, Susan and Anne raked up a big pile of leaves in our backyard just so they could jump in the middle of 'em. Susan said she liked to hear the crackle of the dried leaves."

Eddie nodded. "She told me the same thing last week when we were raking up some leaves. It almost seemed like she was making a game of it."

"I wouldn't be surprised if that was the case," Norma interjected. "She was probably pretending she was a young girl again. I can still hear both girls giggling way back then. They'd come up out of the pile with leaves stuck in their hair. Yes, it was good ole plain, simple fun."

"Whelp, I love to reminisce, and maybe we can do more of that this evening," Henry said, pulling a gold pocket watch from his pants pocket. "But I think we oughta get back outside and finish chopping the rest of that wood, don't you, Eddie? We can take a few of these crackers out for George, too."

Eddie stayed sitting, staring at the pocket watch. He could feel his heart hammering in his chest. There was something about Henry's watch that seemed familiar to him. Could he have had a watch like that at some time? If so, was the watch somehow special to him?

Norma touched Eddie's arm. "Are you all right? You've had a very strange look on your face ever since Henry took the watch out of his pocket."

"I think I may have had a watch like that sometime in my past," Eddie murmured.

"Really?" Henry leaned closer. "Think hard, Eddie. Think about the pocket watch you used to have and where it came from."

Eddie sat quietly, eyes riveted on the watch, trying to recall having had one of his own. Suddenly he jumped out of his seat and shouted, "I think I know my name. It's Luke!"

A VOW FOR ALWAYS

Thou hast turned for me my mourning into dancing:
thou hast put off my sackcloth,
and girded me with gladness.

PSALM 30:11

CHAPTER 1

Darby, Pennsylvania

"Is it true, Eddie? Do you really remember your name?" Susan asked excitedly as she rushed into the living room. "I just got home from my shift at the hospital, and Grandpa gave me the good news."

He looked up at her from his seat in front of the fireplace and nodded. "I'm pretty sure my name's Luke."

"Luke's a biblical name." Susan smiled as a sense of hope welled in her chest. "Do you know your last name, Luke?"

He shook his head, a look of defeat clouding his turquoise eyes. "You'd think if I could remember my first name I'd know my last name, too, but I don't. I still can't remember anything about my past." Luke groaned. "It's so frustrating."

Susan knelt on the floor beside him and touched his arm. "It'll come to you, Eddie—I mean, Luke. Just give it time. Remember what the doctors have told you. Your memory could return slowly. It's been about nine months since your accident. I think it's a positive sign that you're beginning to remember."

He stared at the fire. "You really think so?"

"Of course. Seeing Grandpa's pocket watch jogged your memory. With more time, other things will pop into your mind." Susan hoped she sounded more confident than she felt, for she really wanted to offer him hope. For that matter, she needed hope, too—that Luke would remember everything about his past and that they wouldn't discover he was married.

≈

Bird-in-Hand, Pennsylvania

Grasping a can of insect repellant, Jonah sprayed all around the buggy shop, watching as several spiders came out of nowhere.

"This should have been done a whole lot sooner," Jonah mumbled as he finished spraying. Usually they had this job done before October, but life had gotten in the way. So that morning, Dad had been bitten by a black widow spider. Besides pain and redness, Dad had developed some muscle cramping, a headache, and nausea. At the hospital, he'd been treated with an antibiotic, given some cream for the spider bite, and kept overnight for observation. The doctor had assured them that Dad would be alright, and luckily he didn't have a severe allergic reaction. His hand would probably be sore for a few days, and he was advised not to do any work in the shop until it felt better. Now it was Jonah's turn to carry the load, but he would do it gladly, just as Dad had done when Jonah broke his ankle.

Woof! Woof! Jonah smiled as Herbie, his folks' frisky border collie, darted into the shop with a small squash in his mouth and promptly dropped it on the floor at Jonah's feet.

"That's not a ball for you to play fetch with," Jonah scolded while he washed the bug spray off his hands. "Mom's not gonna like it when she finds out you've been stealing things from her garden."

Herbie looked up at Jonah with his big brown eyes, as though waiting for him to pick up the squash and throw it. When the dog got no reaction, he leaned down on his front legs, tail wagging in the air, and pushed the squash toward Jonah with his nose.

Jonah chuckled. "You don't take no for an answer, do you, boy?"

Woof! Woof! Woof!

He picked up the squash, placed it on the workbench, and looked for Herbie's rubber ball. He found it on a shelf near the door and cleaned it, too. "Here you go, boy—fetch!" Jonah pitched the ball out the door, and Herbie tore across the yard, yipping until he snagged the ball.

Jonah quickly shut the door so he could get back to work. As he finished up the buggy he and Dad had been working on, his thoughts went to

Meredith. He still couldn't believe she'd agreed to let him court her, and he couldn't wait to spend more time with her.

⚬

Ronks, Pennsylvania

"It's been nice visiting you," Meredith told her mother, "but Levi and I really should go. I want to stop by Elam and Sadie's place on the way home and let them know that Jonah and I will be courting."

"I hope it goes well," Mom said, leaning over to kiss the top of the baby's head.

"I hope so, too." Meredith gathered her belongings and carried Levi out to her buggy.

When she arrived at the Stoltzfuses' place a short time later, Elam was home, but Sadie had gone shopping.

"Do you know when she'll be home?" Meredith asked.

Elam shook his head. "You know my Sadie. She likes to shop, and if she ran into any of her friends along the way, she's probably gabbing like a magpie."

Meredith smiled, wondering if she should tell Elam her news and let him relay the message to Sadie. It might be easier. If Sadie had anything negative to say, at least Meredith wouldn't have to hear about it today.

"Why don't ya come in and have a seat?" Elam opened the door wider. "We can visit before Sadie gets back." He grinned. "It'll give me a chance to hold my *kinskinner* without Sadie hogging him the way she always does."

Meredith didn't know whether to laugh or cry. It was true; whenever Sadie had the chance to hold Levi, she was reluctant to let him go.

"I guess we could visit awhile," Meredith agreed. "Although if Sadie doesn't get here soon, I'll have to head for home and get supper started."

"You could stay and eat supper with us," Elam suggested, leading the way to the living room.

"I appreciate the offer, but I invited my friend Dorine and her family over for supper, so I'll need to go pretty soon."

"Can I hold the *boppli*?" Elam asked.

"Of course." Meredith smiled, seeing the look of joy on her father-in-law's face. She'd just handed Levi to Elam, when Sadie entered the room.

"We didn't hear you coming," Elam said, holding his grandson gently, as if he were afraid the little one might break. "Look who stopped by for a visit."

"I'm glad you're here," Meredith said, smiling at her mother-in-law. "There's something I want to tell you and Elam."

Sadie's eyes narrowed. She looked directly at Meredith. "If it's about you and Jonah courting, I already know. What I don't understand is why you kept it from us."

"I was planning to tell you. That's the reason I'm over here now."

Sadie's mouth turned down at the corners. "It's too soon for you to be courting. Luke's only been dead nine months."

"I realize that, but it's not like I've agreed to marry Jonah. We'll just be getting to know each other better."

"Courting can lead to marriage, and it often does." Sadie's voice was edged with concern. "You may not realize it, but I'm sure Jonah has marriage on his mind." When she looked over at Elam for his support, he merely shrugged. "Do you love Jonah?" Sadie questioned, turning her attention back to Meredith.

Meredith dropped her gaze to the floor. "I think I do, although not the way I did Luke."

"Humph!" Sadie tapped her foot. "Guess there's nothing I can do about that, but I don't have to like it."

Meredith felt sick at heart. She'd known the feelings of others would have to be considered, and instinct had told her that Sadie wouldn't take the news well. But did she have to be so rude? Meredith wished everything could be like it was when Luke was alive. She wasn't the type to think only of herself. But things were different now. She had a son to consider. Would Sadie ever accept the idea of Meredith being with any other man than Luke?

<hr />

Hearing the steady *clip-clop* of a horse's hooves, Meredith glanced out the kitchen window the following morning and spotted Jonah's rig pulling in. She noticed the bounce to his step as he hurried across the yard after securing his horse to the hitching rail. A cool, comfortable day such as this would put pep in anyone's step.

Autumn was in its finest glory now that October was in full swing. After the long, hot days of summer, the cooler weather was like a breath of fresh air. The smell of wood smoke wafting from chimney tops meant warmth inside from stoves being stoked, and Meredith could see her breath when she stepped outside each morning.

"*Wie geht's?*" Jonah asked when Meredith opened the door.

She smiled. "I'm fine. How are you this beautiful day?"

"I'm doin' good, but I can't say the same for my *daed*."

"What's wrong?" Meredith asked, noticing the troubled look on Jonah's face.

"He got bit by a black widow spider. Happened while we were working in the buggy shop yesterday."

Meredith gasped. "*Ach*, my! Is he okay?"

"He showed no signs of being allergic to the venom, but his hand's pretty sore, so I'll be working in the shop by myself for a couple of days." Jonah glanced back at his horse, pawing at the ground as though anxious to go. "I'd wanted to take you and Levi for a ride to look at the colorful leaves today, but there's so much work at the shop that needs to be done, I'm afraid our little outing's gonna have to wait a few days. Maybe this Sunday after church we can go—that is, if you're free."

"Sunday afternoon would work fine for us. The leaves are just peaking, and it'll give me something to look forward to." Meredith's gaze dropped to the porch.

"Is everything all right?" Jonah asked, lightly touching her arm.

She didn't want to hurt his feelings but felt he had the right to know about Sadie's reaction to the news that they would be courting.

She lifted her gaze to meet his. "I went over to see Luke's parents yesterday afternoon and told them you'd asked to court me."

"How'd it go?"

"Elam didn't say much, but Sadie thinks it's too soon for me to be seeing anyone. She reminded me that Luke hasn't been gone a year yet."

"What do you think, Meredith?" Jonah questioned. "Are you comfortable with me courting you right now, or would you rather wait a few more months?"

Meredith shook her head. "I don't want to wait. I think once Sadie sees how good you are with Levi and realizes you're not trying to take Luke's place she'll accept the idea."

Jonah's eyebrows pulled together. "Maybe I should have a talk with her—try to make her see how much I care about you and Levi and that I only want what's best for you. I'd like to assure her that even though we'll be courting, I have no intention of changing how often they can see their grandson. I would never come between them and Levi."

"I'm sure Sadie will be relieved to hear that, but I think we should give her some time. If she doesn't warm up to the idea soon, then you might try talking to her about it."

"You're right, that's probably best." Jonah grinned. "You're not only pretty but *schmaert* too."

Meredith felt her cheeks blush. "It's nice of you to say, Jonah, but I don't always feel so smart. I'm still struggling to decide whether to rent out my house. I don't like the idea of leaving my own place and moving in with my folks."

"Would you like my opinion?" he asked.

"*Jah*, please."

"If you put your place up for rent and move in with your folks, that would take a financial burden off your shoulders. Plus, it will generate some extra income for you, and you can concentrate on taking care of Levi."

"You're right," Meredith agreed, "but things are always so hectic at my folks,' and sometimes my younger siblings get on my nerves."

"Well, I wish—" Jonah's words were cut off by the sounds of a horse and buggy arriving. When he saw Alma Beechy, he turned and started down the steps. "I'd better go now, Meredith, but I'll see you and Levi on Sunday afternoon."

Meredith smiled. "I'm looking forward to it, Jonah."

∽∾

Philadelphia, Pennsylvania

"What are we going to do about Eddie—I mean Luke?" Susan asked as her sister, Anne, pulled her car into the hospital parking lot.

Anne's eyebrows arched. "What do you mean?"

"Ever since he remembered his name, he's been depressed—more so than before." Susan frowned. "I'm really worried about him."

"He'll be fine," Anne said, turning off the ignition. "Grandpa's keeping Luke busy with projects around the house, so that should help with his depression. I'm sure that remembering his name has left Luke starving to recall everything else about his life before he came to know us, and that'll happen in time."

"I can't imagine what it's like for him, struggling to grasp details that seem to be just beyond his reach." Susan sighed. "I hope Luke gets his memory back, but I'm also scared."

"Of what?" Anne asked.

"That he might be married."

Anne touched Susan's arm. "You've fallen in love with him, haven't you?"

Tears sprang to Susan's eyes as she nodded slowly. "I've tried not to, but Luke's so sweet. I feel so happy when I'm with him. I never thought there would be someone out there for me like Luke. Even though I don't know anything about his past, what I do know of him. . .well, he's everything I've ever dreamed a man could be." She sniffed. "Maybe we made a mistake inviting Luke to move into Grandma and Grandpa's house."

Anne gave Susan's shoulder a tender squeeze. "You need to stop worrying about this. When Luke's memory returns in full, you might discover that he's not only single, but rich."

Susan snickered, despite her tears, knowing that a man's wealth didn't matter to her at all. "I doubt he's rich. If he were, he wouldn't have been wearing tattered-looking clothes when he was found unconscious at the bus station all those months ago."

⁂

Darby

"You okay, Luke?" Henry asked as the two men worked on some birdhouses in the garage. "You look a little down-in-the-mouth this morning."

Luke shrugged and blew on his cold hands. "I didn't sleep very well last night. Had a weird dream about seeing people with no faces. I've had that dream a few other times, too."

Henry set his hammer aside. "I have a hunch those faces you couldn't make out might be people from your past."

"Then why can't I remember who they are?"

"I don't know, but I think if you give it more time it'll come back to you."

"That's what Susan and Anne keep saying, but I have my doubts. If I was gonna remember, don't you think it would have happened by now?"

Henry scratched his head. "That all depends."

"On what?"

"From what Susan's told me about her work, some folks in your position get their memory back in pieces, a little bit at a time."

Luke groaned. "And some never get it back at all. The doctors have warned me about that possibility."

"Maybe for some that's true, but you've remembered your first name now. I think that's a sign you'll be able to put the rest of the pieces together soon." He thumped Luke's back. "In the meantime, we have some birdhouses to build, 'cause the annual church bazaar is just a few weeks away."

Luke picked up a piece of sandpaper. Despite his frustration, he would try to focus on the job before him and not get pulled back into the black hole of sadness that seemed determined to overwhelm him. Living with Susan and Anne's grandparents had given him a sense of family—of belonging somewhere and doing something meaningful. Even so, he longed to know if he had a family of his own. If so, where did they live? Were they looking for him, or had they forgotten he'd ever existed?

CHAPTER 2

Bird-in-Hand

As Meredith guided her horse and buggy down the road toward Elam and Sadie's house, a chill raced down her back. She was plagued with doubts. It had been two weeks since she'd told her in-laws about letting Jonah court her. In those two weeks, she'd only seen them at church, so she hadn't been able to speak to them privately. Meredith loved Sadie and Elam and wanted their approval.

Well, at least Mom and Dad don't object to me being courted by Jonah. Meredith glanced at Levi, asleep in his carrier on the seat beside her. *It's nice to have someone's support.*

Meredith thought about how Mom and Dad had objected when her sister Laurie had first decided to marry Kevin, who was a Mennonite. It wasn't merely the fact that Laurie wouldn't be joining the Amish faith that bothered them. It was the idea of her moving away and becoming a missionary. The Kings were a close-knit family, and it would be hard to see Laurie go.

But things didn't always turn out the way a person wanted. Losing Luke had been one of the hardest things Meredith had ever dealt with. Yet as Grandma Smucker had reminded her several times, life didn't stop because a loved one died. Meredith had made up her mind to make the best of her situation and keep her focus on raising Levi.

Meredith's thoughts came to a halt when Elam and Sadie's house came into view. She hoped they were home and would be willing to watch Levi for a few hours.

∽◈∾

Hearing a horse and buggy come into the yard, Sadie set aside her mending and went to the door. Meredith was hitching the horse to the rail, and when she reached into the buggy and brought Levi out, Sadie smiled in anticipation.

She added a piece of wood to the slow-dying embers in the woodstove before grabbing a shawl and going out to greet her daughter-in-law and grandson.

"It's good to see you," Sadie said when Meredith joined her on the porch. "It's been awhile since we visited." She reached out and stroked the top of Levi's head. "He's growing so much."

Meredith smiled. "I know. He's doing all sorts of new things."

"Like what?" Sadie asked, motioning for Meredith to come inside.

Meredith took a seat on the sofa and pulled Levi's blanket aside. "Well, let's see. . . He's kicking and pushing with his feet; grabs for anything within his reach; smiles, laughs, gurgles, and coos. Oh, and he's sleeping through the night now."

"I'm sure that's a relief," Sadie said, taking a seat in the rocking chair across from Meredith.

"Jah. I'm finally getting caught up on my rest." Meredith smiled. "Of course, taking care of Levi and trying to get some sewing done keeps me busy. Not to mention all of the household chores that need attention."

"Is your sister Laurie still coming over to help you?" Sadie questioned.

Meredith shook her head. "She's busy getting ready for her wedding."

"What about Alma Beechy?"

"She's not helping me now, either," Meredith said. "But I'm managing to keep up with things inside, and between Jonah and my daed, the outside chores are getting done."

Sadie's forehead wrinkled. "You ought to call on Elam more, instead of asking Jonah. I'm sure he's got lots to do at the buggy shop."

"Speaking of Elam, where is he right now?" Meredith asked.

"He had a dental appointment this morning. When he's done there, he has some errands to run."

"Oh, I see." Meredith sat quietly for a moment. Then she looked at Sadie and said, "I was wondering if you'd be willing to watch Levi while I run a few errands and take care of some business this morning."

Surprised by the offer, Sadie nodded agreeably. "I'd be happy to do that. By the time you get back, Elam might be here, and we can all have lunch together."

"That'd be nice." Meredith handed Levi to Sadie; then she reached into his diaper bag and took out a bottle. "I just fed him before we left home, but if he gets hungry before I return, you can feed him this bottle I've filled with breast milk."

"I can certainly do that." Sadie looked forward to the time she'd have with her grandson. "You can put it in the refrigerator for now, and I'll heat it up if he gets fussy."

"*Danki*," Meredith said as she started for the kitchen. "I shouldn't be gone more than a few hours."

⸎

"Are you sure you don't mind me taking today off?" Jonah asked as he and Dad mucked out the horse stalls. It had been two weeks since Dad had been bitten by the black widow, and he'd been back working in the buggy shop for the last week.

" 'Course I don't mind. We agreed some time ago that Mondays would be your day off, so if you've made plans for the day, just do 'em."

Jonah smiled. He'd been courting Meredith, and even though they'd gone for a couple of buggy rides and done a few other things together, he didn't see nearly as much of her as he'd like. Today, however, before he went to see Meredith, Jonah wanted to pay a call on Sadie and Elam, hoping he might win them over. He planned to do that as soon as he finished up in the barn.

"Anything new on that house you wanted to buy?" Dad asked, pulling Jonah's thoughts aside.

Jonah shook his head. "I made an offer on the place, but they won't come down to a fair asking price, so I decided to give up on it and look for another home."

"That's probably for the best," Dad said. "It wouldn't be good for you to overextend yourself."

"I'll just keep looking, and when the time is right, I'm sure the house I want will be there."

⸎

"*Wa-a-a! Wa-a-a!*"

Sadie paced the floor, patting Levi's back, trying to get him to burp. She'd fed him awhile ago, but he still hadn't burped. All he'd done was scream. She was beginning to wish Meredith hadn't left Levi with her today. It had been some time since she'd had a baby to take care of, so maybe she wasn't up to the challenge.

Sadie continued to pace, while patting Levi's back. "Come on, little fellow, give me a burp."

"*Wa-a-a! Wa-a-a! Wa-a-a!*" Levi cried even harder, setting Sadie's teeth on edge, until she thought she might scream herself. *I wonder if a walk around the yard might do us both some good.* Sadie went to get her shawl before she wrapped Levi in his blanket.

A knock came from the front door.

Draping her shawl over the back of the chair and keeping a tight grip on the screaming baby, Sadie opened the door. Jonah Miller stood on the porch with his straw hat in his hand.

"I'd like to speak with you," Jonah said.

Sadie frowned. "This isn't a good time. I'm babysitting Levi, and as I'm sure you can tell, he's fussy right now."

"What seems to be the problem?" Jonah asked.

Walking out to the porch, where the air was nice and crisp, and wrapping the blanket tighter around her restless grandson, Sadie hoped the change might help calm him down. "I fed him awhile ago, and he's been crying ever since," she explained.

"Maybe he needs to burp."

"Of course he does. For the last twenty minutes I've been trying to get him to do that," Sadie said with a huff as she continued to pat Levi's back.

"Babies don't always need to be patted in order for them to burp," Jonah said. "They need to be relaxed."

Sadie ground her teeth together. Who did Jonah think he was, trying to tell her how to burp the baby?

"Want me to try?" he asked, plunking his hat back on his head and extending his arms.

She shook her head.

"My twin sister has little ones, so I've had some experience burping *bopplin.*"

"And I've raised my own *kinner*, so I've had more experience than you,"

Sadie answered, feeling more than a little miffed.

"I'd like to try."

Seeing the determined set of Jonah's jaw, Sadie finally nodded. Maybe once he saw that he couldn't get Levi to burp or stop crying, he'd give up and leave. She opened the screen door and led the way to the living room then handed Jonah the baby.

Jonah took a seat in the rocker and used one hand to hold Levi so that his backside was supported, almost like a seat. He held the little guy's head with the other hand, tipped him slightly forward, and gently lifted him up and down in a slow bounce.

A few seconds later, Levi stopped crying and let out a loud burp!

Jonah looked over at Sadie and grinned. "Works nearly every time."

Sadie couldn't believe how easily Jonah had done what she couldn't do with all her patting of the baby's back. She was also amazed at how relaxed Jonah seemed to be holding the baby as he gently rocked him. He obviously did have some experience with babies. She forced a smile and said, "Danki for getting him calmed down."

"You're welcome." Jonah cleared his throat. "Is Meredith here?"

Sadie shook her head. "She had some errands to run, so she left Levi with me. Elam's not here either," she quickly added.

"I'd like to talk to you about something," he said, stroking the top of Levi's blond head.

"What's that?"

"It's about me and Meredith."

Sadie grunted. "I know the two of you are courting, if that's what you came to say."

"That's right, and we'd like your and Elam's blessing."

Sadie stared at the floor, unable to form any words. She had a hunch from the way Jonah handled the baby that he'd make a good father. From the things Meredith had told her, she knew Jonah was kind and helpful, but could she accept it if he and Meredith got married?

"I'm very fond of Meredith," Jonah said. "And this little fellow, too." He put Levi over his shoulder and gently patted his back. "But I want you to know that I'm not trying to take your son's place. I know Luke will always hold a spot in Meredith's heart that I'll probably never be able to fill, but I will always be good to her and the boppli."

Tears welled in Sadie's eyes. "Are you hoping to marry Meredith?"

Jonah gave a nod. "When the time is right; if she'll have me, that is."

"Will you stay here in Lancaster County or move back to Ohio?"

"I have no plans of living anywhere but here," Jonah answered. "My folks are here, and I'm happy working for my daed in the buggy shop."

"If you married Meredith, would we still be able to see Levi?" she dared to ask.

"Of course. I'd want him to spend time with all of his grandparents."

Sadie sighed as a sense of relief flooded over her. "You have my blessing to court Meredith, and I'm sure Elam feels the same way."

⁂

Darby

"It won't be long and we'll be done with this project," Henry said as he and Luke sat at the picnic table, putting the finishing touches on the birdhouses they'd been making for the church bazaar.

"It's been fun working on them," Luke said, adding a bit more red paint to the birdhouse he'd made to look like an old barn.

Henry smiled. "You've done a great job with that. If I were to hazard a guess, I'd say you've done some carpentry work in the past."

Luke's jaw clenched as he tried to recall what he had done in the past. Nothing came to mind. Nothing at all. Then a thought popped unexpectedly into his head. "Someone told me once that whenever we do anything, we should make sure we do it well."

Henry set his paintbrush aside and looked at Luke with a curious expression. "Who told you that, son?"

Luke shrugged. "I don't know. Just remember hearing it from someone before."

Henry clasped Luke's shoulder and gave it a squeeze. "See now, Luke, you've just remembered one more thing from your past. That's a real good sign."

Luke started painting again. He longed for Henry to be right but didn't want to get his hopes up, only to be disappointed in the end.

"Look over there," Henry said, pointing across the yard.

Luke followed Henry's gaze and spotted a lazy possum ambling out from behind the woodshed and waddling away. "It's fun to watch nature," he said as a cardinal flew out of the maple tree and landed on one of the birdbaths.

"I agree. Norma and I both enjoy watching the birds in our yard, any season of the year." Henry pointed to the birdbath. "That one I keep heated during the winter months so the birds have fresh water to drink. You'd be surprised how many birds flock to that heated birdbath." He chuckled. "On really cold days, the steam comes up from the water and makes it look like a hot tub."

Luke laughed, too. He could almost picture the birds sitting around the birdbath as the steam lifted into the air. It made him think about the hot tub he'd used during therapy at the hospital and how good it had felt on his sore muscles. "Do the birds actually get in the warm water during the winter?" he questioned.

Henry shook his head. "Not to my knowledge, but they do sit on the rim and drink. Guess you could say Norma and I like to spoil our feathered friends."

"That's nice. Staying connected to nature is what sometimes kept me going while I was in the hospital. That, and the support of your granddaughters, of course."

"They're wonderful girls." Henry grinned. "Guess it's better to say, young women, since they aren't really girls anymore. But then to me and Norma, Susan and Anne will always be our special girls."

Luke was tempted to tell Henry how fond he was of his granddaughters—especially Susan. Just then the back door opened, and Norma stepped out, interrupting their conversation.

"I brought a few nibblies to tide you over until lunch," she said, placing a tray of fruit and vegetables on the picnic table.

"They look good." Henry smiled at his wife.

"There's also a small bowl of vegetable dip, if you want to pep it up a little," Norma said, taking a seat beside the men. "Oh, and I brought a jug of warm apple cider, too."

Henry smacked his lips. "There's nothin' like hot apple cider on a chilly fall day."

Norma pulled her jacket a little tighter around her neck. "It probably won't be long before we see some snow flurries." She smiled at Luke. "I really get into the Christmas spirit when there's snow on the ground."

"Maybe it'll snow on Thanksgiving, like it did last year," Henry chimed in. "But then I guess we shouldn't get ahead of ourselves. Let's just enjoy the beautiful autumn colors 'cause they won't be here much longer."

"Henry's right," Norma put in. "When the fall foliage starts in early October and lasts until early November, there doesn't seem to be enough time to enjoy the magnificent shades of autumn. Right now the mountains and valleys throughout Pennsylvania are ablaze with the most vibrant colors. Many folks like us feel there is no other season of the year more breathtaking than this one."

Luke popped a piece of cucumber in his mouth and thought about the upcoming holiday season. He wished he could remember having celebrated it before. Even more than that, he wished he knew who he'd celebrated the holidays with.

CHAPTER 3

Darby

I've never seen so much food all in one place," Luke said as he took a seat at the Baileys' Thanksgiving table. "Least, I don't think I have."

Henry chuckled. "That's what Thanksgiving is all about—good food, and sharing it with friends and family."

"And remembering to be thankful," Anne put in.

Susan bobbed her head in agreement. "That's right, and we have much to be thankful for."

Luke sat, mulling things over. Even though he didn't have his memory fully back, he had a roof over his head, clothes to wear, and four people who really cared about him. If that's all he ever had, it was enough to be thankful for.

After taking each other's hands, bowing their heads, and listening to Henry's words of devotion and praise, they all finished with a hearty, "Amen!"

Henry stood and began carving the turkey, while Norma made sure everything was on the table.

"My mouth is watering already," Susan said, reaching for the bowl of steaming mashed potatoes. She looked at Luke and giggled. "I always go for these first."

"That's right," Anne interjected with a snicker. "Don't get in the way of my sister and her mashed potatoes. As for me, I can't wait for some of Grandma's stuffing," she added as Norma passed her the corn. "Just wait till you taste it, Luke. It's so moist and good, you'll have to go back for seconds."

"Along with bread, celery, and onions, Norma always adds some diced apple and a few chopped mushrooms," Henry added. "Anne's right—it's scrumptious!"

By now, Luke's mouth was watering. Watching Susan smother her fluffy mashed potatoes in gravy, Luke was suddenly reminded that they were someone else's favorite. But who? Was it him, or someone he knew from the past?

Even though Luke wanted to follow the thought further, everyone was having such a good time, he didn't want to spoil the festive mood. *When it's supposed to happen, it'll come to me*, he decided.

Luke handed his plate to Henry, watching as he scooped some of the stuffing out of the breast cavity.

"How about it, Luke?" Henry asked as he continued to carve the bird. "Would you like a drumstick to start with, or do you prefer some white meat first?"

"That drumstick looks pretty good. Think I'll start with that." Luke grinned, eager to taste the golden-brown skin that covered the dark meat. He could see from the smiles across the table that the Baileys were in high spirits. He enjoyed listening to everyone as they complimented Norma on the delicious meal she'd spent most of the morning preparing.

"We always eat our Thanksgiving meal promptly at noon, because Grandma is traditional when it comes to Thanksgiving, and we wouldn't want it any other way." Susan looked at Norma with appreciation in her eyes. "By eating early enough in the day, we'll have plenty of room for dessert later on." She reached over and patted her grandmother's hand. "You did it again, Grandma. You've made another Thanksgiving feast special for all of us."

"Well now, honey, you know I love doing it. And isn't the day just perfect?" Norma added, looking out the dining-room window. "I could never figure out why, but I love it when the weather's cloudy on Thanksgiving Day."

"Cloudy outside, warm and inviting inside," Henry said, passing Anne the bowl of cranberry sauce. "It looks a bit like snow out there, even though they aren't calling for any. It won't be long, though," he added with a wink in Susan's direction. "Maybe you'd better get out your sled and wax up the runners."

Susan laughed. "I might do that, Grandpa."

After all the food had been passed, Luke started out with the drumstick, but he was eager to taste Norma's stuffing. The sweet potatoes still bubbled in the casserole dish, next to a bowl of fresh green beans.

"Eat slowly now, because later, we'll be having some of the pumpkin and apple pies the girls made this morning," Henry said, nudging Luke's arm with his elbow.

"Dessert is the only thing Grandma will allow me and Susan to help with when Thanksgiving rolls around." Anne winked at Norma, who still had a gleam in her eyes, watching everyone enjoy their meal.

"We can't forget the ice cream, either," Susan chimed in as she reached for a second helping of mashed potatoes. "I got vanilla, and it's a new brand that's supposed to taste like homemade."

Luke felt blessed being a part of this meal. Even though he couldn't remember any of his other Thanksgivings, he knew without a doubt that he'd never forget this one.

⚬⚬⚬

Ronks

Luann's forehead beaded with perspiration as she scurried around the kitchen, stirring kettles, checking on the turkey roasting in the oven, and making sure everything was just right for Thanksgiving dinner. She didn't know why, but she seemed to work best under pressure. A lot was happening in the next couple of weeks. In addition to Thanksgiving, Laurie and Kevin's wedding would take place on the first Saturday of December, and there was still much to do in preparation for that.

Keeping busy helped Luann not to worry so much, and she was worried right now—worried about Laurie becoming a missionary and concerned about Meredith and her relationship with Jonah. They'd been seeing a lot of each other lately. Luann figured it was just a matter of time before Jonah asked Meredith to marry him. It wasn't that she didn't like Jonah; he seemed very nice and was kind and attentive to both Meredith and Levi. She just had this nagging feeling that wouldn't go away, and it troubled her, thinking Meredith might not be truly happy if she married Jonah.

I can't share my feelings about all of this with Meredith, Luann thought as she lifted the lid on the kettle of potatoes simmering slowly on the stove. *I need to keep my opinion to myself and trust the Lord to work everything out for His good.*

She glanced out the window, wondering when their company would arrive. At Meredith's suggestion, Luann had invited Jonah and his folks to join them for Thanksgiving. Kevin and his parents would be here, as well as Sadie and Elam, so the house would be full when they sat down for the holiday meal.

"We're just about done here now," Laurie said when Luann poked her head into the dining room and found Laurie and Meredith putting the finishing touches on the two large tables that had been set up to accommodate their family and guests.

Luann smiled. "Things are getting done in the kitchen now, too, so once our company arrives, we should be able to eat."

Meredith stepped over to Luann. "Before everyone gets here, there's something I'd like to talk to you about, Mom."

Luann's mouth went dry. *Has Jonah already proposed? Is that what Meredith wants to say?*

"Is anyone else in the kitchen?" Meredith asked.

"Not at the moment," Luann replied. "My *mamm* went to her room to change her dress; your daed and brothers are in the barn; and Kendra's keeping the younger ones occupied in the living room."

Meredith motioned to the kitchen door. "Let's go in there so we can talk."

When they entered the kitchen, both women took a seat at the table. "What'd you want to talk to me about?" Luann asked.

"I've found someone to rent my house, and I was wondering if Levi and I could move back here for a while—until things improve for me financially."

Luann took Meredith's hand and clasped her fingers. "You and Levi are welcome to stay here for as long as you like."

"Danki, Mom, I appreciate that. I know you and Dad have your hands full, but with Laurie getting married and leaving soon, I can be here to help out."

Luann breathed a sigh of relief. Since Meredith would be moving in with them, maybe she wouldn't feel the need to marry Jonah, should he ask. She and the baby would be surrounded by their family, and Luann would make sure their needs were met, even if it meant making some sacrifices. After all, that's what families were for.

When Meredith returned to the dining room, she was pleased to see that Laurie had filled the glasses with water and everything was ready. Now all they had to do was wait until their company arrived.

"I think I'd better see how Mom is doing," Laurie said, brushing past Meredith on her way to the kitchen.

Meredith smiled. She knew her sister was getting nervous about her upcoming wedding, which was probably why she wanted to keep busy. Meredith understood that. She'd felt the same way before she and Luke were married.

Meredith moved to the window and stared out toward the barn. She could hear joyous sounds of laughter coming from the yard, where her younger brothers raced through the fallen leaves, chasing each other, as well as the dog they'd recently acquired. He'd been abandoned at the schoolyard, and the boys had brought the mutt home. Of course, Mom couldn't say no to their sad looks, so now Freckles, the brown-and-white mixed terrier, had a new home.

Meredith's thoughts went to Fritz. When she and Levi moved here, she'd have to bring the dog along. She wondered how well he'd get along with Freckles. If it turned out to be a problem, she might have to ask Luke's folks to take Fritz. That had been his home before Luke and Meredith got married, so maybe he'd be happy there.

Meredith was glad Luke's parents had been invited to join them for dinner. Since none of Luke's siblings had been able to come for Thanksgiving, Sadie and Elam would have been alone today if Mom hadn't extended the invitation.

Meredith had been feeling a lot better about things since Sadie now accepted the idea of her being courted by Jonah. She hadn't said anything to Mom or anyone else in the family, but she had a feeling Jonah would ask her to marry him sometime in the spring. She'd begun praying about what her response should be. She cared deeply for Jonah and was sure he would be a good father to Levi. But did she love Jonah enough to be the kind of wife he deserved?

Pushing her thoughts aside, Meredith noticed the low-hanging clouds that threatened to unleash the drizzle that had been predicted for Lancaster County. That was okay with her. She was never disappointed when Thanksgiving Day was overcast or even snowy. It was sort of a prelude to the Christmas season.

Continuing to stare out the window, as her breath steamed the glass,

Meredith looked beyond the yard into the fields, catching sight of the baled hay that was ready to be brought into the barn.

Suddenly, an image of Luke came to mind, and she was reminded of last Thanksgiving, when they'd had the meal at their house. They'd invited both of their families to join them for the feast, and everyone had been in good spirits throughout the day. Even though Meredith had been a bit frazzled getting everything ready that morning, the meal and all the trimmings she'd prepared had turned out quite well.

Meredith rested her forehead against the cool window glass and sighed. When she'd first learned that Luke had been killed, she'd felt guilty for all the times they'd disagreed on things and thought she could never be happy again. Now, just ten months later, she felt a sense of peace, and a reason to go on living. Not only had God blessed her with a precious son, but now she had Jonah and his friendship.

Soon everyone would be sitting around the tables. It would be wonderful to enjoy Thanksgiving with those who meant so much to her.

My son is blessed, even though he doesn't know it yet, she thought. *If things work out between me and Jonah, Levi might end up having three sets of loving grandparents instead of the normal two. Well, I shouldn't let my thinking get carried away; Jonah hasn't asked me to marry him yet.*

Meredith headed back to the kitchen to help with any last-minute tasks. One thing she wanted to make sure was that when all the family sat down to dinner, the bowl of mashed potatoes would be sitting right next to her plate. Everyone knew Meredith got first dibs on her favorite part of the Thanksgiving feast.

CHAPTER 4

Bird-in-Hand

"Where's Dad?" Jonah asked when he stepped into the living room and found his mother on the sofa by herself. "We need to leave now if we're gonna be on time for Laurie and Kevin's wedding."

"He went out to the buggy shop. Said he wanted to check on something before we left," she replied.

Jonah grunted. "He picked a fine time to be doing that. We should be on the road already."

Mom flapped her hand. "Ach, Jonah, just relax. You'd think you were the one getting married today."

Wish I were, Jonah thought. *I'd give nearly anything to be marrying Meredith today. I just need to be patient and wait till the time is right.*

"Think I'll go out and see what's taking Dad so long," he said.

Mom rolled her eyes. "Go ahead if you must, but I think you're being too impatient."

As Jonah headed out the back door, he heard Herbie barking. Then he caught sight of the dog running out of the buggy shop, yipping like his tail was on fire.

"What's the matter, boy?" Jonah asked when Herbie dashed up to him and started pawing at his pant leg.

Woof! Woof! The dog raced back to the buggy shop, as though he was trying to coax Jonah to follow.

Sensing that something was amiss, Jonah quickened his steps. When he stepped into the buggy shop, he found Dad trapped between a buggy and the floor.

"Dad!" Jonah hollered, rushing across the room. "What happened? Are you hurt?"

"Th–the buggy. . .slipped off the prop. . .and has me pinned," Dad panted in raspy breaths. "It's. . .tight against my. . .chest and hard. . .to breathe."

"Stay calm, Dad; I'll get you out of there," Jonah said, trying to compose himself.

Using strength he didn't know he had, he lifted the buggy off Dad and put its frame back on the prop where it had been.

Dad stood, but after a few seconds, he started to fall. Jonah was able to catch him and help him lie on the floor. "It's okay, Dad; I've got you."

Dad's breathing improved, and the color started coming back to his face. "Just stay put," Jonah instructed. "I'm going to the phone shack to call 911."

Just then, Jonah's mother rushed into the shop. "What happened?" she asked, with a look of alarm.

"Go to Dad!" Jonah pointed to the spot where Dad lay on the floor. "He got pinned under the buggy, but he's breathing somewhat better now. Stay with him while I go and call for help."

⟜⟞

Paradise, Pennsylvania

Meredith smiled as she watched Laurie and Kevin take their places at the front of the Mennonite church, in readiness to say their vows. Joy radiated from both their faces, and Laurie looked lovely, wearing a modest, beautiful, white satin dress. Kevin, dressed in a dark suit and white shirt, looked equally handsome.

As the young couple looked lovingly into each other's eyes, Meredith's thoughts went to Luke. It was hard to believe he'd been gone nearly a year. So much had happened since then—Levi's birth, putting their house up for rent, and now being courted by Jonah, a man Luke had never met. But over the last couple of days, Meredith had sensed that if Luke had known Jonah, he would have had a good opinion of him, just like everyone else in their community did.

Continuing to watch her sister's wedding, it was hard for Meredith not to think about the day she'd wed Luke. Other than the birth of her son, her wedding had been the happiest day of her life. She and Luke had been joyous, filled with dreams for the future.

Things had changed the day Luke left for Indiana. No one planned for disaster. Without warning, tragedy had ripped her heart out. But as much as she hadn't wanted it to happen, life had moved forward one step at a time.

Meredith glanced around the church. *I wonder where Jonah is.* He and his folks had been invited to the wedding, and they'd said they would be here. It seemed strange that they hadn't come. It made Meredith wonder if everything was okay. Surely they hadn't forgotten.

She closed her eyes and offered a prayer: *Be with the Millers, Lord, and if they're on the road with their horse and buggy, please keep them safe.*

❧

Philadelphia

"I appreciate you coming with me today," Susan said as she and Luke entered a furniture store on the outskirts of the city. "Grandpa's old chair is getting pretty worn, so Anne and I want to get him a new one for Christmas." She smiled at Luke. "I really need a man's opinion."

He grinned back at her, and her heart nearly melted. Not counting Grandpa, she'd never felt so relaxed and contented with any man the way she did with Luke.

"I'm not sure how much help I'll be," he said, "but I can try out a few chairs and let you know which ones feel comfortable to me."

"That's all I want." Susan led the way through the store to the section where sofas, recliners, and rocking chairs were sold. "Here's a nice blue one." She motioned to a larger recliner. "Take a seat and tell me what you think."

Luke sat down and stood back up almost immediately. "That one's too big, and it wasn't very comfortable. The chair would swallow him up, I think."

"Okay. How about that one over there?" Susan pointed to a tan recliner that also rocked and swiveled.

Luke sat down, leaned his head back, and closed his eyes. He stayed like that for several minutes, causing her to wonder if he'd fallen asleep. Susan was about to give his arm a shake, when his eyes popped open. "This chair feels good to me. I think your grandpa would like it."

Susan smiled. She hadn't expected they would find one so quickly. "Great! I'll talk to the salesman and see if I can put some money down on the chair and then pay the rest before Christmas. You can wait there if you like." She giggled. "Just don't fall asleep."

He wiggled his eyebrows playfully as he started to rock the chair. "I'll try not to."

Susan headed to the counter, where the salesman waited on another customer. When he was done, it didn't take him long to write up the paperwork for Susan's purchase. She returned to where she'd left Luke, but he wasn't there.

Susan glanced around and was relieved to see Luke standing beside a beautiful oak dining-room table that could have easily seated ten or twelve people. He was bent over, looking closely at the table, and rubbing his hand over the wood grain with an odd expression. "Luke, is something wrong?" she asked, approaching him.

He straightened and blinked his turquoise eyes. "I used to work in a furniture store."

<hr />

As they got closer to Darby, Luke stared out the window of Susan's car, barely noticing the snowflakes coming down. All he could think about was the fact that he'd remembered having worked in a furniture store. But where was that store? Did he own it or work for someone else? Had he been a salesman there, or was he a woodworker who built some of the furniture?

Luke leaned his head back and closed his eyes. *Why can't I remember the details? Will my past ever come fully back to me?*

"Are you okay?" Susan asked, reaching across the seat to touch his arm.

"I'm fine. Just thinking, is all."

"About having worked in a furniture store?"

"Yeah. I wish the pieces would come to me. I'm tired of struggling to remember who I am," Luke murmured in frustration. "I know I should be happy that even a little bit is emerging about myself, but I get discouraged when I can't recall the rest of it."

"You know that your name is Luke, and I think you're on the verge of getting your memory completely back, so cling to that."

Susan sounded so sincere, Luke almost believed her. Maybe these little flashes of memory he kept having *were* a sign that he was on the threshold of remembering everything about his past.

"I can't believe how hard it's snowing; especially when it wasn't doing anything when we left home," Susan said, motioning to the heavy flakes hitting the front window. It looked as if they had the makings for a full-blown snowstorm. The windshield wipers could hardly keep up.

"I love the snow, but I don't like to drive in it," Susan said, her knuckles turning white as she gripped the steering wheel.

Luke wished he could offer to take over the driving, but he didn't know whether he'd ever driven a car. Besides, he didn't have a driver's license.

"I don't think the weatherman said anything about getting a lot of snow this morning," Susan observed. "He did say a few snow squalls could move through our area, and sometimes those squalls can give us a couple inches when all's said and done," she added.

Knowing she was nervous and wanting to keep the conversation light, Luke grinned at her and said, "Hey, if the snow keeps up like this, maybe we can build a snowman when we get home."

She nodded and seemed to relax a bit. "That sounds like fun."

⊂⊇⊃

Paradise

"Congratulations to both of you," Meredith said as she greeted her sister and new brother-in-law with a hug. "I hope you'll both be very happy."

"I know we will." Laurie's face beamed as she clung to her groom's hand.

Kevin smiled down at her. "With God at the center of our lives, every day will be an adventure." He nodded at Meredith. "I want you to know that I'll take good care of your sister."

She poked his arm playfully. "You'd better, or you'll have to answer to me."

"I sure wouldn't want that." He winked at Meredith.

"Where's Jonah?" Laurie asked. "I thought he and his folks were coming to the wedding."

"They were planning to," Meredith replied. "Something must have happened." It had started snowing during the ceremony, and now the roads were covered. She didn't voice her concerns to Laurie, but she was worried about Jonah. It wasn't like him to say he was going to do something and not follow through. Maybe he and his folks had been in an accident.

"We'd better go into the fellowship hall," Kevin said, smiling at Laurie. "Everyone's gathered for the reception."

Laurie giggled. "I think you're just anxious to eat some of that good food the women from your church have prepared."

He gave his stomach a thump. "What can I say? I'm a hungry man."

"Are you coming, Meredith?" Laurie asked.

Meredith nodded. "I'll be right behind you."

As the newlyweds headed down the stairs to the fellowship hall, Meredith thought about how different from an Amish wedding their wedding service had been. Besides the fact that it had been held inside a church building, there would be just one meal following the service, not three, like in most traditional Amish weddings. That meant the festivities would be over much sooner.

Meredith was about to head down the stairs, when she caught sight of Merle Raber, who often drove Jonah and his folks places when they couldn't take their horse and buggy. He hurried toward Meredith with a grim expression. "Jonah asked me to come. He wanted me to tell you that he's sorry he couldn't make it to your sister's wedding."

"What's wrong?" Meredith asked, alarm welling up in her chest. "Did something happen to Jonah?"

Merle shook his head. "His dad got pinned under a buggy they'd been working on, and he's at the hospital getting checked over."

Meredith gasped. "That's terrible. I hope he isn't seriously hurt."

"I don't think so," Merle said, "but he was having a little trouble breathing, so they wanted to check him over real good."

"That makes sense," Meredith said with a nod. "Thank you for letting me know. I hope and pray that Raymond's okay."

⟨≈⟩

Darby

"Are you going to come outside and help us build a snowman?" Susan asked Anne after she and Luke returned from their shopping trip.

Anne's curls bounced around her face as she shook her head. "You two go ahead. I just got off work, and I'm gonna curl up in front of the fireplace and finish reading that book I started last week."

"Is it another Amish-themed novel?" Susan asked.

Anne nodded. "I don't know why, but I'm fascinated with the Amish way of life."

Susan smiled. "Maybe we should make another trip to Lancaster when the weather warms in the spring. We can stop at one of the farmers' markets and see what else we might buy."

Anne bobbed her head. "Luke, maybe you'd like to go with us. We could go for a buggy ride, browse some of the shops, and eat shoofly pie."

Luke's eyebrows furrowed, and he rubbed his forehead. "I think I may have had shoofly pie before, but I can't remember where or what it tastes like."

"It has a molasses base," Susan said. "They sell it at the farmers' market in Philly. Maybe you had some there."

Luke shrugged. "Guess that could be. I'm just not sure. Fact is, I'm not sure about anything that took place before I woke up in the hospital and met you two."

Susan's heart ached for Luke. She could see by his pinched expression that he was struggling hard to remember his past. Maybe what he needed was a distraction. She pointed out the kitchen window, where the snow was coming down harder. "Why don't we head outside now and build that snowman before it gets too cold?"

"Sounds good to me. Let's go!" Luke grabbed Susan's hand, and they headed out the back door.

Once outside, they began rolling a snowball. Soon they had three good-sized balls and had formed a snowman. Then they put a carrot in for its nose, two matching rocks for the eyes, and placed Luke's red baseball cap on the snowman's head.

"He looks pretty good, don't you think?" Luke asked, standing back to admire their creation.

Susan nodded. "Let's make some snow angels now."

Luke chuckled when she dropped to the ground, spread her arms and legs, and moved them back and forth through the snow. When she hopped up, the place in the snow where she'd been flapping her arms looked like a pair of angel's wings.

Without warning, Susan scooped up a handful of snow and flung it at Luke. He shivered when it landed on his neck. "Hey!"

Quickly, he leaned down and formed a snowball then tossed it at Susan. It landed on her right arm. "No fair, I wasn't ready for that!" She whirled around, but before she could take a step, Luke threw another clump of snow. This one hit Susan's shoulder.

Soon, there were snowballs flying back and forth, along with peals of laughter. Luke was having such a great time, he forgot about his earlier frustrations. It felt good to run around like a kid, enjoying the fresh-fallen snow while chasing Susan.

Luke watched slyly when Susan scooted behind a pine tree in one corner of the Baileys' yard. *What is she up to now?* he wondered. The white pine's soft needles were covered with snow, and several pinecones still clung to a few of the branches.

Luke glanced up and noticed a low-hanging limb right above where Susan stood behind the tree. *I'll get her now.* Luke smirked and whipped around to the other side of the tree. On impulse, he jumped up and shook the tree limb.

"Yikes!" Susan squealed as a wall of snow fell on her head. "I'll get you for that!" she warned, spitting snow from her mouth.

Before she could get the snow wiped from her face, Luke turned in the other direction, hoping to get out of the line of fire.

"You can't get away from me," Susan yelled with excitement in her voice.

Whap! Another snowball made its mark, sending icy cold fragments of snow down Luke's neck. He whirled around and raced after Susan, quickly grabbing her around the waist.

Panting and laughing, they fell to the ground in a heap of cold snow. As Luke lay there beside her, huffing and puffing, his gaze went to her rosy-red lips. Seeing the merriment in Susan's eyes, he leaned closer as the urge to kiss her became strong. His lips were mere inches from hers, when the back door opened and Anne shouted, "Hey, you two! Why don't you come inside and warm up with a cup of hot chocolate and some of Grandma's melt-in-your-mouth banana bread?"

Luke looked at Susan to get her reaction. Was that a look of disappointment on her face? Had she been hoping he would kiss her? Did she want it as much as he did?

Maybe it's best that we were interrupted, he thought. *Since I haven't put the pieces of my past together yet, I really can't commit to Susan right now.*

Luke's growing attraction to her made him even more anxious to know his past. If he could just find the key to unlock the memories hidden away in his head, he might feel free to express his feelings.

CHAPTER 5

Ronks

I'm glad your daed wasn't seriously hurt," Meredith told Jonah as they sat on the sofa together in her parents' living room.

He nodded solemnly. "It about scared me to death when I found him pinned under the buggy like that. Fortunately the only injuries involved some bruising."

"God was watching over him," Meredith said.

Jonah nodded. "I would say so."

"When you didn't show up for Laurie and Kevin's wedding yesterday, I was worried—especially after seeing the snow come down as hard as it did."

"Well, it wasn't because of the weather, but we did feel bad about missing the wedding." He glanced around. "Where is everyone this evening? I expected to see your sisters and brothers running around like they usually do when I drop by."

"They're upstairs in their rooms," Meredith replied. "Dad thought it would be nice if we had some time alone, without the little ones climbing all over you."

Jonah chuckled. "They do seem to like me for some reason."

"That's because you're such a nice man, and they like those twisty animal balloons you make for them." Meredith smiled. "You're good with Levi, too. He lights up whenever you're in the room."

"He's a special little guy. I have a fondness for him, just like I do his mamm."

Meredith's cheeks warmed. "I have a fondness for you, too, Jonah."

"Enough to marry me in the spring?" he blurted unexpectedly.

She flinched and sucked in her breath, unsure of how to respond.

Jonah took her hand and gave her fingers a gentle squeeze. "I'm sorry for blurting that out. I'd planned to wait till you'd been widowed a year before I said anything about marriage, but the words just popped out of my mouth. Did I speak out of turn?" he asked.

She shook her head. "It's not that. I just need some time to think about it. Can you wait until Christmas for my answer?"

Slowly, he nodded.

~⊗~

Darby

"Where's Luke?" Susan asked when she entered the kitchen and found her grandmother fixing lunch.

"He and your grandpa are outside, shoveling snow off the driveway so you and Anne can get your cars out of the garage. It's a good thing you both have afternoon shifts, because the roads should be cleared by then."

Susan smiled. "Luke's thoughtful, isn't he, Grandma?"

Grandma nodded and reached for the loaf of bread sitting on the counter. "I heard him tell your grandpa the other day that he feels like he's imposing on us."

"What'd Grandpa say in response?"

"He told Luke in no uncertain terms that it's been a blessing to us having him here, and he should quit worrying so much."

"I hope Luke listened to him," Susan said. "I wouldn't want him to leave and go out on the streets."

Grandma tipped her head. "What makes you think he used to live on the streets?"

"I'm not sure if he did or not, but if he were to leave here, I'd be concerned about where he would go."

Grandma gave Susan's shoulder a squeeze. "Don't worry, honey, we won't let him leave. At least not until he gets his memory fully back and we find out where he came from."

Susan swallowed around the lump in her throat. "I'll miss him when that happens."

"You've fallen in love with Luke, haven't you, dear?"

Susan nodded slowly, her eyes filling with tears. She turned and looked out the window toward the pine tree in the far end of the yard. The tracks in the snow were still there, where she had hid from Luke when they'd played around in the snow. She smiled, despite her tears, remembering the cold bath she'd gotten when Luke snuck up from behind and knocked all the snow off the branch above her head. "Last night, when Luke and I were romping in the snow, I think he was on the verge of kissing me," she said.

"Why didn't he?" Grandma questioned.

"Anne came out and called us in for hot chocolate." Susan sniffed, hoping to keep her tears from spilling over. "Maybe it's a good thing we were interrupted. If Luke had kissed me, it would have strengthened our relationship even more, and I really don't want that right now. At least not until I know more about him."

"Is it because you fear he might already have a girlfriend, or maybe a wife?"

"Yeah. If I allow myself to think about a future between me and Luke, and then he remembers his life before and it includes someone else, I'd be devastated."

Grandma slipped her arm around Susan's waist and gave her a hug. "Just pray about it, honey. God will work it all out."

⟡

Ronks

Meredith yawned. She was more tired than usual as she got ready for bed. With the Christmas holiday approaching, she'd been getting more requests for prayer coverings to be made for the store where she'd been taking them. She would have to buckle down during the next couple of days and try to make a few extra. That, and Laurie's wedding with all of its preparations, plus Thanksgiving, had kept her on the go.

On top of that, worrying over where Jonah and his family had been when they didn't show up at the wedding, and then Jonah suddenly asking her to marry him had only added to her fatigue.

"No wonder I'm exhausted," she mused, looking at Fritz lying in his usual spot on the floor by the foot of her bed.

The dog looked up at her, with all four legs stretched out to one side. From the way he was lying, his short tail was just long enough to make little thumping sounds as he wagged it against the floor.

"You look tired, too, pup," Meredith said.

Fritz offered a whiney groan before he laid his head down, looking toward the door. Ever since they'd moved back in with her parents, Fritz had been getting more exercise each day, playing with Freckles, the Kings' new family pet. Meredith was glad the dogs got along well; it was one less thing for her to worry about.

As tired as she was, Meredith could tell she wouldn't be falling asleep any time soon. Lying down with her hands behind her head on the fluffy, down-filled pillow, she pondered Jonah's speedy proposal. Truthfully speaking, it wasn't really such a surprise that Jonah had proposed. Meredith had been expecting it, just not this evening. She'd figured he would wait until she'd been widowed at least a full year.

"Am I ready for this?" Meredith spoke out loud into the darkness of her room. Listening to her son's even breathing coming from the crib across the room, and to Fritz's contented snoring from the floor by her bed, Meredith was glad she hadn't awakened either of them. "Wish I could be asleep like the two of you are right now," she whispered.

Meredith couldn't help being excited about the upcoming holidays. She and Jonah had several things planned besides the usual family gatherings that she was anxious to partake in. Meredith sighed, pulling the quilt up and tucking it under her chin. Christmas was the last holiday she'd spent with Luke before he'd been killed. After that, she hadn't thought she'd enjoy another Christmas. Nor much else, for that matter. But Jonah had proven her wrong.

As she lay staring at the ceiling, Meredith realized that her relationship with Jonah had become more comfortable. She was at ease when he was around. Levi also seemed to gravitate toward Jonah. Meredith's family had accepted him as if he were already part of the family. Even Luke's parents seemed adjusted to the idea of Jonah courting their daughter-in-law. But would the family's acceptance be enough?

As the stillness of the night enveloped the house, Meredith wondered, *Oh Luke, what should I do?*

CHAPTER 6

Ronks

"It was kind of Jonah's folks to invite us to their house for Christmas dinner," Meredith's mother said as they put their fresh-baked pumpkin and apple pies into boxes.

Meredith smiled. "Jah, it'll be a nice afternoon out, and you won't have to cook for a change."

"I don't mind cooking. Never have—not even when I was a *maedel*."

"How old were you when Grandma taught you to cook?" Meredith asked, closing the lid on the box of pies.

"Let's see now. . .for as long as I can remember I enjoyed being in the kitchen, helping my mamm with whatever she would allow me to do."

"That's right," Grandma Smucker spoke up from across the room, where she'd been cutting apples, pears, and bananas for a fruit salad she'd be taking to the Millers'. "By the time Luann was born, her sisters were already in school. So she pretty much followed me everywhere around the house. And since I spent a good deal of time in the kitchen, she was there, too, always asking to help." Grandma smiled. "By the time your mamm was six years old, she was baking cookies."

While Mom and Grandma continued to reminisce about old times, Meredith walked into the living room and looked out the window. Squinting at the bright sunlight hitting the sparkly white snow, she gazed at the beautiful, almost magical scene.

Christmas made her feel more spirited and full of life, and a snowfall close to the holiday made her seem even more energized. It was fun to watch Arlene, Katie, and Owen, her youngest siblings, romping in the snow. It was like someone flipped a switch on their energy level, taking it up a notch. Any other time, their liveliness would have gotten on Meredith's nerves, but she had to admit, she was feeling their excitement as well.

All week, Meredith had heard Mom and Grandma Smucker humming as they baked. Even Dad and her brother Stanley didn't seem to mind the cold as they tended the animals and worked in the barn. To free Mom up for her extra baking, Kendra and Nina had pitched in to help mind the kids and keep the house nice and tidy. Meredith didn't let the idea of her sister Laurie moving away soon get in the way of the joy she felt.

Meredith had promised to give Jonah an answer to his proposal later today, and as the time drew closer for them to load up their buggies and head for the Millers', she found herself feeling anxious to get there. She'd lain awake for several hours last night, praying and trying to decide what her answer should be. In the wee hours of the morning, Meredith's answer finally came, and she felt a sense of peace.

⟲⟳

Bird-in-Hand

"Would everyone like dessert now, or should we let our meal settle a bit?" Jonah's mother, Sarah, asked after everyone had finishing eating.

"I can't speak for anyone else," Meredith's dad said, pushing back his chair, "but right now I couldn't eat another bite."

"Me neither," Jonah agreed. "In fact, I was thinking of taking Meredith on a sleigh ride." He glanced at Meredith and smiled. "How about it? Would you care to join me?"

Meredith hesitated. If she took a ride with Jonah, it would give her the chance to give him her answer about marrying him. However, as much as Meredith wanted to go, she didn't feel right about leaving the other women to do the dishes. She was about to say so and start clearing the table, when Sarah scooped up several plates and said, "Don't concern yourself with that, Meredith. There are enough of us here to get the dishes done, so feel free to join Jonah outside and take advantage of that fresh air. Who knows how long this snow will stick around or when the next snowfall might be?"

"Don't worry about Levi, either," Meredith's sixteen-year-old sister,

Kendra, was quick to say. "If he wakes up from his nap, I'll keep him occupied."

"And if she doesn't, I will," Dad added with a wink. "I never mind holding my grandson."

"Everyone in our family enjoys holding Levi," Grandma Smucker added. "He's such a sweet boppli."

"Shall we get our coats?" Jonah asked, motioning to the jackets hanging on the wall pegs in the utility room.

Meredith nodded and rose to her feet. "Let me tend to Levi first, and I'll be with you in a few minutes."

⸺

When they stepped outside a short time later, Meredith sucked in her breath. "It's been such a lovely day, Jonah. See how the snow glistens?"

"Jah, it's beautiful," Jonah whispered, leaning close to her ear. "Pretty as a picture, just like you."

Meredith shivered, feeling his breath blow against her ear. Hearing his laughter as he skipped over the last two porch steps and jumped into the snow, she, too, felt lighthearted. Then, as he beckoned her to follow, she went quickly down the porch steps and out into the yard.

"All I have to do is hitch Dobbin to the sleigh, and we'll be on our way," Jonah said. "Dad's horse is more accustomed to pulling a sleigh."

Before Meredith knew it, they were heading over the back fields and breaking through new snow. The only disturbances they could see in the snow were a few animal tracks and areas where deer had pawed away the snow, uncovering vegetation to eat.

During the ride, they laughed, visited, and watched the sun set in the west. Meredith enjoyed listening to the sound of the sleigh bells. Hearing them brought back happy childhood memories when Dad used to take the family on winter sleigh rides.

"Are you warm enough?" Jonah asked, looking over at Meredith.

"I'm fine. It's warm and toasty under this thick wool blanket." She smiled, noticing how relaxed Jonah seemed to be, loosely holding the reins. He was obviously having as much fun as she was.

"Look over there!" Jonah pointed across the way. Four deer stood warily watching near a clump of trees, but as the sleigh approached, they turned and ran over the hill.

When the sleigh reached the knoll, Jonah halted the horse. Dobbin pawed the ground a few times as the steam puffed out of his nose and rose off his rich auburn coat. Meredith looked at the view and thought she'd never seen a prettier sight. The blanket of snow gave everything a quiet look, as stillness lay over the land. Smoke coming from chimneys hung heavy in the air, and silos stood tall and visible in every direction.

Jonah reached for Meredith's hand and held it firmly in his. "Meredith, I was wondering if you've had enough time to think about my marriage proposal."

She nodded slowly. "I have, Jonah, and I will marry you."

His face broke into a wide smile. "Now that's the best Christmas present I could ever receive!"

She giggled as Jonah jumped out of the sleigh, ran around to her side, picked her up, and twirled her around. Dobbin whinnied, pawed at the ground some more, and nodded his head as though in agreement. "I was thinking we could be married in early March, if that's all right with you," Meredith said as he gently set her on her feet.

"I wish it could be sooner, but I have no problem with March." Jonah leaned close, and she thought he might kiss her. Instead, he reached for her hand and gave it a squeeze.

"I don't think we should tell anyone yet," Meredith said. "I'd feel better about waiting until my year of mourning is up."

Jonah's smile faded. "Not even our folks? Don't you think we ought to tell them now?"

Meredith shook her head. "I'd rather wait."

Although disappointed, Jonah smiled and said, "Whatever you think is best."

❦

Darby

"You three women certainly outdid yourselves preparing this meal," Henry said, giving his stomach a thump. "I think every year Christmas dinner tastes better."

"Thank you, Grandpa," Susan spoke up, "but Grandma did most of the cooking."

"That's not true," Grandma said, handing Susan the platter of juicy ham. "You mashed the potatoes, and Anne made the fruit salad."

"That's right, Grandma," Anne said in a teasing tone. "Susan likes to lick the beaters when she's done mashing the potatoes. But you prepared everything else."

Grandpa smiled. "That's 'cause my wife likes to cook."

"That's right, I do, and you like to eat my cooking." Grandma chuckled and poked Grandpa's arm playfully. "I've had lots of practice over the years to perfect my cooking skills."

Grandpa forked a piece of ham into his mouth. "Mmm. . .this is so good. Don't you think so, son?" he asked, looking at Luke as he took a bite of the bright red cherry and pineapple ring that had been on top of the glaze, adding flavor to the ham.

Luke nodded.

Susan pursed her lips. It wasn't like Luke to be so quiet. Normally he was quite talkative during a meal. At least that's how he'd been the last couple of months. He'd joined in the conversation early today, too, when everyone had opened their presents.

Susan had been pleased to see how well Grandpa liked the chair she and Luke had picked out for him, and Grandma said she appreciated the Crock-Pot, sweater, and perfume the girls had given her, too. Luke had even made gifts for everyone—a "WELCOME TO OUR HOME" plaque for Grandma, a feeder for George the squirrel for Grandpa, and jewelry boxes for Anne and Susan, all of which he'd managed to make when no one was around. They'd given something to Luke as well: a nicely framed photograph of the four of them. Grandpa said it was so Luke could always remember them.

Could Luke be thinking about his past—maybe wondering what he'd been doing last Christmas, and who he was with? If that's what he was thinking, Susan couldn't blame him. She'd be doing the same thing if she were in his situation. In fact, such questions would probably be constantly on her mind.

Maybe Luke's hoping for a Christmas miracle, Susan thought. *Oh, I wish I could give him the gift of getting his memory back.* If there were any extra miracles to be given, she hoped with all her heart that Luke would regain his past life.

CHAPTER 7

Ronks

By the end of January, Meredith felt ready to announce her engagement but wanted Jonah to be with her. So they'd decided to have a joint family dinner where they could share their good news.

Too bad Laurie and Kevin won't be here, Meredith thought as she set the table. They'd left the first week of January for Mississippi, where they were ministering to a Native American community. In Laurie's last letter, she'd described how much she and Kevin were enjoying their life together and said that working with kids during several church events had made them eager to have children of their own. She'd also mentioned how good it felt to help the elderly with transportation to and from their doctors' appointments.

Meredith smiled. Laurie sounded happy and would be a wonderful mother someday. It would be nice for Levi to have a little cousin to play with, but they might not get to see each other much, with Laurie and Kevin going on missionary trips. Well, at least her son would have his uncles and aunts to shower him with attention, not to mention the love he would continue to get from his doting grandparents. Meredith's siblings, especially the younger ones, loved spending time with Levi. In fact, Katie, Arlene, and Owen were keeping him entertained in the living room while she prepared dinner.

"Is there anything I can do to help you?" Grandma Smucker asked.

"No, thanks, Grandma. I told Mom a few minutes ago to relax in the living room with the kinner and that I had everything under control, so you ought to do the same."

Grandma slipped her arm around Meredith's waist. "You look well rested and happier than I've seen you in a long time. Is there something going on we should know about?"

Meredith's face heated with embarrassment. Was her excitement really that obvious? "I'm just happy to be able to serve my family a nice meal this evening," she said, avoiding her grandmother's question.

Grandma studied Meredith. "I notice you're not wearing black today. It's nice to see you in that blue dress."

Meredith glanced down at her dress and matching apron. "Luke has been gone a year now, Grandma, so it was time for me to put my mourning clothes aside."

Grandma smiled with a knowing expression. "And it's good to see that you're moving on with your life." Did she suspect that Meredith was planning to marry Jonah? The whole family probably suspected what was going on. After all, Jonah visited her a lot these days, and everyone knew they were courting. In any event, Meredith was confident that everyone would be happy for them and offer their blessings.

❧

As Jonah sat beside Meredith on one side of the Kings' dining-room table that evening, his palms grew sweaty. *When should I make the announcement?* he wondered. *Should I tell them during dinner while we're eating? Or would it be better to wait till we're eating dessert?*

Jonah felt like a silly schoolboy. How would he say it? He hadn't even prepared a speech. Should he tell everyone, kids included, or should he and Meredith take their parents aside and only announce it to them for now?

No, he decided. *We should tell everyone at once. Maybe now would be a good time.*

Jonah cleared his throat and wiped his sweaty brow. A shiver ran through him. Why was he so nervous, for goodness' sake?

"Are you okay, Son?" Dad asked. "You look like you're not feeling so well."

"I—I'm fine," Jonah stammered.

Meredith, as if sensing his predicament, tapped her water glass with her fork and said, "Jonah and I have an announcement to make."

All heads turned in their direction.

She looked over at Jonah and gave him a reassuring smile, then she said in a clear tone, "Jonah asked me to marry him, and I said yes. We plan to get married in March."

Jonah held his breath, waiting for the response.

"Congratulations!" the Kings and his parents said. "That's great news," Meredith's father added. And the smiles around the table showed Jonah that everyone agreed.

❧

Darby

"What a beautiful night for stargazing," Susan said as she and Luke took seats on the Baileys' back porch.

"You're right," Luke murmured, staring up at the sky. "The sky's so clear I can see most of the constellations."

They sat in quiet camaraderie for several minutes, and then Luke reached over and took Susan's hand. She looked at him and smiled. He didn't know why, but he felt like he'd done this before—maybe in his previous life with someone else. It was very disconcerting and seemed all too familiar. Maybe he was just remembering a few months back, when one evening he and Susan had watched for falling stars.

They stayed that way awhile longer, then Luke shivered and said, "Sure is cold out tonight. It felt really cold like this before I got on the bus, too."

"What bus?" Susan questioned, tipping her head and staring at him.

He shrugged. "I don't know. Just remember being cold and riding on a bus." He groaned as he leaned forward and cradled his head in his hands. "This not being able to remember things about my past is nearly driving me crazy. It's kind of like trying to put together a difficult jigsaw puzzle and nothing seems to fit."

"I know it has to be hard," Susan said, gently squeezing his arm. "But you're remembering a few more things all the time, like just now when you remembered getting on a bus." She paused. "You had to be going somewhere, Luke, because you were found badly beaten in the Philadelphia bus station."

He lifted his head and offered her a weak smile. "I wonder what I did to make someone mad enough to beat me up."

"Maybe you didn't do anything," Susan said in a reassuring tone. "It might have been some maniac who just liked to push people around." Her expression sobered. "Or maybe the person responsible for your injuries needed money, and when you said no, he beat you up and took your wallet. Remember, there was no wallet or any identification found on you, Luke."

He shook his head forcibly. "No, I don't remember. If I did, I wouldn't be here right now, trying to put the pieces of my life together." Frustration welled in Luke's chest, and he fought to keep his emotions in check.

"I'm sorry. I didn't mean to upset you," she said. "I guess I didn't word things quite right. What I meant to say was, remember what I told you the police said to those they spoke to at the hospital when they brought you in?"

"Yeah, I know what you told me, but it's not the same as me actually remembering what happened in that bus station."

"Luke, I have an idea."

"What's that?"

"Do you think it might help you remember if we went to the bus station where you were found?" she suggested.

"I don't know. Guess it's worth a try."

"All right then, we'll take a ride over there on my next day off."

Sometimes Luke couldn't get over how sweet and accommodating Susan was. He was falling harder for her all the time and wished he could express his feelings. But that would have to wait until he knew for sure who he was and what had transpired in his past.

CHAPTER 8

Ronks

When Meredith looked at the kitchen calendar on the second Monday of March, she couldn't believe it. In just three days, she and Jonah would be married.

A few weeks ago, Jonah had taken Meredith to see a farm he hoped to buy. He'd put money down on the place, and if all went well, the deal would close the day before their wedding. Jonah had put away sizeable savings from working in Ohio and then with his Dad. He'd wanted to use the money toward buying a place when the time came for him to marry. With Jonah's job, plus the rent money they would receive from Meredith's house, they should be able to live quite comfortably. Everything seemed to be falling into place, and she was almost sure that marrying Jonah was the right thing to do. Why then, did she feel a sense of apprehension this morning?

Staring out the window, as her breath steamed the glass, Meredith looked beyond the yard and into the fields. She pictured the day a little over a year ago when she and Luke had been eating breakfast and talking about the business offer Luke had gotten from his uncle in Indiana.

Meredith sighed, resting her forehead against the cool window, as she remembered how her suspicions had been true of being pregnant with her and Luke's firstborn. With the window still fogged over from her warm breath, she drew a happy face with her finger. She had been blessed in so many aspects of her life. Looking up, she said a brief prayer of thanks for the time, however short, that she'd had with Luke, and now their most precious gift, little Levi.

"*Guder mariye,*" Mom said, entering the kitchen. "Did you sleep well last night?"

"Good morning," Meredith replied, turning away from the window. "I slept okay. How about you?"

"With your daed's snoring and the incessant howling of the wind, I didn't sleep so well," Mom admitted.

"I'm sorry to hear that."

Mom yawned. "It's okay; I'll catch a catnap this afternoon and be good as new."

She moved across the room to the propane stove and picked up the teakettle. "Are you getting *naerfich* about the wedding?" she asked, filling the teakettle.

"Not really nervous; just kind of anxious is all," Meredith replied. "But I guess that's to be expected when one is about to get married."

"Were you anxious before you married Luke?"

"Not really. I was excited and couldn't wait to be his bride."

Mom set the teakettle on the stove and moved to stand beside Meredith. "Are you sure you're doing the right thing marrying Jonah?"

Meredith stiffened. "I thought you liked Jonah and had given us your blessing."

"I do like him, and so does your daed. I'm just concerned that you might be rushing into things."

Meredith shook her head vigorously. "I'm not. Jonah will be a good husband to me, and an equally good daed to Levi."

"I'm sure that's true, but if you're feeling—"

"I'll be fine, really. It's just a bit of pre-wedding jitters."

⤫

Bird-in-Hand

"I think I ate too much," Jonah said, pushing away from the table. "Danki, Mom, for fixing such a tasty breakfast."

"Jah," Dad agreed. "The ham and eggs were real good."

Jonah rose to his feet and went to get the coffeepot. After he'd poured himself a second cup of coffee, he sat back down and listened as his folks talked about the buggy business and the strong March winds they'd been having.

Leaning back in his chair, Jonah's thoughts went to Meredith. In just a few days his dream of settling down with someone he loved would begin. Who knew that his teenage friend from years ago would one day become his bride? Meredith was everything he'd ever hoped for in a wife. He admired her parents and the close relationship they had, and looked forward to becoming part of that family as much as he longed for Meredith and Levi to be a part of his.

Jonah smiled, thinking about the other night when he'd stopped by to see Meredith. He'd watched Levi sleeping soundly in his mother's arms and felt overwhelmed with the love he had for that precious little boy. The deep abiding love he felt for Levi's mother was something Jonah had only wished for before. Now it was a reality, and he felt confident that Meredith loved him, too. Maybe not in the same way she'd loved her first husband, but he was certain her feelings were genuine. Jonah looked forward to becoming a father, not only to Levi, but to any other children he and Meredith might be blessed with.

"So what do you think, Son?" Mom asked, breaking into Jonah's thoughts.

Jonah jerked, nearly spilling his cup of coffee. "Uh—about what?"

"About the weather," Dad said before Mom could reply. "Do you think this awful wind we've been having will let up any time soon?"

Jonah shrugged. "I have no idea, Dad. I wasn't even thinkin' about the weather."

Mom poked Jonah's arm playfully. "That's because your mind was someplace else, and I bet I know where. You were thinking about your upcoming wedding, am I right?"

Jonah gave a nod.

"Are you naerfich?" Dad asked.

"No. Well, I guess maybe I am," Jonah admitted. "I want everything to be perfect, but more than that, I hope I can be the kind of husband Meredith needs and a good daed to Levi."

Mom patted his hand affectionately. "You will be, Son. I have no doubt of that."

⌦

Darby

"What's in there?" Grandpa asked when Susan took her seat at the breakfast table beside Luke.

She smiled, placing a small box on the extra chair in the corner behind her. "It's a present for one of my patients."

"Which patient is that?" Grandma asked, sipping her tea.

"A five-year-old girl named Elsie. She and her parents were in a car accident." Susan took a piece of toast and slathered it with Grandma's homemade apple butter. "The poor little thing has a broken arm, several nasty cuts and bruises, and she suffered a severe blow to her head."

"That's a shame," said Anne. "Is she in stable condition?"

"She's getting better," Susan replied. "But she doesn't say much, and I thought it might cheer her up if she had a doll to cuddle. So I decided to give her the little faceless doll I bought at the farmers' market last year." She leaned her chair back and pulled the doll out of the box.

"That's what I've been seeing in these dreams I keep having," Luke said. "At first I thought it was faceless people, but I think it's a doll like this one." He touched the doll where it's face would have been, staring at it as though in disbelief. "Someone I know had a doll like this."

"Who was it, Luke?" Grandpa asked, leaning close to Luke.

Luke made little circles across his forehead with his fingertips. "I think her name was Laura. No, maybe not. It started with an L, though; I'm pretty sure of that."

"Think of some L names," Grandma said, coaxing Luke.

He studied the faceless doll. "Laurie! Her name was Laurie, and she had a doll like this. No, not one doll, but several."

"Susan, wasn't that young woman at the farmers' market who sold you the doll named Laurie?" Anne spoke up.

"Yes, I think it was." Susan turned to face Luke. "Have you ever been to the farmers' market in Bird-in-Hand?"

His eyes widened. "I believe I have."

Grandpa reached over and clasped Luke's arm. "I wonder if you might be Amish."

The look of astonishment on Luke's face told Susan the answer.

CHAPTER 9

The following evening, Luke watched nervously as Anne and Susan searched the Internet, looking for Amish last names. He had never heard the word "Google" before and quickly learned it meant doing a search for information on the computer. He sipped at his hot tea, watching in amazement at what the computer could do.

Susan glanced over at him and smiled. "I'm sure this is all new to you, Luke, but we use computers for just about everything these days. Especially at the hospital."

Luke shook his head, still dumbfounded as Susan added, "Just about anything you want to know can be accessed by the click of a button, as long as you know the right words to search for."

After checking out several websites that didn't help much, they finally found one that listed Amish last names. They started reading the long list out loud. When they got to "Stoltzfus," Luke immediately knew who he was. His name was Luke Stoltzfus, and he was Amish!

His hand went to his forehead, as more memories came flooding back. "I have a wife, and her name is Merrie. We have a home somewhere in Lancaster County, but I'm not sure where." It made no sense that Luke could remember some things and not others.

"So if I live in Lancaster, how and why did I end up in Philadelphia?" he asked Susan, who sat quietly by his side at the kitchen table. "Why was I at that bus station?"

He and Susan had gone there several weeks ago, but it had done nothing to spark any memories.

"I don't know," she said, slowly shaking her head. "But with your memory coming back this quickly, I'm sure that information will come to you eventually, too."

"My name is Luke Stoltzfus," he repeated over and over. It was like music to his ears. He felt like a real person; he was somebody, at last!

He looked back at Susan and noticed that her shoulders were slumped as she took their empty teacups to the sink. Wasn't she happy his memory was coming back?

"It's getting late," Anne said, turning off the computer. "I think we should all go to bed and continue with this in the morning."

"My sister's right," Susan was quick to say. "After a good night's sleep, your brain will be rested, and it'll help you remember more."

Luke nodded. "Jah, maybe so."

"Jah?" Susan asked, looking at him curiously.

He grinned. "It's the way the Amish say yes. It's funny I've never said it till now, though. If I'm Amish, wouldn't you think I'd have been speaking Pennsylvania-Dutch?"

"Not when you had amnesia," Anne said. "Until recently, it was as though your past had been completely erased from your brain."

"Tomorrow, hopefully, I'll remember my phone number—if I have one that is," Luke quickly added. He pushed away from the table and left the room, feeling tired yet exhilarated. He could hardly believe he'd remembered so much of his past in one evening. He was ever so anxious to get back to Meredith. Now all he needed to do was remember his phone number and address.

⟿

"Whew!" Anne blew out her breath. "Can you believe how quickly things started coming together for Luke once he saw your Amish doll?"

"I know." Susan stared at a stain on the tablecloth as a lump formed in her throat. She'd known from the beginning that Luke's time with them had been uncertain and that his memory could come back at any moment. She just hadn't been prepared to fall in love with him; and learning that he had a wife had been a harsh blow.

So much for my fantasies about building a life together with Luke, she thought. Tears welled in Susan's eyes and ran down her cheeks. *I'm being selfish*, she chastised herself. *I should be happy that Luke will be getting his life back with the woman he married, but I know I'll miss the "Eddie" I once knew.*

❦

Ronks

After another restless night, Luann got up before anyone else in order to get a few things done. With just one day before Meredith's wedding, she still had a lot to do.

Her gaze came to rest on the tablecloth waiting to be wrapped. It had been a wedding gift she and Philip had received from his folks. Luann wished her father and Philip's parents were still alive. They'd all loved being included in family gatherings.

Pulling her thoughts back to the issue at hand, Luann quickly wrapped the present so that Meredith wouldn't see it when she got up. She reviewed the menu for the wedding meal: roasted chicken, mashed potatoes and gravy, a fruit salad, creamed celery, cheese, bologna, bread, butter, honey, jelly, fruits, pudding, cakes, and pies—plenty of good food for all their guests.

Her thoughts returned to Meredith. She'd chosen a dark green fabric for her wedding dress and had made it in a day. Of course, she was an excellent seamstress and had caught on to sewing at an early age. It was no wonder she was able to sew women's prayer coverings with such ease. Unfortunately, it hadn't given Meredith enough income, and she'd had to rent out her home.

Luann had told only Philip that she was concerned Meredith might be marrying Jonah, at least in part, for financial reasons. She knew Meredith felt like a burden for having to move in with her family. Luann's biggest concern, however, was that Meredith might not be over the pain of losing Luke, and if that was the case, it could affect her marriage to Jonah.

At least Luke's parents had accepted the idea of Meredith getting married again. Even so, it would be hard for them to attend the wedding and see their daughter-in-law marry another man.

Luann glanced out the window. The sky was gray, threatening to unleash the drizzle that had been predicted. She hoped the weather would clear by Thursday.

"I just need to relax and stop fretting about things," she murmured.

"Meredith's life is in God's hands, and so is the weather. May His will be done."

⁂

Darby

Luke sat up in bed with a start. He remembered his phone number. After quickly writing it down, he hurried to get dressed, anxious to tell the Baileys this good news.

"Guess what?" he shouted, sliding across the kitchen floor in his stocking feet a short time later.

"What's up?" Henry asked from his place at the table, where he sat drinking coffee. "You look like George when he's swiped some seed from one of our birdfeeders."

"I remember my phone number," Luke said excitedly.

"That's wonderful, Luke," Norma said, joining them at the table.

"Are you going to call your wife or just surprise her by showing up?" Anne asked, placing a cup of coffee in front of Luke.

"I don't know. What do you think I should do?" Luke didn't know why he felt so confused. Everything seemed to be happening so fast, and yet he still couldn't quite remember some details—like how long he'd been gone or what he'd been doing at the bus station in Philadelphia. Maybe it wasn't important. Maybe he should just find a way home to Meredith as quickly as possible. But he couldn't really do that until he remembered exactly where he lived. All he knew was that he lived in Lancaster County, and he wasn't even sure what town.

"I think you should call your wife right away," Susan said, entering the room. Her eyes were red and swollen. Luke wondered if she might have been crying.

"Are you all right, dear?" Norma asked. "You look as if you've been—"

"I'm fine." Susan moved over to the desk, picked up the cordless phone, and handed it to Luke. "You'd better make that call now, don't you think?"

Luke slowly nodded. A chill of nervous anticipation ran through him as he quickly entered the number. It rang several times, then a recorded message came on, saying the number had been disconnected. He hung up, feeling defeated. He'd thought sure the phone number had to be his, but his memory was still sketchy about certain things, so maybe he'd been wrong. "All I got was a recording," he mumbled. "The number's been disconnected."

"Maybe you dialed incorrectly or had the wrong number in the first place," Henry spoke up. "Why don't you try again?"

Luke dialed the number once more and got the same message. "It's no use," he said with a groan. "It can't be my phone number."

Norma stood in front of Luke and put her hands on his shoulders. "Don't worry, Luke. Once you remember your address, you can surprise your wife in person. It might be better that way."

"Let's have breakfast first," Henry said. "Then we'll get things figured out. You'll be home before you know it."

The Baileys' optimism gave Luke a sense of hope. Maybe by this time tomorrow, he and Meredith would be reunited. Of course, he first had to remember exactly where he lived in Lancaster County.

CHAPTER 10

Bird-in-Hand

As Jonah prepared for bed the night before his wedding, he prayed that all would go well and that the weather would turn sunny. It could rain all it wanted tonight, but hopefully by morning it would clear out and start to dry things off so that his and Meredith's wedding would be perfect. Of course once tomorrow arrived, he probably wouldn't care what it was like outside.

All Jonah wanted was to begin a new life with Meredith and Levi, and even though the house he'd wanted to buy had suddenly been taken off the market, he'd be content to live with his folks a bit longer until he found another place. Meredith got along well with his parents, so he didn't think she'd mind living here awhile either. They could move into the house Meredith had shared with her first husband, but that wouldn't seem right—at least not to Jonah. He didn't think Meredith needed the reminders from her past, and living in the home she'd shared with Luke might come between them. Maybe after he and Meredith were married she would decide to sell the house. After all, there wasn't much point in keeping it. She'd probably make more in the long run by selling the place than if she kept renting it out.

That can all be worked out down the road, Jonah told himself as he climbed into bed. *What I need now is a good night's sleep so I'll be well rested in the morning.* He turned down the gas lamp and closed his eyes. The last thing he remembered before drifting off to sleep was a vision of Meredith standing beside him, responding to her wedding vows.

<hr />

Darby

Luke had spent most of the day trying to remember his address. He'd almost given up when, shortly before bedtime, it came to him. "I know where I live!" he shouted, dashing into the living room, where the Baileys sat, drinking hot chocolate.

"You do? Where?" Henry asked, rising to his feet.

"It's crazy how it all of a sudden came to me," Luke said in amazement. "I was flipping through the pages of a tree magazine you got the other day. You know—the one that also has flowers and vegetables you can send off for."

"Yes, I've ordered a few things from that catalog over the years," Norma said. "But tell us, Luke, how did that help you remember your address?"

"Well, I was reading about a beech tree, and I suddenly remembered the name of the road where my wife and I lived. We live on a farm on Beechdale Road in Bird-in-Hand, just off Route 340." He started pacing the floor, nervously running his fingers through his hair. "I need to go home now. Would it be possible for me to borrow enough money from you for a bus ticket to Lancaster?" he asked, looking at Henry. "I'll pay you back as soon as I can."

Henry shook his head. "No way, Luke. We'll drive you home; we wouldn't want it any other way."

"Really? When?" Even though Luke was excited to get home, he felt a touch of sorrow in his heart that he would be leaving these wonderful people who had opened their arms and shared a piece of their life with him.

"Let's go tonight," Susan said. "I don't have to work tomorrow, so I can take you there now."

"You would do that for me?" Luke could hardly believe Susan would offer to drive him home. They were a good hour and a half from Lancaster, and by the time they got there, it would be midnight or later.

"Of course I'll do it. That's what friends are for," she replied.

Luke noticed tears in Susan's eyes. Could it be that she would miss him? Had she been experiencing the same feelings for him as he had for her?

Good grief, Luke thought, rubbing his forehead. *I'm a married man in love with my wife, yet I almost allowed myself to fall in love with Susan. What would have happened if I had? What if I'd made a commitment to her?*

"I start work early in the morning, so I can't go along," Anne said. "But I want you to know that it's been a pleasure to know you, and I wish you all the best."

"Thanks. It's been my pleasure knowing all of you." After returning

Anne's hug, he looked at each of them and knew this goodbye wasn't going to be easy. The Baileys were the "salt of the earth," and even though he'd had a rough road for all these months, Luke had been blessed with the friendship he'd found with the Baileys.

"I appreciate all of you and everything you've done for me these past several months," he said. "You'll never know how much it's meant to me. You've been the family I needed all this time."

Luke could see the gloom in everyone's eyes and noticed how tenderly Henry took Norma's hand when her chin began to quiver. It seemed as though their feelings matched the cold rain falling outside.

"Look," Anne said, as if trying to lighten things up, "this isn't going to be goodbye, you know."

"That's true," Norma said, wiping her nose with a hankie. "We won't be living that far apart. We can visit whenever we want, because Lancaster is only about seventy miles from here and not even a two-hour drive."

"Yeah," Luke chimed in. "It's not like I'm goin' across the country. There's a lot to see in Lancaster County, too, so you might enjoy visiting sometime." His eyes stung with tears as he looked at everyone and said, "I have a home that I can share with you now, and boy, does it ever feel good to say that." A lump formed in Luke's throat, and he bowed his head as he tried to find his voice. Looking up, all Luke could do was swallow and whisper, "Thank you, everyone. Thanks a lot."

❧

Philadelphia

The rain had stopped, and the roads were drying off. In less than two hours, Luke would be in Lancaster. Although time seemed to drag, waiting these couple of hours didn't compare to the months he'd been away, trying to remember who he was.

Luke looked down at his jeans, along with the flannel shirt and his red baseball cap. That hat had become part of his daily attire since he'd seen it hanging on the closet door of his room when he'd first arrived in Darby. Luke had gotten used to the English clothing that had been uncomfortable to him

350

at first, but he couldn't wait to get back into his own Plain clothing. He realized that was why these other clothes had never felt quite right.

Luke leaned his head back and closed his eyes. Suddenly, he remembered that he'd been on the bus over a year ago because he'd been heading to Indiana to learn a new trade from his uncle. By now Uncle Amos must have sold the headstone engraving business to someone else.

I'll worry later about how I'm going to support Meredith, he thought. *Right now I just want to get home to her.*

Another thought popped into his head. *Will Meredith be happy to see me? Will she even recognize me in these clothes, with no beard?*

"I'd better pull in here and gas up," Susan said, directing her car into a gas station. "If anyone needs the restroom, now's a good time."

Norma and Luke stepped out of the car, but Henry had his eyes closed and appeared to be asleep.

When Luke was about to leave the restroom a short time later, he stepped up to the sink to wash his hands. He took a quick look in the mirror, and more memories came flooding back. He remembered going to the restroom at the bus station in Philadelphia and seeing a rugged-looking man approach him. The fellow had asked for Luke's clothing and then his wallet. That was the guy who had assaulted him and put him through months of pain and rehab. In those few minutes, Luke's life had changed. The only thing good that had come from the attack was the new friends he had made during his recovery.

I wonder where the attacker is now? Luke thought. *Guess I really don't need to know, now that I'm finally heading home.*

⚬⚬⚬

Bird-in-Hand

"What are ya doin' out of bed?" Elam asked Sadie as she stood in front of their bedroom window, staring into the darkness.

"I couldn't sleep," she replied, turning to face him.

"How come?"

"I was remembering the day Luke and Meredith got married. It wasn't that long ago, but it seems like forever."

Elam stepped up to Sadie and slipped his arms around her waist. "It's hard not to look back and remember our youngest child's wedding day. Especially since this is the eve of Meredith and Jonah's wedding."

"Jah. Levi is a part of our Luke, and I know Meredith and Jonah will make sure Levi knows his father, even though he never had the opportunity to meet him."

"Meredith and Levi are lucky to have Jonah in their lives." Elam paused. "I've seen with my own eyes how Levi looks at Jonah and wants to be held by him."

"You're right. It's hard not to see and hear the love Jonah has for Meredith and Levi." Sadie sighed. "It couldn't have been easy for Jonah to come here and approach me about his feelings for Meredith and Levi some months ago, but I saw right then that Jonah was a sincere, genuine person. How could I fault him for loving Meredith, or deny her and Levi the happiness they deserve?"

Elam gave her a hug. "Luke would be happy to know that his wife and son will be well taken care of. Tomorrow, when we go to the wedding, let's make sure we let them know how happy we are for them, okay?"

Sadie nodded and leaned into her husband's embrace. For the first time in a long while, she felt a true sense of peace—like everything was right in the world.

CHAPTER 11

Ronks

Lying in bed that night, Meredith was having a hard time falling asleep. Was it the anticipation of tomorrow? Was it from all the week's activities? Her whole family was exhausted, but everything was ready for tomorrow.

So why wasn't she asleep? Was she getting cold feet? She didn't remember feeling this way the night before she and Luke got married.

"Stop it," Meredith murmured into the darkness of her room. "I can't compare the way things were with Luke to how they are now; it wouldn't be fair to Jonah."

But could she extract Luke from her heart, even now on the eve of her marriage to Jonah, and go forward? While Meredith wouldn't admit it to Jonah, deep down, she knew she'd never love another man like she had Luke.

After what seemed like hours, she felt her eyelids growing heavy. *Please Lord*, she silently prayed. *Please let this be right, and help me not to be afraid.*

Afraid of what? she asked herself. She knew the answer but couldn't say it out loud. *You're afraid of making the wrong decision.*

She rolled over and punched her pillow. *I will not let my doubts get in the way of my happiness—or Levi's. Tomorrow morning I will marry Jonah, and that's the end of it.*

Lancaster County, Pennsylvania

The ride to Lancaster went faster than Luke imagined it would. As they got closer, Henry and Norma became more talkative. Listening to them gave

Luke a reprieve from practicing what he would say to Meredith. He still didn't know how he would explain everything.

Soon, they were pulling into the driveway. "This is my house," Luke said, opening the car door and getting out. He could hardly believe it, but he was finally home!

"After I speak to Meredith, I'd like you to come in and meet her," Luke said, leaning in the open window of the driver's side.

"Take all the time you need," Henry assured him.

Norma and Susan nodded their agreement.

Luke didn't want to scare Meredith, so he knocked softly on the door. Even so, he expected to hear Fritz bark, like he always did when someone came up to the house.

He was surprised, when a middle-aged English man answered the door.

"Can I help you, sir? Are you lost?" the man asked, looking at Luke with a dubious expression.

"Uh, no, I don't think so. This is my home."

The Englisher shook his head. "My wife and I have been renting this place for a couple of months, so you must have the wrong house."

Luke was completely baffled. Why would Meredith rent out their house, and where was she now? Something wasn't right. Maybe he did have the wrong house. He quickly thanked the man and headed back to Susan's car.

"My memory must not be as clear as I thought it was," he said, opening the car door. "I've gotta be at the wrong house."

"When we pulled in, you said this was your home," Susan said.

"It's the middle of the night," Norma interjected. "Luke, maybe you mistook the place for your own." She motioned to the house. "We saw you talking to a man. What'd he say?"

"Said he and his wife are renting the place."

"Now what? Where do we go from here?" Susan questioned.

With the dome light on in the car, Luke could see how tired she looked.

"Let's head up the road a ways," he said, getting back into the car. "My folks don't live too far from here. At least, I'm pretty sure this is the road their place is on."

After they'd driven past a few homes, Luke pointed to a mailbox up ahead. Susan pulled over, and Luke got out. It was hard to see in the dark, but using the flashlight Henry had brought along, he was able to see the name on the mailbox: STOLTZFUS.

It was after midnight, and Luke was anxious to see his folks. He didn't want to scare them, yet by the time he got to the door, he was almost desperate. He needed to see someone from his old life—family, friend, anyone.

Luke removed his ball cap and pounded on the door.

After a few minutes, his dad answered. He looked at Luke as if he were a complete stranger.

"Oh Dad, it's so good to be home." Luke could hardly hold back from throwing himself into his father's arms. He needed to be held, comforted as if he were a little boy again.

Dad pointed the flashlight he was holding at Luke and said, "Who are you?"

"It's me, Luke." Luke knew his voice had taken on a raspy sound from the injury he'd sustained when he was hit in the throat by the mugger, but he was sure his own father would know it was him.

"You're not Luke. Who are you, and what kind of a trick are you playin' on me? My son is dead."

"I'm not dead, Dad. It's really me—your son Luke. I was beat up real bad at the bus station in Philadelphia, and I didn't know who I was until recently." Luke stood, squeezing the red ball cap in his hands.

Dad took a step closer to Luke, studying his face. "Ach!" he shouted, with a catch in his voice. "You've got turquoise eyes just like my son."

"That's right, Dad. I do have turquoise eyes, and I'm telling the truth. I am Luke Stoltzfus, and I'm very much alive."

Dad's eyes widened as though seeing a ghost. Finally, he reached out and grabbed Luke in a hug.

From behind his father, Luke heard a gasp. Mom stepped onto the porch, threw her arms around Luke, and sobbed. "Praise be to God! Our son has been brought back to us!"

"I can't believe I'm sitting here in my kitchen with my son and husband on one side of me and the wonderful people who took my boy in and nursed him back to health on the other side," Sadie said, dabbing at her tears. "It's a miracle beyond belief." She could hardly pull herself away from touching Luke's arm and making sure this was real. Luke was really sitting beside her.

For the last hour, they had listened as their son told of his ordeal—getting mugged, never making it to Indiana, and being in the hospital all those months with no memory of who he was. Susan, Luke's nurse, explained about the surgeries he'd had and the weeks of rehab in the hospital and as an outpatient.

Sadie quickly realized that Luke had been in good hands, treated as if he were part of the Baileys' family. She and Elam owed them a debt of gratitude for taking such good care of their son.

Then Sadie and Elam explained to Luke what they had endured since he'd left. They said the bus he was supposed to have been on had crashed and that all the bodies were burned in the collision.

Henry remarked that the mugger who'd assaulted Luke at the bus depot may have died on that bus, since he'd taken Luke's clothes and his wallet, which held Luke's bus ticket to Indiana.

Elam described the memorial service for Luke and how everyone in their Amish community had grieved, especially Meredith.

Luke nearly jumped out of his chair. "Meredith thinks I'm dead?"

Sadie nodded. "We all thought that, Luke."

"Oh no," Luke groaned. "I went to my house to see Meredith and was greeted by an English man who said he and his wife were renting the place. Did Meredith move out after she got the news that I was dead?"

Elam shook his head. "Not right away. She had a hard time financially and has been living with her folks for the last couple of months."

Sadie clasped Elam's arm and mouthed something Luke couldn't understand.

"What is it? What's wrong?" he asked. "Is Meredith all right?"

Sadie swallowed hard. "Do you want to tell him, or should I?" she asked, looking solemnly at Elam.

He shrugged. "Whatever you think's best."

Sadie moistened her lips with the tip of her tongue. "A few hours from now, Meredith plans to be married."

Luke's brows furrowed. "What do you mean, Mom? She's already married—to me."

Sadie drew in a quick breath and started again. "As we said, Luke,

Meredith believed you were dead, and she grieved for many months until a man named Jonah Miller came into her life. Now she's—"

"Meredith's planning to marry this man?" Luke shouted.

Elam and Sadie nodded. She glanced over at the Baileys and could see the shocked expressions on their faces.

"Luke, you'd better get over to the Kings' place right away," Dad said. "You've got to tell Meredith you're alive!"

CHAPTER 12

Luke couldn't believe it. Meredith, believing him dead, was on the brink of marrying another man and starting a new life with him. Even though it was the wee hours of the morning, he had to get to his wife!

Dad offered to hitch his horse to the buggy and take Luke to the Kings' house, but Susan said she would take Luke, as it would be faster by car.

Luke's mother had insisted the Baileys stay with them for the night, and his dad was quick to agree. So while Norma and Henry were shown to their room, Luke and Susan headed to the Kings' place.

Luke was excited to let Meredith know he was alive, yet he was fearful of her response. *What if Meredith loves Jonah now? What if she loves him more than me?*

When they arrived at Philip and Luann's place, Susan said, "Luke, there's something I need to say."

"What's that?" he asked, turning to look at her.

"I want you to know that I'm happy for you—happy that you're getting your life back."

Luke was tempted to give Susan a hug but thought better of it. Instead, he touched her arm and said, "Thanks, Susan. You've become a good friend, and that means a lot to me."

She smiled and motioned to the house. "You'd better go now. I'll see you before we head back to Darby."

Luke hesitated a moment, then he opened the car door, raced up to the house, and pounded on the door with all his might. "Wake up! Somebody, please answer the door!"

Was she dreaming, or was it time to get up already? Meredith felt like she'd just fallen asleep.

It couldn't be her wedding day already, could it?

Someone was pounding on the front door. Had there been an accident? Did a neighbor need help? Was there a fire somewhere?

She quickly got up when she heard her parents heading down the stairs. Her brain was still fuzzy from waking out of a deep sleep, but Meredith was alert enough to check on Levi. Oblivious to all the noise, her son was sound asleep under his warm blanket.

Meredith slipped into her robe and looked out the window. She couldn't see any blinking lights or flames in the distance. Fritz was whining and waiting for her in the hallway.

Meredith walked to the head of the stairs and went down quietly, as her parents had done minutes ago. She saw them standing at the doorway, but no one was saying anything.

"Mom. . .Dad," Meredith said. "What is it? Who's at the door?"

Her parents turned to face her with unreadable expressions on their faces. Fritz started barking, his tail wagging.

Meredith looked beyond them. A young man stood on the porch. He looked English, right down to the red ball cap he wore on his head. For a fleeting moment, the image of the guy in the hot air balloon she'd seen several months ago crossed her mind. *Silly to be thinking of him at this moment*, she thought.

"What's going on?" Meredith asked, reaching down to grab Fritz's collar.

The young English man hesitated then stepped in front of her.

She clasped her robe tightly, watching as the man removed his ball cap. His hair was short and very blond. She'd never seen hair that blond before, except on Luke.

"Meredith," he said in a raspy voice, "it's me—your husband, Luke."

The ringing in Meredith's ears and Fritz's frantic barking blocked out all other sounds. She glanced quickly at her parents and then looked back at the young man. All she saw was some guy who didn't look or sound like her husband, proclaiming that he was Luke. Who was this man, and why was he playing such a cruel joke?

Speechless, Meredith looked long and hard at the blond-haired man, and that's when she noticed the color of his eyes. Deep turquoise. Her eyes widened, as realization slowly hit—it truly was her husband, Luke. She tried to fight the dark veil of blackness as it came over her from some far-off place. The last thing Meredith remembered was the sensation of being scooped up and looking into those beautiful eyes she'd thought she'd never see again.

❦

"Merrie, wake up!"

What a wonderful sound! She had to be waking up from a dream. Meredith reached out, following the voice. Although a little different, she was sure now that it was indeed her husband's voice.

Slowly she opened her eyes and gazed into the pool of blue that was looking back at her.

Luke had carried her to the sofa and held her in his lap as she came to from her fainting spell.

"How are you feeling, Merrie?" Luke smiled, running his fingers gently over her face.

Meredith smiled back, knowing this was not a dream. No one but Luke had ever called her Merrie. It was like music to her ears.

She sat up quickly, and the most wonderful, euphoric feeling— something she hadn't felt in what seemed like eons—filled her spirit and bubbled over. "Luke, oh Luke! I thought you were dead." Meredith went into her husband's arms and didn't care if she stayed there forever. It felt wonderful being in Luke's warm embrace; she held him so tightly she could hardly breathe.

"Everything's going to be all right now, Merrie." Luke murmured as he held on just as tight.

Meredith leaned back and held on to his precious face, looking into those brilliant eyes. She thought of Psalm 30:11: "Thou hast turned for me my mourning into dancing: thou hast put off my sackcloth, and girded me with gladness."Yes, God had certainly turned her mourning into gladness today.

"I don't know where to begin," she said softly.

"Neither do I," he whispered against her ear. As Luke held Meredith's hand, he relayed to her all that had transpired: the assault at the bus station; his memory loss, surgeries, and rehabilitation; and the time spent with the Baileys. Luke also mentioned how the Baileys, all except for Anne, had driven him home all the way from Darby.

Meredith leaned into Luke's hand as he gently cupped her face. "I'd like to meet them."

"You will," he assured her.

Meredith shed tears, hearing what Luke had gone through, but now she had something wonderful she wanted to share with her husband. Something she knew would erase the weeks and months of pain they'd both endured.

Before she could voice the words, Luke lifted her chin so she was looking into his eyes and said, "Meredith, I need to ask your forgiveness for the things I said to you before leaving on my trip."

She sniffed deeply. "I forgive you, but I need to apologize for my part in the disagreements we had, as well."

"No more regrets," he told her. "It's just you and me now, and we have our whole lives before us. We can start over with a clean slate."

"It's not just you and me anymore," Meredith said, feeling so happy she thought she'd burst. "There's someone I'd like you to meet." She reached for Luke's hand. "Come with me to my room."

When they entered Meredith's bedroom, she led Luke over to the crib that held her precious surprise. She watched Luke's expression as he looked from Meredith to the little angel sleeping soundly while sucking his thumb.

"Luke," she whispered, "meet your son, Levi."

Luke drew in a sharp breath. His face broke into a wide smile. "We have a little *bu?*"

She nodded. "I suspected I was pregnant before you left on the bus, but I didn't want to tell you until I knew for sure. I was planning to give you the news as soon as you returned from Indiana." Her voice faltered. "Of course that never happened."

"Meredith, I'm so sorry," he apologized, slipping his little finger into Levi's grasp.

Levi's small hand held tight to his daddy's finger, as if feeling the love pass from father to son. It was a beautiful moment, and among many she would never forget.

She took Luke's hand, and they sat on the bed, watching Levi's even breathing, while Meredith explained everything to Luke about the birth of their son. Then, as if everything else had disappeared, Meredith remembered that her wedding to Jonah was supposed to happen in a few hours. Now she knew why those voices of doubt had kept troubling her about marrying Jonah. She realized what she felt for him had more to do with how good he was to her son and the fact that Levi needed a father. Even though Meredith knew it would hurt Jonah, she had to tell him right away. Jonah was kind and sincere and had been a good friend. She hated the thought that she was about to bring him pain.

As the sun rose, Meredith explained the situation to Luke, and when she said she needed to tell Jonah right away, Luke nodded with understanding and said, "I'll go with you, Merrie."

<hr />

Bird-in-Hand

Jonah had been awake since early that morning, unable to sleep. Finally his wedding day had arrived. He looked outside and whistled, seeing a beautiful day unfolding. The rain had moved out, and the fog was lifting, forming white wispy clouds against the bluest of skies. It looked almost too perfect for words. Today he would marry his true love, and he could hardly wait.

Jonah took a seat at the kitchen table. He was the only one up, but his parents would be coming down shortly; he'd heard them stirring in their room upstairs.

Herbie started barking, and Jonah glanced out the window, seeing a horse and buggy pull up. When he opened the front door, he was surprised to see Meredith.

"Come in." He smiled at his soon-to-be wife. "I didn't expect to see you this early."

"Jonah," she said, biting her lip, "I need to speak with you about something."

Jonah stiffened. Something was wrong. He could see the wary expression on Meredith's face. "What's going on?" he asked. "Why are you here so early?"

She motioned to the kitchen table. "Please, sit down."

Jonah did as she asked, and she took a seat across from him.

"I don't know any other way to say this, but Luke isn't dead," she said, speaking softly and slowly. "He came to my folks' house late last night." Meredith paused. "Jonah, my husband has returned to me."

Jonah didn't believe her. "Are you making this up because you've changed your mind and don't want to marry me?" he asked. He had always sensed a bit of reluctance in Meredith, even when he thought they had everything worked out.

Meredith shook her head forcibly. "It's the truth, and I feel bad telling you this way. The last thing I'd ever want to do is hurt you, Jonah."

"How can Luke be alive? I mean, the sheriff told you that Luke had been killed when the bus was hit by a tanker full of gas."

She nodded. "It's true. The bus exploded. But Luke wasn't on it."

"He wasn't?"

"No. Some man wanting Luke's money beat him up at the bus station in Philadelphia. When Luke regained consciousness, he didn't know who he was. He was injured quite badly and spent some time in the hospital. After that, some really nice folks took him in, and that's where he's been all this time. It's just been recently that Luke's memory returned."

"If this is all true—"

"It is, Jonah. Luke's outside in my buggy right now."

Jonah went over to the window. He could see the silhouette of a man sitting in the buggy, holding the reins. "He doesn't look like an Amish man," Jonah protested. "He's not wearing Amish clothes, and where's his beard?"

"It's a long story," Meredith said, "but my husband has returned, and we can't be married." She blinked, as though fighting back tears. Not wishing to make things any harder for her, Jonah decided to deal with her news the best way he could, although inside his heart was breaking. Jonah wanted so badly to be Meredith's husband. Obviously, that was not meant to be.

⁓

Luke waited nervously in the buggy, wondering how things were going with Meredith and the man she was supposed to marry—a man Luke had never met. Luke had watched as Meredith knocked on the door. She'd turned back and waved reassuringly to him.

Out of the blue, another image entered Luke's mind. On the day he'd gone up in the hot air balloon, he'd noticed a woman walking toward the parking area. For a moment she had turned, watching him, and then she'd waved back as the balloon he was in went higher and higher. Luke would have to share that story with Meredith later on. It was wonderful, knowing they had the rest of their lives ahead of them to plan, share, and grow old together. God had given them both a second chance.

But how would Jonah take the news? Would he be upset? Would he wish Luke really were dead?

The front door opened, and Meredith came out of the house with a man walking behind her. The guy looked nice enough, although even from this distance, Luke could see a hint of sadness in his eyes.

When Meredith and Jonah approached the buggy, Luke got out and tied the reins to the hitching post. It was an odd situation, and Luke struggled for something to say.

Jonah stared back at him with a startled expression.

Luke, unsure of what to do, extended his hand to the man. They shook hands, but Jonah continued to stare at him strangely.

Meredith glanced at Luke, and after a few more awkward moments, she introduced them to each other. Once the introductions had been made, she turned to Jonah and said, "Are you okay?"

Jonah glanced at Meredith and then back at Luke. His voice cracked as he stammered, "It—it's you! You're the one. I'd remember those turquoise eyes anywhere."

Luke, feeling quite confused, asked what Jonah meant.

"A long time ago when I was a boy, I nearly drowned."

"Jah," Meredith said. "I remember you told me what a lasting impression that boy had made on your life."

Jonah nodded. "Being pulled to the surface of that deep cold pond, I saw these kind, caring eyes of such a different color. They looked into my own eyes and gave me silent encouragement to hang on. I never thought I'd come face-to-face with that boy again, and yet, here you are."

Luke rubbed the bridge of his nose as he thought hard and long. When he was thirteen, he'd spent a week with his aunt and uncle in Ohio. He'd gone fishing one day with his cousin and had saved a boy from drowning. He hadn't thought much of it because he'd always been a good swimmer and his parents had taught him to offer help whenever he could.

Jonah pointed to Luke and said, "You are that boy, aren't you?"

"I guess so." Suddenly, Luke realized he and Jonah had a special connection—what could be a lasting bond.

Jonah clasped Luke's shoulder. "You have a very special wife, and I know you two will be happy together for the rest of your lives. I'd be lying if I didn't say that I love her, but I've always known she's never loved me the way she does you."

Tears welled in Meredith's eyes, and Luke felt moisture on his cheeks, too. No wonder Meredith had agreed to marry Jonah. He truly was a fine man.

Luke shook Jonah's hand once more, and then as he and Meredith climbed into their buggy, he thanked God for bringing them together again.

Luke realized that if he hadn't been mugged and had continued on the bus ride to his uncle's, he wouldn't be alive today. Maybe that was God's way of saying thank you for saving a young boy's life a long time ago. Some things were hard to figure out, but no matter what the future held, he and Meredith would make it through, because they had each other and God.

EPILOGUE

Six months later

"Come sit with me as I read the letter we just received from Jonah," Meredith said, motioning Luke to the sofa.

Holding Levi, Luke settled down beside her, anxious to hear what Jonah had to say. Just a few weeks after Luke had returned home, Jonah had moved to Illinois, where his twin sister and her family lived. He'd started a buggy-making business and was doing quite well. It would have been difficult for Jonah to stay in Lancaster County, where he'd be reminded of his love for Meredith every time he saw her.

"Jonah's found a girlfriend," Meredith said, smiling at Luke. "Or at least he's found someone he's interested in. He says he's not sure if she returns his feelings, but he's going to pursue her and see what develops."

"That's great." *A new life for Jonah, and a second chance for me*, Luke thought. "Isn't it amazing how the difficulties we experienced for more than a year turned into blessings for everyone involved? I not only have my life back with my beautiful wife"—he smiled at her—"but I also have an adorable son and a future full of plans and dreams. And let's not forget the Baileys," he added.

"Jah, that's right." Meredith rested her head on Luke's shoulder.

The Bailey family had become special to everyone in Meredith and Luke's families. Several visits had occurred over the summer, and Luke was happy to learn that Susan had someone special in her life whom she'd met at church.

And Luke didn't have to worry about how to provide for his family. Fortunately, Uncle Amos had not sold his business when Luke was presumed dead, so Luke had taken it over just as they had originally planned. But true happiness didn't come from financial security, Luke had learned. It came from being with those he loved and letting others see God's love through his actions.

ABOUT THE AUTHOR

New York Times bestselling author, Wanda E. Brunstetter became fascinated with the Amish way of life when she first visited her husband's Mennonite relatives living in Pennsylvania. Wanda and her husband, Richard, live in Washington State but take every opportunity to visit Amish settlements throughout the States, where they have many Amish friends.

Wanda and Richard have been blessed with two grown children, six grandchildren, and two great-grandchildren. In her spare time, Wanda enjoys beachcombing, ventriloquism, gardening, photography, knitting, and having fun with her family.

To learn more about Wanda, visit her website at www.wandabrunstetter.com.

Let's Keep In Touch!

Want to know what Wanda's up to and be the first to hear about new releases, specials, the latest news, and more? Like Wanda on Facebook!

 Visit facebook.com/WandaBrunstetterFans